Outstanding praise for Rich Merritt and
SECRETS OF A GAY M...

"Merritt's sincerity and his will...
on the pages wins out in the end.
—*Just Out* (Portla...

"*Secrets of a Gay Marine Porn Star* covers a spectacularly diverse life."
—*XY* magazine (San Diego, California)

"An engaging, intriguing read."
—*Gay People's Chronicle* (Cleveland, Ohio)

"An engagingly enthusiastic memoir . . . Merritt clearly cherished his military service and his memoir makes a strong case that gays ought to be able to serve honorably and openly."
—Bookmarks/Q Syndicate

"In a society where honesty is not always the best policy and information can lead to power, what is one to do when his suspect past comes back to haunt him? Rich Merritt brilliantly tackles this subject in his insightful memoir. Merritt's voice is as stalwart as his military demeanor; his story, as gripping as any bestselling fiction novel. *Secrets of a Gay Marine Porn Star* establishes an edge to the memoir genre."
—*X Factor Magazine*

"Well worth a read."
—*HX Magazine*

"Rich Merritt writes an honest, inspiring, sexy, funny, and courageous story. It is filled with insights into military life and the workings of the media, but what truly resonates is the account of one man's journey to self-acceptance and the welcoming, joyous embrace of gay culture."
—William J. Mann, author of *All American Boy*

Please turn the page for more praise for
Secrets of a Gay Marine Porn Star!

CODE OF CONDUCT

RICH MERRITT

KENSINGTON BOOKS
http://www.kensingtonbooks.com

This is a work of fiction. Although the book refers to public figures of the era in which the story takes place—including but not limited to Bill and Hillary Clinton, Sam Nunn, Les Aspin, Barney Frank, Colin Powell, Oliver North, etc.—all references to such well-known persons relate to their roles in shaping the laws, policies and direction of the nation.

If any character portrayed within the story resembles an actual person, living or dead, the similarity is purely coincidental and accidental.

KENSINGTON BOOKS are published by

Kensington Publishing Corp.
850 Third Avenue
New York, NY 10022

All Kensington titles, imprints and distributed lines are available at special quantity discounts for bulk purchases for sales promotion, premiums, fund raising, educational or institutional use.

Special book excerpts or customized printings can also be created to fit specific needs. For details, write or phone the office of the Kensington Special Sales Manager: Kensington Publishing Corp., 850 Third Avenue, New York, NY 10022. Attn. Special Sales Department. Phone: 1-800-221-2647.

Kensington and the K logo Reg. U.S. Pat. & TM Off.

ISBN-13: 978-0-7582-2274-9
ISBN-10: 0-7582-2274-2

First Kensington Trade Paperback Printing: January 2008
10 9 8 7 6 5 4 3 2 1

Printed in the United States of America

In honor of
*all who have served in the armed forces
of the United States of America,
including the lesbians and gay men.
You know who you are—
so should everyone else.*

We shall be remembered
We few
We happy few
We band of brothers.
For he today that sheds his blood with me
Shall be my brother.

—William Shakespeare,
Henry V (paraphrased)

Prologue

Clinton Reaffirms Campaign Promise
To End Military's Ban on Gays
By Kathryn Angel, *Washington Herald*

LITTLE ROCK, ARKANSAS, November 12, 1992—In his first major policy address to the nation since his election last week, President-elect Bill Clinton today reiterated his campaign promise to issue an executive order overturning Department of Defense Directive 1332.14, which bans homosexuals from the military. Directive 1332.14 states:

Homosexuality is incompatible with military service. The presence in the military environment of persons who engage in homosexual conduct or who, by their statements, demonstrate a propensity to engage in homosexual conduct, seriously impairs the accomplishment of the military mission. The presence of such members adversely affects the ability of the armed forces to maintain discipline, good order, and morale; to foster mutual trust and confidence among service members; to ensure the integrity of the system of rank and command; to facilitate assignment and worldwide deployment of service members who frequently must live and work in close conditions affording minimal privacy; to recruit and retain members of the armed forces; to maintain the public acceptability of military service; and to prevent breaches of security.

Governor Clinton delivered a Veterans Day speech today and afterwards told reporters he has no intention of backing away from his controversial pledge to allow gays and lesbians to serve openly in the military. He plans to issue the executive order as soon as he takes office January 20.

Already there are grumblings among the military's leadership, Republicans and even some Democrats that the president-elect is "challenging the military's most entrenched traditions," although no one seems to know precisely what those traditions are. Ironically, when Winston Churchill was accused of threatening the British Navy's traditions during World War I, he is widely reported to have said, "And what are those traditions, save rum, sodomy and the lash?"

Part One

Winter Winds

1

"You goddamned lying son of a bitch!"
Don Hawkins showered Giles's face with spittle but the hospital corpsman made no move to wipe it away. Don's glare was pure rage. He waited. The stench of fear overpowered the Balboa Naval Hospital's pungent odors of antiseptic, fresh paint and linoleum wax. "Spineless motherfucker! How many jams have Eddie and I helped you out of when you had nowhere else to go?"

Retreating, Giles sideswiped a roller cart and knocked over a stack of empty urine cups. "Look, y-y-you can't—"

"I should drag you in that utility closet and beat your ass."

"Easy, killer." Eddie stepped in, putting his hand on the tall Marine's shoulder. "Our boy Giles here, he's just following his orders."

A bead of sweat dripped from Giles's nose, splattering his scrubs. "That's r-r-right. I-I-I'm just following orders."

"My ass." Don lowered his voice, spying a high-ranking officer entering the opposite corridor. "You followin' orders when you light up a joint? Huh, Sailor? How 'bout when you hand in somebody else's piss and tell the Navy it's your own?"

"It's the new executive officer," Giles hissed. "She's triple-checking everyone's work. We're not talking about a slap on the wrist. If I get caught, it's a court-martial and a dishonorable discharge."

Eddie hooked Don's coiled bicep. "Come on. We asked nice. If Giles doesn't value our friendship, we'll go to Plan B."

Don shook him off. "He doesn't get off that easy. He *promised* he'd take care of this. He *owes* us."

"It's a felony offense," Giles whispered. "Yeah, you've helped me out—a lot—but not enough to get thrown in the brig at Fort Leavenworth. *Doin' hard labor.*"

Eddie smiled at the trembling Sailor. "I been in the Navy fifteen years. Don's got that much time in the Marine Corps. We understand how the military works, okay? You got a new hospital XO who wants to show everyone she's the boss. It'll all blow over in a week or so. Besides, Clinton just became the president two days ago! Soon, none of this will matter."

"Why don't you just wait on Clinton? Why do I gotta stick my neck out now?"

"Because, asshole," Don said, "this is the military and deadlines matter. Eddie's got one more week to submit his sample. It's pretty fucking simple—even for a squid like you. Draw my blood, 'accidentally' label it with Eddie's name and social, and turn it in."

The high-ranking officer at the opposite end of the hall looked impatiently at her watch, calling out: "Petty Officer Giles, you were *supposed* to be at the ER ten minutes ago. I assume you'll conclude your business here and report there immediately!"

"Yes, ma'am," Giles replied. He turned back to Don and Eddie. "Friday. Payday. Everyone in the military will be out in San Diego. It's gonna be a long fucking night."

Giles started to walk way, but Don grabbed him by the arm one last time. "Hey, *'Doc.'* Think you're gonna show up on the battlefield, taking care of my Marines? *Think again*—or *you're* gonna be the one needin' a corpsman."

2

"You seen enough?" Oliver Tolson asked his trainee. "I don't want to waste my whole Saturday watching other people have fun on their day off."

From his boss's car, Agent Jay Gared viewed the homosexuals playing in Balboa Park. Perverts cared nothing for nature and proper gender roles. They wasted their lives chasing pleasure; Jay's dad had called them "hedonists." They failed to contribute to society and they corrupted young people, poisoning tomorrow's citizens. Jay couldn't show his true feelings too strongly, though, because Director Tolson had commented that he seemed obsessed with the military's homosexual problem.

"Not yet, sir." Jay watched a shirtless young man rub sunscreen on the back of a larger guy. The younger man joined a volleyball game across the field while two other men—one black, one white—sat at a picnic table. The black man had a dachshund, reminding Jay of his grandmother's Porky, and the few happy memories of his teenage years. The volleyball player shouted, bringing Jay out of his reverie. The man was short, muscular and handsome, and didn't display the telltale effeminate characteristics of a homosexual. "The most dangerous kind."

"What're you looking for, Jay?" Ollie asked. "What're you trying to show me? Naval Investigative Service resources are scarce and the political climate is too volatile for us to chase gays out of the service. These 'witch hunts'—a phrase I hate because it was legitimate work—used to pay off. Homos were an easy target. We caught one, they turned on each other like jackals and NIS achievement records looked good. That's not the case anymore. They stick together. Times are different and NIS reports all the way up the chain to the friggin' president. We know *his* story. He got elected *because* of the gays. I'm telling you, Gared, *leave them alone!* If they admit they're queer, we got them, but if they don't, proving it's too much trouble." Ollie paused and shook his head. "Besides, we have enough problems in San Diego with drugs and gang activity near—hell, even *on*—the bases. Keeps us busy twenty-four/seven."

"With all due respect, sir, sodomy is still a criminal act under Article 125 of the Uniform Code of Military Justice. I intend to be the best damn agent you ever had and I plan to catch, prosecute, and lock up as many violators of *every* article of the UCMJ as possible."

"I got six months till retirement. No way in hell will you be the best damn agent I ever had. I've worked with the best and they end up fired, in jail—or dead. Just do what I tell you."

Jay hoped Ollie would think his silence was consent. Drugs and gang-related activity were problems anyone could handle. Only the most dedicated agent would do the unspeakable things Jay was willing to do in order to nab his villains. Jay saw the big picture. America was great only because her military was great. America's military had been in trouble for twenty years—since the fall of Saigon—and the pro-military heyday of the Reagan years was over. Clinton and his unacceptable elements threatened to erode the military; if they succeeded, they would ruin America. The military was the last stand; if its leaders caved, America would no longer be the world's greatest nation. And God intended America to remain great. NIS Agent Jay Gared was determined to do his part to ensure that America never fell from greatness.

"Enemy missile positions! Straight ahead!"

"Damn it!" said Colonel Leonard Spencer. Intelligence had briefed the pilots that these scruffy desert mountains were friendly territory. "What kind? How many? How far?" He fired the questions into his mouthpiece. He pushed the helicopter's stick forward, dropping the Marine Corps AH-1W Super Cobra close to the ground where the earth's heat and light sources would interfere with the hostile detection systems.

"Looks like two—*shit*—three shoulder-fired missile teams. First is over the ridgeline nine clicks," came the low, gravelly voice of the pilot in the Cobra ahead to Leonard's right.

"Nine kilometers." Leonard instantly performed the calculations in his head. "Good, we're still out of range. We have just enough time. Sledge, bypass team one to the south. Fly in low through the saddle. Take out team two. We'll hit team one and search for team three. Copy?"

The voice hesitated. "We should go toward the sun, Royal. The glare will defeat the heat-seeking guidance systems in the missile warheads."

"Negative. Your mission is to go low. Take out the second missile pos. *Copy?*"

Another hesitation. "Roger." Lieutenant Colonel Melvin "Sledge" Hammer's Cobra veered low and disappeared from sight.

Leonard couldn't be distracted by his suspicion that his subordinate commander was about to disobey his order. He'd already spent too much time, a deadly extravagance in the face of this grave enemy threat. He turned his attention to his copilot. "Jungle, you copy?"

"Roger, Colonel—I mean Royal."

"How many rounds in the one-niner-seven?"

"Seven-fifty, sir—a full load. We firing the gun?"

"Roger." Leonard liked Jungle's attitude. Some pilots felt safer using the Cobra's rockets or missiles but Jungle eagerly faced the enemy from behind the barrel of the airborne machine gun.

Leonard sighted the first missile team. His mind went into high-speed mode. *Jink hard left then fast right toward the large rock formation jutting from the mountain at two o'clock. Shift direction. Pop over the edge. Jungle will have two seconds to—*

"Royal! Incoming missile! Eight o'clock! Fired from three clicks—two point five—two!"

"Sledge! We missed a team," Leonard shouted. "Double back from behind. Take him out before he gets off a second shot." Leonard and Jungle had stumbled into an angry hornets' nest of enemy missiles and the only way they could defeat them was to pull Sledge back into the area. "Sledge! Do you read? Sledge?" Silence.

"One point five—one—first team in sight."

"Fire when ready!"

"Ready to fire—fire!"

Leonard watched as his forward-seated copilot began the rapid-fire assault against the enemy on the ground. But it was too late. Because they'd failed to see a missile team, Leonard and Jungle were seconds away from death and there was nothing they could do about it.

"You Marines never miss a chance to show off your naked bodies, do you?" Eddie asked.

Karl Steiger tossed his shirt onto Eddie's head. "Americans have a constitutional right to see who's protecting them." The twenty-three-year-old Marine flexed his pecs and kissed his bulging biceps. "Their tax dollars at work, right here, baby!" He winked at Eddie. "They catch you Navy boys without your shirts, they'll demand a refund."

"Hell, I actually *work* for a living, else I could spend three hours a day in the gym." Eddie fished in his glove compartment for his Ray-Ban sunglasses and put them on.

"Don't you squids burn off any calories walking to and from the vending machine all day?"

"Ladies, please don't make me referee," said Don.

"Here, Don, take this before he leaves it behind." Eddie tossed Karl's shirt and opened his car door to put the leash on his dog. "Give me any more lip and I'll sic Rocky on you!" They laughed at the idea of a twelve-pound dachshund attacking a Marine.

Karl turned to a volleyball game in progress. "Go ahead, Karl. We'll rotate in later."

Rocky yanked on his leash as Karl took off across the small field in San Diego's Balboa Park. "No, Rocky, over here, boy!" Eddie

CODE OF CONDUCT   11

said. Karl joined the team in formation facing their opponents. The eleven men—allies and foes alike—gawked at Karl's physique. When Karl wore baggy shorts and nothing else, every-one—gay, straight or bi—stared at his chiseled body.

"Where'd he get that tan?" Eddie asked. "Today's January twenty-third, not July fourth."

Don grabbed two beers from the cooler. "That tan cost the boy a big chunk of his paycheck, so just admire like everyone else." He passed one to Eddie.

"Marines in tanning beds," Eddie grunted. "We're in the Clinton era for sure."

"About the fuck-up at the hospital yesterday—a buddy at Miramar can help us." Don popped the top off his Miller Genuine Draft. "Shoulda gone to him first. He's straight, but more reliable than that shitbird Giles. Says he can meet us at Balboa Tuesday morning."

Rocky found a piece of real estate to his liking and did his business. "This HIV test is a lot of trouble." Eddie pulled a plastic bag from his pocket and cleaned up after his pet. "You gotta be away from your battalion. Your friend's gotta come all the way to Balboa."

"Let me worry about that. Besides, we didn't make these fucked-up rules. You're healthy. You've got every right to keep doing your job until you reach your twenty and retire."

"*If* I make it to retirement," Eddie said as they turned to walk back toward their cars.

"Prepare to get creamed! Zero serving zero." Karl put the ball cleanly over the net.

"They'll find a cure soon," Don said. "You're gonna make it way beyond retirement."

"Yeah right. Some politician's tryin' to pass a law discharging *everyone* with HIV."

"Not gonna happen. Clinton's the president, not that asshole Coughlin. Besides, no one's gonna know you have HIV, so it won't matter," Don said. "That's so fucked up—there's a lot of jobs positive people can do where it won't make a bit of difference, even in wartime."

Eddie tied Rocky's leash around a picnic table and the two men sat across from each other. "Next time there's a *real* war—not just a Kuwaiti skirmish—they'll take anyone they can get. I don't care who's got AIDS, leprosy, a criminal record—nymphomania—whatever, they'll take 'em. They discriminate in peacetime 'cause they ain't got nothing better to do." He drank his beer and Rocky jumped into his lap to get a taste. "You don't need that." Eddie laughed. "Got enough alcoholic friends and Sailors to tend to. Don't need no drunken dog." Turning serious, he asked, "What if they find out? We got the same blood *type*, not the same blood."

"How long we been doing this? Six years? Ever since they started requiring these goddamned HIV tests. All the lab does is check the blood for antibodies. That's it. When they see it's negative, they look at the name on the vial and enter it into the computer as negative."

"I was thinking about what Giles said. You could get in a lot of trouble."

"Damn it, Eddie, we have this conversation every year!" Don lowered his voice. "Not another word about it. This is what we're doing."

Eddie scratched Rocky between his ears. "I'm glad I picked out an old dog 'cause I sure as hell don't got the energy to chase a young one all over the park."

"Like you told Giles yesterday, Clinton's changing things for the better. This might be the last year we have to do this."

Eddie smirked. "Don Don Don. I love that you're still the same naïve teenager from Missouri I met on ship in the Arabian Sea. But man, get real! I said all that bullshit about Clinton just to get Giles to go along with us. You read the paper this morning? Bill Clinton ain't gonna change a thing. If he tries, he'll only make it worse."

"In fifteen years, you ever known me to read a paper?"

"I know, stupid question. The new Defense Secretary met with the Joint Chiefs Thursday. All they did for two hours was bitch about Clinton's promise to lift the gay ban."

Don faked surprise. "Well, yippie ki yea, mothafucka! I guess that means we fixed all the other problems, you know the ones in Somalia, Bosnia and Iraq."

"That's what I'm sayin'. We can all pack up and go home."

"What about the general running the Pentagon?" Don asked. "He's black. Don't he understand the ban is just another way to discriminate?"

Eddie almost laughed. "You mean 'Uncle Colin'? Hell, he's the main man *against* Clinton. If he *had* a set a balls, he'd stand up to the rest of the generals and support the president." Eddie shook his head and drank more of his beer. "All he's doing is gearing up to run against Clinton in four years. What better way to do that than lead the lynch mob against the fags?"

"Guess we shouldn't expect anything better from an Army general. Someday, we'll get a Marine general as Chairman of the Joint Chiefs and he'll have a backbone." Don enjoyed the last of his beer as his temper cooled. "I disagree with you about Clinton. I think he's going to change things. Maybe not as fast as he—or we—would like. So what if he's a pot-smoking draft dodger and none of the generals respect him. He's committed to helping gays and lesbians. He knows he wouldn't be president without our votes." Seeing Eddie's continued look of disbelief, Don said, "Have a little bit of hope, man. Clinton's the *man* from Hope!"

"I lost my hope on April 4, 1968. I was eight."

"What happened? I don't know—"

"Of course you don't, white boy." Eddie's usually gentle tone was tinged with bitterness. "That's the day they killed Martin Luther King. If they'll kill a man who preaches peace just 'cause of the color of his skin, things ain't never gonna get better for gay men or lesbians. Especially not for gay men with a deadly, incurable, infectious disease."

Don believed his optimism was merited but he respected Eddie's pessimism. "Want another beer?" Don tossed his can into a trash bin as he walked to his jeep.

"I'm good, but if you have any water, Rocky could use a drink, couldn't ya, boy."

Don smiled at the sight of his friend petting his little companion. "Aren't you glad I talked you into getting a dog? How long has it been, a year?"

"Let's see now. Ray died in November of 'ninety-one and I rescued Rocky from that nasty shelter four months later, so yeah, almost a year. How could *anyone* give up a sweet handsome fella like you, Rocky? Their loss is my gain."

Don returned to the bench as he watched Karl's team rotate. "No hope? Things aren't that bad. Saturday afternoon in Balboa Park in the middle of winter. Santa Ana winds blowing the warm desert air down to the ocean. The war is over and everyone we care about made it home. Life couldn't be better." He grunted and gulped his beer. "What do we even need Clinton for?"

Eddie knocked on the wooden table. "My bayou superstition must be actin' up 'cause it scares me when you talk shit like that. Maybe things *aren't* that bad but don't upset the balance by flauntin' our good luck. We both got five years left to go. Look how many people we know who got screwed out of their pension just before hitting the magic twenty-year mark."

"They got caught 'cause they got careless. Can't let down your guard, not for a minute."

"Who are you talking about?" Eddie asked. "Jeanne? You want to tell her—to her face—that *she* got careless? If you do, you're a braver man than me."

"It's different for the women, you know that. People assume—"

"It's not any different for women. Where'd you get that shit? Wanna talk about careless? Look where you're at. The *gayest* part of Balboa Park, which is smack dab in the *gayest* part of San Diego. Hangin' out with some obvious queens—*no*, I don't mean me," Eddie added, preempting Don's jab. "Karl rubbin' sunscreen on your back in broad daylight."

"Oh come on, straight guys smear lotion on each other's bare backs all—the—" Don and Eddie broke into laughter before Don could complete his sentence.

"No they don't, not here in the park. Anyone from your unit could drive by and wonder why Gunny Hawkins is hangin' out with a bunch of 'mos. We've *all* gotten careless but some of us have been luckier than others. I have hope—hope that your luck and mine lasts until 1998." Eddie walked toward his car. "Be right back. I'm gonna get Rocky's rubber ball."

"You still trying to teach that old dog to fetch?" Don looked around, wondering if Eddie was right. The park was crowded with the usual inhabitants—dogs on leashes and their owners, babies in strollers and a few homeless folks happy for the break from a wet winter. Joggers and roller-bladers—male *and* female—circled the volleyball area checking out the shirtless players. Nothing looked dangerous but it *was* very gay. They'd grown comfortable with their lives and perhaps a little careless. Southern California, with its perpetual sunshine and reputation for laissez-faire attitudes, lulled people into the fantasy that life was always easy and grand. But with earthquakes, mudslides or wildfires, paradise was never more than seconds away from purgatory. Likewise, for gay men and lesbians in the military, a slip in an unguarded moment or an ill-timed encounter with the wrong person could send all of their lives into a tailspin.

Eddie untied Rocky from his leash and tossed the ball. "Go get it, boy!" Rocky, refusing to play the game, used his freedom to stretch and lie down in a different patch of grass.

"Give it up!" Don changed the subject by asking, "How're you holding up?"

Eddie raised his head. "Okay, I guess. My T-cell count is as high as ever."

"Good. But I meant," Don said, leaning across the table, "how're you doing—without Ray?"

Eddie sighed. "It never gets easier, does it." He stared through his sunglasses into empty space. "I'm gonna wake up one day and the pain won't be as bad. So far that hasn't happened."

"We're glad you're going out again. We missed you," Don said sympathetically. "Besides, don't you think Ray would want you to get back into life?"

Eddie wiped his shades clean with the tail of his tank top. "Don't know what that means anymore. All I remember about 'life' is Ray getting sick and me taking care of him without the Navy finding out. Then he died. Other than that, I don't have a fucking clue what 'life' is."

"We're all here for you—Karl, me, Robbi, Jeanne. Let us know what you need."

"What I *need* is to get past this grief." Eddie's face projected raw pain. "I was sad when my father died but I didn't feel *physical* pain. But now it feels like someone's swingin' a crowbar against the inside of my skull, that's how painful the grief is. I was twenty-two when we met and we spent ten years together. I appreciate that y'all are here for me." He looked at his pet, who sensed he was experiencing emotional trauma. "I've got Rocky—don't I, boy—even if you won't fetch. But I don't know how anyone could help, other than what you're already doing."

"I've been there."

"I know." Eddie's tone mellowed. "Does a day go by that you don't—you don't—?"

"That I don't think about him?" Don turned his head away from Karl's volleyball match and stared at Eddie, his closest friend for almost half his life. "When I'm busy, I might go a few hours without thinking about him. But that just makes it more painful when things slow down and I remember his little half-smile, with a corner of his mouth turned up, remember that?"

"Yes, very much." Eddie nodded and smiled. "You two were quite the pair."

"And a million other little things about him. I think about those all the time. It gets different. Life goes on. But honestly? I wouldn't say it gets easier." They sat, silently losing track of time.

"Don't you think that *he* would want *you* to get back out there?" Eddie finally asked.

A cool breeze blew up the steep hill from the bay, and a salty ocean scent wafted gently across the park. "The wind's shifting direction. It'll get chilly again as the sun sets."

"Quit changing the subject," Eddie ordered. "Let you get away with that too many times. We *both* gotta get back into life. This is something we could do together." Eddie seemed surprised at his switch from emotional paralysis to action, like he'd found a reservoir of strength.

They'd helped each other in rough times. "We're young—maybe not for the military—but who cares? They *would* want us out there." Both men were misty-eyed, sad over their past losses but happy they had each other. They hugged, sealing their agreement to get back into life.

"Your protégé is trying to tell you something." Eddie pointed over Don's shoulder.

Don cupped his hand over his ear. "What'd you say?" He pointed toward a jet just a few hundred yards above their heads. "Can't hear you over the noise of the plane landing!"

"Too bad there ain't always a plane landing when Karl's around," Eddie said.

The plane passed. "Unless you wanna go somewhere to lick each other's pussies in private," Karl said, "Dominic and Jack gotta leave. We need more players, even you sorry old asses."

Don tossed his half-full can into the trash and looked at Eddie. "What do you say?"

"How about you, boy? Wanna go play with the big dogs?" Rocky, realizing things were changing, sprang to life. For the first time in over a year, Eddie looked hopeful. "I'm ready to get into the game if you are." The men and the dachshund headed for the sandy pit.

3

"Flight attendants, please prepare the cabin for landing." After studying the ground from thirty thousand feet for over an hour, Patrick McAbe questioned how a city existed between the vast barren desert and the Pacific Ocean. His first impression of the Southwest was that it resembled an extraterrestrial world. As the plane approached San Diego, though, he was happy to see lush green suburbs, creeks and ponds and a large park near downtown, signs that life thrived at the edge of a hostile environment. His new home looked nothing like Chicago just as his new life looked nothing like his old one.

Nearing his destination, his mind raced back in time eight months.

Hundreds of cars filled the parking lot, leaving four spaces open in a corner. Patrick parked but remained seated for ten minutes. His pulse raced and the heat soared. *I'm thirsty.* He searched for a bottle of water. *Shit! What kind of Marine forgets water?* His flight instructor had advised the students to steer clear of Pensacola Beach over the weekend, or else thousands of guys from all over the South would hit on them. The conservative religious town in Florida's panhandle seemed like an unlikely gay destination but he said it happened every Memorial Day. *What kind of Marine goes where everyone knows the place will be packed with gay men?*

It doesn't matter because I'm not—I'm not—but he knew better. Now that he'd decided not to marry Karen and had broken their engagement, nothing stood between him and the truth. He could *be* it, *do* it or even *say* it out loud if he wanted. "I'm—g—gay." His voice was sheepish but he'd said it, and saying it aloud gave him new energy. Each breath was deeper and easier, and his shoulders and spine felt relaxed. He'd said it! He started laughing. "I'm gay!"

A voice with a heavy Southern accent outside his open car window said, "Well, honey, I'm just *overjoyed* that you're gay but I need to know if you're coming or going." The remaining three spaces were taken and a large man in a red Cabriolet convertible wanted Patrick's spot.

Patrick opened the door and waved apologetically. "Staying," he said as the man sped away. *There's nothing wrong with this*, he assured himself. *I'm at a warm beach on a sunny day and I'm just looking for a concession stand to buy a bottle of water. That's all.* As he stepped onto the pavement, he grabbed his towel—just in case he wanted to stay—and headed for the ocean. Several cars had Department of Defense decals. *Are there other military guys on this beach?*

Before May 1992, Patrick had never cared much about politics and he didn't know anyone who paid attention to the subject of gays in the military. By now, though, everyone in the armed forces was aware that the Democratic Party's nominee for president had vowed to end the ban that prevented gays and lesbians from serving. Although the Arkansas governor's promise had set off a firestorm within the military, no one believed he stood a chance against President Bush.

Patrick glanced nervously at another DoD sticker. *Why are military people here? Are they investigators?* Ignoring his fears, he walked toward the pounding surf. With each footstep, he grew more comfortable about his decision. To his surprise, most of the men on the beach seemed to be in decent physical shape—*excellent* physical shape actually. He liked what he saw. Guys emerged from the sea, and saltwater glistened as it rolled down their hardened six-pack abs. Twenty feet away two men kissed out in the open. Patrick

smiled. He'd wasted too much of his life feeling guilty for his desires. Beginning now, at the ripe old age of twenty-five, he'd pursue what he enjoyed. He regretted that he hadn't experienced this
epiphany ten years earlier.

The afternoon was sunny and beautiful. Except for the absence
of kids and the skewed ratio of men to women, the crowd seemed
like most other places. Given the abundance of twenty- and thirty-
something in-shape guys, the resemblance to a military crowd was
striking. Everyone was having fun. A few looked like Sailors and
one or two sported a Marine haircut.

Patrick hadn't satisfied his thirst but no concessionaires were
nearby. Not wanting to risk being spotted by a military person, he
stopped walking, spreading his towel close to the vegetation near
the parking lot. He stripped off his T-shirt. A clump of weeds partially shielded him from the view of the men between him and the
ocean. He tied a bandana around his head, making him feel incognito, and he leaned back to watch the parade of people. *There sure
as hell are a lot of them—I mean a lot of us.* Thinking of himself as
part of this group seemed bizarre at first, but oddly, the more he
saw, the more he liked the idea. *Maybe I can be gay.*

"I *knew* you'd be the one!"

An electric shock rushed from Patrick's lower spine to his neck
and his lungs wouldn't take in air. He thought he'd been hit with a
stun gun but his reaction came from inside. As his head cleared, he
recognized the voice. He turned to face its owner. *Think, Patrick.
Why am I here?*

"Second Lieutenant McAbe, leader of Marines. What brings
you out to Pensacola Beach?"

Patrick reflexively jumped to his feet to address his instructor.
"Sir, I—is this—what beach did you mean? Pensacola? I haven't
been—?"

"Hey! McAbe! Relax. Call me Chris." Navy Lieutenant Ashburn—Chris—started to sit. "Mind if I use a corner of your
towel?"

"No sir, not at all. Pl—please be my guest." Patrick's mouth had
gone from dry to parched.

Chris sat cross-legged and Patrick followed, facing the other man across his beach towel. The instructor held out a bottle. "Want a drink?" Patrick nodded and grabbed the water.

Patrick forgot his bewilderment as he enjoyed the ice-cold liquid going down inside him but the feeling was temporary and his questions returned with urgency. *Why is Lieutenant Ashburn, the instructor who warned us about this beach, here? Why did he say I would be "the one"? Does he think I'm—gay?* Chris looked at him blankly. As Patrick returned the bottle of water, he inadvertently let his eyes roam over Chris's tanned and muscular legs, his flat stomach and his appealing upper body. When he looked up, Chris was smiling at him.

"Your first name's 'Patrick,' isn't it? Mind if I call you 'Patrick'?"

"Um, yes sir, you can call me Patrick."

"You have to stop that 'sir' shit." Chris laughed. "Answer the question."

"I—it's, um, what was the question? Why am I here?"

"No need to turn it into an existential crisis. What I meant was, why are you here—on this *beach*?" Chris smiled and winked as he tilted the bottle to extract the last drop.

Patrick inhaled and launched into his rehearsed explanation. "It's Memorial Day weekend. I'm at the beach and there's nothing wrong with that." As awkward as it might've sounded, Patrick relaxed. *It's a free country and an open beach. If Lieutenant Ashburn wants to tell the other pilots he saw me at a gay beach, then, well—what the hell is Lieutenant Ashburn doing here?* Patrick suddenly realized what should've been obvious from the start. *Why* is *he here?* "So—Chris," Patrick said, his courage strengthening by the second, "why are *you* here?"

"Because I like this part of the beach the most. How about you? With miles of beaches to choose from, why pick this one? Don't you rent a place with Tim Roberts on the beach at Perdido Key? That's right, you do. Why drive twenty miles to this beach?"

"Thirty, actually," Patrick offered absently.

"Is Tim here? Why didn't he come with you?"

"Because Tim's not—" Thankfully, Patrick stopped before he said "gay." "Because Tim's not in town this weekend. He's in Seattle. Getting engaged. To Melanie."

"I see." Chris dragged out "see" until it faded into the sound of the birds and the waves.

Patrick hypnotized himself with the rhythm of the surf. *Crash, come in, cover the sand, ebb, go out, repeat.* He felt calmer than before. *Can I trust Chris? I feel like I can—but can I trust* anyone? A hard crash of the waves brought him back. He still hadn't answered the lieutenant's question but it didn't matter because Chris also seemed to be in harmony with the waves. Patrick thought he knew his instructor well but now he realized he didn't know him at all. Chris was friendly, good-natured and well liked by his students but he rarely talked about himself. Maybe that's why he was their favorite. Most Navy and Marine Corps aviators—especially the ones proficient enough to train new pilots—talked about themselves a lot.

"Don't worry. I'm not with the Naval Investigative Service." Chris scanned the beach and squinted into the sun, which was on its downward arc. He removed his sunglasses, inched closer to Patrick and stared into his student's eyes. "I'll start a special friendship between us by saying that I'm a very open-minded type of guy. You can tell me anything you need to. I'm sure I told you who comes to this beach on this particular weekend and most of my students wouldn't go near a gay beach. But you *chose* to come here, and I ask myself 'Why?' Are you a gay-basher here to beat the crap out of some '*fags*'? I've known you for eight months and you don't seem like the Neanderthal type. Or are you a fundamentalist Christian here to tell the sodomites about Jesus?" Chris leaned forward. "Or are you 'curious and confused'? Isn't that the expression?" He brushed sand off his leg. "I don't care—unless you're a Bible thumper. Now *that* would really annoy me."

"You haven't told me why *you're* here." As Patrick's trust grew, his suspicion that Chris was toying with him diminished. "Which are you?"

Chris mulled over the different groups. "None. I'm a nonviolent agnostic combat-ready helicopter pilot. All that I'm curious or confused about is why Second Lieutenant McAbe is at a gay beach. Now *that* puzzles me." The sun's rays penetrated the outer layers of Patrick's skin but the Gulf breeze kept him cool. He returned Chris's stare. The man had vocalized the "g" word, and for the first time in Patrick's life, he hadn't heard "gay" uttered as a slur. Chris moved closer. "Mind if I take these off?" He removed Patrick's sunglasses. "You're handsome. I've never seen a man with such sparkly green eyes."

Patrick suddenly felt his temperature rise in a wonderful way. He was immobilized. All he could do was smile at Chris, a man whose face seemed warm, friendly and, best of all, sincere. Chris wasn't playing a game. The rules required him to use vague words. Maybe Patrick really *could* tell him anything. "I—I guess—"

"Shhh." Chris covered Patrick's mouth with his hand. In a strong swift motion, he leaned forward, put his lips firmly against Patrick's, and gently placed his hand on the back of Patrick's neck. Patrick wanted to melt. His body tingled as he felt Chris's fingers brush his ear. Before this kiss, Patrick had planned every move his muscles dared to make. But in this instant he willingly surrendered to his instructor. For the first time in his life, Patrick was spontaneous and it felt natural. Finally, he understood the meaning of the word "euphoria." He moved his lips against Chris's and let Chris's tongue ply its way into his mouth. Chris's mouth tasted salty and gritty, but it was also hot, and Patrick loved the whole experience of kissing a man. As he wondered how high this natural rush could go, Chris backed away. "So you're not a homophobe and obviously not a fundamentalist. What are you? Besides an excellent kisser."

"I—" Patrick tasted his lips and grinned. "I don't think I'm 'confused' anymore. But you've—aroused—my curiosity." Patrick almost added that "curiosity" wasn't all Chris had aroused but the comment seemed too overt and, given the tightness of his shorts, unnecessary.

Chris seemed flattered and smiled. "Don't take this wrong—I mean it in the best way, but I had you pegged from the start. When you've been around awhile, it gets easier to spot family."

"'Family'? What do you mean by that?"

"That's what you are now, right? Family? Or do you plan to spend the rest of your life in this 'curious' phase?" Patrick nervously scanned the area for military spies. Chris threw his head back, laughing. "You're hysterical. Considering what we just did, eavesdropping is the least of our worries. And do you mind if I take that stupid-looking bandanna off your head? You have a great energy about you. You shouldn't hide it." Without waiting for Patrick's permission, Chris slid around, put his arm around the younger man's waist, and slipped the bandanna off. "That's *much* better. Now I can see you. *Completely.* And I mean this sincerely— you're *very* easy to look at." He whispered, "Don't be so nervous. We're safe here. No one's listening, no one's watching—except a few voyeurs, but no one to worry about."

The other man's embrace felt comfortable and secure. "Um, th—that's not why I'm nervous. I—this is—new—" He realized then how much he loved the warmth of Chris's tough skin against his own softer exterior. Patrick felt safe with Chris because they were both under the military's rules. *Rules that we're both breaking.*

"Do you want to go somewhere and talk? Let's go downtown for a drink at a little place I know. I'll introduce you to people."

"Sure." Patrick knew his life would never be the same and that he'd never regret this day.

During Patrick's final seven months in flight school, he and Chris forged a close friendship, slipping into the roles of mentor and protégé. In mid-December, on Patrick's last day in town, Chris treated him to a high-class dinner celebrating Patrick's graduation from flight school and promotion to first lieutenant and, sadly, to bid each other farewell. "I can't believe you're leaving Pensacola a virgin," Chris joked. Before Patrick could protest, Chris held up his hand and qualified his statement. "I'm sorry, I mean a *gay* virgin."

"I'm just—I don't know, Chris—"

"Patrick, I'm kidding. I admire how patiently you've adjusted to gay life. Promise me you won't get bitter. The gay world has enough jaded old queens—many are under the age of twenty-five. All of us were cheated out of our adolescence. No use trying to get it all back in one circuit party weekend. Take it slow and easy— stay young and naïve as long as possible."

"I'm usually not this much of a prude."

"You're cautious. Deliberateness is a valuable skill. It's what makes you the top pilot in your class. It also makes you think about sex before you do it, a very good—but rare—trait these days. Too bad some others I've known weren't as deliberate. They might still be alive."

"Do you mean pilots? Or gay men?"

"Come to think of it, both."

"I still feel guilt over breaking my engagement with Karen, without telling her the truth."

"The rules are wrong and they force us to keep secrets. Sometimes they cause us to hurt the people we care about without explaining why. It's not your fault. Do like I do—blame it on George Bush. Makes me feel better." Chris poured more wine. "I predict you'll get over that guilt when you see the men in California. Which reminds me." He fished in his pocket. "Here's my buddy's number. Look him up." He handed the paper to Patrick. "Told him all about you."

"Thanks." Patrick glanced at the number suspiciously. "'Don Hawkins.' So you told him about me—what's his deal?"

"Thought I taught you better than that. I didn't tell him *anything* about you, except that your good looks are both boyish and manly. But no, I didn't tell him your rank, or what you do, or anything like that, although Don's smart enough to figure out a lot of things. Coming from here—and knowing me—he'll assume you're a pilot. You two can share all that girly chitchat when you meet. Besides, it'll give you something to break the ice. Don isn't—let's just say he's not the most socially sophisticated person. But he *is* one of the best all-around guys—honest, loyal, dependable—a real Boy Scout, except with gigantic muscles and a hairy chest. Oh, I can hear you two Marines now—'what's your MOS'? 'I'm a pilot. Ooh, what's *your* MOS?'"

Patrick laughed. "You love to crack yourself up, don't you?"

"Someone's got to do it." Chris added somberly, "Especially now that we're leaving. Wish I could take you to Patuxent River, Maryland, to be a test pilot with me."

"I should learn how to fly the Cobra before I try testing stuff that hasn't even been built yet."

"You're right," Chris said. "I'm going to miss you, though, and I don't say that to very many people. I can tell that someone in San Diego is going to be the luckiest guy alive."

"Flight attendants, please take your seats for landing." The captain's voice brought Patrick out of his thoughts. Going to the beach that beautiful day in Pensacola had changed his life forever. As he looked out onto sunlit Coronado Bay and the palm-tree-lined streets below, he couldn't help but wonder what other surprises—maybe some lucky guy—were in store for him.

4

"Captain Pfeiffer, how did you get the callsign 'Jungle'?"

"Good question, sir. My first squadron commander pronounced my name like 'fever'—"

"'Jungle fever.' " Leonard laughed. "Clever."

"I was a wild lieutenant back in the day. He said I made him sicker than a case of malaria. So 'Jungle' stuck."

"'Back in the day'? Christ! How old are you? Twenty-nine? Thirty?" The two men carried their helmets, notepads and maps as they walked across the tarmac from their Cobra into the squadron's hangar at Camp Pendleton. The maintenance area smelled of aircraft fuel, grease and machinery, a mixture that made Leonard feel at home.

"Thirty-two, Colonel. Makes me an old man in the Corps. But thank you."

"Thirty-two?" Leonard feigned shock. "That old?" As he and Jungle climbed the steps to the second floor, he hoped the power of suggestion emanating from their discussion of age made him feel winded and not age itself. This evening he felt all of the fifty years he'd be this year.

"How'd you get the callsign 'Royal'?"

"My father was British and I grew up in London. He died when I was sixteen and my mother and I returned to her native New

York. I suppose I still had a trace of an accent when I joined the Marines. *My* first squadron commander was from Texas—"

"—and to him anyone with an accent *must* be part of the monarchy. No wonder we always carry a special love for our first commanding officer." Jungle laughed. "I hope I fly half as well as you do when—"

"When you're my age?" Leonard asked. "Captain, if I were you, I'd stop talking now."

Jungle's faced reddened several shades. "I admire the way you flew the aircraft today, sir. I don't know many pilots who can handle a helicopter as skillfully in fierce Santa Ana winds."

"Do you know where the name 'Santa Ana Winds' originated?"

"The Santa Ana Mountains? Or—is it because they blow down the Santa Ana Canyon?"

"That's what most people believe," Leonard said. Jungle stepped forward to open the door. "The truth is we Anglos mispronounce it as we do many things. The correct term comes from the name the Spanish missionaries used centuries ago: '*Vientos de Santanas.*'"

Jungle followed Leonard into the pilots' "ready room." "I don't know Spanish, sir."

Seeing Leonard, Lieutenant Colonel Hammer leapt to his feet and shouted, "Attention on deck!" The twelve or thirteen officers in the ready room jumped to the position of attention.

"'Winds of Satan.'" Turning to the group, Leonard said, "At ease!" He stepped to the chair they'd left vacant for him in the center of the front row. "Please, please, take your seats."

Despite Leonard's order, the officers in the room waited until he was firmly in his seat before they moved. Sledge waved and a Marine delivered Leonard an ice-cold bottle of water from the back of the room. He thanked the officer but kept his eyes firmly on Sledge, one of six squadron commanders who reported directly to him. Leonard had flown today primarily to evaluate Sledge's performance as squadron commander, a fact of which Sledge was no doubt aware.

"Let's begin," Sledge said from the lectern, "as we have a lot to talk about and I'm sure everybody has a better place to be on a

Saturday night than here. I know I do." The pilots laughed, nodding their heads. Leonard smiled but mentally prepared for the looming confrontation. "Let's begin with our favorite pastime—beating up on intelligence. Intel officer? Where are you? Since you were our first total fuck-up of the day, you get to go first."

A woman shouted from the back row, "Here, sir!" She made her way to the front of the room as Sledge stepped to the side. She had a determined look on her face despite the badgering by her squadron commander, treatment that probably wasn't new for her. "Good afternoon—or evening, gentlemen." She smiled, nodding toward Leonard and Sledge. "I'll engage in a pastime we enjoy even more than beating up on intelligence. Because this was a *joint* training mission, we were required to rely on intelligence gathered and provided to us by *Army* units from Fort Huachuca, Arizona."

The men howled in agreement. "Fuckin' Army—sticks it to us every time!" a pilot shouted. No matter how much the Corps evolved, some things, like Army-bashing, never changed.

She continued. "Field units reported the 'enemy' shoulder-fired surface-to-air missiles—in actuality our own Marine Stinger teams from Camp Pendleton—should've been thirty miles east of the hills where they 'shot down' Colonel Spencer and Jungle. The winds delayed our launch, giving the Stingers time to relocate further west. The intelligence wasn't updated."

The debrief ended almost an hour later. After the other officers left the room, Leonard said, "Sledge, Jungle, can you stick around for a few minutes?"

"Yes sir!" Jungle shouted.

"Sure—Colonel." Sledge seemed annoyed that his Saturday night plans would be delayed even further.

Leonard looked at Jungle, "How many rounds were you able to fire out of the 20-millimeter machine gun before we were 'killed'?"

"Enough to wipe out one of the teams." Jungle spoke with the typical overconfidence of a Marine Corps captain. "If it hadn't been for the faulty intelligence and the 'phantom missile team,' sir, we would've won the day. I'm absolutely sure of that."

Sledge was more subdued. Looking at the captain, he nodded with satisfaction. "I believe Captain Pfeiffer is correct, sir. If we'd received proper intelligence—and if we'd spotted that first team—we wouldn't have had any problems."

"Captain Pfeiffer," Leonard said, "may I see the logbook for that particular machine gun?"

The captain hesitated then realized what he had to do. "Yes sir!" He darted out of the room, heading for the stairwell to the maintenance department.

Sledge gulped and sweat beaded on his forehead. "Why do we need that, Colonel?"

"I'm not sure," Leonard answered. "Perhaps we don't." Now that he and the squadron commander were alone, Leonard said, "You questioned my order during a hostile engagement. When I restated your instructions, you pretended to follow them. When you were out of my sight, you went against my command. Why did you disobey my order?"

Sledge braced. "You know as well as I do that the best way to counteract shoulder-fired infrared heat-seeking missiles is to position the aircraft between the missile and the sun."

"That's not what I asked. Flying toward the sun was your second decision and one I understand—you thought you'd be safer, even though you were mistaken. What I *don't* understand was the decision you made first—the decision to disobey my order!"

Leonard was near his boiling point when Jungle returned with the maintenance records. "Here you are, sir," he said, stopping to catch his breath.

"Do you mind if I look at that?" Sledge asked.

"Go ahead." Leonard passed the unopened logbook to the squadron commander.

Sledge opened the book, glanced at its pages and slammed it closed. "Goddamn it, Pfeiffer!" He thrust the book at the captain. "Look at this. Tell me what you see."

The captain opened to the most recent entry. Confused, he flipped back several pages. "Sorry, sir. Don't see anything."

"That's just the point, Captain!" Sledge snarled. "The most dangerous threats are the ones you *don't* see. What I *don't* see in this logbook is any evidence that the maintenance department replaced the rotor and breech bolts in that gun by the end of fiscal

year 'ninety-two as required by DoD specifications. You know
what that means?" Jungle looked at the floor. "It means that you,
supposedly my best flight instructor, took a gun out flying today—
with the *group commander no less*—that was defective. When you
simulated firing that gun, not only did you *not* kill the enemy, you
blew yourself and the colonel all the way from the halls of goddamned Montezuma to the shores of fucking Tripoli! I mean you
would have, except that a phantom Stinger team had already blown
you to pieces. I'd say we all had one hell of a day, wouldn't you,
Captain Pfeiffer?" Sledge screamed so loudly that the sergeant of
the guard popped in to check on things.

A look of realization crossed Jungle's face. "But Colonel
Spencer—*you* told me to go ahead and use the 20-millimeter gun
instead of the rockets and missiles." Leonard nodded, satisfied the
captain had learned a valuable lesson. "So you knew that the gun had
a defective part—before the flight. You did that to make a point."

"You're dismissed, Captain Pfeiffer," Leonard said calmly. The
sergeant, not wanting to get involved with the senior officers, disappeared with Jungle. Leonard continued. "The combat readiness
of that machine gun is just as much your responsibility as it is his
and it's just as much my responsibility as it is yours. If General
Neville had discovered the error, I would expect and deserve the
same reprimand from him that I'm giving you. You *damn* well
should've known about it, Sledge, but you didn't. I can only wonder what else in this squadron is defective. The next time I fly
with your squadron, which will be soon, I expect everything to be
current with all specifications."

"Yes, Colonel," said the dejected commander.

"About your direct disobedience of my order—"

"You can't fault me for that, Colonel." Sledge regained some of
his earlier confidence. "I was protecting my crew and my airframe.
Your order was—"

"My order was what?" Leonard shouted louder than before and
Sledge's head reared back in surprise. "Do you honestly think I'm
so stupid that I've either forgotten or never knew the capabilities
of heat-seeking missiles? If I believed for a *second* that flying into
the sun was the best way to accomplish our mission, don't you

think I would've ordered it?" Sledge stared in wide-eyed disbelief at his commanding officer's sudden display of anger. "Or perhaps since the first of October—*last year*—heat-seeking missiles have also had the capability to track a helicopter's silhouette as well as its heat. When you violated my order and flew toward the sun, you sacrificed yourself, your Cobra, your copilot, and most of all, the mission."

While Leonard paused to catch his breath, Sledge stammered, "I—I—how—I don't know how we were supposed to know about silhouettes."

Leonard, fearing he'd reached his cardiovascular breaking point, lowered his voice and recomposed himself. "I routed a classified update about missile systems to you and the other squadron commanders last September." He removed a red-covered folder from his bag. "It's now the end of January, Lieutenant Colonel Hammer. By Monday afternoon, you will call to let me know you've read this memo and any others from me you may have missed last year."

The chagrined lieutenant colonel took the pages and stared meekly at the cover. "Yes, sir."

Leonard picked up his equipment and headed out of the room. He paused at the door and turned around. "Sledge, your advice to Captain Pfeiffer was sound."

"What advice was that, sir?"

"'The most dangerous threats are the ones you don't see.' But there's a more specific way to state the point you were trying to make."

"How's that, Colonel?"

"'If you know the enemy and you know yourself, you need not fear the result of a hundred battles. If you know yourself but not the enemy, for every victory gained you will also suffer a defeat. If you know neither the enemy nor yourself, you will succumb in every battle.'"

"Sounds like wise advice," Sledge said. "Is that a 'Colonel Spencer original'?"

"Hardly." Leonard continued out the doorway. "I may be old and wise, but Sun Tzu is a little bit older and a whole lot wiser."

* * *

"Put your shirt back on," Don said to Karl after their volleyball team's short victory celebration in the parking lot. "The air will cool fast as the sun sets. It's still January."

"Yes, Daddy." Karl thrust his short but thick arms through the sleeves in his tank top. "It's January? I'm glad you told me because I can't read a calendar for myself."

"Smartass," said Eddie.

"Enough outta you, boat driver. You coming with us to WCPC's tonight?"

"Probably not." Eddie's clothes were drenched with sweat from the afternoon's matches and he grunted as he leaned over to help his short-legged dog into the car. "I doubt if I could handle a night out dancing with you young boys at the West Coast Production Company. But shower and change at my apartment if you'd like. Beats driving back up to Vista."

"Sounds like a plan." Don scanned the area around his jeep for trash or anything they might've dropped. "Karl, what are you doing? Get out of the jeep and come here."

"Damn it! I hate when you act like a gunny." Karl pulled his sweatshirt over his tank top as he slid out of the vehicle. "You're right about the temperature drop. And I'm showering first."

"Earth to Steiger! I *am* a gunny. It ain't no act. Now aren't you glad I told you to bring that sweatshirt? And even if you shower first, you still gotta clean your nasty pubes outta the drain."

"Quit your bitchin', Karl. You the one always leaving shit behind," Eddie said. "Remember Laguna Beach? You left a bag of condoms and lube under your chair at that restaurant."

"Jesus! I forget shit once and you'd think I left top-secret gear with the Iraqi army."

"That was a *family* restaurant. 'Look at this, Mommy. What's this, Daddy?' And it wasn't just one time! You'd lose your head if it weren't—if you *had* a head to lose."

Don picked up an object from the grass, holding it high to show the others. "It's a good thing I made us do a police call of the area but I'm afraid Eddie owes Karl—"

"Ha, motherfucker, take that!" Karl jumped to grab the item out of Don's hand. "Look who's leaving shit behind now, chief."

Eddie squinted and said, "What is that? My eyes are going bad."

"Rocky's ball!" Hearing his name, Rocky barked inside the car as Karl ran his ball over.

"That's about got it," Don declared. "Eddie, sure you won't join us? A night like this—weather's perfect—guys will be itchin' to go out. WC's will be packed."

"I don't—"

"Come on! Quit being such a pussy and take the skirt off! Or in your case," Karl said, "put the skirt on! Let's hit the town—there's fresh meat out there, ripe and ready to pick."

"If Uncle Sam required you Jarheads to graduate high school, you'd know what a 'mixed metaphor' is." Eddie grabbed Karl around the neck and rubbed his knuckles across the younger Marine's high-n-tight haircut. "Know what, you little runt? I was hitting this town when you were playing with Legos, eating Apple Jacks and watching Saturday morning cartoons."

"Runt? Who you callin' a runt? Check out these huge guns— even through my sweatshirt!" Karl flexed his biceps. "You wouldn't be able to call me a runt if I wasn't just five six."

"But 'ch *are*, Blanche, ya' are!"

"Who the fuck is Blanche?" Karl asked. "And what's she got to do with anything?"

"Oh my God," Eddie said as he and Don looked at Karl in dismay. "We're failing our child. Next rainy weekend, I'm hosting a Bette Davis and Joan Crawford marathon at my house."

"Sounds like a party that'd be too wild for me." Karl rolled his eyes.

"Come on now, princesses, be nice." Don was glad to see Eddie energized and having fun. Today had been a good day for him—for *all* of them—and maybe tonight would be even better. "Think about it during dinner. On me."

"Great!" Karl rebounded quickly from his pouting. "You paying for me, Uncle Donnie?"

"Why should tonight be different from any other Saturday?" He and Karl hopped in the jeep.

"Just kidding," Karl said. "I've got my *own* money tonight and I think it's time I treated."

Don placed his arm across his chest, feigning a heart attack. "You got paid over twenty-four hours ago and you still got money? What the fuck?"

Ignoring Don, Karl asked, "Hamburger Mary's?"

"Is there any other place?" As Don turned the key, he noticed Karl counting twenty-dollar bills in his wallet and he became curious as to how a Marine corporal could have that much cash. Karl came from a poor family, though, and money was a delicate topic so Don kept quiet. He secretly suspected that Karl was always broke because he sent money to his mom in Idaho.

Don rolled to a stop at the park's exit. He checked over his left shoulder for traffic on Sixth Avenue when something across the street caught his eye. Two men sat in a car just inside the entrance to the park. By itself, this wasn't a show-stopping scene but the face of the younger guy grabbed Don's attention and the look in his eyes stopped Don cold. Although they stared at each other only briefly through two automobile windows forty feet apart, Don sensed the other man's intensity. He wasn't sure if the man's passion was from fear, anger or lust—or a combination of the three—but it was certainly in overdrive.

"What are you doing, Agent Gared? There's no regulation against a Sailor or Marine playing volleyball without a shirt in a public park."

"I know, Ollie. Just to be safe, I'll check the system Monday to see if they have a record."

"Fine. But we're calling it a day." As the jeep pulled out of the lot, Jay quickly wrote down its license plate number. He'd been at his new job for less than a month but he already knew that these seven alphanumeric characters were all he needed for the next step in an investigation. Using the military's vehicle registration system, he had access to information on every automobile on file with the Department of Defense in Southern California, such as name, address and military unit.

That was all the information on the jeep that Jay needed to make its owner's life a living hell.

5

After renting a car and checking into a cheap hotel, Patrick ventured to Hillcrest—according to Chris, San Diego's most gay-friendly neighborhood. He stumbled into the Obelisk, a gay-and-lesbian-themed bookstore, a type of place he hadn't known existed. After Patrick had browsed novels, memoirs and magazines for hours, the manager recommended a dance club called the West Coast Production Company. He advised Patrick that WC's started late, which Patrick assumed meant ten o'clock. After a quick bite at a diner, he followed the manager's directions to the bar.

"Holy shit!" he exclaimed. Less than two hundred yards separated the main gate of the Marine Corps's recruit training base from the entrance to the gay dance club. Patrick drove around the industrial neighborhood, almost deciding the proximity was too dangerous. But he'd arrived a day early for the sole purpose of checking out San Diego's Saturday scene and WC's was the only place he knew to go. While weighing his options, he drove aimlessly around the dark warehouse district. If he stayed, his choice was between parking on the well-lit street or in a back alley. He chose the latter, risking muggers rather than military investigators.

"ID?" Patrick's military ID was hidden in the rental car with most of his cash. As he waited for the bouncer to search his Illinois driver's license, he faced the building to protect his identity from drivers heading to the base. "You just missed the free cover period before ten," the man said, "but you're from out of town. You can slide this time." The burly guy gave Patrick a friendly jab on the shoulder, saying, "Welcome to San Diego, Patrick. Have a good time."

"Thanks." The doorman's friendliness partially allayed his anxiety. Nodding politely, he hurried through the door away from Marine motorists. A short hallway led to the club's interior.

"What can I get you?" asked a bartender.

Patrick scanned the mostly empty space. "How about some men? Where are they?"

"You're early." The man flashed a devilish smile. "Have a drink—on me—while you wait."

Jay studied the naked form staring back at him in his bathroom mirror. He looked good for thirty-three. Every year on his birthday, he paid the exorbitant cost and measured his body-fat percentage at a water-immersion tank, the only sufficiently accurate method. He smiled. The percentage of his body weight attributable to fat was a healthy nine percent, a half-percentage point lower than a year ago. More importantly, he'd added four pounds of pure muscle onto his lean form, a personal record and quite a feat for a man who'd been a skinny kid.

Youth had once been Jay's only asset, and losing it had terrified him. He'd replaced youth with discipline, and to his surprise, he looked better than ever. He'd been born with average looks but now, after fifteen years of daily workouts, healthy diet and abstinence from alcohol and drugs, he'd been rewarded with the stunning physique standing in front of him. As his self-confidence had improved, so had his looks.

"Don't forget why you've been blessed," said a voice Jay recognized painfully well.

"How can I?" Jay asked as he toweled himself dry. "You won't let me."

Helicopter pilots are brooding introspective anticipators of trouble. They know if something bad hasn't happened, then it's about to. Leonard recalled the quote from a speech the late Harry Reasoner had given to senior military aviators. Reasoner's message had been right on point. Helicopter pilots and jet pilots were as distinctive as their respective airframes. Propelled by rearward thrust, a jet's wings glided effortlessly, relaxing on top of nitrogen, oxygen and the other air molecules. A jet was *supposed* to fly, and barring an unforeseen accident—or as Reasoner deftly observed, an incompetent pilot—it would. Jet pilots approached life as their aircraft went through the sky—they were astounded when things didn't go well.

Helicopters were different. They flew by sheer force of will. Rather than soaring like a plane, a helicopter's rotor blades, says an old joke, beat the air beneath them into submission. According to the laws of physics, helicopters—like bees and hummingbirds—weren't supposed to fly. Somehow, they remained aloft but the process required a lot of attention, work and tender loving care. Thoughtless incompetents like Sledge weren't up to the task. Leonard's drive from Camp Pendleton to his house in La Jolla was long but it gave him the solitude and time to process the day's problems. Sledge, as the cause of many of his headaches, had consumed much of his car time over the last eighteen months.

At a quarter past ten, Leonard entered his favorite restaurant. Sitting at the bar, he ordered a large Cobb salad. His reading glasses had the annoying habit of disappearing and he searched in his bag for several minutes. "I put them in the side so I'd remember where they are."

"Don't you hate it when that happens?" asked the bartender.

"Don't know which is worse, Jimmy. The fact that I have to wear these things to read or that I forget where I put them." Despite the forty-minute drive, Leonard's altercation with Sledge continued to rile him. Fortunately, he had plenty of work as a distraction. "Thirty-eight e-mails and that's on a Saturday." He flipped through the printouts his adjutant had stuffed in the bag. "How did we ever win a war before the computer was invented?"

"I don't know, Colonel," Jimmy said sympathetically. "I don't have any use for the things."

At least one message made him smile. His daughter had recently obtained a computer—no doubt a gift from her stepfather—

and had learned to correspond with him using something she called "America Online." Although he didn't understand "AOL," she communicated with him now more than ever so he liked it. *Hi Dad! I was writing to say 'Hi' but also I wanted to let you know . . . I GOT INTO CORNELL!!!!* He was proud of his little girl but sad he wasn't there to help her celebrate. He pulled the message out of the stack, putting it in his pocket to remind him to call her as soon as he was home. On second thought, he remembered it was after 1 A.M. in New York. He'd congratulate her tomorrow.

Most of the pages were junk mail, but one that caught his attention was a personal message from a close friend in Washington. *The Commandant of the Marine Corps sent the selection list for brigadier general to the president for signature on Thursday.*

Leonard recalled a mentor's advice. "Lieutenant colonel is the last promotion you'll achieve on the basis of merit. After that, it's as political as running for mayor."

The e-mail continued. *No one's sure if Clinton will sign the list this week. The White House is in total chaos right now. I hear the Democrats don't even know how to work the phones.*

"Well, of course not," Leonard grumbled. "They haven't had to since Jimmy—"

"What was that, Colonel? You need somethin'?" the bartender asked.

"I meant 'Jimmy' as in *Carter,* not you, Mr. Sabo. Sorry to distract you, Jimmy. Must be talking to myself over here. Isn't that another sign of old age?"

The message concluded with a friendly piece of encouragement. *Wish I had more reliable information for you but with Bush losing the race no one knows what will happen to the promotion list. Still, I think your chances are better than most.* Leonard was aware what the message *didn't* say. Only four percent of eligible colonels would be promoted to general and many worthy women and men would be passed over. With an untested president in the White House, a fortuneteller's prediction was as good as anyone's was.

"Here you go, Colonel." Jimmy placed a glass of Dewar's in front of Leonard. "On the house. It's a small token of my appreciation for what you do for this country."

"On the rocks. Thanks, Jimmy." At least he could count on some things without waiting.

Patrick circled the interior of WC's to become familiar with its layout. The windowless club smelled of beer-soaked moldy carpeting. Without people, it seemed cavernous, especially compared to the small gay bar in Pensacola. The ceiling over the dance floor was two stories high. Pool tables overlooked it from a second-story pool bar. Patrick found a staircase to an open-air patio bar on the roof. Under a protective awning behind the bar, television screens showed videos of mellower songs. The chill in the air made him glad he'd brought his jacket. Over the ledge to the south, the city's skyline and the bay glowed and sparkled in the dark. Compared to his hometown, San Diego's downtown was modest, but the magnificence of the bay—with cliffs forming a protective peninsula on the other side—blew Lake Michigan away.

"Damn." As Patrick scanned northward, his admiration for the city's natural beauty reverted to anxiety as his eyes rested on the Marine Corps' flag flying over the recruit training base.

"Scary—yet oddly ironic—how close the Marine Corps Recruit Depot is, isn't it?"

The strange voice over his shoulder caused Patrick to jump. A second ago, he'd been the only person on the roof but now a dozen other customers milled about. The man who'd spoken to him, though, looked like a club employee. "I'm sorry—I—"

"I'm Lance." The young man extended his hand. Patrick's initial feelings toward Lance—a mixture of lingering surprise at his sudden intrusion and fear of being recognized as a Marine in a gay bar—changed to physical attraction. Looking at the strapping young man, he realized how horny he was. "Come over to the bar," Lance said. "Keep me company until more people show up. Want something to drink? On the house. You look like a beer drinker— premium beers."

"Don't think I've ever been to a friendlier club." Patrick followed Lance the short distance to the bar, where he sat on a stool. "'Premium beer'? Do I look pretentious?"

"No. You look like a man with taste. I can tell a lot about people.

Been doing this for four years." Lance stocked bottles from cardboard cartons into the cooler below. He leaned across the bar and whispered, "Don't tell anyone 'cause I'm only twenty-three. Lied about my age to get this job. Owner thinks I'm twenty-six." He grabbed a bottle. "Heineken?"

"That's a first—a gay man claiming to be *older* than he is." Patrick smiled. "Sam Adams."

"My second choice for you." Lance reached deep into the metal cooler and exchanged the brews. Opening the bottle, he asked, "How do you know I'm a gay man?"

Patrick was stumped. "I'm sorry. I—I shouldn't make assumptions—"

"No, you shouldn't," said the bartender jokingly.

"I'm sorry I assumed you're a man." Patrick flashed what he hoped was a mischievous grin.

"Ouch!" Lance laughed. "Guess I deserved that. Yes, I'm a man, and yes, I'm gay. Now I'll make some more assumptions about you. Hmm, you're an officer, right? If I played the odds, I'd say you were a Navy ensign, *maybe* an LJG 'cause I think you're a couple of years older than you look, which would put you at twenty-five. But my instinct—and the way you were looking at MCRD—leads me to say you're a Marine lieutenant, probably a first lieutenant, for the same reason I said you might be an LJG." Lance had a self-satisfied smile.

"Neither confirm nor deny." Patrick gulped his beer. "What's with the mind-reading shtick?"

Lance took some orders and laughed. "Buddy, I don't have to read your mind—just your clothes." He handed the other customers their drinks and leaned over the bar close to Patrick. "No one else wears khakis, a rugby shirt, docksiders and a college jacket. Not to *this* bar."

Suddenly Patrick felt stupid. He'd grabbed his favorite—and most easily recognizable—jacket. Anyone here who assumed he was a Marine officer and who had access to military personnel records—not a stretch in this town—could end his career by searching for officers from Northwestern. Process of elimination would lead them straight to his doorstep.

"Sorry I said anything," Lance said, interrupting Patrick's self-flagellation. "Get a sexy—yet tasteful—pair of jeans and shirts that show off your pecs. You work out so let us see it! Then no one will know you're a Marine officer. Just trying to help you out, my fellow Devildog."

"'Fellow *Devildog*'? You still in the Marines too?" Patrick realized he'd just confirmed Lance's suspicion that he was a Marine.

"Not anymore. But yeah, I worked here the last two years I was in. I was stationed about two hundred yards away at MCRD. Got out with an honorable discharge and now the GI Bill pays my way to UC San Diego. The GI Bill and this job."

"You got a set of balls."

"That's what all my ex-boyfriends tell me." Lance grinned as Patrick caught the expression's double—or true—meaning. "Funny how all those things Marines say to each other take on a whole new definition in here."

"Or do they?" Patrick took another drink from the bottle.

"Good point. Yeah, every time another Marine said 'Eat me!' or 'Suck my dick!' it crossed my mind, 'Does he really *want* me to or is he just saying that?'" Glancing at the growing number of patrons, Lance said, "Time to get busy. Been a slow month, but tonight will be pumpin'! Before I deal with these queens the rest of the night—am I right? You a Marine officer?"

Picking up his drink, Patrick extended his hand. "Nice to meet you, Lance. My name's Patrick. I'm sure I'll be seeing a lot more of you." Lance's wink communicated he understood Patrick's need to be coy. Grabbing some glasses, Lance backed away to the other end of the bar. Patrick turned to face the crowd, amazed at how rapidly the roof had filled with customers. He could only imagine what it looked like on the lower two floors. Realizing there was only one way to find out, he descended the staircase into the dark and loud space below.

"Bitch, I done told you if you so much as *look* as my man again, I'd slice your damn throat."

Jay hated waiting in lines and paying cover charges but the afternoon's reconnaissance with Ollie had delayed his plans, forcing

him to stand outside with these obnoxious fairies. He hoped the
effeminate homosexuals would get into a fight, providing some entertainment, but the one who'd spoken sashayed to the back of the
line without carrying out his threat.

The line into the club was fifty yards long and snaked down a
sidewalk adjacent to a row of parked cars. Two had the telltale
DoD decals, similar to the jeep's Jay had copied earlier. No other
businesses in the vicinity were open, leading Jay to the conclusion
that the owners were in the club. He decided against writing down
the numbers so as not to arouse suspicion.

"Mmm good!" Jay turned around to see a large guy with a beard
leering at him. "De-lic-ious!" The man licked his lips. Jay turned
to the front, glad he was at the door to the club.

"Need to see some ID." Jay handed the doorman a Virginia license. "What's with all the out-of-state IDs tonight?" He studied
the picture and then scrutinized Jay. "Go on in."

6

"Wondered when the dream team would show up tonight."

"Makes two of us," Don said as Lance handed him a beer. "Thanks. Just what I needed. Getting the ladies—and the lesbian—moving on a Saturday night wore me out. Karl had to call his fan club to tell them where he could be seen." Don looked around. "Looks busy."

"Thanks to all the rain, tonight's the first Saturday the patio's been open since New Year's Eve. If I lost any more tips, I'd have to reenlist."

"Admit it. You miss the thirty-mile marches with a seventy-pound pack and mortar plate."

"My molecular biology textbook is as heavy as that plate. My parking lot's gotta be thirty miles from my eight A.M. class." Lance poured vodka in a tumbler, giving it a shake. "When your Marines bitch about how bad they got it, tell 'em the 'First Civ Div' ain't no bed of roses."

"Really? You trying to tell me that in the 'First Civilian Division' they don't wake you gently every morning at ten with harps and flutes and violins?"

"Maybe—but I'm awake no later than seven thanks to garbage trucks and the neighbor's Pomeranians." Lance divided the mixture from the tumbler into two glasses.

"What about the wine and cheese and caviar they serve you

civilians every evening," Don said. "Don't tell me that's bullshit too."

"Buddy. Try ramen noodles and nasty coffee so I can stay awake studying till three A.M."

"Damn! Remind me again why you got out?"

"Don't worry about investigators snooping in my life," Lance said. "These are for Eddie and Robbi." He gave Don the martini glasses. "Karl wants a drink, tell him to come get it himself."

Don took the three drinks. "You're not over him? Man, never seen you smitten like this."

"Karl hasn't left with anyone in months. He's just waitin' for a chance to tell me he's sorry."

"You sound like a country song." Don laughed as he walked away from the bar.

His friends had gathered under a large heater. Lance was right. Don couldn't remember the last time Karl had hooked up. There wasn't anything wrong with Karl taking it easy sexually—it was just a definite change in his young friend's behavior. When Don recalled the wad of twenty-dollar bills in Karl's wallet, he wondered what might be going on in Karl's life.

"Hey!" Karl said. "Where's my drink?"

"Drink some of mine," Robbi said. "You *are* about to become my lawful wedded husband."

"You're really going through with it?" Eddie shook his head. "Fake marriages can backfire."

"I don't want that girly drink." Karl motioned toward the bar. "He knows what I like."

"And according to him," Don said, "you know what he likes."

"Christ! Don't tell me I have to fuck him again just to get a god-damned beer in this dump." Karl left the group, Don presumed, to make peace with his ex-boyfriend.

"Gimme a break. Like Karl's a top." Eddie sipped his beverage. "Damn! Lance makes 'em strong. Or maybe I just ain't had none in a while."

"Did I hear Karl say 'Christ'?" Don asked. "How long's he been swearin' with that word?"

"Who knows," Robbi said. "He picks up bad habits like you or

I pick up the dry-cleaning." To Eddie, she explained, "Half our unit thinks we're married already and the rest assume we're a couple. The ones who're smart enough to guess the truth are already on our side and won't talk. We'll make more money *and* get permission to live off base. The system's such bullshit."

"No argument from us." Don scanned the patio and waved to friends and acquaintances.

"*Why . . . waste yo' time? You know you gonna be mine!*" Karl screeched as he danced back to the group. "*I'm gonna get choo, YES I AM . . . !*"

"That was fast," Don said. "And I see you got your beer."

"My man just couldn't stay away from me more than five minutes." Robbi feigned passion. "Honey, where's your sweatshirt?"

"He's gotta show off that tan," Eddie said. "A wife beater undershirt in January. Could you be any more of a gay cliché?"

"Homo say what?" asked Karl. "It's hot beside the heater with all you pussies—not talking about you, old lady. Chill. Don't let me forget. I left the sweatshirt with my boy at the bar. He misses me very much by the way."

"What *do* Marines do in bed with each other?" asked Eddie. "I mean besides wear out a double-headed dildo?"

"Ha Ha Ha, that's so fucking original, sailor boy!" Karl said mockingly. "Ooh, quick, I need to write that down. 'all . . . Marines . . . are . . . nelly . . . bottoms . . .' there. Can I use that? I'm sure no one's ever heard it before."

"Smart ass."

"Speaking of Devildogs," Karl said, "Lance says there's a newby here tonight."

"Where?" the other three asked in unison.

"Whoa, you think I was throwin' meat to starving wolves," Karl exclaimed. "He's just another dime-a-dozen Marine 'mo."

"You mean another conquest for you," Eddie said.

"Naw, I'm through with officers," Karl said.

"An officer?" Don asked. "Did Lance tell you his name?"

"Yes."

"Okay, little buddy, I'm tired of playing twenty fucking questions. What's his name?"

"Why don't you go ask him yourself? He's been cruisin' you ever since we got here."

"Hello, handsome. Don't think I've seen you here before. Buy you a drink?"

Jay twisted his body to see who'd approached him, keeping his arms folded, though, as a way of retaining control. If the man was a worthy target, Jay would unfold his arms, lean against the bar and open up his body. He returned the man's smile but replied, "No thanks."

The long-haired man walked away, leaving Jay to his profiling. Of the dozens of men who'd cruised by, only a few could be servicemen. Fifteen years in Washington DC, with its heavy concentration of military personnel, had taught Jay how to weed out the real thing from the fakers in less than five seconds. The haircut wasn't a good indicator—only amateurs believed they could spot a Marine or a Sailor that way. Hell, most sailors wore their hair *longer* than civilians did.

Jay was no amateur. He looked at a man's gait and posture as the initial signs of legitimacy. Military men carried themselves with a unique combination of confidence and caution. They'd been taught to walk bravely through a dangerous world. Beyond that, though, were a man's speech patterns and, most of all, his eyes. If Jay talked to a man and looked into his eyes, within ten seconds he knew with a ninety percent degree of accuracy if he was military or a wannabe.

Ten minutes later Jay spotted his first targets. Gay military men hung together in tightly knit groups. While that aided catching many of them at one time, infiltrating the clique was challenging. Through years of experience he knew how to gain their trust, always the key.

Prying himself between dozens of sweaty shirtless guys, Jay stepped onto the dance floor, where he removed his shirt and tucked it into his jeans. He smiled at a thin young man with a Navy tattoo on his chest. The man returned the smile, pointing Jay out to another Sailor. As much as Jay hated gay men's music, he laughed at its appropriateness for his mission. *I know what I want, and I want it NOW!*

"Lance says that he's hot but needs new clothes," said Karl. "Gotta agree with my crazy ex."

"Boys," said Robbi, "go meet him before you strip him and play dress-up. I swear you act like high school girls. And stop calling Lance crazy just 'cause he tried to run over you."

"I'm all for stripping him." Eddie's comment caught his three friends off guard. For a rare moment, the group was silent. They couldn't remember the last time Eddie had expressed anything mildly sexual. "Go ahead, Don. I see that look in your eye."

"Oh my God, Don," shouted Robbi. "I've never see you blush before! This is so—*cute!*"

"What're you waiting for?" asked Karl. "Take charge! If you don't, someone else will."

Don recovered from his momentary loss of composure. Patrick's handsomeness wasn't manufactured. Many men in Southern California worked hard to create an appealing—but ultimately clone-like—image for themselves, but not Patrick. *He looked real!* Don thought he'd lost the ability to be nervous about meeting another guy. He'd met hundreds of them, many on this patio, but seeing Patrick tonight proved him wrong. He felt like a jittery kid. As his conscious mind stalled, his instincts took over and he operated by reflex. Stepping forward, he saw that Patrick's drink was empty. Grabbing a five, he sidestepped toward the bar, passing it to Lance. Lance, quick on the uptake, traded him a cold Samuel Adams.

Don paused then approached the other man. "Um, excuse me, is your name Patrick?" He raised his voice, emphasizing the name. As the man spun around, Don paid extra-close attention to his eyes. An unexpected greeting was as genuine as any moment of human interaction. In those seconds, before others had time to deploy their defenses, Don learned volumes of honest information about their soul.

"Yes—that's—" the man stammered.

To Don's delight, he saw the look. Men, even the most calculating and emotionally secretive, were universally bad at hiding signs of physical attraction. When men saw something they desired, an unmistakable and undeniable fire ignited in their eyes. Don was thrilled to see it in Patrick. "I'm Don, Chris's friend. He said you were on your way out here."

"Right! Hi—Don—I hoped that was you—I mean, from how he described you, I thought that might be you. Across the bar. With your friends."

Don almost choked. Patrick was even more authentic than he looked. *I hoped that was you.* Don felt a giddiness he hadn't experienced in a decade. His well-rehearsed pattern was to squelch unfamiliar emotions. Not tonight. He heard Eddie's voice from earlier in the day telling him to get back out there. Rather than kill the tingling sensation and ignore the happiness, he decided to enjoy it all—ride it out and let it carry him someplace new. Maybe he'd go nowhere or maybe he'd get hurt—hell, he *knew* he'd get hurt somehow. Hurt was unavoidable over the long term—but hurt had to be better than the feelings of nothingness he'd suffered for years.

Patrick shifted nervously and Don wanted to put him at ease. "Hear you met my good friend, Lance. He's another one of 'The Few, The Proud.'" His voice trailed as their eyes met.

Visibly relaxing, Patrick smiled warmly and in a deep, soft voice said, "So you're versatile?"

"What?" Don hadn't expected a sexually forward comment from the reserved-looking man.

"MGD *and* Sam Adams—at the same time?"

"Oh—shit. Sorry, this one's for you." Don offered the premium beer to Patrick and took a swig of his own. He'd been so taken with the man's warmth, dimples and eyes that he'd failed to use his prop. Then again, he hadn't needed to. Patrick leaned back and rested his elbows on the bar, opening himself to Don, a sign Don didn't miss. As he slid next to Patrick, Karl winked and gave him a thumbs-up sign.

"Don't take this the wrong way," Patrick said. "You don't look like a gunny." Don remained silent as Patrick inched nearer. Shyly, he clarified his statement. "Meant that as a compliment."

"Thanks. You mean I don't look thirty-three going on sixty-four? The Corps's a hard life. Many of my peers haven't learned that chain-smoking and nightly binges don't make it any easier. And don't take this the wrong way, sir, but you *do* look *exactly* like a pilot."

"Because I dress like an officer?" Patrick laughed. "So I've been told."

"No. I don't mean you *dress* like an officer—which you do, but that's okay. You can tell I'm not exactly Calvin Klein. I meant it as a compliment. Seriously Patrick—you're very—" Don feared he was crossing a line—that his swirling emotions had carried him too far on their introductory meeting. *Fuck it.* "You're very handsome."

To Don's surprise, Patrick leaned closer in and their faces were only inches apart. He grew quiet and even more alluring. "I'm *never* this forward, but I'd kiss you right now—except something tells me you're not into public displays of affection."

With no hesitation, Don kissed Patrick. The younger man's lips felt firm and pliable and Patrick eagerly received Don's caress. Don wondered if time had come to a screeching halt for Patrick as well. How he wanted this sensation to last! He set his beer on the bar behind the slightly taller Marine and firmly embraced the younger man. Patrick's tongue found its way into Don's mouth and it tasted bittersweet but delicious from the rich beer. Behind Patrick, from across the patio, Don's friends made loud comments and clapped. The sudden attention caused his emotions to retreat. He pulled his head back a few inches and stared deeply into Patrick's green eyes. "I'm not into PDA at all—but there are exceptions to every rule."

Patrick nodded. "I'd say that was quite exceptional."

"I'm—" Don prided himself on his usually perfect bearing but right now he had none. He didn't care, though, because somehow he knew that Patrick didn't care. A mutual understanding passed between them that simply staring and smiling at each other was okay. They didn't need to say or do anything to impress the other. Don assumed Patrick was twenty-four or twenty-five, the age of most lieutenants coming out of flight school, but he looked a couple of years younger. He'd probably been a later bloomer in puberty, as well as in coming out. Don tried to recall the few details Chris had shared with him. Whatever Chris had said, it was understated. "You were Chris's student? How'd you figure each other out? He must be even brighter than I thought 'cause I never would've pegged you as gay. Well, not until I kissed you."

"Chris said he guessed I was gay early on—I don't know if he's just saying that or what. But he laid the bait for me and I followed it—eagerly—out to the beach, Memorial Day weekend."

"He still pulling that trick? We gotta get him some new material." Don laughed. "Or not. It's still working—I'm very glad to see. He didn't tell me much about you, though."

"Didn't tell me much about you, either." Patrick whispered. "If he had, I would've cut my leave short and made it out here a hell of a lot sooner." Goose bumps formed on Don's arm and neck. He whiffed Patrick's aftershave, an off-the-shelf drugstore brand that was earthy and masculine. "Please forgive me if I'm being a little—aggressive—but something about you brings that out in me. I want to see you again, like, tomorrow."

Don gulped, "Okay." Part of him wanted to say, *I want to see you again in less than an hour, under my sheets with all your clothes off.* Instead, he said, "Tomorrow's great."

Eddie said, "Pardon us for interrupting—"

"Fuck that—I'm Karl, this is Robbi and our token squid here is Eddie. Patrick, I presume?"

"Meet the family," said Don. "Guys, this is Patrick."

"Chris's friend from Pensacola?" Eddie asked. "His friends are our friends."

"Welcome to San Diego, Patrick," Robbi said as she shook Patrick's hand. "I'm Robbi."

"'Robbie?'" Patrick asked.

"'It's spelled R-O-B-B-I," said Karl. "But you can call her Roberta."

"Call me Roberta one more time, Karl, and I'll fucking slice your nuts off with a dull razor."

"Ouch!" said Patrick. "Sweet to sassy in under two seconds! I *like* you!"

Just as quickly as she'd turned on Karl, Robbi regained her earlier cuteness. "I wish I could've charged admission to that little show you put on. You're the hottest ticket at WC's!"

It was Patrick's turn to blush. "Um—great to meet all of you—"

"It's a little overwhelming, I know," said Eddie in a reassuring voice. "New city, new—"

"You a top? Or a bottom?" Karl asked. " 'cause if you're hookin' up with Don, then—"

"*Karl!*" Robbi punched Karl hard. "Oh my God! You are *absolutely* impossible!"

"Do I need to tell you to ignore him?" Don asked Patrick. Staring at Karl, Don's eyes gave a clear order. *Not this time!* Karl's submissive expression told him he got the message. Don usually tolerated Karl's bluntness but he wouldn't allow anything to screw up his chances with Patrick. As he watched and listened to Patrick converse with his friends, he fell even deeper for the guy. Looking back over his life, there were many twists and turns Don hadn't seen at the time. This was different. He knew that right now, in the moment, he'd never be the same again. And he was glad.

7

"You're strong," the Sailor said. "I like that in a man." Jay wrapped his arms around the man's waist and gave him a firm squeeze. "You twenty-one?" He hoped his playfulness seemed sincere. "They gonna arrest me for buying you drinks?"

"Well, thank you!" The Sailor slurred his words. "You're so sweet! I'm almost twenty-two!" Turning his glass upside down, he swallowed the last of his vodka. "Whoops! All gone."

Jay ran his hand through the Sailor's hair. "What's your name, handsome?"

"I told you already. It's Jerry."

"Just 'Jerry'? No last name?"

"My my, you ain't supposed to ask that until the second date," Jerry whispered in Jay's ear. "Tell you a secret. It's Giles. With a G." Jay grabbed him as he stumbled. "Wanna know another secret? My last name ain't all I'll give up on the first date."

"Something tells me it's no secret you're easy, 'Jerry Giles.' Your name is easy, too. Easy to remember." He pointed to the anchor and USN on Jerry's chest. "Like your tattoo."

"That old thing?" the drunken Sailor asked. "You can lick it if you want."

"I'll wait." Jay winked, asking, "Your friends in the Navy?"

"Why? You interested in them?" Jerry pouted. "I thought you liked me."

"I do. But I like to hang out with you military guys. You're so sexy."

"We are? Aw, you say the sweetest things." Jerry looked across the pool table and pointed. "He is. He used to be. That hottie's a SEAL. That one pretends to be whatever will get him laid. And this one's a Marine." Jay congratulated himself on his correct assumptions. "A lot of the military guys are stuck up. They hang out on the roof."

"The roof?" Jay asked. "They let people on the roof?"

"Oh yeah!" said Jerry. "It's nice up there. Want me to take you?"

Before Jay could say "yes," one of Jerry's friends interrupted. "No you don't, Jerry. Time to go. You been falling down for an hour. We're taking you home and putting you to bed." Jerry mumbled his dissatisfaction.

"See ya next week!" Jerry waved as his friend helped him leave. "I want my second date."

"Will I see you tomorrow?" Patrick prayed the answer was "yes."

"Tomorrow? Um, sure," Don said. "What're your plans?" Patrick rattled off a list of moving-related activities. "I'll give you my number. Call and tell me what time to come over. I'll pick up dinner and sneak into the Bachelor Officers' Quarters."

"Sounds like an outstanding plan," Patrick said. The two men smiled at each other for a few seconds before Patrick asked, "Do—you—want to give me your number?"

"Oh, shit. Yeah." Don searched his pockets and looked frantically at the bar for paper.

Karl smirked and handed his friend a book of matches. "These come in handy."

"You'd be the one to know," Eddie said.

"Thanks," Don said as Patrick handed him a pen from his jacket. "This looks nice."

"What kind of pen is that?" Eddie asked. "A Mont Blanc?"

"Yep. Too high class for me," said Patrick. "Graduation gift from my fiancée's dad." Don's expression told Patrick he should've broken the news of his former engagement more gently.

"Robbi's *my* fiancée," Karl said. "We're dropping her off at her girlfriend's lesbian bar later. You and *your* fiancée swing that way?"

Robbi rolled her eyes. "What? What'd I say now?"

"I assume your fiancée situation is—real?" asked Don.

"No. I *meant* to say *ex*-fiancée. Karen is—was—I just broke our engagement."

"Ah." Don gave the matchbook to Patrick. "Can you read my writing? More important—do you know where Vista is? It's just a few miles inland from Oceanside."

"A map came with my rental car."

"Oh shit!" Karl exclaimed. "A lieutenant with a map? Alert the search team now."

"Is he *always* like this?" Patrick asked. "Or is this my initiation?"

"Always!" Don, Eddie and Robbi said in unison.

Patrick repeated the number aloud. He fumbled with the matchbook. "I don't want to go but I need some rest. I'll see you tomorrow." Waving good-bye, he turned toward the exit.

"Good night," said Robbi and Eddie while Karl scoped out the dwindling crowd.

Don followed a few steps behind. "Want me to walk you to your car?"

Patrick squinted and gave Don a look of embarrassment. "I parked far—to be discreet."

"I did that when I started going to gay bars. It's smart. All the talk about Clinton lifting the ban has made our nightspots visible. One of the network news shows was here last night trying to talk to active duty military people."

"Military people talking to a reporter? Isn't that a little dangerous?"

"You get tired of the forced silence. Other than that, I—don't—" Don's words faded as he edged closer to Patrick. They gave each other a goodnight kiss, which, to Patrick's delight, was even more passionate than before.

"Tomorrow," Patrick said, bounding down the stairs with a huge grin.

As he drove to his motel, he couldn't stop thinking about Don—not that he tried. The memory—Don's musky aroma, the thick five o'clock shadow, his tan skin and deep-set eyes—excited Patrick in a way he'd *never* felt. His hands sweated, requiring extra effort to hang on to the steering wheel. He'd loved Karen, but she'd never made him feel like this. He knew so little about Don but couldn't wait to learn more. "Guess that's what tomorrows are for," he said, turning into the motel's parking lot. Even though he felt too excited to sleep, he wanted to hurry up and try so that tomorrow would arrive as soon as possible. Tomorrow was a chance to see Don again. He wanted to know the man who'd awakened him to this unknown ecstasy. Parking the car near his room, he looked at Don's number, with its bold swift strokes. In the room, the clock showed it was past midnight. "Awesome! Tomorrow's already here!"

"And the party continues," Eddie mumbled to himself as the men danced in front of him. WC's lower bar held good memories of the days when he and Ray had been the life of the party. He laughed as Sheffy, an old friend from the South, took the stage as Elton John, along with a stunning black drag queen. They did a remake of Elton's "Don't Go Breakin' My Heart," with someone named RuPaul taking the place of KiKi Dee. "Even the music's *kind of* the same."

"What?" a bartender he didn't know shouted over the noise. "You want something?"

"No—sorry." Eddie didn't realize he'd vocalized his thoughts.

He'd been away from the scene and it had gone on without him just as Ray had gone on without him. He didn't miss the scene but he missed Ray more than he could bear. Now he wondered why he'd stayed at WC's after his friends left. Maybe the magic between Don and Patrick had given him some optimism. He couldn't think about finding someone else, but maybe the sparkle that had returned to Don's eyes was a sign that overdue good times were on their way. Perhaps Clinton's inauguration and his promise to lift the ban were good omens. Or maybe Eddie should go home and rest. Tomorrow he'd clean the gutters and fix a window because there'd be no football games. The Cowboys and Bills were prepping for the Super Bowl.

"I see your friends abandoned you." Eddie assumed the voice behind him was addressing someone else so he sidestepped out of the way. To make certain, though, he glanced over his shoulder. To his surprise, a man looked at him. "Your group. Upstairs it looked like you were joined at the hip." The man moved closer. "Glad I caught you alone. Name's Stephen."

Eddie hesitated. After fifteen years in the Navy, he was suspicious about meeting people, *especially* unfamiliar faces in gay bars. He'd seen too many careers destroyed after people became overly friendly with beautiful strangers too quickly and he'd survived too much to suffer the same fate. "Good to meet you, Stephen." He measured his friendliness. "New in town?"

"Pardon?" Stephen scowled at the speakers, indicating the music was too loud.

Sheffy had left the stage and the DJ had switched to nonvocal techno that sounded like someone was beating pots and pans. Leaning forward, Eddie shouted, "Wanna go upstairs?"

"Upstairs would be great!" Stephen grabbed his beverage.

A thirty-minute conversation couldn't hurt. Eddie motioned for Stephen to follow him. The crowded stairway forced the two men to climb single file. Glancing back, Eddie said, "It's easier to hear up top and the music's better. I can't stand most of this crap anymore. Never thought I'd miss *Blondie* so much." On the second flight of less noisy stairs he said, "For lack of a wittier question, I asked if you were new in town."

"You could say I am. Been here a few weeks. I've gone out—till tonight, every bar and club was dead. I was beginning to think San Diego didn't have any nightlife."

"It's different. We're a lot more laid back than L.A. or San Francisco. And proud of it." Eddie waved to Lance as he and Stephen located an isolated spot at the edge of the patio. Lance smiled and nodded as he handled bottles and mixed drinks for WC's thirsty gay men and women. "Time for another drink. Get you anything?"

"A diet soda. Whatever they have."

"Smart man. These cops like to go after guys leaving gay clubs."

Eddie found a vacant spot at the bar. To the annoyance of the men in line, Lance stopped to make his friend a martini. "Those girls have had too much already," said Lance.

"Easy killer." Eddie motioned for Lance to hold back on the gin. "I'm a lightweight compared to what I used to be. My judgment's already off tonight."

"You kidding me? Your judgment's right on! Your friend is the catch of the day."

"My friend will have a diet soda." Eddie smiled in Stephen's direction. "Seems decent. He just moved here. Appears level-headed and reasonably sane."

"Reasonably sane? That's a rare find at this hour." Lance handed the drinks across the bar. "It's great to see you. You're one of the few guys I miss when you don't come around."

"Thank you, Lance. You'll be seeing more of me." Taking the glasses, he added, "Karl was a damned fool to let you go."

"You're a kind soul for saying that but I was the fool to think I could domesticate the boy. That's a job for someone with a much more forceful personality than mine. But yeah, he's a fool too. I'm quite a catch, ain't I? Shit! Speaking of Casanova—" Lance pulled a brown paper bag from under the bar. "He left his sweatshirt here. You'll see him before I will."

Eddie grunted as he tucked the package under his arm. "Always picking up after Karl."

"Embrace it. We exist to serve the gods. It's our destiny!" Lance returned to his customers.

Eddie preferred the roof, not only for the music, but also because the patio lights and the moon allowed him a clearer look at Stephen than in the dim lights below. "Here's your drink."

"Thanks," Stephen said as they leaned against the ledge. "You didn't have to get me a gift."

The comment threw Eddie until he remembered the paper bag. "This? My friend has a habit of leaving his clothes all over San Diego."

"Here's to good friends looking out for each other." Stephen clinked his soda glass against Eddie's and they sipped their beverages. Eddie maintained a semialert posture but he warmed to the new guy. Stephen had a dark—but not artificial—tan and big brown eyes. He wore the de rigueur faux-butch club outfit of tight T-shirt and jeans, but on him, they had the intended effect. With his masculine features and lean body, he fit into most gay men's "desirable" category. Physically desirable men, though, were commonplace at WC's on a Saturday night, especially after he'd had three strong martinis.

Stephen's most alluring feature was his eyes. Eddie knew the look well. All the masquerading in the world couldn't hide sadness from someone who shared it. Stephen had known real hurt and his big smile couldn't cover the pain. "What brings you to San Diego?"

"Same as everybody. The sun, the ocean, the climate—and the men. I was a security guard in Baltimore when I had this revelation. I was newly single and one morning I woke up and said to myself, 'I can do this same fuckin' job someplace a hell of a lot nicer than Baltimore.'"

Eddie raised his martini glass. "Here's to sky-high rents, low-paying dead-end jobs and perfect weather." Stephen laughed as he touched his glass to Eddie's. "Welcome to San Diego."

"And to friendly men." Stephen scanned the busy roof. "You know the bartender?"

"You interested in Lance? I'll introduce you. He's a great guy—smart too—has a goal of getting a Ph.D. in nuclear physics—or molecular biology, somethin' brainy like that." Eddie's slight buzz was just enough to override his rule against divulging friends' personal information.

"Really? He looks too sexy to be that intelligent."

"He showed up about five years ago. I think I was on my second tour here—I mean it was the second time I worked in San Diego." Eddie cursed inwardly for his slip. The distinction was that when civilians "toured," they went on *a* tour, as in going on a tour of the Sistine Chapel while on vacation, as he and Ray had done years earlier. When they changed jobs, though, civilians "moved" or "relocated." It was a stupid mistake and he should've known better.

If Stephen caught Eddie's sudden word change, he didn't let on. "I left Michigan at seventeen. Like a fucking idiot, I moved to Baltimore to live with a cousin. All the places in America, I had to move to goddamned Baltimore."

Eddie liked laughing again. "Good old seventeen. We're expected to make all these life-changing decisions at the very age when we're *least* capable of making them."

"Ain't it ironic? What life-changing decision did you make at seventeen?"

Eddie had set a trap for himself. At seventeen he'd joined the Navy. Maybe it would be easier to trust Stephen with the truth than to continue the game. *Loose lips sink ships.* The mantra repeated itself in his mind and he decided the game was safer. "Ran away from home."

"Where'd you run to?"

Eddie stared at Stephen for a moment to determine if he was nosy or genuinely interested. It was a thin line but he settled on the latter. "Florida for a while. Then Virginia. After that I went to Europe and then here—twice." He omitted his stint in Japan because that would be a dead giveaway. Few Americans—and no African-Americans he knew—ever ran away to Japan.

"That's a lot of running."

"You're right," Eddie said, sipping his martini. "But this is home now."

Several minutes of comfortable silence passed. "You haven't said your name."

"You never asked."

"Didn't want to pry." Stephen's smile was coy. "If you wanted me to know, you'd tell me."

"That's mighty polite of you. It's Ed." He chose the name he always gave new acquaintances. After Stephen spent time with his friends, Ed would become "Eddie."

The music changed and the volume increased. Eddie scowled at a video screen when a dance-techno group played a song he didn't like. "Thought we'd be away from this music here."

Stephen moved in, his body touching Eddie's. "Wanna go someplace where we can choose our own music?" he whispered. Eddie bristled. In the world of gay men, Stephen's question always meant one thing and *only* one thing. Perhaps it was the same between men and women, but among gay men, it was gospel truth. *Wanna go someplace* translated directly to *Let's fuck.*

"Stephen, you're a *very* good-lookin' man, I'm just not into any-thing sexual. Haven't been for a while. Probably won't be in the near future. Nothing to do with you. Back in my day, I woulda been all over you."

"Back in your day'? You're young." Stephen rattled the ice in his empty soda glass. "I'm not looking for sex. I'm new in town. Just looking for friends, that's all."

"Uh-huh." Eddie had heard this line before but judging from Stephen's face, he was sincere or a great actor. He decided to vio-late his rule against bringing strangers home. "I'm ready to go and I don't live far. You can follow me to my house if you'd like to come over and talk for a half hour or so." In a tougher tone he added, "But I mean it, Stephen. I'm not interested in sex. If that's what you're after, there are a lot of guys in this place who'd oblige you."

"I hear you, Ed. No sex. Been around the block enough times to know the value of my currency in the meat market. Not being vain when I say I could hook up with ninety percent of these guys if I wanted—just being realistic." Looking at Eddie intently, he explained, "What you and your friends have—*that's* what I want. It's what I had in Baltimore. I almost didn't move 'cause I didn't want to leave my friends. It's hard to find quality people."

"How d'you know we're quality people? I think we are. But you don't know that."

"It's what I want to find out—why I want to get to know people outside of bars. Come to a place like this, meet nice people, get to know them someplace else."

Eddie liked Stephen. What he said made sense and Eddie felt that perhaps he'd make a good friend and addition to their little family. He wasn't a military person but being in the service wasn't a requirement—it just happened that way most of the time. "Sorry if I implied you're just another horn-dog but come on—it's almost last call at WC's." Stephen laughed, his nod communicating Eddie had nothing to apologize for.

"Y'all ready for this?" said a voice on the television.

Eddie smiled at Stephen and said, "I'm ready if you are."

8

"I thought you two might fuck on top of the bar."

"Sorry, sport. I'm not you," said Don to his friend in his jeep's passenger seat.

"That's right." Karl laughed. "Forgot I told you how, at the end of Lance's shift, I'd pull his jeans down and flip him over the bar. He'd get off work then we'd both get off! Damn, I miss that ass. Too bad it's attached to someone so needy."

"Of course you told me. You *used* to tell me everything, remember?"

Karl was quiet for a few minutes but it was too dark for Don to see his facial expression and tell what he was thinking. "I tell you—like, I told you about those two behind Peacock Alley."

"That was nine months ago. Buddy, it's your life. No law says you gotta tell me about your business. But for three years you hooked up with a lot of guys and you always gave me the gritty details. Lately you haven't said shit about *anyone*. Makes me wonder, that's all."

"Fuck you. You get on my case for too much sex. Now you're telling me I don't have enough. What the fuck?"

Karl's sudden outburst caught Don by surprise. Because he was still enraptured by his experience with Patrick, he wasn't up for a verbal brawl. "Forget it. Sorry I upset you." He reached across the interior of the jeep and gave his friend a gentle squeeze on the shoulder.

"I'm not upset. It's just—it's just there are some things—things I can't tell you."

Karl's comment was alarming. "You can tell me anything. I thought you knew that." He diverted his eyes from the darkened interstate long enough to see Karl look out the passenger's side window into the night air.

"No, Don," Karl sighed. "I *want* to, but there are some things I can't tell even you."

Jay's simple plan was to earn the Sailors' and Marines' respect by passing himself off as something similar to a serviceman—a cop, a fireman or a security guard. He didn't speak the military's language with its thousands of unique phrases, acronyms and abbreviations. Only the men and women who endured the armed forces' intense initiation rituals were fluent in what he thought of as mil-speak. Fortunately, being in the military wasn't necessary for his purposes. His goal was to earn their trust, allowing him to infiltrate the military's tight-knit community of gays. Once he was accepted, he'd gather vast amounts of information like names, addresses, photographs and maybe even tape recordings and videos. He hoped to become a legend within the agency by busting the largest ring of homosexuals in the history of the armed forces.

But he had to hurry. American society degenerated more each day. Soon the new president would allow gays to serve openly. Starting tonight, Jay would use tougher and smarter tactics than the NIS had ever used to get rid of the homosexuals.

If Ed lived near the dance club as he'd said, their two-car convoy should be nearing his house. Jay had recognized Ed from his afternoon's surveillance in the park with Ollie. He had the opening he needed when Ed's friends left him alone at WC's. Initially, Ed's stoicism had been a hurdle but the Sailor was outmatched. Over the years, Jay had learned how to harness his charm and apply the right touch at the best time to win over the hardest-hearted men.

Although Ed was more disciplined than most, the Sailor had inevitably dropped his guard, revealing too much. Only a Sailor would've gone to Florida—boot camp in Orlando—then Virginia—many Navy bases there—and finally to Europe on a Mediterranean float. Ed's use of the word "tour" and his recurring moves to San Diego were also giveaways. Outside the club, Jay tried to glimpse Ed's DoD sticker but he'd shielded it. Regardless, tonight's progress with his networking plan was satisfactory.

Jay wasn't familiar with San Diego's neighborhoods. "Washington Street to Park Boulevard." From there they'd driven down two smaller side streets. Ed turned into the driveway of a small and quaint bungalow-style house. Jay parked by the curb and hurried across the street, following Ed to his front door. "Looks like a nice place, Ed. You live here alone?" An enlisted person couldn't afford a house in San Diego. Jay hoped Ed was an officer.

"Yes," Ed said curtly.

Jay feared he'd crossed a line by asking Ed a question that was too personal. He looked around, quickly trying to think of something generic to say. Fortunately, a bright porch light gave him the chance. "You've got an amazing green thumb. Or your gardener earns his pay."

Ed brightened. "Thanks. My yard is my therapy. More productive and cheaper than a shrink *or* a gardener." He opened the door. "Come on in, Stephen. Can I get you a diet soda? It's a mystery to me why you physically fit types stick to diet drinks."

"No thanks." Jay studied the room. "I'll be up all night from caffeine or pissing or both." As he'd suspected, Ed's house was immaculate and the smell was a combination of pine-scented cleaner, lemon furniture polish and a citrus potpourri. No hint of a dog.

Ed laughed. "Suit yourself. Have a seat on the sofa. Back in a sec—have to look after the dog, let him know I didn't abandon him."

"I don't mind if you let the dog in."

Ed disappeared through a doorway into the kitchen. "He gets crazy around strangers."

A door opened and shut. Jay heard Ed's muffled conversation with his pet in the backyard. "Hey there, boy! Ya' miss me?" Jay took advantage of his host's absence to look at his personal items. Photograph albums were stacked on shelves next to books like the kind seen in lawyers' offices. Framed pictures covered the walls displaying a large number of men in decent shape with military-style haircuts.

"Jackpot," Jay muttered. Ed's house was a gold mine of information. Many photographs showed Ed with the same man. One shot of the couple was at the 1984 Los Angeles Olympics. In the earlier photographs, Ed and his partner stood in front of landmarks like the Eiffel Tower and Buckingham Palace and they looked young and happy. The group photographs were at beaches, in bars or at parties. In the later photographs, Ed's partner was in poor health. If pictures were worth a thousand words, these walls spoke volumes about Ed's life. The story they told, and Ed's living alone, gave Jay the impression Ed's lover had died of AIDS.

Despite Jay's beliefs about homosexuality, he empathized with tragedy. His prior work had connected him with men who'd endured this awful disease. Even though Jay always used condoms when his work required him to have sex with men, he still took anonymous HIV tests every six months. His sense of duty, though, outweighed his sympathy. Their immorality corrupted the soul, and his emotions couldn't become entangled in their humanity or he'd lose sight of his mission.

Although the photographs were eye-catching, they weren't the best evidence in the room. A desk occupied the far corner. On top, under Ed's sunglasses, was a small notebook. On closer inspection, Jay realized he'd hit the mother lode. He became mesmerized as he thumbed through the pages. Ed's address book contained hundreds of entries listing names, ranks and addresses in military towns and bases around the world. Ed had updated many of them in pencil, increasing the information's accuracy and value as evidence. Telling gay from straight was impossible based on the entry alone but the odds were high that a significant percentage would be gay military men and women.

Jay wondered what else Ed might possess. The desk's top drawer contained useless bill stubs and receipts. He closed it and opened the second drawer. Suddenly he froze. "*Holy—!*" He was shocked to see a dull black Beretta 9-millimeter pistol, the kind the military used, with an ammunition magazine in its handgrip. The only way Jay could tell if the magazine held any bullets was to pick it up and visually inspect its chamber.

As Jay reached for the gun, the kitchen door slammed. He shut the drawer and slung the address book across the desk. As he stepped across the room to sit on the high-backed sofa, something hit the wooden floor but he didn't have time to see what it was. Ed entered the room. "The dog's fine and he still loves me. You can meet him next time. He's too unpredictable around people at first. This late he might wake the—"

Jay's heart pumped at a dangerous rate. He'd let himself get carried away. He cursed himself for failing to pay attention to Ed's location and to how long he'd been gone. "My grandma's dachshund was the same way." Ed had stopped mid-sentence. Jay followed his host's gaze across the room.

Ed's demeanor changed. Before, he'd been cautiously friendly but now he was tense and rigid and he moved deliberately across the room. He raised his eyes from the floor, looking directly at Jay. "Stephen—or whatever your name really is—"

Jay braced himself against the back of the sofa. His mind searched for an explanation for why Ed's address book was open. Too late, he realized his major mistake.

"I never told you my dog was a dachshund." Ed stepped toward the desk. "Why are my sunglasses on the floor? Why is my address book open? How *did* you know—?"

"The pictures," Jay blurted. "I was admiring your—your photographs—and—the dog is in—" Although Jay couldn't recall if he'd seen a dog in any photographs, the gay men he'd known in DC took pictures of their dogs like parents took pictures of their children.

Ed's anger grew more severe with each word. "There *are* no pictures of a dog!" he shouted. "We never *had* a dog. My partner was allergic to animals. I rescued a dog from a shelter because I wanted the company. Believe me, whoever the *fuck* you are—I haven't taken a picture since *way* before the dog came along!"

Jay remained silent as both his body and his mind froze. Usually he operated at his best under pressure but this situation stupefied him.

"So—*Stephen*. I'm asking you again. How did you know that my dog, which you haven't seen—is a dachshund? And why are my sunglasses—which were on top of my address book—on the floor?"

Jay continued to draw a blank and the only thing he knew to do now was leave. "Maybe—maybe I should—" He reached down to zip up his jacket, but the zipper became stuck and he tugged on it. Terror overcame him as Ed's hand inched downward. When Ed opened the desk's second drawer, Jay blacked out.

"Fuckin' A, dude. Pound my hole! Shove that big cock up my ass! Shoot your load! I want all your cum inside me, man!"

Don laughed as he grabbed the remote to lower the volume. His bedroom television backed against the wall his condo shared with the next. He doubted his neighbors could hear the loud moans and grunts of the guys who appeared on his television every night but he saw no reason to take a chance. Besides, he didn't watch porn for the dialogue—or the music.

He stripped off his jeans and T-shirt and threw them in the laundry basket. As he plopped down on top of his bed, he grabbed a bottle of lube and a small towel out of the nightstand. As tired as he was, he wouldn't be able to sleep without executing his nocturnal ritual. He squirted a small dose of the lube in his right hand and leaned into the pillow, raising his head high enough to see the hot guys having sex. After years of practice, operating the remote had become one of his ambidextrous skills. He massaged himself slowly. His hand was cold at first but after a few strokes, it felt good and warm.

The scene began where he'd left off the night before. It was a six-man orgy in the back room of an auto mechanic's shop, an image existing only in gay porn and in the imaginations of gay men. The video was one of two or three dozen Don owned and it was his favorite because two of the porn "stars" were Marines he'd known. Years earlier, they'd enjoyed a series of three-ways but he'd lost touch with them after they got out of the Marines and moved to L.A. to pursue their careers. Another reason he liked these videos was that they'd been filmed in the early eighties and the guys didn't use condoms. Although Don never had sex without a condom now, he saw nothing wrong with jacking off to pre-AIDS bareback group sex.

Every guy was stoned. One knelt on all fours and fell over laughing several times before another guy, one of the Marines Don knew, stayed hard long enough to penetrate him. Usually Don laughed with the duo as they tried to fulfill their commitment to the director, but not tonight.

He closed his eyes and smiled as his focus shifted away from the worn-out tape to the stunning man he'd met just a few hours earlier. Patrick had said, "I hoped that was you." Instantly, Don's dick sprang to life and became hard as metal. "*Patrick.*" Don squirted some more lube. He relived the scene when their eyes first met— the unguarded unforgettable moment when he'd caught "the look." He smelled Patrick's aftershave and he imagined how delicious Patrick's crotch smelled and tasted after a day of flying his helicopter. Nearing orgasm, he imagined Patrick on top of him, his penis sliding into Patrick's tight hole. Don stroked himself harder and harder and—"*Oh Patrick!*" he shouted at the ceiling as cum landed on his face.

"Wow." He lay still for a moment, enjoying one of those special orgasms, the kind that takes its time subsiding. He sat up in the bed and cleaned his torso as the porno played on, showing the two Marines sixty-nining each other on the floor. He laughed, remembering when the pair had made these low-budget flicks. He tried to recall how much cash they'd made. He'd been surprised at how little it was. Still, it wasn't bad for easy and fun work.

An image from earlier that day flashed across his mind. "*Karl's extra cash.*" Don visualized his friend counting the huge stack of twenties in his wallet. "Oh no." Don sighed as reality set in. He'd seen the pattern many times. Every day the military sent young, good-looking and hard-bodied guys to Southern California, where the alluring Golden State became a jungle of temptations. Many of these underpaid, hormonally driven and adventuresome guys from America's heartland fell prey to the triple threats of drugs, prosti-

tution and pornography. Some of the guys were gay, but most identified themselves as straight. They were restless and needed
money and the predators around the bases had perfected the art of
catching them in their webs. At least that's how *Don* thought of
porn producers. The unsuspecting young men—many just barely
out of boyhood—were no match for men who'd practiced their seductive craft for years.

Eddie had disagreed. In his opinion, the producers provided a
service that many men enjoyed. The video "stars" were adults ex-
ercising free will, and if they messed up their lives, they had only
themselves to blame. He'd called Don a hypocrite for enjoying the
porn while condemning the producers and looking down on the
actors. Don and Eddie had argued this point many times in the
past, and no doubt, their debate would continue in the years
ahead.

Don turned off the television and he crawled under his sheets.
He recalled Lance's comment that Karl hadn't left WC's with any
guys in a long time and that he'd noticed the same thing. Another
memory suddenly surfacing was that Karl had disappeared for
whole weekends recently without explanation. Don hadn't
thought anything of it at the time—Karl was a grown man with the
right to do his own thing. Taking all of these factors together,
though, Karl's behavior had changed. Most worrisome of all was
Karl's statement tonight.

I want to but there are some things I can't tell even you.

"Not you too, little buddy." Don lapsed into a night of fitful
sleep.

Eddie's first observation after entering the room was that his
sunglasses were on the floor. Then he spotted his address book
askew and opened, leading him to conclude that the stranger he'd
invited into his home had been snooping. Eddie's initial reaction
was to throw Stephen out of the house and advise his friends to
avoid the good-looking new guy from Baltimore—or who *claimed*
he was from Baltimore. But Stephen's knowledge that Rocky was
a dachshund alerted Eddie that the man's motive for being in his
house was far more sinister than simple nosiness.

He was furious that he'd been so gullible. Outwardly, though, he directed his rage at the lying scumbag sitting on his sofa. The sofa was an antique family heirloom Ray's parents had given them when Ray became a partner at his law firm. In his mind, he raced through his night's conversation with Stephen just to be sure. No, he'd never said that Rocky was a dachshund. Eddie's introverted and reclusive nature prevented him from giving away unnecessary details about his life, and his dog's breed fit that category. Eddie had to solve this mystery now. His and his friends' careers and livelihoods were at stake.

That's when he remembered the gun in the drawer.

As part of his pro bono practice, Ray had represented lesbians and gay men in some high-profile employment and housing discrimination cases. After receiving a number of death threats, he'd purchased the pistol and Don taught him and Eddie how to shoot it. When Ray died, Eddie left the house exactly as it had been. Ray's clothes hung in the closet, his law books were on the shelves and his loaded gun remained in the desk.

Eddie wondered how he could've fallen for Stephen's "I'm just looking for friends" line. Eddie wasn't some twenty-year-old just off the bus from Baton Rouge—he *knew* better or he *should've* known better. Stephen had spied on him—he'd probably watched Eddie's house for a long time. Maybe it wasn't too late. If Eddie put the fear of God in the man, Stephen might leave them alone.

"So—*Stephen*. I'm asking you again. How did you know that my dog, which you haven't seen—is a dachshund? And why are my sunglasses—which were on top of my address book—on the floor?"

Eddie didn't plan to pull the gun out. He didn't think the situation through at all. Going into an anger-induced hypnosis, he leaned against the desk and slid his arm down to the drawer with the gun. He was furious at the world for being so homophobic and bitterly despondent because Ray had died so young. He was enraged at this stranger for spying on him, for being in his house, for snooping in his address book and for sitting on a sofa that had been so special to Ray. Stephen didn't answer his questions but stared blankly ahead.

Eddie's eyesight had steadily worsened over the last year and Stephen was slightly out of focus. When Eddie saw him reach into his jacket, Eddie feared he had a gun of his own, a fear that sent Eddie over the edge. Stephen said something but Eddie wasn't paying attention. In half a second, he opened the desk drawer and grabbed the pistol.

Before Eddie could raise the gun into position, Stephen lunged at him from the sofa, a reaction Eddie hadn't expected. He jerked away from his attacker, and as he stepped back, his left foot crushed his sunglasses. When the metal frames slid easily across the polished floor, Eddie's left leg flew out from under his body and he lost his balance. As he fell backward, he pointed the gun directly at Stephen. Before he could pull the trigger, though, Stephen grabbed Eddie's gun arm, forcing it up toward Eddie's head.

As Eddie's forearm hit his chest, he heard the gunshot. He felt nothing as the bullet entered his throat on an upward arc. He never knew that a 9-millimeter piece of metal had penetrated directly into the center of his head, where it tumbled and turned his brains to mush before blasting out the back of his skull. Because it happened so quickly, or because he went into instant shock, he didn't feel it. In the last seconds of his life, Eddie saw a horrified expression overcome the stranger's face as he stepped away from Eddie's dying body in terror. In the background, Eddie heard Rocky bark and he smiled because he knew his friends would take care of the little guy.

9

"Ladies and gentlemen, rounding out our threesome, it's the fashionably late Colonel Spencer!"

"Glad to see you again, too, Pete," Leonard said. "At our age, though, we shouldn't refer to each other as 'the late,' fashionably or otherwise. Someone might claim our parking space."

The other two colonels laughed. "With your wit, you should've been a standup comedian," said Colonel Joseph Watkins. "Or a politician." As commanding officer of a Marine regiment, Joe was Leonard's infantry counterpart at Camp Pendleton.

"But not a general?" asked Leonard.

"Hell, no!" said Colonel Peter Williams. Leonard, Joe and Pete—and their wives and ex-wives—had been friends since Vietnam. "Generals don't need wit. Just a good caddy, a fifth of bourbon and an oxygen tank close at hand."

"Now, Pete," said Leonard in a taunting voice. "Are you referring to our boss, General Neville?" Pete, like Leonard, was the commanding officer of a Marine Aircraft Group, but Pete's MAG consisted of F-18 jet fighter squadrons at Marine Corps Air Station El Toro. Pete's bull-headedness frequently put him at odds with their superior, the commanding general of the Seventh Marine Aircraft Wing. It had also effectively ended his career in the Marine Corps.

Pete didn't bite. "You won't get me started today, you son of a bitch. Are we gonna play some golf or sit here and start the local chapter of the Women's Christian Temperance Union?"

The men strolled out to their cart and clubs. Looking at the sky, Joe said, "Glad yesterday's winds died down. Wouldn't be able to play much of a game today if they hadn't."

Leonard climbed into the front passenger seat. "Did you know that in almost every ancient civilization, an eastern wind was a bad omen?"

"Aw, Jesus, Leon!" Pete took his usual spot in the driver's seat. "We ain't even made it to the first hole yet and you're already philosophizin'."

"I'm serious," Leonard protested. "The Mayans lived in fear of an ancient prophecy: 'They shall also be smitten with the east wind.' The North African proverb was: 'A western wind carrieth water in his hand; When the east wind toucheth it, it shall wither.' The Bible is full of dire references to east winds. So is Chinese history."

"You're just a bundle of joy this Sunday morning," said Pete. "I'm takin' you to some Angels games this season. You need to get out more."

"Down here in SoCal we don't have to wait for something bad to happen when the east winds blow. Wildfires break out right away." Joe took the rear-facing seat. "Last October we almost lost two Marines when a fire spread faster than we could get the platoon out of the field."

"Fortunately January was wet, preventing the winds from doing their usual damage," Leonard said. "Unless keeping pilots on the ground counts as damage."

"When was the last time you flew?" Pete's foot hit the pedal and the cart jolted forward.

"Yesterday. Sledge arranged for Stinger teams to act as aggressors. I showed up at the last minute and flew with a captain alongside my squadron commander." Leonard grabbed the cart for support. "Are you insured to drive this thing, Pete?"

"Glad to see the east wind didn't ground you at all," Pete said. "Wish I coulda seen the look on Sledge's face when you showed up to fly with his boys."

"Pilots and your callsigns," said Joe. "Who's 'Sledge'? What's his major malfunction?"

"Besides bein' a drunk-driving wife-beating philanderer?" Pete said sarcastically. "That would be none other than the infamous Lieutenant Colonel Melvin 'Sledge' Hammer. Other than his—*minor*—problems, he's one of the Marine Corps's finest leaders."

"How do these unsatisfactory officers remain in the Marine Corps?" Joe asked as they rounded a sharp curve. "More worrisome—how the fuck do they get command of a squadron?"

"And a training squadron at that," said Leonard. "Christ, Pete! Sure *you're* not the drunk driver this morning?"

"Now Leon, you know I don't need to be drunk to drive this bad." Reverting to the topic, he answered, "I know how he got the job. General Laker *loved* the man. Treated him like a son."

"Say no more," Joe said. "General Laker. *There's* a name I hadn't heard in ages. His antics were legendary even among us ground-pounders." Leonard quietly offered thanks as Pete stopped the cart at the first hole. "Now that General Laker's retired, will Sledge get selected for colonel?" Joe asked, pulling a club out of his bag.

"Retired, my ass," said Pete. "General Laker's not only retired, he's on life support!"

"So is Sledge's career," said Leonard, "if I have my way."

"Shit." Pete put on his gloves. "If a Jim Beam–drinking certifiable moron like Paul Laker can wear three stars, Sledge Hammer can certainly get his sorry ass selected for an eagle. Hell, all of us made it, didn't we?"

Leonard squinted in the sunlight as he fished for his sunglasses. Finding them, he grinned at his close friend. "I disagree. Sledge and his kind haven't faced reality. The days when the General Lakers of this world could whore about in every port and drink all day are over."

Pete practiced his swing. "Well, then I say good riddance to bygone days and the dinosaurs of the past. Of course, it won't make any difference for me. But you, Leon, hell, you got your star. That means you gotta start actin' and thinkin'—which means *not* thinkin' at all—like one of them—*a general*!"

Joe looked surprised. "Is the list out?"

"Not that I'm aware of," answered Leonard. "Anyone who claims to know when President Clinton will sign it is delusional."

"Just saying what everyone knows," said Pete. "I'm sure you're on it, too, Joe, but I don't know how things work on the ground side of the house. Aviation I know."

Joe was first to tee off. As Leonard swapped clubs, movement in the direction of the clubhouse distracted him. He looked up as a shop manager drove a cart in the direction of their threesome. At the same time, a pager went off. "Who brought his goddamned pager to a golf course on a beautiful Sunday morning like this?" asked Pete.

"We're about to have company," said Leonard as the manager approached.

"Colonel Spencer!" shouted the manager from a hundred yards away.

"A pager *and* a pro shop manager." Leonard grew apprehensive. "I'd say we have a two-alarm emergency on our hands." Without leaving his cart, the manager explained that Leonard had an urgent phone call at the club. Joe said he also needed to return to the club to make a call.

"You two are just gonna leave me out here by myself?" Pete moaned, lighting a cigarette.

"Yes," Leonard yelled as they drove away. "I know what's in my bag, you worthless jet jockey. If you take anything, I *will* find out."

Within minutes, they were back at the clubhouse. "Colonel Spencer," Leonard said as he took the phone. He listened as his command duty officer briefly explained the emergency. "What? Lieutenant Roberts, you mean that's it? You're in squadron 707, aren't you? Good. Please give this so-called emergency message to Major Burr. Thank you, Lieutenant." Leonard handed his phone to Joe, who dialed the number to his infantry regiment's headquarters. "I'd wager we have the same message." Leonard watched Joe's face for clues. Sure enough, Joe's look changed to one of disbelief and he slammed the phone down in its cradle. "Coughlin?"

"Coughlin," replied Joe. "That meddlesome bastard."

The manager drove Leonard and Joe back to the first hole, where they happily resumed their game. "Will someone tell me what in God's name is goin' on?" asked Pete. "What the fuck am I? Road kill? No one pages me and no one sends a damn pro shop manager after me."

"Calm down, Pete," said Leonard. "This doesn't concern your jets—not *this* time, at least. Be glad. It appears that the Honorable Mr. Coughlin desires a helicopter flight Tuesday."

"And a full-fledged ground-based dog-and-pony show," Joe growled.

Leonard sympathized. "I hope your operational tempo isn't as bad as mine."

"Sounds like all Coughlin wants to do is show his face at Camp Pendleton for some free press time with Marines in the field," Joe said.

"Coughlin?" asked Pete. "That lunatic? You gotta be shittin' me! Both of you have to jump through hoops for that pompous—?" Pete grew red-faced. "You're right, Joe. My predecessor loved the guy and gave him joy rides in our jets. Don't ask me to do it, that's all I got to say. I have more important things to do with my F-18s than play Disneyland to Congressmen and Senators—especially *that* bloated bastard!"

"Sounds like we're all singing the same song," said Leonard.

Joe's voice lacked enthusiasm. "Let's play the game and worry about this later."

"Certainly," answered Leonard. "Nothing we can do to help the Congressman now."

"You're damn right we're continuin' the game!" Pete declared. "No politician is screwin' with my golf schedule."

As they resumed, Leonard said, "Our predecessors were pulled from *their* golf courses with news like, 'Colonel! The Japanese are bombing Pearl Harbor!' or 'Colonel! The North Koreans have crossed the thirty-eighth parallel!' or 'Colonel! Krushchev has ships bound for Cuba!'"

"I know what you mean, Colonel," lamented Joe.

"This is the down side of the *Pax Americana* in the new world order. 'Colonel! You can kiss a politician's ass!'" The colonels laughed, albeit somberly, at Leonard's perspective.

"Well, Leon and Joe," advised Pete, "maybe—just *maybe*—

when *you* two put those stars on your collars, you can change the new world order!"

"Perhaps." Leonard pierced the ground with his tee, lining up his shot. "But unless we're in the four percent selected, all we'll be changing is the filter in some general's coffeemaker."

"Excuse me—hello! Son? You all right?"

"What?" Jay slowly came out his daze. "I'm sorry. What did you say?"

The clerk had a concerned expression. "The total is nineteen dollars. You gave me a ten."

"Oh, sorry." Jay gave the elderly man two fives and retrieved his change. He took the bag, griping to himself that snacks, sodas, dog food and the Sunday paper cost so much. His legs were heavy as he walked to his car, and his back and shoulders ached. His watch showed two o' clock in the afternoon but his body and brain were in a twilight zone. He hadn't slept in thirty-two hours and the lack of sleep had dulled his mind. Focusing was a challenge and his co-ordination was gone.

The clerk informed him that the name of the quaint neighborhood was University Heights, although a university didn't seem to be anywhere in the vicinity. All Jay saw were early-twentieth-century houses and a scattering of postwar structures. Many were in the same California bungalow style as Ed's, but Ed's—now his heir's—was the nicest one on his street.

Jay drove to the spot of the vigil he'd maintained for the previous twelve hours. He shut off the ignition, wincing as Ed repeated his last words: *How did you know that my dog, which you haven't seen— is a dachshund? And why are my sunglasses—which were on top of—*

"Stop!" Jay shouted. He put his head down and rubbed his eyes but nothing halted the video. Although he'd blacked out at the time, the scene had lodged itself in his subconscious. Each time it replayed, the images were more ferocious than before.

Ed reached for the drawer containing the pistol, sending Jay into automatic pilot. All he'd meant to do was take the gun from Ed. *That's all!* Gunmen had pulled weapons on Jay in the past and he'd vowed that no one would ever point a gun at him again. A man was never more powerless than when he was staring at the wrong end of a loaded firearm. Jay's intentions—seemingly reasonable at the time—had been to immobilize Ed's shooting arm with his left hand and wrest the gun from Ed's grip with his right. Once Jay had the gun, he'd remove the bullets and reach a truce with the Sailor. Looking back, peace was probably what Ed wanted too, but Jay's instincts wouldn't let him give away that much power. No, Jay *had* to control the gun.

But everything had gone wrong. Instead of immobilizing him, Jay had slammed Ed's gun arm against his chest. Because his right finger had been on the trigger, the Beretta fired, launching a bullet into his skull through his throat and sinuses, the softest part of the head. Jay watched helplessly as the chain reaction unfolded. The strangest part was Ed's smile just before he died. The smile unsettled Jay most of all. *Why had he smiled? Did he see something? Did he learn some—truth? Some truth that only death teaches? If so, what was it?*

Jay didn't have the luxury of dwelling on Ed's serene face at the moment of his death. Jay assumed that a neighbor heard the gunshot and called the cops, giving him little time. His mind, never at rest, went into hyperdrive. Ed's blood and brains had splattered the wall behind his lifeless body, resembling a typical suicide scene. The investigators wouldn't find a note but fewer than twenty percent of people who committed suicide left a note. Looking around, Jay realized a note wasn't necessary. The room—filled with pictures and mementos of Ed's recently deceased lover—was a visual suicide note.

Two pieces of evidence might divert an investigator from the conclusion that Ed's death was a suicide. Jay picked up the crushed Ray-Bans from the floor near Ed's feet. No one would miss the Sailor's sunglasses. Next, Jay removed his jacket and stripped off his T-shirt, using it to wipe his fingerprints off the front and back covers of the address book. Although its information seemed too valuable to leave, he decided against taking it as Ed's friends would notice it was missing. To be safe, he wiped the desk, the sofa and the other furniture clean. Backing away from the death scene, he used his shirt as a mitt and opened the door, wiping prints from the doorknob. He gasped when the chilly early morning air hit his bare chest and he hurried to put his shirt and jacket back on. Racing across the front lawn to his car, Jay heard the dog bark, a bittersweet reminder of Porky's unconditional love. If only he'd used his head, he wouldn't have mentioned his grandma's dachshund! Too late, though—the dog's owner was dead.

As stealthily as possible, Jay drove his car around the corner, parking by a curb where he had a view of Ed's house. He slid low in the seat and dreaded the inevitable siren. But as the hours went by, the sun arced overhead and the community remained at rest. Jay's world was the opposite of peaceful as he relived that final gruesome scene dozens of times throughout the early morning hours. By late morning, his stomach ached and he felt like his bladder would explode but he remained motionless for a few more hours. By Sunday afternoon, his discipline was no longer enough to stave off Mother Nature. He found a store with a public toilet and purchased some food for himself and the dog. The poor thing had to be starving by now.

But back at Ed's house, after seeing the death scene in his head again, Jay decided feeding the dog was too dangerous. "Sorry, little guy. You're going to have to wait until it gets dark."

10

"Always wondered what the inside of the bachelor officers' quarters looked like."

Patrick laughed. "I don't mean to insinuate anything by what I'm about to say—"

"That means you're *totally* about to insinuate something." Don set the bag of Chinese takeout on a cheap faux-wood table and playfully pushed the young officer onto the bed.

"—something tells me you've seen the inside of a BOQ room before."

"But I've never seen *your* BOQ room." Don fell onto the dusty bedspread inches away.

"That's because we just met last night." Patrick turned sideways, propped his head on his hand and scanned Don's torso.

Reaching across the bed, Don took Patrick's hand into his own. "Was it really just last night?" Their lips touched, and to Don's delight, their kiss was slow and long. They had time. With no reason to rush, he wanted to savor every minute with this man. "You know—I—" Don's cheeks grew warm and he was sure he was blushing. "I was afraid you might not call."

"What?" Patrick massaged Don's palm. "You couldn't see how crazy I was when we met?"

"Yeah, guess I could." The two men laughed and kissed again. "But you didn't call today until after fourteen, I mean two o' clock—listen to me! 'You didn't call!' I sound pathetic, not like a gunnery sergeant in the United States Marine Corps."

"Woof! Say that again."

Don got on his knees. As loudly as he dared in the officers' building, he shouted, "Gunnery Sergeant D. A. Hawkins, United States Marine Corps, reporting as ordered, sir!" As he said "sir," he whipped his shirt off over his head, leaned across the bed and ripped Patrick's off as well. As he disrobed the lieutenant, he feared he might be going too fast. But when Patrick's head popped out of his shirt, Don saw the most charming—and willing—smile he'd ever seen on a man. "Awesome." He ran his hand over Patrick's tight and lean abs.

"What's the 'A' stand for?" Patrick asked.

Don hesitated. "I could tell you—but then I'd have to *eat* you."

"What're you waiting for?" Patrick pulled Don down to the bed. "Tell me now!"

"Antonio."

"Antonio," Patrick said. "That's a great name. You Italian? That'd explain your looks."

"My mom was." Patrick's face winced at Don's use of past tense. "Died when I was a baby. Hodgkin's. Today she coulda been treated, but in the early sixties, it was different."

"I'm so sorry—"

"Stop it. No downers, not today." He ran his hand over the smooth skin covering Patrick's shoulders and arms. "Tell me about your day."

"Well . . ." Patrick began, "I *wanted* to call you sooner, but I got a late start. Checked out of the hotel in San Diego. Drove up here. Gosh, I didn't realize what a long drive that is."

"Don't have to tell me. It's thirty-eight miles from my condo in Vista to WC's. After a few hundred times it's not so bad. Ask Robbi. She drives it daily from her girlfriend's in Hillcrest."

"Then I checked into this room." Patrick waved his hand around the drab space with Spartan furnishings. "Not the Ritz. But if you stand on the bed, you can see the ocean."

"It *is* the Ritz compared to what we enlisted folks get. Only one of your chairs is broken." Don sniffed. "Hell, you can hardly even smell the asbestos." They laughed and stared into each other's eyes. "Did you find an apartment?"

"Yep. Got a great deal on a place next to the beach thanks to California's real estate slump."

Don threw his head back. "Listen to Machiavelli over here! Homeowners—me included—have lost millions in property values since 1989. Foreclosures force children into the streets. But Patrick's happy. He gets a cheap apartment on the beach in beautiful downtown Oceanside."

"I can't remember when I laughed this hard. There *was* that time when Chris Ashburn tried to pick up this twenty-year-old. Watching him get shot down was fucking hilarious." Patrick ran his fingers through Don's dark, curly chest hairs. "I like the way you groom this. Just right." He leaned in for another kiss. "Then I started looking for a car."

"Not a 'lieutenant-mobile', I hope."

"Of course. A shiny new sports car is a rite of passage. I've earned it—*and* I'm doing it the right way and *not* going in debt. My dad's buying it for me as a present for getting my wings."

"That's awesome. Glad you gotta dad like that. Wanna know the only thing my dad ever bought me?" Patrick nodded. "When I turned twelve, he bought me a six-pack."

"I assume it wasn't a six-pack of root beer? God, Don, again, I'm sorry—"

"Who's complainin'? I enjoyed the six-pack," he said, trying to lighten the mood. "At seventeen I enlisted. Corps's turned out to be the best dad in the world."

Patrick became sullen. "What's always on my mind, though, is that my dad would disown me—if he knew—like, if he knew I was on this bed—with you right now."

"So would my dad."

"Really? Your dad's like that—?"

"I'm not talking about 'Dad the Drunk.' He wouldn't give a crap if I fucked sheep. 'Dad the Marine Corps.'" He gently stroked Patrick's cheek with his hand. "There's some things we can *never* tell our dads." He paused. "Thought we agreed no downers."

Patrick rolled on top of Don. "Agreed." He propped his elbows on Don's shoulders and put his head in his hands. "After I looked at a few cars I *didn't* like, *finally* I could call you."

"Thank God. I sat by the phone like a sixteen-year-old girl, waitin' for some guy to ask her to the prom. I was so excited. After we hung up, I called Eddie."

"What'd he say? That we just met last night and don't fall too fast? That you need to slow down and be careful? Don't get hurt?" Patrick rolled off Don and lay beside him on the bed. "Best friends give the best advice. Wonder why we never take it."

"He wasn't there so I left a message on his machine." Don fished in his pocket for his pager. Looking at the device, he said, "Strange. Eddie never waits this long to return a call."

"He seems like a good guy."

"He's the best. Helped me through some stormy times, especially after we met. Not too long ago I helped him—as best I could—through the worst thing imaginable." Don returned the pager to his pocket. "But all that's ancient history." He slid his finger down the center of Patrick's chest. "Bet he worked around his house all day. Took the pooch to the park, the usual Sunday routine when football's not on." Don sat up. "Permission to take my shoes off, sir."

"Granted." Patrick removed his as well.

Grabbing Patrick firmly by the shoulders, Don rolled him on his back and straddled his torso. "Back to *us*. Where were we?"

"Don, um, I got a confession." Patrick feigned guilt.

"What? I've known you less than twenty-four hours and you got something to confess?" He grabbed Patrick's nipples and gave them a little squeeze.

"When I got back to my hotel room last night—" He paused.

"Yes?" Don pinched Patrick's nipples harder.

"I thought about you."

Don let go of Patrick and rolled over beside him. "And I thought about you."

Patrick gave Don a mischievous-looking half-smile that brought back a flood of wonderful memories. "I thought about you—while I beat off."

"Then we've got a lot in common, sir."

"You think about yourself while you beat off?" Patrick laughed.

"No, silly boy." Don rubbed his knuckles across Patrick's head. "I mean, no, smart-ass lieutenant!" The two men engaged in a bout of wrestling-as-foreplay for a few minutes when Don thought of something he should've realized from the beginning.

"What's—is something wrong?"

"No. Nothing's wrong, not at all. But—did you say you just broke an engagement?"

Patrick put his arm around Don's neck and rubbed Don's whiskers. "Yes. That's—it's not a problem, is it?"

Don smiled and tapped his forehead against Patrick's. "Of course not. But forgive me if this is too personal. Have you ever—you know—had sex with a guy?"

Patrick bit his lower lip. "No. Not with a guy. But—it's only because I never met a guy I wanted to have sex with, well, I mean *really* wanted. Until last night. When I met you. Am I making sense? Guess what I mean is, I *really* want you."

Don felt a lump in his throat. "Wow, Patrick. That's—that's the most romantic thing anyone ever said to me." Don gently squeezed Patrick's firm upper arm. "And yes, it makes sense. I figured out you're the guy—and I'm breaking every rule in the gay men's dating handbook by saying this so soon, but you're the guy I've been waiting for."

Patrick laughed. "You mean you haven't had sex?"

"Very funny, flyboy." Don leaned over and whispered, "I've had sex before but I've gotta feeling compared to what's in store for us, I've never made love before."

Patrick's face brightened. "Now *that's* the most romantic thing anyone ever said to me. Being new to all this—are we crazy? Feeling this way and saying these things so soon?"

"Only as crazy as we think we are. I know what I want when I see it. My only concern is that you haven't had a chance to sample the big gay smorgasbord."

"Shhhh." With a strong burst of energy, Patrick pushed Don onto his back and unbuttoned his jeans. "The only smorgasbord I wanna sample is in front of me." He kissed Don hard and full, his lips thrusting into the other Marine's mouth. "I can't wait to get lost in this hairy chest."

Don unbuttoned Patrick's jeans, feeling Patrick's washboard abs again. "What *do* they feed you officers at Quantico?" Don rolled Patrick over and slid Patrick's jeans over his lean hips and legs. Patrick put his hands behind his head, lying on the bed in a position that said, *Take me.*

"You are one handsome man," Don said as he removed what was left of his clothing. Patrick also removed his boxers. "Wow." Don slid his naked body on top of his companion. "You really are the whole package, aren't you?"

"Good boy! There you go." Jay emptied the last of the dog food onto the concrete patio and looked around Ed's backyard. Fortunately, the moon was bright and he located the empty water bowl near a spigot. "Here's some water." He scratched the little dog. "You're two dogs long and half a dog high." Thankfully, Ed's pet hadn't barked when Jay jumped over the small fence between Ed's house and his neighbor's. "That's all, fella. Don't bark." The dog looked both satisfied and curious.

As Jay leapt over the fence, returning to his car, he heard the muted ringing of Ed's phone. In his sleepless delusion, Jay had begun to fantasize they'd never find Ed's body. Maybe the Sailor would decompose into nothingness and no one would be the wiser. How he wished that were the case! His problems would be over. The phone's ring, though, brought him back to reality. Ed had family, friends and a job. Even though his body had been lifeless for almost twenty-four hours, tomorrow was Monday and someone would miss him.

Jay returned to his car. Against his will and better judgment, he fell asleep for a few hours. When he awoke, he realized that *tomorrow* wasn't Monday—*today* was. He looked toward the southeast and saw the faint early glows of the crisp winter sunrise over the mountains east of San Diego. As desperately as he wanted to remain at the scene of the crime—no, this wasn't a crime, it was just an incident—and learn what would happen, he had to be at his office soon. Now that he'd slept, his mind worked again and a plan formed in his head. Fortunately, the sun remained low on the horizon. Grabbing a pen and a slip of paper, he darted across the street and copied the DoD decal number from Ed's Oldsmobile.

As Jay stared at the windshield, an item on the front seat caught his attention. He eyes became riveted to the brown paper bag Ed said held a friend's clothing. Suddenly, Jay had an idea that might solve his problems. He tried the door but, as expected, it was locked. He turned his head to look at the house, dreading what he had to do. Repeating his drill, he took off his jacket and laid it on the car. Steeling himself to the cold, he stripped off his T-shirt and wrapped it around his right hand. He hurried to the front door because he was running out of darkness.

The door was as he'd left it—not locked. The body was also as he'd left it—not alive. From Jay's limited knowledge of forensics, he didn't expect the smell to be overpowering after only thirty hours, and thankfully, it wasn't. Kneeling beside Ed's corpse, Jay thought about all the microscopic processes taking place inside the body. Bacteria had begun spreading, breaking down tissues and blood vessels. Black spots had formed on the white parts of Ed's open eyes, the only visible sign, other than the pool of drying blood, that his body was decomposing. In the cool, dry room, he'd decompose slower than average; regardless, putrefaction would set in soon.

Ed had used his right hand so Jay, using the T-shirt as a glove, reached into the right pocket of Ed's jeans. He grimaced. Ed's leg felt like a piece of steel and his joints were frozen. Rigor mortis was at its peak at twenty-four hours. Suddenly, a noise startled Jay. It was only a fly buzzing by his ear, landing on Ed's lips.

Seeing light through the open front door motivated Jay to hurry. He found the keys, snatched them out of Ed's pocket and ran outside, where he retrieved the paper sack from the Oldsmobile's front seat. Relocking the car, he returned the keys, this time setting them on the desk. He couldn't bring himself to touch the stiff corpse a second time.

Safely outside, he dressed and stuck the paper sack under his jacket. As stealthily as possible, he returned to his car. After a short detour home to clean up and change clothes, he drove to work, smiling along the way. Work is where he had to be to take care of this mess.

Thank you, he prayed, *for giving me this plan.*

Patrick looked in the mirror and adjusted the khaki necktie, a required part of all Marines' "winter service alpha" uniforms. "Alphas" were the uniform Lieutenant Colonel Oliver North wore when he testified before Congress about his role in orchestrating the Iran-Contra scandal, making it almost as recognizable as the Marines' Dress Blue uniform. The alpha coat—or blouse, as Marines called it—had an exterior belt worn tightly around the upper part of the waist. Patrick's was snug on his lean frame. His only medal had been easy to affix—as dictated by Marine Corps uniform regulations—one-eighth of an inch above his rifle and pistol shooting badges and centered on the pocket.

While his uniform adhered perfectly to standards, as it always had, Patrick's face looked different. Was this "afterglow"? It seemed strange that the excitement and serenity he felt inside radiated on the outside. Technically, he was still a gay virgin. He and Don had decided to wait until next time to "go all the way," but if last night was the appetizer, he couldn't hold off much longer for the main course.

"What's so funny, my handsome Devildog?" Don approached him from behind, naked, and much to Patrick's enjoyment, semi-hard. "Damn, Lieutenant, I thought I got up early! It's not even zero-five-thirty yet."

"Can't be late for my first day at the new squadron. Besides, I didn't sleep much—not that I wanted to between our three times. I couldn't take my eyes off you sleeping."

"Spoken like a real hard-charger," Don said, using "Marine-speak" for "overachiever." He tugged at the flaps of Patrick's blouse, straightening a few wrinkles on the back. "Perfect."

"Where'd you go last night when you stepped out? I missed you."

"To the pay phone in the lobby. Seemed safest to go when none of your fellow officers would be awake. Didn't see anyone but the clerk. He was asleep."

"Who'd you call?" Patrick frowned at the off-center knot in his tie.

"Eddie." Don sounded concerned. "He always returns my calls. I'm a little worried." He moved his nude body in front of the mirror. "Let me help you."

"Maybe he went somewhere and hooked up." Don looked even better first thing in the morning and Patrick felt *his* penis getting hard. "Like his best friend."

Don retied the knot, smiling when he brushed against Patrick's bulge. "It'd do him some good. But he wouldn't be away this long. Not with Rocky at home."

Patrick let his eyes enjoy every square inch of his overnight guest. "Wish I had a camera." He squeezed Don's meat as Don finished adjusting the necktie. "Me, in my alphas, getting ready to check into my new squadron. You, helping me, standing there naked as when you were born, but *hot* as hell. And they say homosexuality isn't compatible with military service."

Don finished the tie and squeezed his young lover gently on his upper arm, carefully avoiding the lieutenant bars pinned to the shoulder epaulets of his uniform. "I'd say we're compatible." Giving Patrick a tender peck on the cheek, he said, "I won't touch you because this uniform is flawless. And you're right, you should—and will—make a great impression this morning." Don searched the room for his boxers and jeans. "Make half as good of an impression on them as you've made on me and they'll meritoriously promote you to captain."

"If officers *could* be meritoriously promoted, the ass kissing would be even worse than it already is." Patrick picked up his garrison cap to walk with Don out to his car.

"Aren't you a little young to be so cynical?" Don asked, putting on his socks and shoes. "Besides, you're a damn good ass kisser yourself, from what I remember." He winked and pulled his shirt over his head. Picking up his coat, he added somberly, "I know it's the 'officer and a gentleman' thing for you to walk me to my car, but we can't risk it. No one can see us together. *Especially* not here at the BOQ."

Reality crashed into Patrick's room like an uninvited guest. What he and Don did last night was illegal according to the Uniform Code of Military Justice. But it felt right and in Patrick's heart he knew there was nothing wrong with it. Unfortunately, their government and their Corps held a different opinion. "What the fuck? What business is it of theirs?"

"None. That's why we don't tell them and we don't let them figure it out." Putting his hand on the doorknob, he said, "I haven't felt this good in years. What you and I did last night—what we have here, right now—is ours alone. No one can take it from us and it's none of their goddamn business. But we gotta be smart."

Patrick nodded that he understood even though the situation infuriated him. "I feel the same. And I hope—I hope that—"

Don gave Patrick a "can't wait to see you again very soon" kiss. "Hope is good. Give me a call tonight. Tell me how your first day goes." He smiled and opened the door. Seeing the hallway was vacant, he stepped outside.

Patrick remained in the room. He couldn't have gone outside anyway because he had to wait for his erection to go down. "Damn. Feels like I'm a teenager again," he said, grinning. "Only nothing like this ever happened to me in high school, that's for sure."

11

"Ollie will be in by eight thirty, but he has a conference call with Washington as soon as he arrives. Anything requiring his immediate attention?"

Jay had been at the low end of hierarchies. He'd learned which people in organizations had the most influence—and posed the greatest threat. The younger agents straight out of college gravely underestimated Esther Wilson's power in the NIS, but not Jay. Esther knew as much as Ollie about the office's investigations but now was too soon to involve her in his plan regarding Ed. "I need to talk to Ollie—but I'll be out of the office for a few hours."

"After his conference call he has a ten o' clock and a late lunch appointment but I'll make sure he's free, say at eleven thirty? Will that work?"

"Yep. Thanks, Esther."

"Sure thing, Agent Gared. Give me a call if you need to change it."

Jay hurried to his cubicle. He didn't bother to remove his sports coat because he planned to be out the door in less than five minutes, assuming the computer systems worked. The machine booted up, asking him for his log-in information, which he hadn't yet memorized. He'd written his ID and password on a slip of paper he kept in his wallet. As he thumbed through his cash and receipts, he saw another handwritten number. "Where did this—?"

CODE OF CONDUCT 91

He vaguely remembered copying a license plate number in the park on Saturday. That seemed like a lifetime ago but staring at the paper jogged his memory. The number belonged to Ed's friend—the one driving the jeep.

After getting on to the NIS's link to the military's database, Jay entered Ed's DoD decal number. While the system slowly searched for the information, he grabbed a folder and located the proper forms to open the file. A few minutes and several keystrokes later, he had all the information he needed on "Chief Petty Officer Edward 'Eddie' Lamont Johnson." As badly as he wanted to search for information about the jeep, he didn't have time but would follow up later. "Have a good morning, Esther." Jay ripped the paper out of the dot matrix printer. "Back at eleven thirty," he shouted as he ran out the door.

"Be right with you, sir. Please have a seat beside the first desk— that's mine. I have to brew the coffee before the squadron commander gets in."

The clock above the doorway showed seven-twenty A.M. Patrick had been told that enlisted Marines arrived at work no later than seven thirty, but Marine officers should be in no later than seven. Obviously his new squadron commander didn't follow that rule. "Take your time, Corporal. Don't think I'm on the flight schedule today." Patrick sat in a dull gray metal chair. In a photograph on her desk, Corporal Delarosa's long black hair hung beautifully over her shoulders. She, a man and a crinkly-faced infant smiled from the picture frame. "Beautiful family you have here."

"Thank you, sir." Corporal Delarosa smiled as she scooped the military-issued coffee grounds into the percolator. "You pilots. All you think about is flying." She pushed the button to begin the coffeemaking process, wiping a few loose grounds from the table. "I wish I could fly. The executive officer, Major Burr, promised to take me up in a Huey someday but I don't know when." The squadrons at Camp Pendleton flew Hueys—the light Vietnam-era cargo and passenger helicopters, as well as Cobras, the small, highly maneuverable and lethal combat attack helicopters. Patrick was interested only in the Cobra. "You're very efficient," she said as she sat at her desk and glanced at his forms, "and looks like you have all your receipts and records in order and the proper forms completed."

Two male Marines entered the office. "It's about time you showed up," she shouted. "I don't care if you had a formation run. So did I. You two take longer to get in uniform than women Marines. Get those messages downloaded by seven thirty. Lieutenant Colonel Hammer will want them on his desk as soon as he gets in!" To Patrick she said, "I say the same thing to those two every morning." Studying his papers, she filled out a travel claim form. "Wow, I'm impressed. You found an apartment already. What a great location."

"McAbe! You dirt bag. About time you showed up."

Recognizing the voice, Patrick turned to see Tim Roberts, his close friend and Pensacola roommate who'd graduated three months earlier. Patrick jumped to his feet and the two men shook hands. "Tim! How've you been?" He took a step back, giving his former roommate a good look. "Why the hell are you in cammies and not a flight suit?" Tim wore the woodland camouflage-patterned trousers and jacket that Marines in the ground community usually wore. "Ah," said Patrick. "Never mind. It's amazing what a guy forgets on leave. Ouch! You got stuck being the duty officer on a Sunday?"

"Yeah, man. Like a fuckin' dumb-ass I volunteered, thinking it'd be a slow day, you know, to force myself to study for a test coming up." Tim set the duty officer's logbook on a clean edge of the corporal's desk. "Talk about getting fucked royally. Yesterday morning, right after I showed up, I got the call that some congressman will be here Tuesday. I spent the rest of the day and last night running around like a bat outta hell working on that."

The corporal interrupted. "Sir, does the commanding officer know about the congressman?"

"Don't know, Corporal Delarosa. I got Major Burr on the phone but I couldn't get the CO. I assume the XO reached him." Turning to Patrick, Tim said, "Well, buddy, my day as duty officer is officially over. Now it's someone else's problem. How the hell are you? You look great in your alphas, man. Of course, checking in is the last time we wear them until we get out of this bullshit training squadron and check into something permanent."

"Thank God," said Patrick. "If I wanted to wear a suit, I wouldn't have joined the Corps."

"Sir," said the corporal, "let's get you checked in before they pull me aside to work on this congressional visit. What time did you arrive in San Diego on Saturday?"

"Fifteen thirty." The corporal jotted the time down on Patrick's form.

Tim shot Patrick a quizzical—and hurt—expression. "You motherfucker! You been here all weekend and you didn't call?"

Patrick searched for an explanation as quickly as his mind could work on a Monday morning. "You know how it is, buddy. Jet lag, and apartment hunting—looking for a new car—"

"Fuckin' A! You got rid of that shitty old Chrysler?" Patrick knew his friend well. By switching the subject to cars, he'd caused Tim to forget about his failure to call. But the episode was disturbing. Patrick had reconciled himself to hiding his gay life from the Marine Corps because that was the policy but he hated deceiving his friends. "Hey! Now that you're here, we need a fourth pilot in our house since our roommate deployed to Okinawa."

"Oh shit, I signed a lease yesterday."

"Why'd you do that?" Tim's pained expression returned. "We talked about this in Pensacola, you know? How cool it'd be if four of us lieutenants got a house here? Remember? I thought you liked living with me, buddy. Can you get out of your lease?"

"I don't think so. But I got a nice place. Come over anytime. Bring Melanie when she's in town. I move in Friday. Right off the beach—great view of the ocean."

"Sounds good, but if it doesn't work out, we can always make room for you at our place." Tim's disappointment was obvious and Patrick began to see that it was the military's *ban* on gays that created a wedge between him and his fellow Marines. The half-truths and secrecy diminished unit cohesion more than his homosexuality ever could. But he hadn't made the rule, and because of the DoD Directive banning him from service, Patrick couldn't offer his buddies an honest explanation for his seeming aloofness. The lack of understanding hung between the two friends like a thick invisible barrier. "You gotta come to our Super Bowl party on Sunday. You'll change your mind about living at the house when you see how great it is."

"I'm sure I will." But he knew he wouldn't. "Of course I'll be at the party."

"Also, sir," said the corporal, "the officers have a mandatory dining-in this Friday evening."

"There's a dining-in this Friday?" Patrick asked Tim. "And you blame *me* for not calling *you*? You shoulda given me a heads-up. Hope I can get my dress blues ready."

"Oh yeah, sorry about that, bro'. It's at the U.S. Grant Hotel in downtown San Diego. I know I shoulda called but—but I didn't wanna disturb your leave. Melanie's flying down—"

"Gunny! Where the fuck are the messages from Headquarters Marine Corps?" Patrick lurched backward as a voice boomed through the open doorway across the personnel office.

"Oh shit!" Corporal Delarosa dropped her pen. "He's early. Thank God the coffee's ready." She stood to face the man approaching from the back of the room.

Tim said quietly, "Remember all the shit they told us to expect from Sledge when we got here?" Patrick nodded. They'd hoped the stories weren't true. "For once, the Marines didn't exaggerate. He's a goddamned bastard." Tim turned to leave. "I don't feel like dealing with that asshole after what I went through the last twenty-four hours." Backing out of the room, Tim put his thumb to his ear and pinky to his lips and mouthed, "Call me!"

"Sir!" Corporal Delarosa said to Lieutenant Colonel Hammer as he stepped into the large open office. "Gunny's at the pistol range this week. We're printing the messages now." Patrick saw signs of both nervousness and determination in her response to the large man.

"Goddamn it! Major Burr's off to God-only-knows-where, the gunny's not here—where the hell is my worthless adjutant?"

"I don't know where the adjutant is, sir."

"I oughtta fire the whole friggin' bunch of 'em!" Sledge yelled, walking across the room to the coffeepot. "Any phone messages?"

Corporal Delarosa fumbled through a small stack on her desk. "Yes sir. The duty officer dropped these off a few minutes ago." She carried the slips of paper to the man.

Patrick and the other Marines had been standing at attention since Sledge's bombastic entrance. As the squadron commander snatched the messages from the corporal, he turned his attention to Patrick, much to Patrick's dismay. "Who the fuck are you?"

"Sir, I'm Lieutenant McAbe." Patrick stared straight ahead into empty space. He hadn't felt this anxious around a superior officer since leaving Officer Candidate School at Quantico, Virginia, several years earlier.

"What? You a goddamned squid masquerading in a Marine's uniform? Last time I checked, the Corps didn't have any 'lieutenants.'" Patrick was confused. *No lieutenants in the Marine Corps?* "Well? Are you a fucking mute?" Lieutenant Colonel Hammer bellowed in Patrick's face. "What are you? First lieutenant? Second lieutenant?—*Lance* lieutenant?"

The two young lance corporals in the back of the room laughed at their commanding officer's use of the fictional—and derogatory—rank of "lance lieutenant." Patrick finally grasped the squadron commander's point. While the Navy had an official rank of "lieutenant," the Marines Corps' "lieutenants" were either "second" lieutenants or, once they were promoted as Patrick had been recently, "first" lieutenants. Patrick's mistake was minor and Sledge's type of harassment usually disappeared after boot camp or OCS. But some officers enjoyed humiliating their juniors and Patrick's choice was to play along or go to the brig for insubordination. "*First* Lieutenant McAbe, sir!"

"There. Was that so fucking hard?" Sledge's sarcasm was annoying. Laughing, he added, "It's my job to cure you of that Navy bullshit after you leave Pensacola. Now, *First* Lieutenant McAbe, you're a Marine again. Welcome aboard!" He shouted the last statement in an apparent attempt at motivation but it came across as sadistic. Patrick's peers had warned him about the "You're not in the Navy anymore" attitude from senior Marine pilots but Sledge overdid it.

The Marines in the outer room exhaled audibly as their CO

walked away, sipping coffee with one hand and reading the phone messages with the other. "Corporal Delarosa, you got five minutes to get me the official messages from headquarters off the system."

"Aye, aye, sir!" the corporal responded as the Marines returned to their seats. "Hey, Devildogs, print those messages *now*!" She calmed down and said, "Whew. Please check over your Record of Emergency Data sheet, sir, and if everything is correct, sign here." She stepped away to assist the Marine at the noisy printer churning out pages of documents.

"Holy Mother of God!" shouted Sledge from his corner office.

"Damn!" she said. "He read about the congressman before I could break it to him gently."

Sledge stormed into the outer office and the Marines returned to standing positions. "Delarosa! Did you know a goddamned congressman would be here tomorrow?" Sledge Hammer was a large man, both in height and in girth. Patrick wondered how he passed the Marine Corps's annual physical fitness test, met the strict weight standards or even fit in the cockpit of a Cobra. He didn't doubt the man pulled strings to get around the rules.

"I just found out about it, too, sir. Five minutes before you did."

"Why didn't you tell me? This should've been the first thing out of your mouth. Which congressman is it?" His question stumped the corporal. "Well, you better find out—*now!*"

The woman's face brightened as she grabbed the logbook Tim had dropped off. Flipping through the pages, she stopped at the most recent entry. "The name is 'Edward Coughlin,' sir, from Orange County, California." Patrick congratulated her quickness with a smile and a wink.

"Coughlin?" Sledge calmed down as he repeated the name. "At least he's one of the good guys." Reading the message in his hand, he added, "I don't see why the fucking infantry can't provide their own goddamned escort officer." He stopped halfway across the room. "Hey, you there—*McAbe*—you ever been an escort officer before?" Patrick said he hadn't. "You ever heard of a Congressman Coughlin?"

"No sir." Sledge's questions couldn't be leading him to a good place.

"Today's your lucky day. I've got to put together a whole god-damned dog-and-pony show and you get to help me since you're the newest man in my squadron. Tomorrow morning you'll be the escort officer for the Honorable Mr. Coughlin when he visits Camp Pendleton. If that piece-of-shit adjutant ever shows up for work, he can help you." Sledge turned toward his office, but stopped midway. Looking directly at Patrick, he said, "McAbe—"

"Sir?"

"Don't fuck this up. You're not at flight school anymore—this is the real shit. Tomorrow's your first impression in the Fleet Marine Force that counts for anything, you understand?"

He'd entered the legendary—even mystical—FMF. So much for being broken in easily. Suddenly he was nauseous. "Yes sir."

"Delarosa, don't let *anyone* interrupt me this morning. I've got my own goddamned assignment to complete. If Colonel Spencer calls, tell him I'm working on his project." Sledge refilled his coffee mug, stepped into his office and slammed the door. Once again, the Marines returned to their seats.

"Damn, sir! Ever hear of the 'Big Green Weenie'?" The corporal used a common Marine expression referring to the Corps's habit of screwing over individual Marines.

"I have now." Patrick laughed but wondered what kind of shit he'd stepped in.

"I request permission to come aboard."

"Need to see some identification sir," said the Sailor standing guard over the USS *Cayuga*'s entry point. Jay hoped the Sailor couldn't discern that this was the first time he'd ever boarded a Navy vessel. Novices attracted too much attention, and requesting permission to come aboard exhausted Jay's knowledge of embarkation protocol. He said as little as possible and remained alert. Showing the Sailor his NIS identification, he awaited instructions. "Sign in." The Sailor pointed to a logbook beside the American flag. "What's the purpose of your visit?"

"Urgent business with the captain involving a criminal investigation."

"Very well, sir," the Sailor said as Jay entered the required information into the logbook. "Wait here and an officer will be down to escort you up to the bridge."

"Fifteen-mile forced march this Friday. Helmets, flak jackets, rifles and packs. Here's a list of gear that *every* Marine will have in his pack."

"Is the whole battalion marching?" asked Staff Sergeant George. "Or just our company?"

Don remained calm even though he wanted to punch the whiny staff sergeant in the face. Instead, he kept his voice firm and steady as he answered Charlie Company's second platoon sergeant. "What do you think?"

"Damn it, Gunny! This is bullshit. You gotta talk to the captain. Charlie Company goes on more fifteen-, twenty- and twenty-five-mile humps than any infantry company I ever been in. Hell, Alpha Company ain't been on a hump since—"

"You're out of line, Staff Sergeant." Don said, anger seeping into his voice. "First of all, I'm not Alpha's Company gunny and I don't give a shit what those fuckin' slack-asses do. Second, you must be confused on how the chain of command works so let me explain it to you. The captain gives the orders around here and I make sure they're carried out. I don't tell him what to do—I tell *you* what to do and you tell your squad leaders and they tell their team leaders. Is that clear?" Don's office was a cubbyhole in an old building tucked away in a remote section of Camp Pendleton. He barely had room for himself, his desk and the four cheap government-issued chairs he used for his daily meetings with Charlie Company's platoon sergeants. The closeness of the space added to the tension between him and Staff Sergeant George.

"Damn it, George. Have your men ready to go Friday morning," said the platoon sergeant for first platoon. "Try not to lose any Marines this time."

"I'll be doing random inspections at zero five hundred Friday morning," Don said. "Be—"

Without warning, the wooden door to Don's office smashed open. He jumped to his feet immediately. Only two people he knew dared to open his door without knocking. This time, though, the Marine leading the charge into his office was neither the captain nor the first sergeant, although both men followed closely behind. The man in front was the commanding officer of the battalion, Lieutenant Colonel Ritter.

"Gunny Hawkins, please forgive me for intruding on your meeting like this but we need to discuss something with you. In private."

Staff Sergeant George looked relieved to be off the hot seat. He and the other platoon sergeants took their cue. "Pick it up with you later, Gunny."

Don, standing at the position of attention, nodded to the staff sergeant. To the battalion commander he said, "It's no intrusion, sir. What can Charlie Company do for you and the Marine Corps?" Don's face remained stoic and his body stiff but he trembled inside. Moments like this reminded him that no matter how well he hid his personal life from the Corps and no matter how careful he was in his off-base behavior, a part of him lived in terror that the military would find out he was gay. He'd suffered terrifying nightmares with this scenario. The battalion commander—or higher—bursting through his door followed by military police. Some of his nightmares had been so real he'd felt the cold steel of handcuffs on his wrists as the MPs arrested him for sodomy and carted him off to the brig.

Lieutenant Colonel Ritter looked grim. "We learned about a serious problem this weekend, Gunny Hawkins—and I'm afraid it's your problem."

Don clenched his jaw tightly. *So this is it. This is how it ends.*

12

"I'm sorry, Agent Gared, but who did you say you had under surveillance?" The captain of the USS *Cayuga* sat behind a large desk covered with souvenirs from ports all around the world.

"Edward L. Johnson."

"Is this a joke?" The skipper stopped laughing. "Seriously, you have the wrong man."

Jay was prepared for the dismissive reaction. He waited calmly until he had the captain's attention and then continued. "You won't object if I ask to speak to Chief Johnson?"

"Considering your allegations, agent, I'll advise Chief Johnson not to say anything to you unless an attorney from the Judge Advocate General's office is present." The captain crossed the room behind Jay's chair. "But I'll send for him. Let me speak to him privately. If he wishes to talk to you, you may question him about this ridiculous charge." The captain opened the hatch to his ship's administrative spaces. "Commander Pittman, have Chief Johnson—"

From Jay's seated position, he couldn't see the activities in the outer office. The tall and lanky captain standing in the doorway blocked his view. Jay heard a commotion, though, and in a hushed but forceful tone, the captain asked, "Are you—are you *certain?* Commander, this can't be—we have to verify this information—" The remaining words were unclear.

Moments later, the captain returned. "Agent Gared, I have to step away. I apologize. I'll be back as soon as possible." The captain left and closed the hatch, leaving Jay in the room alone.

Jay smiled. Slowly his breathing returned to normal and his muscles relaxed. His plan was working and he was regaining control. "I can wait all day."

In fifteen years Don had never known a battalion commander to set foot in the office of a company gunnery sergeant. Lieutenant Colonel Ritter had recently taken over as battalion commander and Don hoped his presence here was nothing more than an indication of a new and unique leadership style. Still, part of Don feared that MPs stood outside to cart him away.

"My boss, Colonel Watkins, handed me a huge problem, Gunny Hawkins, which I've just passed along to your boss, Captain Bruce. But knowing Captain Bruce, my guess is that he'll hand the problem to you. So I thought I'd come here and cut out the middleman."

"And I do appreciate that, sir," Captain Bruce said in his Oklahoma twang.

"Truth is, Gunny, I've heard so many great things about you from all the officers, I wanted some face-to-face time—and to get out of my office and see who really runs this battalion."

"You're in the right place," said Captain Bruce. "Operationally and logistically, Gunny Hawkins keeps Charlie Company running like a well-oiled machine." The first sergeant, who remained standing behind the two officers, agreed. Don was relieved—his secret was safe.

"You sound like the best man for the job, Gunny," said Lieutenant Colonel Ritter, "because that's what Congressman Coughlin expects to see tomorrow—a well-oiled machine."

Don flinched. "Coughlin?"

"We don't have much time so I'll cut right to the chase. We all know these VIP exercises are a complete waste of time. But regiment just shafted us with a big one."

Now Don understood the purpose of the battalion commander's visit. Marines frequently staged tactical demonstrations for media-savvy dignitaries—it was the longest running show on base. Don had earned many awards for his past roles, and that didn't make him proud. He joined the Corps to be a Marine, not a camouflaged-covered backdrop for vote-hungry politicians—*especially* not for Edward Coughlin, the politician Don despised the most.

"Ain't Coughlin the one making the biggest stink about Clinton's plan to let queers in the military?" Captain Bruce asked.

"He's the one," answered Lieutenant Colonel Ritter. "As the senior minority member on the House Armed Services Committee, Coughlin is *very* important. If his party regains a majority in Congress, Coughlin would become committee chairman. He could be the most powerful ally—or the worst enemy—the Marine Corps has ever had. As luck would have it, Colonel Watkins selected our battalion to put on a dog-and-pony show for him tomorrow morning."

"Tomorrow?" Don asked. "Amazing. Can't believe regiment gave us so much notice."

The battalion commander raised his eyebrows. "Normally I'd agree with your sarcasm but regiment has a good reason. The congressman didn't decide on this visit until the weekend."

"Why is he coming here, sir?" asked the first sergeant.

"Because he found out President Clinton will be off the coast of San Diego tomorrow visiting an aircraft carrier—the USS *Zeeland*—and Coughlin hopes to upstage Clinton in the local and national media. It's no secret that Coughlin wants to run against Clinton in 1996." Don's earlier fears turned to dread and he felt nauseous. Of all the despicable lowlifes in the world, Coughlin was the worst. "Sounds like you're the company to put a show together in a hurry. Nothing fancy. Helicopters will fly the congressman to combat town. Alpha Company will simulate an assault. This company will stage a platoon at combat town as aggressors. If we impress the congressman, maybe he'll add a few hundred million to the Corps's budget next year."

"At least there's no pressure," Don said with a smile.

"There's always pressure dealing with these thousand-pound egos from Washington." The battalion commander's jocular tone turned serious. "Rumor is, Coughlin's writing a bill to turn the

DoD Directive banning gays from the military into federal law. His sole purpose for coming here is to use your men to make it look like he has the support of the average Marine." Lieutenant Colonel Ritter looked at his men. "He probably has their support—or he might not, I don't care. What I *do* care about is that the Marine Corps—the men and women we lead—gets the support we need from Congress to accomplish the missions they give us."

"Sir," said the first sergeant. "Reporters ask the men about Clinton or his plan. What then?"

The battalion commander shook his head vigorously. "They don't say a word. Remember there are liberal politicians in Washington who control our budgets and set our policies. They're in the majority—have been for forty years. They listen to what your men say to the press, Gunny. When the cameras are rolling, it's not just Coughlin your men are talking to."

"None of my men will have any comment on the matter, sir. I can assure you of that."

"We have to maintain a delicate balance with the civilians. They can be partisan—we can't. We took an oath—it's our constitutional duty as Marines to keep our personal opinions about homosexuals to ourselves." Don's nod showed that he understood the commanding officer's message. "Good. Charlie Company has its work cut out. Let me see your plan in four hours, Captain Bruce. The major says you did one of these three months ago. Adapt that plan for Coughlin." Don and Captain Bruce jumped to their feet, anticipating the battalion commander's exit from the room. Lieutenant Colonel Ritter stood and said, "Carry on."

"Aye, aye, sir," Captain Bruce said as his commanding officer departed. The first sergeant also departed to ensure the other Marines in Charlie Company showed the battalion commander proper courtesy. The captain closed the door. "What d'you think? First or third?"

"Neither, sir. Let's go with second platoon."

"*Second* platoon? Hell no!" The captain paused reflectively then asked, "What—why send second platoon on somethin' this important?"

"Not 'send,' sir. I'll go with them. I'll take Staff Sergeant George and we'll put on a show for the congressman and the cameras. We need to raise our expectations for second platoon."

Captain Bruce sat silently, processing every angle. "We been together a long time, Gunny. You never let me down. I'm trying to understand what you're thinkin'." He paused. "If we give an important mission to second, it'll send 'em a message we still have some confidence in them."

"Yes, sir, that's it. Unless we give them challenging tasks, they'll never improve."

Captain Bruce tapped the leg of the steel chair with the heel of his boot, a sign he was stumped. "You have another reason for doing this? You hope second fucks up so bad, I'll fire George and ship him off to work in some shit job until he gets out. That's not like you, though."

"I don't think second will fuck up." Don answered truthfully. He'd begun plotting a scheme. Don couldn't waste an opportunity to get back at a potent enemy like Coughlin. Even second platoon could handle a simple dog-and-pony show. Officers were the ones who complicated everything—well, except for the one particular officer who'd rocked Don's world over the weekend. Don smiled, recalling the fun he'd had with Patrick last night and remembering how uncomplicated everything seemed when they were together. No, his reason for using second platoon was strategic—and personal—a reason he couldn't reveal to the captain.

"Okay, Gunny Hawkins," the captain said, signaling a change of heart. "I've staked my career on your recommendations before and I haven't regretted it yet." As he stood, he added, "But don't make tomorrow the first time, okay?" As the captain opened the door to leave, he asked, "By the way, Gunny, what *are* you so damn cheerful about today? I mean, we just got this dog-and-pony—and you look as if you won the lottery."

"Maybe I did, sir. But I love the Marine Corps so much I'd stay in anyway."

* * *

"You can go on in. He's expecting you."

"Thanks, Esther." After exchanging a friendly smile with his boss's assistant, Jay opened Ollie's door. "Got a minute, boss?"

"Sure, Jay, come on in." Ollie closed a folder and placed it in a corner of his desk.

Jay had planted the seeds of his plan. His purpose for this meeting was to nurture those seeds, helping them take root. Fortunately, Ollie looked more rested than after their surveillance training on Saturday. Taking a deep breath, Jay dove in. "A Sailor killed himself this weekend. A chief on the *Cayuga* by the name of Johnson. Shot himself at home in University Heights."

"Does it concern us? It should go to the Navy's internal Criminal Investigative Division."

Launching into the next phase of his plan, Jay said, "Usually CID would handle it but this is different. I've had Johnson under surveillance since last week. Drug trafficking. Saturday night I observed him in some suspicious activity. This morning I went to his command, the USS *Cayuga*, to find out background information. While I was there, someone called the Naval Station's police unit, who called the ship. When shore patrol went to Johnson's house, they found his corpse. Looks like a self-inflicted gunshot wound to the head. He'd been dead for over twenty-four hours." Jay paused to let his supervisor absorb this information.

"You had this guy under surveillance for over a week—?"

"No sir. *Since* last week." Jay had rehearsed this part of his story several times because it was the most precarious. "Got a phone call late Friday afternoon. Caller wouldn't identify himself but it was about Johnson. So I looked up Johnson's information on the system."

"Did you enter the call into the log?"

"No." Fortunately, Jay was still within the undefined period of time when he could plead his status as a novice and get away with minor policy infractions. "I'll know better next time."

"Did you open a file?"

Jay nodded. "This morning. Then I went to the ship. That's when I learned of the suicide."

"You shoulda logged the call and opened the file on Friday. Jesus, Gared! Why didn't you say anything to me about this on Saturday? We were in the field together over eight hours and you didn't mention an anonymous caller—or suspected drug traffickers—one goddamned time."

"I'm—I'm sorry, Ollie." Jay looked at the floor, a gesture he'd choreographed with his apology. "I didn't know for sure that the call would lead to anything—I didn't want to involve you with something that most likely was a dead end." Jay hoped his acting skills were solid.

While Ollie fidgeted with his pen and stared out the window, Jay studied the office. Boxes, papers and books cluttered the floor and the odor of stale cigarette smoke oozed out of the walls even though smoking had been banned in government buildings for years. Ollie had tacked a photograph of himself shaking hands with President Nixon to a wall a few feet away and its plastic frame hung crookedly to the right. "All this anonymous shit—I don't like it." He looked at Jay. "Where'd you see this alleged drug deal?"

Jay bit his lip, another rehearsed motion, but also a genuine indicator of his deeply felt anxiety. He was mixing truth and lies. The lies didn't bother him but keeping them all straight required focus. His slip about Ed's dachshund had caused the Sailor's death and put Jay in this bind. He couldn't afford another mistake. "I observed the suspicious activity at a nightclub called the West Coast Production Company."

Ollie's eyes widened. "Holy shit, Jay. The gay bar near the Marine recruit depot?" He shook his head. "What were you—? Never mind, ain't none of my business. But didn't I tell you that we have too many problems without—?"

"I know, Ollie, I know. But—"

"'But' nothing. This issue—gays in the military—it's exploding like a neutron bomb in DC. I saw the new Defense Secretary, Les Aspin, on *Face the Nation* yesterday morning talking about how controversial this debate will be." Ollie rummaged through the papers on his desk and pulled out a newspaper clipping he'd marked in ballpoint pen. "Look at this. A *New York Times* poll says forty-two percent of Americans are in favor of lifting the ban, forty-eight percent want to keep it in place and the usual ten percent don't have a fucking clue what planet they're on. The country's split on this. Both sides will be looking for something—*anything*, no matter how minor—to prove their side is right." Ollie folded his hands and leaned across his desk. "This office will *not* draw national attention. *Leave the queers alone!*"

"I understand you completely, Ollie. But it wasn't—it wasn't like that. This was a drug investigation that happened to lead me to a gay establishment. After we left the park Saturday afternoon, I went home and changed clothes, then drove to the suspect's house. I sat outside until shortly after eleven P.M. He drove away from his house and I followed him to the gay bar."

Calming somewhat, Ollie asked, "And you went inside? What'd you observe?"

Jay smiled. "*Many* things—"

"I bet you did." Ollie laughed, much to Jay's satisfaction.

"Johnson interacted with a bartender, guy by the name of Lance. Around one A.M. Lance handed Johnson a small package wrapped in brown paper. I followed Johnson out of the bar and back to his home. I waited an hour—then went home. My plan this morning—"

"You didn't think the anonymous phone call and the package were substantial evidence for probable cause?" Ollie raised one eyebrow. Jay shook his head. "Good call."

"My plan was to contact his command, check out his disciplinary record—"

"Dammit, that's *not* how we do things around here. You go snooping around a Sailor's command and all kinds of red flags will go up." Ollie rubbed his bare head with his hand. "Anonymous phone calls, exchanging packages—which could be anything, by the way—*at a gay bar*. I don't like this. And the kicker is that the guy's dead."

"If we can take the case from CID, I want to be in charge," Jay said as intensely as he could.

"I could call over there. Our reasons for wanting the investigation would be—?"

"Possibility of drugs in his house, or large sums of cash although it's doubtful. Still, I need to search for bank records. If Johnson was in a drug ring operating on military bases, he may have names, addresses and numbers of others." Lowering his voice for emphasis, Jay added, "What if it wasn't a suicide? We should be in charge if it was a drug murder." The last point was the most convincing. Judging from Ollie's silence, Jay had persuaded him to intervene.

"It's not just CID." Ollie looked at a large city map tacked to his wall. "Because it happened in town, officially it's within the city's jurisdiction. Maybe even the federal vice squad."

"I talked to an investigator for the city. I'll call back this afternoon to find out what they pulled on Johnson. My guess is he's clean or the Navy wouldn't have promoted him to chief."

"Good point," said Ollie. "Why would a Sailor, this late in a successful career, get messed up in drug trafficking? I've seen stranger things, but—okay, Gared, I'll call CID. They'll probably hand it over to us. I assume the body's at the coroner's?"

"This just happened. No one could answer me. I'm sure the body's been picked up."

"I'll call the city." Leaning forward, Ollie spoke resolutely. "This'll take lot of coordination. Get busy and please tell Esther to move this to the top of my agenda."

As Jay left the office, Ollie pressed the buttons on his phone. Jay's plan was in motion.

Don drove as fast as he dared along Camp Pendleton's narrow, hilly and winding back roads. If he used the pay phone near Charlie Company's headquarters, he could avoid the trip, but that was too risky. Because the phone was out in the open, any Marine waiting in line to use it could overhear his conversation. Don preferred driving ten miles to the miniexchange near the interstate exit on the rare occasions he made a personal call during the day.

He called his answering machine first and was disappointed Patrick hadn't phoned, but it was early afternoon. The poor guy was probably trapped in his squadron's tedious check-in process. More worrisome was the absence of a call from Eddie. Don called Eddie's house again but, just as before, reached the machine. "Hey, Eddie. It's me. Listen—why the fuck haven't you returned my calls from yesterday? I'm worried about you. Something's come up here and I have to postpone the appointment we scheduled for tomorrow morning until Wednesday or Thursday. Your cutoff isn't until Friday so it shouldn't be a problem, right? I'm stuck at work overnight. No point in paging me 'cause I'll be outta range. Leave me a message at home. Let me know you got this, okay?"

Don returned the receiver to its cradle. He was more disturbed than ever but the next sixteen hours of his life he was preoccupied with preparing his men for Coughlin's visit. He felt helpless—trapped by the situation. The clock ticked toward Friday's deadline for Eddie's HIV test but Eddie couldn't be found. "Fuck Coughlin!" Don said as he hopped into his jeep.

13

I'm not here to take your call. Slowly and clearly leave your name, phone number and the time. I'll return your message as soon as I can.

Hearing Don's voice reminded Patrick of their night of passion. Don's message was also a glimpse into the way he handled his complex life. By not identifying himself in his machine's outgoing greeting, he could use the same number for his Marine world, where he was "Gunnery Sergeant Hawkins," and his gay world, where he was known only as "Don."

But I'm the lucky guy who gets to know all *of him*, Patrick thought. Anticipating the beep, he cleared his throat and lowered his voice. "Hey, buddy—it's—well, you know who. Wanted to say, I checked in this morning. Now, um, I'm getting ready to move into my apartment Friday. I have a phone number—but I'll catch you tonight when you're at home. Okay? Hope you're having a good day. Oh shit! Almost forgot. I got tasked to be an escort officer for the governor or mayor, or somebody tomorrow. Don't know what it's about. Anyway, I'm rambling so bye."

Patrick shook his head and laughed. Thinking about Don made him feel great inside and out. As awkward as their communications had to be—leaving cryptic nameless messages without identifying information—it was worth it to know the future was wonderful and limitless. Perhaps *their* future together. Because of Don, Patrick's cheerfulness transcended even the mundane tasks associated with a cross-country military move. Patrick walked from the lobby of the BOQ into the bright Pacific coast sunshine, smiling as he put on his shades.

"Who's been inside?" Jay asked the police officer outside Johnson's house.

"Just myself, my partner and two paramedics. Can you tell me who's running this show?"

"I am," said Jay. "Apologies for the delay, Officer. Because of the unusual facts—a Navy person, off base, possible criminal activity or foul play—the agencies were confused about who'd be in charge of this investigation."

"Fucking bureaucrats." The officer shook his head. "A man's dead and they fight a turf war."

"I hear ya' on that—I'm a field agent too. But they sorted it out and now I'm in charge."

Jay's attempt to bond worked and the officer's disposition mellowed. He pulled out a notebook. "What's your name? I'm entering that at fifteen thirty I turned this over to you."

"Agent Jay Gared. With the Naval Investigative Service." Jay handed his card to the officer. "Before you go, I need to ask you some questions, if that's okay, Officer—?"

"Baccari." The man extended his hand. "Good to meet you, Agent Gared. What d'you need to know?" Jay wrote that Baccari and his partner were in the neighborhood when, at 8:12 A.M., the dispatcher sent them to Johnson's. An anonymous caller heard a gunshot earlier in the night but didn't say why he waited to phone in the tip. "We were here at eight seventeen."

"Did your partner come in at that time?" Jay asked.

"Yes, but only to cover me. I waited on the front porch. Shouted a warning, per department regs. No one answered. So I was prepared to bust the door open but it wasn't locked." Jay feigned a puzzled look, even though he would've been worried if the door *had* been locked. "I entered and saw the body laying by the desk. My partner covered me from the doorway. When I saw the Navy paraphernalia—awards and plaques and things—I assumed he was a Sailor. Didn't look like anyone else was present, so she called it in."

"What did you do then?"

"Called the paramedics. They confirmed Johnson was dead and took him. I sealed the house and waited here. For six hours. 'Cause the desk jockeys couldn't decide who's in charge."

Jay looked around the area but didn't see anyone else. "Where's your partner?"

"Back at the station. The city can't afford two officers baby-sittin' an empty house."

"There's been no activity since you put the yellow tape up this morning?" Jay asked.

"No. Neighbors walking by, staring, asking questions. That's it." Jay heard the dog and Officer Baccari added, "He's got a little mutt in back that won't stop barking." Jay finished writing the information. "Agent Gared, if you don't mind, I'll turn this over to you."

"Roger that," Jay said as the officer started down the steps. Hearing the dog bark again, he asked, "Officer Baccari, did anyone feed the dog? Give him fresh water?"

"No. But I don't think the Sailor would care if you took care of his pooch."

After the police officer drove away, Jay put on a pair of skin-tight rubber gloves. Ducking under the tape blocking Johnson's doorway, he wanted to see the scene before the forensics team investigated. He'd delayed them as long as possible without creating suspicions.

Jay stepped into the living room. As the unnerving realization sank in that he was back in the space where he'd experienced so much trauma, the dog barked for a third time, distracting him from the nightmare. "Okay, little guy, gimme a minute." In Johnson's kitchen, he found a bag of dog food. He opened the back door and the dog propped himself on his hind legs and rested his front paws on Jay's pants. "There you go, little fella'! You shouldn't have to starve. Not your fault your owner was a homosexual." The dog began crunching his food and Jay refocused his mind on the task.

His eyes slowly readjusted to the dim indoor lighting as he

scanned the kitchen. Johnson's answering machine flashed a large red "04." Removing his notebook from the inside pocket of his coat, he pressed PLAY. The first and second caller was the same person—a friend of Johnson's. Neither message provided any helpful information for hunting gay servicemen, but to Jay's relief, they also didn't present any evidence contradicting his conclusion that Johnson's death was a suicide. The third message was left at 8:04 A.M. by a yeoman in the *Cayuga*'s personnel section asking Chief Johnson why he missed roll call.

The first three messages were neither helpful nor hurtful, and when Jay recognized the final caller was the same as the first and second, he almost deleted all four messages. But when the voice said, "*Something's come up here,*" it grabbed Jay's attention. Copying furiously, he pressed REPLAY. *Something's come up here . . . postpone the appointment . . . tomorrow morning . . . Wednesday or Thursday . . . Your cutoff isn't until Friday.*

A voice in the other room said, "Agent Gared! You here? We're the forensics team."

"'Your cutoff isn't until Friday.'" Jay smiled, convinced the last phrase was the key to something important he should know. Tucking the piece of paper in his coat pocket, he turned to greet the two investigators. "Let's get to work."

"Come in," the gruff voice said.

"Here's your letter, Ollie, ready for your signature." Esther slid the paper across the desk.

"Thanks, Esther. And thank you for working through your lunch hour today. That was a big help considering all the last-minute emergencies." Ollie put a few swirling lines of ink at the bottom of the page and returned it to his assistant. "If nothing else is urgent, take off early." Looking at his watch, he said, "Damn! Four thirty? Take off a half hour early anyway."

"You know me better than that. I don't leave till you do. All I need is fifteen minutes to cross the street and grab a late lunch. Or early dinner."

"Don't know what I'd do without you, Esther. Of course. Take all the time you need."

Before leaving the office, she asked, "Want anything?"

"Just smoke a cigarette for me, since I can't get away from my desk at the moment."

"Sure thing, boss." Esther closed the door behind her as Ollie continued to work. They'd faced crises before but Ollie always had time for a smoke. "Wow, this must be *really* serious," she mumbled, pulling some money out of the bag she kept locked in her desk drawer.

"Back in fifteen," she said to another assistant, who waved in acknowledgment.

Esther crossed the Naval Station's main street, which was clogged with base personnel hurrying home. She entered a recreation center housing several fast food restaurants. Fast food wasn't what she needed, though. Instead, she headed toward a row of pay phones.

"The Flame, this is Jeanne."

"Jeanne, it's Esther."

"Hi, Esther, how are you? You sound—exhausted."

"I am. Can't talk long but something's going on down here I should pass to you. Not sure if you would've heard, but you might know who to call."

"Okay," Jeanne said. "What's NIS up to *this* week?"

Esther turned her body away from the other pay phones. "A Sailor shot himself in his University Heights house. It appears to be a suicide. Early Sunday morning."

"Family?" University Heights was a neighborhood with a large lesbian and gay population.

"Looks that way," Esther said.

"Damn! Why won't they get help? It's not so bad anymore— there's the gay and lesbian center, support groups and other places." Jeanne sighed. "How do they know he was gay?"

"That's why I called you soon as I could. Our agent was at WC's on Saturday night."

"Shit!" Jeanne exclaimed. "So much for our hope that NIS's bar-snooping days were over."

"No, Jeanne, I've told you—ever since the Gulf War, Director Tolson's policy has been that agents are *not* supposed to go into gay bars. But apparently this particular agent observed the Sailor make a drug deal at WC's."

"*If* the charge is true. Because we're talking about the NIS, we shouldn't make that assumption. How did your agent know the drug deal was supposed to happen?"

"The agent received an anonymous call on Friday. The caller said the Sailor would make a drug deal at WC's on Saturday night. So the agent put the Sailor under surveillance." Esther looked over her shoulder to ensure no one was listening . "He followed the Sailor to WC's, where he claims he saw the Sailor take a package from a bartender named Lance—"

"Are you kidding me? I know Lance. I find that hard to believe."

"The agent claimed he distributed drugs. Next he followed the Sailor from the bar to his house. Watched it for a over an hour. Nothing happened so the agent went home. This morning the agent was at the Sailor's ship when they found out the Sailor's body was discovered—"

"How'd the ship find out?" Jeanne asked. "Who reported the body?"

"Another anonymous tip."

"This sounds really strange. Anonymous tips—NIS agents in gay bars—suspicious drug deals. Sounds to me like there's a witch hunt on. Then again, I might be paranoid—"

"In your case, I'd say paranoia is justified," Esther said.

"Well, I've got more questions but they'll have to wait. Now I need to decide what to do."

"What do you want me to do?" asked Esther.

"Nothing I can think—oh, except the obvious. Tell me the Sailor's name."

"Edward Johnson. Chief Petty Officer." Esther waited for Jeanne's comment, but hearing nothing, she asked, "Jeanne? Are you there? Is—is anything—wrong?"

"Oh my God, Esther. Eddie Johnson? Eddie is—was—*is* one of our closest friends. This can't be right. No. No—you've got—you've got to double check the information."

"Oh Jeanne. I'm so sorry. But I've typed his name a hundred

times today. I hate to tell you but I'm sure the name I just told you is right. His ship is—"

"The *Cayuga?*" asked Jeanne.

"USS *Cayuga.*" Her heart ached for her friend. "I'm afraid it's him, Jeanne."

"I doubt if Don even knows yet. They were closer than brothers—going back fifteen years."

"Your Marine friend from Parris Island?"

"Yeah, that's Don. Oh my, this will kill him," Jeanne sighed. "Wait one fucking minute, Esther! No way in *hell* Eddie Johnson was involved in a drug deal. Absolutely not. In fact, I think—I *know* Robbi was with him Saturday night at WC's."

"Maybe she can answer—"

"Esther, I've got to make some calls—try to reach Don somehow. Stay in touch. You're doing an excellent job. Don't know what we'd do without you."

Esther said good-bye and hung up the phone. "Seem to be hearing that a lot today," she muttered as she left the food court to return to her desk. First, though, she needed that cigarette.

"Cut 'em loose for chow. We'll rehearse some more tonight."

Don rethought the plans for Coughlin's visit. Although he wanted his Marines to get some solid training out of it, he'd stopped focusing on the quality of their performance primarily because it was already stellar. Also, Coughlin didn't care how well the Marines performed. His only concern was the media. And if Don's scheme was a success, when Coughlin left Camp Pendleton tomorrow, no one would remember how well or how poorly the Marines performed.

"Sure thing, Gunny," said Staff Sergeant George. "Back at eighteen thirty."

Don returned to the company office, pulled a frozen meal out of the minirefrigerator and threw it in the microwave. Tonight would be a late one and tomorrow would begin well before sunrise. He'd crash in his office using his cot and sleeping bag as he had many times.

As hard as he tried to focus on tomorrow's mission, his thoughts kept swinging between Patrick and Eddie. He checked his pager, a futile act because it was out of range in this part of the base. He wanted to use the base phone sitting on his desk to check his answering machine at home. His curiosity was at its boiling point—he *had* to know if his lover from the night before had called and if Eddie had received his message postponing tomorrow's hospital appointment. But his discipline and survival instincts prevented him from taking the risk.

Cutting into his Salisbury steak, he thought about his situation. This was exactly the type of scenario that'd kept him single for so long. Civilian guys didn't understand—when duty calls, a Marine answers. Without question. That was another advantage of becoming more serious with Patrick. *He's a Marine. He understands me as only another Marine can.*

"I've never heard of this Coughlin but I'm so proud they picked you to show him the base."

"Mom, my CO stuck me with this because I was in the wrong place at the wrong time."

"Patrick, you're too modest. I knew the Marines would see what a fine gentleman you are."

"I can tell you who Coughlin is," said Sean McAbe. "He's one of the few politicians in Washington who's not afraid to say what's on his mind. He's got the right idea about things."

"Oh, Sean, stop," said Carol McAbe. Patrick could tell she was on the kitchen extension.

As usual, his dad ignored her and continued. "Coughlin's the only one not afraid to call that bastard Clinton what he is—a pot-smoking, cheating, lying—"

"Sean!" Patrick's mom silenced her husband with her volume. "Let's not go into that. Patrick isn't paying for this call to listen to your politics." The familiar conversation of the McAbe clan helped ease the homesickness Patrick felt. Back at the dinner table, he'd tuned out the political debates between his folks. He missed his mom and dad, and hearing their voices made him feel like he was eating a homecooked meal instead of a microwave dinner.

"Carol, your son doesn't want to work with a bunch of queers. If that president of yours has his way, fairies will infiltrate the military. Coughlin is the one trying to stop that." Sadly, this wasn't the first time Sean McAbe's comments had silently stung his son. In the eight months since Patrick had evolved beyond self-denial about his sexual orientation, his father's antigay comments had intensified, or at least that's how it seemed. He wondered when—or if—he'd ever be able to tell his dad that he was gay.

Patrick ended the call and tried Don's house once more but no luck. He didn't leave another message and found himself feeling less buoyant than before. He wanted to speak to Don so much that it physically hurt. He'd *never* felt that way with Karen, or with any girl he'd dated. Twenty-five seemed to be an old age to begin having these feelings but he supposed being a late bloomer was better than withering on the vine.

Jeanne dreaded this call. She couldn't talk to Don on his base phone but she had to let him know about Eddie. Maybe she'd catch him at home, although he rarely left the base until he'd put in an eleven- or twelve-hour day. She wasn't surprised to get his answering machine. "Don, it's Jeanne. When you get this, give me a call at the office. I'm here the rest of the evening."

Next, she had to let her girlfriend know that one of their closest friends had died. Calling their house, she left a message for Robbi. "Hi, doll. When you get home, can you come over to the bar? Love you, bye." She put down the receiver, laid her head on her arms, and cried.

"Jeanne! We're outta vermouth," shouted an employee from the front. Instead of responding, Jeanne closed the door to her small office. Something was brewing. She'd worked hard to become a respected member of the business community so she could use her money and influence to save others from these nightmares. Drying her eyes with a tissue, she said, "Now's the time to get busy." She called a number from her address book.

"*San Diego Gay and Lesbian Times*, editor speaking."

"Hi, Ricky, it's Jeanne. Afraid I've got a story for you."

14

"Stay between ten and fifteen feet from Congressman Coughlin at all times."

"Yes, ma'am," said Patrick.

"Be attentive to his needs." The major giving orders was Camp Pendleton's protocol officer.

"Uh, ma'am. Couldn't I be more attentive to his needs from closer than ten feet?"

"You graduated from The Basic School, right, Lieutenant?" Patrick nodded, but he was confused. If officers didn't complete TBS, they didn't remain in the Corps. "So you know common sense rarely applies in these settings." The major's tone was sarcastic and she hadn't answered his question. "All you officers in combat arms jobs think staff work is for pussies. Today you'll learn the truth."

Patrick's haze was partly because he'd never heard a woman say "pussies" but mostly it stemmed from his fear of the day's unknowns. His lack of sleep didn't help. Sunday night was because of Don, but last night, tension had kept him up. In ten minutes, he'd be around VIPs and his instructions weren't clear. "Doesn't he already have people attending to his needs?"

"Yes. If you're lucky, you'll deal only with his staff." That was the first encouraging news he'd heard all day. "This is your Bible," she said, giving Patrick the schedule. "Here's some extra copies. Don't let anyone know you have them. *Especially* don't let the colonels order you to give them one. If you give it to one, you gotta give it to all of 'em. Then they start haggling over the itinerary, fucking up the plan. It's only for the generals and the congressman's staff."

"How do I stop a superior officer from giving me an order?"

"What did I say about common sense, Lieutenant?" The major laughed and smirked over her shoulder as she walked away. "You were smart enough to finish TBS. You'll find a way."

Looking at the schedule only added to his anxiety. He was slated for every event, including the helicopter flight to combat town. Glancing at the clock in Camp Pendleton's small passenger terminal, he estimated Coughlin's plane would touch down in five minutes. He used the restroom quickly as he doubted he'd have another chance soon. Checking his uniform—the long-sleeved khaki shirt and tie with a tanker jacket—in the mirror, he wondered if other lieutenants had as many uniform changes in such a short time. Today, at least, was more casual.

"Flight inbound!" shouted the Marine working at the operations desk.

Twenty or twenty-five captains and above—including three generals—departed the terminal, taking their places at one end of a red carpet. The small jet touched down from the east and roared by the entourage before taxiing to a stop at the other end of the red carpet.

As a crewmember opened the plane's door, a colonel standing in front of Patrick said to another, "Leonard, how does Coughlin rate a coast-to-coast military flight?"

"Armed Services Committee, Joe. Same way he rides in my helicopters anytime he wants."

A man, presumably the congressman, stuck his head out of the plane's doorway and waved both his arms. A three-star general, the highest-ranking Marine on the West Coast, led the procession down the red carpet to greet Coughlin and a woman, presumably Mrs. Coughlin. As the two VIPs approached the generals, staff members spilled out of the plane.

"*She's* not on the damned Armed Services Committee," said the colonel named Joe.

Leonard, his companion, laughed and said, "Maybe *you* should run for office."

"Good to see you, General! That's the best flight I've *ever* had," the congressman said loudly as Patrick tried to maneuver to a spot ten to fifteen feet away. "And Major General Neville, what I meant was, that's the best flight I ever had in any aircraft *other* than one of yours!"

"Are you the escort officer?" A young woman surprised Patrick.

"Um, yes, yes, that's—I'm First Lieutenant McAbe."

"Thought so. You look like the youngest—and probably the lowest-ranking—person here. I'm the congressman's deputy chief of staff. Where do we go now?"

Patrick took a deep breath and prayed he didn't screw this up. "We'll board the Hueys immediately. You hear them spinning over there. We'll fly out to the assault on combat town."

"Great," she said. "Come here. I'll introduce you to Congressman Coughlin."

"No, ma'am, that's not—" Patrick's attempt to halt the introduction was futile.

"Congressman Coughlin, this is First Lieutenant McAbe. He's your escort officer for today."

"McAbe, eh?" asked the congressman. "That's a good Irish name."

Patrick was relieved that was the extent of his interaction with the Honorable Mr. Coughlin. The deputy directed the party to the waiting helicopters. "Mrs. Coughlin should follow the general's wife," Patrick shouted and the deputy guided her toward a car. Fortunately, the generals and colonels monopolized Coughlin's attention. If all Patrick had to do was work with the deputy, he might survive the day.

Hueys over there! A lot of Hueys.

It was the AirCav, First of the Ninth, our escorts to the mouth of the Nung River. But they were supposed to be waiting for us another thirty kilometers ahead. Well, Air Mobile, those boys just couldn't stay put.

Don had seen *Apocalypse Now* at least fifty times and he'd memorized most of the lines. Whenever a flight of Hueys came in low, Wagner's "Flight of the Valkyries" played in his head as it had heralded the movie's awesome beach scene. Don always heard the distinctive *whomp whomp* of the helicopter's twin-bladed rotors before he saw the rounded nose of the small trusty aircraft in the distance. Today was no exception—only this time it meant Coughlin was near.

"Staff Sergeant George!" he shouted at the platoon sergeant and pointed. "See where the reporters have stationed their vans? Move your riflemen closer. This congressman will go for the cameras. I want those two men nearby."

"Don't look at the cameras, don't look at the cameras . . . Go on through . . . Don't look at the cameras . . . Go by just like you're fighting," said the director. Francis Ford Coppola had included shots of a movie crew filming the attack as part of his Vietnam War epic. Considering all the media events Don had participated in during his fifteen years of service, Coppola was a genius.

"Don't tell me real life doesn't imitate art."

"What'd you say, Gunny?" asked Staff Sergeant George. "Don't tell you what?"

Don shook his head. "Move your team near the cameras." The staff sergeant didn't want his men near the generals or the media but Don had an agenda. Minutes later, the helicopters popped above the southern hills. A Marine exploded a canister of green smoke to point the pilots to the landing zone as well as to impress the congressman with a pyrotechnic display.

"Coughlin." Don spat the name with all the contempt he could muster. No politician reveled in his hatred of gays and lesbians as much as the man who represented California's Fifty-Seventh congressional district. Jeanne and Eddie kept Don informed on political matters that affected their lives and what they'd told him about Coughlin pissed him off. He was their public enemy number one. He'd introduced bills in Washington to prevent progressive states like California and New York from protecting gay employees from workplace and housing discrimination. He'd helped pass laws barring people with AIDS from broad categories

of government jobs. He'd proposed a bill to automatically kick all HIV-positive people out of the service and he was the most vocal opponent of Clinton's plan to lift the ban on gays in the military. History would revile Coughlin as it did segregationists and slaveholders, but in 1993, he was a powerful man.

The Hueys landed, and Coughlin, the three-star general, and four others deplaned from the first helicopter. True to form, the congressman walked toward the group of reporters. The second helicopter landed closely behind the first. Despite the overpowering noise of the Hueys, Coughlin tried to talk. Don shook his head as the reporters told the congressman they couldn't understand him. "Fucking moron," Don mumbled.

The passengers stepping out of the second helicopter caught Don's attention. A female civilian carried a big briefcase as she tried to talk on a large portable phone. A young officer attempted to assist her, but he looked lost. Suddenly Don realized who the man was. "Patrick!" He couldn't take his eyes off the tall blond Marine lieutenant. Just as Coughlin had pursued the press, Don reflexively left his observation point to chase the object of his desire. Patrick was even more handsome in his service bravo uniform than in the alphas he'd worn yesterday.

Don was within twenty feet of Coughlin and his party. The helicopters departed, moving some troops, but they'd return soon to whisk Coughlin to the next show. Looking at his watch again, Don estimated the general had twelve minutes to get the congressman a hundred meters down the road and on the roof of the first building, where they'd observe the assault.

Patrick hadn't noticed Don, but when everyone started walking, he hoped to slide in for a few discreet minutes with the lieutenant. An aide spoke to Coughlin and the party moved across the street. Now was the optimal time. "Good morning, sir." Not surprisingly, Patrick didn't recognize him. The last time the man had seem him, Don was nude. Today, not only did he wear a camouflage uniform, he'd also painted his face, neck and hands shades of green and brown.

Patrick's eyes widened. "D—I mean—Gunny Hawkins! What're you doing up here?"

"We're the aggressors. I'm here so my men do what I've told them." Coughlin set a fast pace for his entourage and the two gay Marines fell in step at the end. "How'd you get this job?"

Patrick looked around. No one was within earshot, and in a low deep voice, he said, "I'm so glad to see you. I left a couple of messages on your machine last night—"

"I got stuck with this morning's 'show.' Spent last night in my office after rehearsals."

"Then we're in synch," Patrick said. "I'm here 'cause my squadron commander offered me as the sacrificial lamb for this bullshit assignment."

"I bet you hadn't even completed the first item on your check-in sheet," Don said.

The group stopped at the first of twelve cinderblock buildings comprising the "combat town" constructed to teach Marines how to fight in an urban environment. "How did you know?"

"Because I know the Marine Corps." This was the first time the two men had been able to stare directly at each other since their good-bye at the BOQ. "It refreshes my soul to see that officers get shafted just like us enlisted men. I'm just sorry it had to happen to you."

"But I'm not sorry now. I get to see you all dressed up like a gunnery sergeant."

The pair halted as the gaggle entered the three-story building, climbing the narrow cement staircase taking them to the roof. As they took their places, the squadron of medium-sized CH-46 helicopters that had been waiting on the ships off the Southern California coast swarmed low overhead. The machine gunners fired strings of blanks to the obvious delight of the congressman. His staff members looked displeased with the noise and the proximity to danger. The generals and colonels were unfazed.

Don viewed the remainder of the assault with his critical eye for tactical and quasitactical evolutions. For the first time in years, though, he was distracted. He wanted desperately to wink at Patrick, letting him know how strongly he felt about him. But even a wink could be dangerous if the wrong person saw him. Instead, Don focused on the simulated warfare.

The assault took the allotted twenty minutes and the three-star general turned, leading the group away. "General, hang on." Coughlin said. "I'd like to talk to some of your Marines."

"You will, sir. The assault force will return to the ships but the aggressors remain here to defend the town from another attack. You may speak to them."

"Very well. You've got this show under good control, General. Looks great, I tell ya'! Wish I could get you to do a raid like that on the Capitol next time Congress is in session!" The group laughed politely as they descended the steps to exit the vacant structure.

"Congressman," said the general, taking advantage of a rare opportunity to catch Coughlin between words, "the Hueys return in five minutes to take us to the next destination."

"Well, let me have a talk with some of your Marines here on the ground. How about these fine young men guarding us from the liberal media?"

"Perfect," Don said softly.

Lowering his volume to match Don's, Patrick tilted his head and asked, "What is it?"

"Watch this, sir. Things are about to get very interesting."

"We're waiting on some other results to complete our analysis. Right now I'd estimate—with a ninety percent degree of certainty—Chief Petty Officer Johnson committed suicide."

"Why only ninety percent?" Jay asked.

"Oh—some blood work isn't back from the lab," said the analyst.

"I don't understand," said Jay. "What can blood tell you in a case like this?"

"A lot. In one suspected suicide incident last year, later tests showed someone had poisoned the victim hours before his death. Then they shot him, making it look like a suicide. But that's rare. I doubt if there's anything in the Sailor's blood that would lead us to a different conclusion. How about I give you a ninety-nine percent degree of certainty. Is that better?"

"Sure," Jay said. "Maybe if I stand here long enough, you'll reach one thousand percent."

The analyst smiled. "None of the evidence points to foul play, coercion or the presence of a passive bystander—a person to provide comfort at the time of death. We don't see those with gunshots to the head. Only pills or the like." Despite Ollie's initial skepticism, the evidence analyst had just given them a verbal report in one day. Best of all, the report was good news. Jay owed his boss gratitude for expediting the process without alerting anyone to the case.

"What type of evidence would a—a comfort person leave behind?" Jay asked.

"Well, like I said, I've *never* seen a suicide where family or friends were present where a person shot himself. But in the case where they ingested pills, the person might hold the victim's hand well after death, possibly leaving a mark. Or they'll tidy up the place—or the body. When the body dies, the bladder muscles relax, causing urination. This might surprise the other person. They may clean the body before slipping out and calling the police or ambulance."

"But that didn't happen here?" Jay said, more of a declaration than a question.

"In this case the only remote possibility that comes to mind is— the investigators found some hairs in the back of the sofa. They appear to belong to a Caucasian male."

This revelation stunned Jay and he cursed himself for failing to check the sofa. Maybe they weren't his. Johnson had white male friends and had even been in a relationship with one. "What can the hairs tell you?"

"Johnson kept a clean house. For instance, there's almost no evidence of the dog inside the home. The hairs indicate someone had been in the house recently. Perhaps that person knows Johnson's motive. Unfortunately, there's no way of knowing who the hairs belong to."

"What will you do with them?"

"Store them with the weapon, the bullet and any other evidence. If there's an arrest relating to this incident, which doesn't seem likely, we'll run DNA tests to see if it's a match."

Jay wasn't happy with this news and his earlier fear turned to anger at his carelessness. He'd allowed a part of this case to escape from his control. He couldn't do anything about it now, but down the road, he'd think of something. "Nothing indicates this case involves anyone else?"

"Not at this time, no."

"No evidence of criminal activity?"

"No," the analyst said. "Not at this point. It's doubtful my conclusion will change. I assume you want to rule it as a suicide as quickly as possible and close the whole matter?"

"That's correct," Jay said absently, his mind racing to the next phase of his plan. "Here's my card. Please give me a call when all the test results are in."

15

"That's a good Irish name, Lance Corporal O'Doherty. My name's Edward Coughlin."

Cameras recorded the exchange, journalists copied the words and someone extended a long microphone between the congressman and the nervous Marine. "Who's your buddy over here?" Coughlin asked, sidestepping to the other rifleman.

The second Marine jumped from his defensive position and stood at attention. "Sir! My name is Lance Corporal Nogales."

"It's my honor to meet you too, Lance Corporal Nogales. You Marines make me proud to be an American." Turning to O'Doherty, Coughlin said, "I have a question for you, son."

The general bristled at Coughlin's mention of an impromptu question-and-answer session with the Marines. For the first time in years, Don prayed. *God, I'll be good—at least I'll try. Please let this go just like I planned.* Opening his eyes, he saw Patrick laughing quietly.

Coughlin continued with his question's setup. "Let's say you and Lance Corporal Nogales have been out here for more than a week. You were ordered to remain in this spot. You'd dig your foxhole and stay in it the entire time, isn't that right?"

The two lance corporals didn't answer but stared blankly ahead. The general chimed in. "Can't dig fox holes here, Congressman. Against EPA regulations."

"You're kidding me!" Coughlin shook his head. "Our men can't train properly because of the environmental wackos?" As he shook his head a second time, he looked at the cameras. "Guess foxholes somehow cause 'Vice President Ozone's' so-called global warming. Geez." Returning to the Marines, he said, "Lance Corporal O'Doherty, let's assume it's a perfect world and the EPA has been abolished. You and Lance Corporal Nogales have been living in the same foxhole for a long time. Bullets are flying over your heads and incoming rounds blow up on the ground in front of your foxhole." The crowd was silent and the cameras and recording devices remained fixed on the storyteller.

"I hope he gets to the question before the Hueys get back," Don whispered.

"In the middle of this war," Coughlin said in a hushed tone, "Lance Corporal Nogales decides to tell you a secret." Coughlin leaned close to O'Doherty's face. "He tells you he's *gay*. When he thinks about what the two of you could do together in your foxhole, he gets excited. He says he's fantasized about doing things with you the whole time you've been out here." To add emphasis to his delivery, Coughlin straightened. As the cameras rolled, he asked, "What do you think about that, Lance Corporal O'Doherty? Think you could concentrate on fighting if you shared your foxhole with a queer Marine?" Shifting his posture, Coughlin looked directly into the camera as if he were about to embark on a tirade.

Don nodded at the Marine and mouthed, "Say it, Devildog, just like we rehearsed."

Lance Corporal O'Doherty resumed the position of attention and shouted, "Sir, as long as Lance Corporal Nogales can shoot his rifle and hit the target, I don't care what he thinks or says!"

Several of the reporters exhaled sharply and one giggled with delight to have such a raw and embarrassing situation on tape. A stunned hush fell over the generals and their aides. Edward Coughlin, though, hadn't survived years in Washington by allowing momentary surprises to knock him out of the ring. "What about you, Lance Corporal Nogales. How'd you feel if O'Doherty wanted to do all kinds of disgusting perverted things in your foxhole?"

"Does Coughlin know what he's saying?" Patrick laughed softly. "Can he hear himself?"

"He doesn't listen to anyone—not even himself," Don whispered. "I need to get closer, sir. I'll talk to you tonight." Breaking his rule, he allowed a quick "see you later" wink at Patrick and then edged closer to his men to coax them if necessary. He knew them well and he'd handpicked them for this assignment. Nogales's explosive temper was both an advantage and a disadvantage. For the second time today, he prayed. *Dear God,* please *don't let this backfire.*

Lance Corporal Nogales returned to the position of attention. "Sir, I want to know why you think my parents should not have the right to vote, sir!"

"Holy Jesus!" whispered a general to no one in particular.

"I believe in every American citizen's right to vote," Coughlin answered gingerly.

Don had done his homework and he knew that Coughlin was an equal-opportunity bigot. Not only had his discrimination against gays earned him their wrath, but he'd infuriated the nation's Hispanic community by placing armed guards at polling places in precincts with large Latino populations. Observing the cameras were still rolling, Coughlin asked, "Where are you from?"

"San Fidelis, California, sir!"

"What a—*coincidence.* You're from my district." Coughlin spoke slowly, giving him time to think of a way out of this situation. "If your parents are properly registered to vote, I fully support their right to do so and I hope they will take advantage of every election and cast *legal* ballots. Preferably for me." Laughing, he turned toward the cameras and reporters, who'd recorded every sound and action. He began to sweat and he searched the sky for the helicopters.

"My parents *are* here legally. I don't understand why they were investigated last year."

Coughlin sounded both uncomfortable and condescending. "Son, in a democracy, we must ensure we run elections fairly and according to the rules. Sometimes there are occasions where we have to go to great lengths ensuring that everyone follows the regulations. I know that a fine American like yourself—who is a Marine and willing to die for his country—might not understand why it would be necessary for his parents to be questioned or—or investigated. But as long as I am your representative, they will never be denied their right to vote. As long as they are here legally and are properly registered."

Coughlin scurried away from the young Marines who'd ambushed him but he wasn't leaving Camp Pendleton without a soundbite on national news. "Here's a rugged Marine who's been around for a few years." Coughlin pointed to Don. "Come over here and give us an honest, 'old Corps' opinion about Mr. Clinton's plan to let queers into the Marine Corps."

Don hadn't expected this moment, but now the spotlight—the world's attention—was focused on him. His men had carried out their orders superbly. They'd diverted Coughlin from his agenda by reminding the media how he'd subverted elections by harassing citizens likeliest to vote for his opponent. Now Coughlin—and fate—forced Don to make a choice.

In the past, Don would've deflected the attention with a polite ambiguous comment such as: "As a Marine, I follow the orders of the commander-in-chief whether I disagree with those orders or not." He was tempted to give that response now. But something felt different. Recalling his conversation with Eddie at the park on Saturday, Don realized the world wouldn't change until people like him took advantage of moments like this, as Rosa Parks had done decades earlier. Raising his head to answer, Don glimpsed Patrick standing to the side. Handsome, young and sexy, Patrick looked to him, not only for love, but also for leadership. Don made up his mind.

The helicopters approached from the far side of the ridgeline. Don would have only one chance to say what he wanted, and if he paced himself correctly, noise would prevent Coughlin from responding. Speaking in his most forceful military voice, he said, "Congressman Coughlin, I'm against any law or rule or Department of Defense Directive that forces any member of the military to hide or lie about who they are. The ban preventing gays and lesbians serving in the military is as unjust and undemocratic a law as

I can think of. It goes against our core values of honor, courage and commitment. It's a violation of our code of conduct. This is a democracy and the military exists to protect equality, not reinforce discrimination. I hope our president, Mr. Clinton, will carry out his campaign promise and end this embarrassing, un-American law and let gays and lesbians serve their country openly and without fear."

Coughlin's face turned an ashen white. Ignoring Don's response, he looked toward the noise of the incoming helicopters and appeared to pray that they'd take him away from this debacle. When the Hueys circled the zone, preparing to set down and retrieve the passengers, Coughlin shouted to the senior general, "Get me outta here!" Nodding, the general guided Coughlin by the arm toward the aircraft. Don stood at attention and saluted the helicopters as they flew away from combat town. His pulse raced, both from the tension of the encounter and the exhilaration he felt about what he'd accomplished.

"Hey you! Can we get your name?" The reporter's question jerked Don back to reality. He was a Marine. He was subject to the Uniform Code of Military Justice and he might've just committed the gravest error of his career. He looked at the reporters and at the lance corporals who remained standing where they'd just put a congressman on the spot.

"No, thanks," Don said. "Think I've said enough. O'Doherty! Nogales! Grab your gear and throw it into the back of the Humvee. Let's get outta here!"

Patrick couldn't believe what he'd just witnessed. Don had put a US congressman in his place! Best of all, he'd done it on network news. Patrick was also impressed with the stellar way Don's Marines had ignored Coughlin's stupid questions.

As the party moved toward the helicopters, Coughlin's deputy screamed her displeasure. "What the fuck was that all about, Lieutenant?"

"I don't know, ma'am. Guess the Marines spoke their minds."

"Don't you screen the people you present to a person as important as a congressman?"

In the past, Patrick would've avoided a confrontation by disregarding the statement but Don's example had inspired him. "We do. It's called boot camp. Anyone who's earned the title 'Marine' is worthy to be presented to any member of congress."

Fortunately for Patrick, the woman was next in line to step into the helicopter and she hadn't worn the correct shoes for field maneuvers. Before she could retort, he shouted, "Let me give you a hand!" He lifted her from behind, easing her into the Huey. Next, he jumped in and turned around, just in time to see Don with his men. Even though he'd known Don only a few days, he'd never been prouder to be a part of anyone's life. As the Huey lifted off, Patrick recalled the thoughts he'd had when his plane landed in San Diego on Saturday. Then, he'd wondered what surprises might be in store for him. Less than seventy-two hours later, Don Hawkins was the best surprise Patrick had ever had. And they were just getting started.

Don and his two lance corporals rode in silence from combat town to Charlie Company's headquarters. Before getting out of the vehicle, Lance Corporal Nogales said, "I'm glad we did that, Gunny. I didn't like that bastard."

"I didn't either," said Lance Corporal O'Doherty. "Motherfucker had bad breath."

Don laughed. "You men did an outstanding job today and you don't need to talk about it with anyone, understand?" Both men nodded. "Let me take the fall for this. If anyone asks, you tell them to come see me. Now, go report to Staff Sergeant George."

"Aye, aye, Gunny," the Marines said in unison, grabbing their equipment.

Don studied the sky as he walked alone across the expansive asphalt-covered field the Marines used for parades and other ceremonies. Even though a small fog layer hovered over the coast near combat town, the sun shone brightly on the east side of the steep hills cutting through Camp Pendleton. But the change from fog to sunshine inversely reflected Don's moods. His sense of satisfaction at embarrassing the most notoriously antigay politician in

Washington was about to be challenged. He steeled himself mentally and emotionally.

Charlie Company's headquarters was empty. According to the training schedule, the Marines were cleaning their weapons at the armory. Wondering how long it'd be before he was summoned, he walked down the short hallway to his office. A note was pinned to his door: *Gunny Hawkins, see the battalion commander <u>immediately</u>!!!*

"That didn't take long," Don muttered. A pressed utility uniform hung in his wall locker, shielded in dry cleaner's plastic wrap. He was saving the uniform for the next battalion formation, but considering the scrutiny he was about to endure, he needed to look his best.

While changing uniforms, Don heard Captain Bruce's car come to a screeching halt. Five seconds later, the company commander rushed in. "Good, you'll need a clean uniform." The captain shook his head and stared. "I don't know what possessed you to do that."

Nothing Don said would vindicate his actions and statements in the eyes of his superiors, but he had to say something. "I don't know, sir, I couldn't keep my mouth shut. The whole thing was pathetic, the way Coughlin used our men and wasted our time for his own good." Don pulled clean trousers over his boxers and sat down to put on his boots.

The captain sat in a metal folding chair. "You saved my ass in the Philippines—"

"Twice."

"Right. Twice. And then off the coast of Kuwait more times than I can count. If anyone else had—had sky-lined himself out there the way you did this morning, I'd hang 'em out to dry. But for you, because I owe you, I'll go to bat for you on this one. But if I get your ass out of this sling, consider it as repayment for all those IOUs from years gone by."

As he put on a green T-shirt and camouflage blouse, Don said, "Captain Bruce, sir, I don't think the legendary General Chesty Puller could get my ass out of the sling it's in now."

Standing, the captain said, "We should go see the old man before he sends for you."

"Too late, sir." He handed his captain the note he'd found pinned to his door.

"Aw, shit. I'll say whatever I can. But I might not be able to help you one bit."

"Thank you, sir," Don said as they hurried across the gravel parking lot into the battalion's headquarters building. He followed Captain Bruce down the corridor to the command suite, where the sergeant major, the executive officer and the battalion commander's offices were located. The three men were waiting in the hallway for their errant gunnery sergeant.

"Gunnery Sergeant Hawkins!" barked the sergeant major. The senior enlisted Marine in the battalion was a hardened, leather-skinned twenty-six-year veteran of the Corps, similar to Clint Eastwood in the movie *Heartbreak Ridge*, except with more intensity and volume and less hair. "Report to the commanding officer!" The sergeant major's ferocity caused the captain to jump.

"Aye, aye, Sergeant Major!" Don said in his gruff drill instructor voice. He locked his jaw and braced for the agonizing ordeal.

"You too, Captain Bruce," said the major who served as the executive officer, the battalion's second-in-command. When all five men were in the room, the sergeant major closed the door and Lieutenant Colonel Ritter took his seat behind his desk.

"Gunny Hawkins, what was the last thing you said to me yesterday as I left your office?"

Don centered in front of the CO's desk. Captain Bruce stood slightly to his left and a step behind. "Sir, that my men wouldn't say anything to the congressman."

"You assured me of that, Gunny." Lieutenant Colonel Ritter toyed with a pencil. Suddenly he threw it down and rubbed his hands across his eyes. "I just got off the phone. Guess who you—I mean *we*—have the pleasure of visiting at thirteen hundred tomorrow,"

"Colonel Watkins, sir?"

"Well, you're a regular Einstein, aren't you, Hawkins? You're damn right it's Colonel Watkins. And you know what? I just hope and pray that this ends with him because I sure as hell don't want to stand tall in front of a goddamned general!" Don hadn't heard the lieutenant colonel shout like this. From the reaction of the Marines in the room, neither had they. After a pause, he continued. "You realize, Gunny," he said in a quiet voice as he studied Don's face, "you might be ordered to apologize to Congressman Coughlin."

Don bristled at the idea. "With all due respect, sir—"

"Don't give me any of that 'with all due respect' bullshit!" Lieutenant Colonel Ritter thundered. "If you're ordered to apologize to the congressman, you will! Do you understand?" Sweat trickled down the back of Don's neck. Apologizing to a man like Coughlin was against his principles. "What do you have against Coughlin? True, he's a conceited, self-righteous prick but he's only one out of 535 representatives and senators and they're *all* like that. Why pick on him?" Lieutenant Colonel Ritter walked to the window. Don kept his eyes locked straight ahead. "You crossed a line, Gunny Hawkins. The whole episode was unprofessional." He turned and in a softer tone said, "Look at me." Don obeyed and the two men locked eyes. "Why? Is it just him? Or would you deliberately embarrass *any* VIP who wanted to visit Camp Pendleton? Why him?"

In Don's heart, he knew his commanding officer was right. He'd been unprofessional but he couldn't let his CO know why. Somehow, Don had to fix this. "I would challenge *any* person who tried to use my men to his or her advantage in such a—a hypocritical way. Sometimes, yes, I get carried away and cross lines. But the congressman came here pretending to view our capabilities. All he wanted to do was use our Marines like they're trained monkeys to get his opinions in the press. He should have more respect for these men and realize their training time is limited. I don't like that, sir, and I hope you don't either."

"Damn it, Gunny! Of course I don't like it. Believe it or not, I want these men trained and ready for combat even more than you do and I don't like wasting valuable time. But guess what? I'm nothing but a goddamned lieutenant colonel in the United States Marine Corps! That means I don't get to say whatever the hell I want when I want to say it! Neither does the commandant—hell, no one in the military can just shoot their mouth off to the press. If the Chairman of the Joint Chiefs can't spout off his personal opinions whenever he likes, neither can Gunnery Sergeant Hawkins. Is that clear?"

"Yes, sir," Don said.

"Hawkins, you're the best gunnery sergeant in this whole battalion. I almost put you on my staff to be the operations chief when I took over, I'd heard so many good things about you. But Captain Bruce convinced me to let you stay in Charlie Company." Lieutenant Colonel Ritter glanced at the captain. "Perhaps that was a mistake. I hope I don't lose you, Gunny Hawkins. To be honest, I don't know what's going to happen. People are really pissed off right now. People at *much* higher pay grades than mine."

Looking at the men in the room, the lieutenant colonel said, "Everyone meet here at noon tomorrow. We'll ride down to regimental headquarters together. Sergeant Major, arrange for a driver and a van. Everyone *except* the driver will be in the winter service alpha uniform. We'll be early but that's of little consequence right now." To Don he said, "You're dismissed."

Don had been standing at attention throughout the entire episode. "Aye, aye, sir," he said. He took a step back, executed an "about face" movement and marched directly out of the battalion commander's office. The others followed closely behind.

As Don expected, the sergeant major said, "Not so fast, Gunnery Sergeant Hawkins."

Captain Bruce took the cue that the next confrontation was exclusively between the two enlisted Marines. "Gunny, I'll see you back at the company office."

"Aye, aye, sir." Don wondered how many times he'd have to repeat that archaic Naval phrase before this ordeal was over.

16

"Charlie Company, Gunnery Sergeant Hawkins."

Patrick didn't know what to say—he'd never phoned another gay Marine at his command. In the same tone, Don repeated his greeting. "Charlie Company—"

"Gunny," Patrick said, wondering if the base monitored all calls, "It's Lieutenant McAbe."

Don paused. "It's good to hear your voice. But aren't you with Congressman Coughlin?"

"I am. We're at the officers' club for a lunch meeting. I'm calling from a phone in the hall."

"Their reaction's pretty bad, isn't it?"

Don seemed like the type who preferred the truth, no matter how brutal. Patrick said, "Hate to say it, but Coughlin's like a mad dog. He ranted to the general about his 'planned attack at combat town.' The general promised Coughlin that the matter would be looked into and the, quote, 'appropriate parties would be disciplined,' end of quote. What did they say to you?"

"My battalion commander verbally reprimanded me. That's nothing compared to what's on the way. We see my regimental commander, Colonel Watkins, tomorrow at thirteen hundred."

"I saw him this morning," Patrick said. "He looks like a tough SOB."

"He is. He was also my regimental commander in *Desert Storm*."

"What's he like?" Patrick asked. "A solid leader? Will he treat you fairly?"

"In Kuwait, he was the best but I heard he's up for promotion. Sad, but that changes people."

Patrick peered into the dining room, where the three-star general introduced the Coughlins to the hundred or more top officers finishing their lunch. Looking at the schedule, he saw Coughlin had fifteen minutes. "Coughlin told the general that only a 'closeted faggot'—his expression—would set him up like you did. He recommended that you be investigated for homosexuality."

"Doesn't matter what Coughlin recommends. How'd the general respond?"

"He agreed it was a 'valid consideration'—those were his exact words."

"'Valid consideration,' huh? Sounds kind of weak. Not 'we'll look into it and get back with you,' or worse, 'I will personally call you with the results of an investigation'?"

"No," Patrick said. "Nothing like that."

While waiting for Don's response, Patrick heard a few lines of the congressman's speech. "Yesterday the Joint Chiefs of Staff, including your very own brave Commandant of the Marine Corps, met with Clinton for two hours. Do you know what they discussed? Was it protecting America? No! Clinton's promise to the homosexual activists who put him in the White House dominated the meeting. Neither President Clinton—nor her husband—care about your Marines or military readiness—their only goal is to advance the radical homosexual agenda!"

"Good. Maybe I'm safe. Did Coughlin ask any more Marines about gays in the military?"

"No. He's done with ad lib interviews." Patrick listened to Coughlin. "You scared him."

"Out-fucking-standing," Don said. "Mission accomplished."

"But he's giving an antigay speech now," said Patrick. "Betcha he doesn't take questions."

"What's he saying?" Don asked.

Patrick held the phone toward the room, where amplifiers blasted Coughlin's words through the building. "Today the *New*

York Times—or as I call it, 'Pravda on the Hudson,'—ran a lead ed-itorial with the headline WHO'S IN CHARGE OF THE MILITARY?" Raising his voice even louder, Coughlin said, "I'll tell those liberal editors at the *Times* who's in charge of the military—*you are!*" The officers in the room leapt to their feet, shouting and applauding.

"*Heil, Fuehrer,*" Patrick said softly as he stared at the frightening spectacle. Speaking into the receiver, he said, "Don, regardless of what happens, I think what you did today was brave."

"But stupid?"

"No, just brave." Patrick wanted to add that he'd been really turned on by his lover's display of boldness but he'd save that for a more intimate setting than the telephone booth. "Just wish I had the guts to do something like that. Maybe someday."

"Thank you, sir. Sounds like all of us have a rough road ahead—and what you said means a lot. It makes what I did worth the risk."

Coughlin said, "Before my wife and I return to Washington, I'd like to say one last thing—"

"Shit, he's wrapping up early," Patrick said. "Don, I think they're—"

Don said, "Lieutenant McAbe—"

"Damn, I mean, Gunny. Keep you posted. Hope all goes well with your colonel tomorrow."

"Thank you for the call. I'll—return the favor, very soon. *Semper Fi*, Devildog."

Patrick returned the receiver to its cradle and stepped to the double doors to the dining room, where Coughlin's deputy chief waited for him. "Where've you been? I've looked for you for ten minutes. We're canceling the remainder of the events and return-ing to DC—*immediately.*"

"Very well, ma'am, I'll call the flight line to see how soon your plane can depart."

"I said 'immediately,'" she snapped. "As in *immediately* right now."

"I'm sure it can." Patrick's promise was more hope than cer-tainty.

After a few calls, Patrick initiated the early retrograde and, min-utes later, found himself seated in the back of a large van on its way to the flight line. He sat next to the deputy as she tried in vain to use her portable phone. "Doesn't this base have any fucking cell towers?"

Speaking to the three-star general, Coughlin said, "Did you know that by six P.M. yesterday, Powell's office had received 681 calls to keep the ban on homosexuals and only 21 to lift it?"

"Yes." The general barely feigned enthusiasm. "I read it in today's 'Early Bird.' That's a compilation of military-related newspaper clippings the Pentagon faxes to senior officers."

"Oh, very well," said Coughlin, "so you know that Clinton is in way over his head on this issue." The general simply smiled, nodded and looked out the window of the van.

Half an hour later, Patrick and the other Marines saluted as the plane ascended, carrying the congressional delegation away. "Talk about a single-issue—" said the three-star general. "Not one of our better productions, ladies and gentlemen," he said to the group. Looking at Colonel Watkins, he asked, "Joe, how do you plan to handle this?" Taking their cue, the other Marines departed. Patrick, unsure of his duties, followed to learn Don's fate.

"General, I've instructed his battalion commander to have him at my office at thirteen hundred tomorrow. Beyond that, I plan to—"

"Just a minute, Joe." The general interrupted his subordinate commander. Patrick froze as the fifth highest-ranking Marine in the Corps addressed him. "Your duties are completed, Lieutenant. You may return to your unit now."

Patrick stiffened to the position of attention. "Aye, aye, sir!" He saluted the pair of senior officers and left as fast as possible. He was relieved to be done with this assignment, but sorry he wouldn't learn any more information. "Sorry, Don, I tried," he mumbled and exited the area.

The worst part was what he didn't know. Don didn't understand why the officers couldn't tell him what they planned to do with him. Then again, he *did* understand. He'd been around enough senior officers to give him insight into their thought processes. The Uniform Code of Military Justice gave them wide latitude, and considering the political pressure, they might punish him severely. If they prosecuted him for disrespect and direct disobedience, he could go to jail for a few months or a few years. Worse, they could investigate him and find links to Eddie, Karl, Robbi and his other gay military friends. Maybe even Patrick. The irony was that Don had taken this risk partly to be an example to Patrick and to make things easier for the men and women following in their path. Unfortunately, his rashness may have placed Patrick in jeopardy.

But Don had an exemplary record and the other Marines in the battalion respected him. His immediate superiors would face a morale crisis if they dealt harshly with him. He'd put Captain Bruce, Lieutenant Colonel Ritter and even Colonel Watkins in a difficult bind. In the isolation of his office, Don realized how he'd endangered everyone he cared about or who'd treated him fairly. His high-minded motivations aside, he'd embarrassed the congressman because he had an insatiable need to inflict damage on a person he despised. Don had allowed his hatred of Coughlin to bring him down to Coughlin's level.

Pacing in his tiny office, Don barely noticed when the phone rang. He didn't have a separate line, as that was an unheard-of luxury in a rifle company. Halfway through the third ring, the corporal picked up and knocked on Don's door. "Gunny. Telephone. It's your wife."

The time was fifteen forty-five—or a quarter till nine Wednesday morning in Okinawa, where his lawfully wedded wife—and her girlfriend—were stationed. "Thanks, Corporal."

Listening to the exchange outside his office, Don smiled. "I didn't know Gunny had a wife!"

"Yeah, dumbshit! And she's a gunnery sergeant, too, in Japan. That's why I told you never to say anything bad about women Marines. The worst ass-chewing gunny ever gave was because some stupid private first class was in here shootin' his mouth off saying bad shit about WM's!"

"Got it, Corporal." Don listened to ensure the company's clerk had hung up the other phone. "Good morning, hon. How've you been?" Don communicated with Erin over the military's intercontinental phone system on a regular basis. The calls didn't cost the individuals or the command any money, and because Don and Erin were husband and wife, Captain Bruce turned a blind eye. The calls also helped substantiate his alibi—he didn't date women because he was already married to one. Besides, he and Erin had been friends for years and talking to her would be a welcome distraction from the events of the last few hours.

The problem with the phone system—besides the likelihood the military monitored the call—was the five-second delay. "Just fine, Don," Erin said gently. "How're you holding up?"

The question caught him by surprise and he wondered how she'd heard about his run-in with Coughlin so quickly. "I'm—I'm holding up fine. I dread what's going to happen next, naturally, especially since I don't have a fucking clue what that is. But—how did you hear already?"

"Don, we're so *so* sorry. Jeanne called us last night. We couldn't stop crying and I haven't slept at all. I'm just upset we can't be there with all of you."

The delay in the line added to his confusion. "Erin? Erin? What're you taking about? Did you say 'last night'? There's no way—do you mean my run-in with Congressman Coughlin? That just happened a few hours ago."

Delay. "What? No—Don. I'm calling about—what's this about Coughlin?"

"So you haven't heard. Good. Short version. I got tasked with providing a 'dog-and-pony' show for our favorite congressman. Didn't go according to Coughlin's plan. You would've been proud of your husband." He was determined to put the best face on the episode, no matter what its consequences might be.

Waiting the usual amount of delay, he was surprised when Erin didn't laugh or reply. Finally she said, "Oh my God, Don. You haven't heard, have you?"

"Four o' clock P.M., Tuesday, January 26."

Jay stared at his logbook. Over sixty hours had passed since Johnson's death, and finally Jay felt some relief. As he parked along the street beside Johnson's house, January's early sunset shot its orange rays brilliantly over the roof, giving it an ethereal outline. Ollie had instructed Jay to lock the house and give the keys to the captain of the USS *Cayuga*. The captain would give them to Johnson's mother when she arrived in San Diego tomorrow morning. Before Jay could do that, though, he had an unfinished item on his agenda.

A kind neighbor had agreed to take care of the dog until Mrs. Johnson arrived. Without the little dog's bark, an eerie silence greeted Jay when he opened the door. Stepping slowly into the room, he stopped in the middle, all at once realizing this was the last time he'd ever be in this space. Jay's mind recalled Johnson on the floor, blood spurting out of his head as he lay dying. Then the bizarre smile crossed his face.

"Who do you think you are?"

Jay jumped then froze in terror as a voice called out from the doorway to the kitchen. Instead of lying on the floor, Johnson's corpse was resurrected and floating toward Jay from the back of the house. "Who the *fuck* do you think you are?" Johnson asked.

"I—I'm just doing—"

"You think *you're* doing *God's* will? You think *God* wants you to hunt down the homosexuals? To *kill*—in his name?" Johnson suddenly morphed into a different ghost on the other side of the room. Jay spun around, facing his new inquisitor. "Is that your plan, Jay?"

"Pastor Stephen!" Jay smiled. "I—isn't that what—*God* wants?"

"Is that what you think, my precious Jay—or 'Stephen'? I'm honored you chose my name."

"Why did this happen?" Jay blurted out. "I thought I was doing the right thing."

"You blame me for your life and that's the fire that keeps you going. But it's not really me you blame, is it? Don't you know whose fault this is?"

Jay put his hands over his ears as tears welled up in his eyes. "Yes."

The apparition stood in the spot where Johnson had died. "Who told you to do this? Who told you that if you chase—and *murder*—these people, that somehow, *some way* God will forgive you for what you and I enjoyed together. Who told you that, Jay?"

"You know who." Jay's tears were only partly from sadness. Mostly, he felt trapped by a helpless form of rage. He'd hoped his ghosts were gone forever. But the demons were back. He knew they weren't real—but they *were* real because he could see them. "No!" he repeated, "You—are—*not*—real!"

Trying to ignore the images, Jay focused on his mission. He reached into his bag and removed Johnson's address book, which he'd taken from the house yesterday and had photocopied after the forensics investigators had finished. He laughed at the irony— everything had unraveled because he'd been obsessed with the address book. In the end, though, he got what he wanted. He always did. "What the *hell* are you laughing at?" Pastor Stephen's ghost had disappeared and in its place, Johnson had returned, standing inches away from where Jay had last seen him alive. "Fuck with my friends, and so help me God, I'll torture you the rest of your life."

"You aren't real either," Jay said through clenched teeth. Setting the address book on the desk where he'd first seen it three nights ago, he reached into the bag once more and grabbed a pair of Ray-Ban sunglasses he'd purchased at the Naval Station's Exchange.

"Damn," said Johnson's ghost. "You think of *everything*, don't you, Agent Gared?" Jay ignored the voice and the image.

"It's my mind," Jay said. "I'm doing what I have to. I'll deal with this later." Using a rag he'd brought for this purpose, he rubbed his fingerprints clean from the book and the glasses.

"Oh, no, Agent Gared. You're mistaken. I'm not just in your mind. I'm *real* and I'll be everywhere you go. And you forget my friends are real. They won't let you get away with this."

Halfway to the front door, Jay spun around. "Really—Ed— *Eddie?* Where *are* your friends? You've been dead three days and no one's come to your house. If *I* hadn't made an anonymous call to the Naval Station, you'd still be on the floor, decaying in a pool of your own blood! Your dog would've starved if it hadn't been for me. So, Chief Johnson, *I'm* your only friend."

With a solemn voice the fading spirit said, "You're not on *your* time now, Agent Gared. You're on *my* time. You can be certain—when the time is right, my friends *will avenge me!*" Jay stared into space as the room cleared of any nonphysical images.

Using the cloth, an unnecessary precaution since the forensics team had done its job, Jay turned the doorknob and let himself out of the haunted house.

"I'm okay," he said. "I'm okay."

"Corporal," Gunny Hawkins said, emerging from his office, "I have something to take care of and I won't be back until noon tomorrow. Tell the captain and the first sergeant I'll call them tonight."

"Okay, Gunny." The corporal stared out the door as his boss walked to his jeep. "That's the first time I've ever seen Gunny leave work early—*or* say that he'll be out for half a day."

"Seemed really upset about something too."

"Friggin' amazing," the corporal said, shaking his head. "Ten thousand miles away and your old lady can still fuck up your world."

17

"If you're driving in on the 8 west this Wednesday morning, watch out for that three-car pileup just before the Fairmont exit," said the cheery voice on the radio.

"Now you tell me." Sitting still on the interstate gave Jay time to fret. The rearview mirror showed how bleary-eyed he was from stress and lack of sleep, and the ghostly visits hadn't helped. He tapped the steering wheel. He'd never admit it but fear weighed him down the most.

He blamed himself for dropping the ball on a few details. Consciously, he recited everything he'd done correctly. *Replaced the address book. Check. Substituted a new pair of sunglasses for the broken ones. Check. Pitched the broken ones. Check.* He'd also verified that none of Johnson's neighbors saw him return home with anyone early Sunday morning. Jay had covered every base and the chances were almost nonexistent that anyone could link the death to him.

The nature of tragedies, though, was that closing all the loose ends was impossible. Hairs from the back of Jay's head were in the evidence locker. Lance the bartender might be able to recognize him. Jay had to tolerate these untidy remnants. Another loose end was on the seat beside him. Reaching inside his gym bag, he fingered the brown package that had inspired him to accuse Johnson of trafficking in drugs. Luckily, another bartender corroborated

Jay's story that Lance had stored a brown paper sack and then passed it to an African-American customer.

If he followed his instincts, Jay would drive far out of town, discarding the package in a random Dumpster just as he'd done with Ed's broken sunglasses. Even better, he should burn the shirt out in the desert, and when he had time, he would. Right now, though, he countered his instincts with the satisfaction the shirt gave him. He liked having a physical reminder of his quick-thinking abilities. He'd turned a potential career-ending situation into an opportunity to pursue his goals. The package was evidence of his resourcefulness despite his mistakes.

A musical introduction announced the seven o' clock news. "Orange County Congressman Edward Coughlin felt as though he'd stumbled into an ambush yesterday at Camp Pendleton," said the serious but pleasant woman. Jay smiled, recalling his introduction to Congressman Coughlin at an NRA convention several years earlier. Coughlin was unafraid to express his opinions, which happened to be in line with Jay's. "At the conclusion of a Marine training exercise he had viewed, Congressman Coughlin asked several Marines their opinions about the controversy surrounding President Clinton's plan to allow gay men and lesbians in the military."

"Good for you, Congressman!" Jay's laughter indicated his unrequited appreciation.

The broadcaster continued. "The first two Marines all but ignored the congressman's questions, instead asking him some questions of their own." The segment cut to a recording of the conversation between Coughlin and the Marines with the anchor's voice periodically interrupting. "'Sir, I want to know why you think my parents should not have the right to vote, sir!' One of the two junior Marines that Coughlin questioned was from the congressman's district and has parents who were investigated as part of a probe into election fraud. The investigation stemmed from the congressman's allegations of voter irregularity in the heavily Latino precincts in his district. That investigation is still ongoing. The last Marine Coughlin questioned was a member of the senior enlisted ranks."

The reporter again cut to a recording, but this time the voice belonged to an older Marine. "'I'm against any law or rule or Department of Defense Directive that forces any member of the military to hide or lie about who they are." Jay's earlier joy turned to fury as he listened to the belligerent Marine disparage the congressman and—*support Clinton's promise to let gays serve!*

"Neither the Marine who made the statement nor Congressman Coughlin was available for comment. Camp Pendleton's public affairs office also refused to comment on the matter. Congressman Coughlin and his staff reportedly cut their trip short and have returned to Washington DC. Now for an update on that accident on the eight west—"

Jay switched the radio off. Something about the Marine stuck in his mind. He'd heard that voice recently. "Johnson's answering machine!" Jay was convinced it was the same voice as the first, second and fourth messages on the dead Sailor's machine. As he crawled toward the accident, he fumbled through his notes until he found the final message. *Something's come up here . . . Postpone the appointment . . . tomorrow morning . . . Wednesday or Thursday . . . Your cutoff isn't until Friday.* The rage Jay had felt only minutes ago at the Marine's insubordination turned to delight. He and the dead Sailor were coconspirators, and no doubt, their scheme was part of their homosexual agenda. Jay had proof of their collaboration and he was determined to get to its roots. "Assuming this traffic ever moves again."

"How much do you think this dignified gathering will cost the American taxpayer? Nine? Ten thousand dollars?" Leonard joined his two golfing companions at their table. "Excluding the cost of the food, of course. No telling how badly these soggy croissants broke the budget."

"Hell, you gotta pay for the croissants yourself," replied Pete.

Leonard dreaded the tedious monthly conferences at the officers' club but he hoped this morning's would be interesting given the buzz surrounding Coughlin's visit. "Joe, what happened yesterday? Apparently I missed one hell of an assault by your men."

"How did you know they were in my regiment?" Joe looked both surprised and distraught.

"Well, I don't know. Maybe I heard it on the news," Leonard answered. "Or perhaps I overheard it from one of the Marines."

"I hope it was from the Marines. As far as I know, we've kept the regiment out of the press." Leonard was curious. In three decades, he'd never known Joe to be concerned about publicity.

"Ladies and gentlemen, the breakfast buffet is open. Twenty percent off for club members."

"Gents," Pete said, "if I'm paying $4.80 for this grub, I'm gettin' first pickin's."

"Maybe I read it in the paper, Joe. Didn't the *San Diego Post* identify your regiment?"

Patrick wondered if this nightmare would ever end. Just when he thought he was done with his stupid duties as an escort officer, Lieutenant Colonel Hammer ordered him to put on his short-sleeved khaki shirt and green trousers, the Marines' "Service Charlie" uniform, and attend this breakfast meeting. "Day number three—uniform number three," he murmured as he straightened the few wrinkles on his shirt. "Hopefully tomorrow I can finally put on a goddamned flight suit." Sledge said Patrick should be at the club this morning on the off chance the generals had questions about yesterday's botched congressional visit.

"Hell, too bad the *Post didn't* name your regiment. The *Post* would've printed the wrong regiment and thrown everyone off track."

"Good point, Pete," said another colonel Patrick recalled from yesterday.

Standing against the wall in the back of the room, Patrick thought he was inconspicuous until the senior officers walked to the rear. To his dismay, the position he'd staked out wasn't incognito; it was at the starting point of the most high-powered buffet line in California.

"Colonels, Colonels," said the man Patrick remembered as Colonel Watkins, the same officer Don would meet with later today. "What happened to the time-honored Marine Corps tradition of allowing the junior men to eat first?" Suddenly Patrick realized Colonel Watkins was talking about him. "Pete, you just barge right in and the lieutenant standing there hasn't had a bite to eat. And between the two of you, he needs this breakfast a lot more than you do."

"I'm sorry, Lieutenant," said the colonel identified as "Pete." He stepped back, offering Patrick the first place in line.

"Oh, no, sir," said Patrick. "I—I ate breakfast before I came here this morning."

"Smart man," said the third colonel. Like "Pete" and Patrick, he wore aviator wings. "Are you in Marine Aircraft Group Seventy-nine, Lieutenant?"

"Yes, sir, I am."

He extended his hand. "I'm Colonel Spencer, your group commander. What's your name?"

"I'm First Lieutenant McAbe," answered Patrick, shaking hands. "Pleased to meet you, sir." He suspected the group commander knew that no lieutenant was ever pleased to meet a colonel, but courtesy was an essential part of being an officer and a gentleman.

Colonel Spencer smiled and asked, "Which squadron are you in?"

"Seven-oh-seven, sir,"

"Ah, Lieutenant Colonel Hammer's training squadron. How long have you been here?"

"This is my third day, sir," Patrick answered.

Colonel Spencer looked concerned. "Weren't you the escort officer yesterday?"

"Yes, sir, I was."

"Well, I should quit holding up the line or these field grade officers will start a revolt. Good to meet you, Lieutenant McAbe, and welcome aboard!" Patrick nodded politely at the three colonels as they walked away.

"Damn, sir. You're at Camp Pendleton for three days and already you're sucking up to your group commander," said a vaguely familiar voice behind Patrick. "I've heard of officers kissing ass, but this might be a new world record."

* * *

Returning to the table with their food, Pete said, "That lieutenant back there is one of your pilots, Leon? Hell, thought we had a minimum age to fly helicopters."

"You only feel that way because *your* children now have children of their own, Grandpa Petey." Laughing, Leonard turned back to Joe and said, "As much publicity as Coughlin attracts, someone will mention that the Marine was from your regiment. What difference will it make?"

"The general left it up to me to decide what to do to the gunnery sergeant," Joe answered. "I don't need any more pressure—you know what I mean—so-called 'advice' from Washington. The less attention the better. People I've never met have told me to hang this gunny out to dry."

Pete stopped eating. "Hang the gunny out to dry? What the hell did he do besides piss off a congressman? We should give him a medal! You can't punish a man for speaking his mind."

"You can't?" asked Leonard, playing devil's advocate. "That's mighty liberal of you, Pete. We've all seen good people fall by the wayside because they couldn't keep their mouths shut."

"It's not just what he said. Out of the whole Congress, if you think it's a coincidence that the marine standing nearest Coughlin was from his district, I've got an Army battalion for sale."

"No matter what you're asking for it," Pete joked, "I'm sure it's overpriced."

"So the gunny set up an ambush for the congressman?" asked Leonard. "Is that a crime? They *do* call it 'combat town' after all. It exists to train Marines in urban assault techniques."

"I agree with Leon," said Pete. "If the gunny is clever enough to make a plan like that work, hell, promote him. Make him a warrant officer! Seems to me his worst crime is that he's a fag lover. What'd you think, Joe? Is your gunny queer? What kind of a record does he have?"

"I remember him from *Desert Storm* and he was a water walker," said Joe. "He's married—"

"That don't mean he ain't a homosexual," Pete interjected.

"Speaking out in favor of homosexuals doesn't mean he is," countered Joe.

"And thanks to our new president," said Leonard, "being a homosexual might no longer be a basis for separation from the service. Did anyone read the Early Bird this morning?"

"I haven't read that piece of shit in two years." Pete smeared grape jelly on a piece of bread and took a bite. "Why? What did it say?"

Pulling the newspaper clippings from his bag, Leonard put his reading glasses on the edge of his nose. "According to all the major newspapers, 'Mr. Aspin, in proposing to suspend enforcement of the military's ban on homosexuals for six months while he consults with the chiefs and lawmakers on an acceptable way to carry out the new policy, is trying to address the military's concerns, senior aides say.' "

"Damn," said Joe. "See what I'm up against? 'Proposing to suspend for six months?' What the hell does that mean? Nobody knows what the fuck is going on."

"That's the thickest Early Bird I've ever seen. No wonder I quit readin' the damn thing," Pete said, taking the pages from Leonard's hand. "The stories are from all over the country, about gays in the military! Listen to this: 'Mr. Clinton has promised to end discrimination against homosexuals in the services but has also pledged to order the Secretary of Defense to write a strict code of conduct to govern behavior for homosexuals and heterosexuals alike.' Someone ought to tell the draft-dodging son-of-a-bitch we've already got a code of conduct."

Leonard retrieved the Early Bird from his friend. "Both of you—I'm curious about your opinions. Apparently, 'Some Marines have gone so far as to suggest the Corps be disbanded rather than accept avowed homosexuals.' " Leonard looked at his friends to gauge their reactions.

"Holy shit," said Pete. "That sounds a little—melodramatic."

"How does one 'avow' oneself a homosexual?" asked Joe. "A sign-up sheet at City Hall?"

"Good point," Leonard said, laughing. Continuing in a more serious tone, he said, "And a sergeant major wrote in *The Marine Corps Gazette,* 'The Bible has a very clear and specific message towards homosexuals—"Those that practice such things are worthy of death."'"

"My opinion?" said Joe. "These senior Marines are shooting their mouths off—or typewriters—on *both* sides of this issue. They have no business publicizing their opinions."

"What does the Bible have to do with the Marine Corps?" Pete asked. "I don't know about you two but I signed on with this outfit to protect a *demo*cracy—not a *theo*cracy."

"We're in for a long debate," Joe said. "What a waste of time. Homosexuals already serve, and honestly, we probably need them more than we realize. What's your take on it, Leonard?"

"It's purely a generational issue. As we die off—or fade away— the next generation will look at us the same way we look at 'separate but equal,' child labor, the imprisonment of Japanese-Americans in World War II or those who opposed women's suffrage. Archaic, unenlightened cretins of the past, sent off to the dustbin of history and the graveyard of shame."

"Here's to fading away—to the golf course!" Pete raised his coffee mug in a mock toast.

Leonard touched his mug to Pete's. Joe said, "But back to my urgent problem. The gunny and his battalion commander will be in my office this afternoon. What would you do, Leonard?"

"I thought you didn't want any more opinions," Leonard answered.

"I don't want any more unsolicited opinions from lazy rear-echelon assholes who've never led anyone anywhere except maybe the Xerox repairman to the photocopier. What I need is opinions from real leaders and survivors of these political scrapes. Like you, Leonard."

Leonard glanced at the lectern, where the announcer began the program. "Let me give you a ride to your regiment when this meeting is over. We can discuss it in the car."

Patrick spun around and was startled when he recognized the Marine who'd just spoken to him. A corporal at the officers' club chowing down on a croissant would've been a surprising image by itself. The most astonishing part, though, was that the corporal was Karl, one of Don's friends he'd met at WC's Saturday night. "Good morning, Corporal—" It occurred to Patrick he didn't know Karl's last name.

"Steiger." Smirking, Karl extended his hand. "Pleased to meet you—Lieutenant McAbe." Karl must've sensed Patrick's unease at meeting another gay Marine in such a high-profile place because he motioned for Patrick to follow him into the hallway just outside the dining room.

"Why're you hanging around the officers' club?" Patrick asked when they were away from the crowd. "How'd you get in? *Why* would you want to get in? I'm an officer and I don't want to be around a crowd with this much rank."

"I'm here a lot," said Karl. "I'm Colonel Spencer's driver."

"*Holy shit*," said Patrick in a low voice. He remained in a visible spot in case the officer in charge of the conference called on him. "So you hang out with these guys all the time?"

"Yep, that's me. A 'VIP magnet,'" said Karl. Patrick noticed Karl was much more somber than he'd been Saturday night, but he attributed the corporal's subdued demeanor to their present location. "I saw you yesterday. At the flight line."

"You should've said something."

"What was I supposed to say to you?" Karl gave Patrick a sarcastic look. "'Hey, Lieutenant, I hoped you fucked my friend Sunday night because he really needs to get laid!' Yeah, that'd go over well. Besides, you looked like you were going out of your mind."

Patrick scanned the area and was happy no one was within listening distance. Even somber, Karl was brash and daring. "Good observation. Probably best you didn't talk to me yesterday."

Looking more glum than before, Karl asked, "Did you talk to Don last night?" Patrick shook his head. Rather than look up at the taller Marine, Karl continued staring around the corner into the dining room. Patrick presumed he was watching to see if the colonel needed anything.

"No. I don't have a phone yet. But I called him—from right here, as a matter of fact—yesterday after his run-in with Coughlin.

I was planning to call him tonight to catch up on things. Why?" Patrick sensed the situation was far worse than Karl's expression had let on.

Karl inhaled deeply. "Something—something happened." Lowering his voice to a whisper, Karl looked up at Patrick. "You remember meeting Eddie, right? Don's best friend for the last—I don't know—twelve, thirteen years?" Patrick nodded. "They found his body Monday morning. He didn't show up for work at his ship. They said he shot himself—a suicide." Karl gritted his teeth. "But we know better."

Patrick remained still. He didn't know Eddie. At the most, he'd spent thirty minutes with him at the bar Saturday night but Eddie meant the world to Don.

"Don called me from Jeanne's house. He stayed there last night," said Karl. "He went over to Eddie's house—he's got a key—to 'straighten' it up, but he was too late. Investigators had already been there." Karl raised his head and looked nonchalantly away from Patrick as another Marine passed them on his way to the restroom. "Eddie's ship is having a memorial service for him at the base chapel in San Diego tomorrow. I'm driving down with Don."

Now Patrick understood the difference in Karl. Saturday night he'd been confident and on fire. Now he was sullen and withdrawn. Looking directly into Karl's eyes, Patrick saw they were bloodshot. "Karl," Patrick whispered, "I'm so sorry for you and Don and your friends. I—I don't know what—I can't believe this happened. I'm here for you, whatever you need." Patrick wasn't sure if that helped but it was all he could think of to say. "Shit. Don's got his meeting with the colonel this afternoon." Patrick's heart ached for the man he'd slept with Sunday night. He was stunned by how much the guy's life had changed in the short time since then.

Karl bit his lip and nodded. "Looks like this meeting is over." He backed away as the roomful of officers exited. As a parting comment, Karl said, "She really likes you, sir, and she'll need you now more than ever. So don't hurt her."

"Corporal Steiger." A distinguished-sounding voice that Patrick now recognized as Colonel Spencer's called out from behind. "We're giving Colonel Watkins a lift to regiment." Patrick spun around quickly, pretending to wait on another officer. "His driver will follow us."

"Aye, aye, sir," said Karl.

Although Karl and Patrick had done their best to appear unaware of each other, Patrick was sure Colonel Spencer caught him fraternizing with Karl. The colonel didn't seem upset, though, and gave Patrick a welcoming nod. "You have a pleasant day, Lieutenant McAbe," he said, disappearing out of the club.

18

"Since you asked for my opinion—"

"Yes I did, Leonard. I trust your advice the most." The two colonels rode in the back seat of Leonard's government sedan along the windy roads through Camp Pendleton's hills.

"For those who'd like to 'hang the gunny out to dry,' ask them what article of the Uniform Code of Military Justice he violated." Staring into the front of the car, Leonard locked eyes with Corporal Steiger in the rearview mirror. "The only possible charge I can see is disrespect—"

"To a congressman?" asked Joe. "Is that in the UCMJ?"

"Precisely. The situation is vague." Launching into a plan he hoped would help the Marine, Leonard looked at his friend. "What do *you* want to do? Save his career?"

"Yes." Joe hesitated. "He *was* out of line. If Coughlin decides to be vindictive, it could hurt the Corps a lot. This Marine is one of our finest and we should protect him. But how?"

"Here's what I'd do. Inform your general that the gunny will face Non-Judicial Punishment for disrespect. It will be at the regimental level and you will be the presiding officer."

"What if the general insists I convene a summary or special court martial?"

"Argue that a court martial would attract attention and be chaotic. Also, point to his stellar record. If he were an average Marine, you'd go with a court martial. Because he's made only one error in fifteen years, the punishment doesn't warrant a trial. That might be persuasive."

"What then? Won't they still expect to see the Marine's head on a platter?"

"Stall for a couple of weeks. Claim you're waiting on all the incident reports. By then, the furor will have subsided. Then bring him before you and drop the charges. From what I saw on TV last night, he seemed respectful." Leonard paused, letting his friend mull over his proposal.

"Know what? That might work. Divert the pressure then let the gunny off the hook quietly."

"Some might say this plan is a political copout," Leonard said. "Guess what? They're right! To hell with politics. Your goal is to protect your Marine. The general gave you the decision-making authority. If you let the gunny off right away, the general might take that power back and the gunny's career is over. If you wait two weeks, everyone will forget about the incident."

"Except Coughlin. The division chief told me a rumor that Coughlin will follow up on this. He wants the Corps to investigate to see if the gunny's gay. I told the chief, 'Fuck Coughlin!'"

"Then Coughlin and the division chief would be the ones under investigation, wouldn't they?" Leonard said, causing his driver to laugh. "The solution to the threat of an investigation relates to the Early Bird articles we read. Clinton's placing a six-month moratorium on discharges for homosexuality. Why should we waste taxpayer dollars on an investigation if we're restricted by presidential order from acting on a possible outcome?"

"That makes sense. Use the present ambiguity of the situation—the fabled 'fog of war'—as justification for inaction," Joe said. "Colonel Spencer, you, sir, are a genius."

"Thank you, Colonel Watkins, but keep that opinion a secret from my ex-wife's attorney."

"I hate to leave Gunny Hawkins hanging in the wind for two weeks," said Joe. "Wish I could let him know nothing bad will happen to him."

"You can't," said Leonard. "No one can know what you've

planned. If word gets out that all along, you were dropping the charges, your general will take the decision away from you and make it himself." Leonard looked up front and once again locked eyes with Corporal Steiger in the rearview mirror. "We can't tell anyone. You know how Marines love to spread rumors."

"Jay, got time for a quick chat?"

Jay's plate was full this Thursday morning. As desperately as he wanted to say "no," Ollie's question was clearly rhetorical. "I— I've got—an appointment, Ollie, but—"

"Won't take more than ten minutes." Sighing, Jay followed Ollie into his office and closed the door. Ollie leaned back in his chair and laced his fingers together behind his head. "Before we close the Johnson investigation, I have some questions."

"Sure." Jay suddenly felt uncomfortably warm.

Reading from a file on his desk, Ollie asked, "You received an anonymous tip last Friday?"

"Late Friday afternoon," said Jay. "Correct."

"On Saturday afternoon, after I dropped you off here at the office, you went to Johnson's house and placed him under surveillance."

Jay ran through the details of the last four days, reminding himself to go slowly and keep his story straight. "I went home first. Changed clothes."

"What time did you arrive at Chief Johnson's?"

Ollie's tone wasn't confrontational, but Jay's sense was that his boss was leading him into a trap. "Um—eight? Maybe nine o' clock."

Ollie looked up from the file. "Which is it?"

"I don't remember exactly." Jay's frustration was visible. "It's in the—what difference—?"

"Was he alone?" Ollie's volume increased.

"Yes. He was alone." Jay tried to remain as calm as possible. "What's with these questions? This information is in my re—"

"I'll tell you why!" Ollie stopped masking his irritation. Standing, he said, "Because there's a goddamned reporter from the *Gay and Lesbian Times* asking if we talked to any witnesses. He specifically asked who might've seen Johnson and two friends having dinner at a place called Hamburger Mary's until after eleven Saturday night. *He's* interviewed restaurant employees—a hostess, a waiter and a busboy—who knew Johnson well. They recall talking to him Saturday night. All three said he was laughing, joking and having a good time. He didn't behave like someone who'd kill himself four hours later. They said Johnson and his party didn't leave until after eleven o' clock, on their way to the bar where you saw the drug deal take—"

"The West Coast Production Company? Did they name the two friends?"

"'WC's' as he calls it." Ollie returned to his seat and rubbed his temples. "No, the witnesses refused to name the two friends. I assume they're military as well." He stopped rubbing and glared at Jay. "The statements conflict with your report. You wrote that you parked outside Johnson's house at nine, waited for two hours then followed him to the club."

"Don't you get it, Ollie?" Jay's intensity matched his boss's earlier level. "They're sticking together! This is what *they* do. The—the waiter—they're queers and they protect each other."

"Do you want to add that to your report?" Ollie rummaged through the file. "Something else that's odd—no one found the bag of drugs you claim the bartender gave Johnson. I assume you didn't find it?" Jay shook his head. "The police, paramedics, forensics—never located it."

"Damn it, Ollie. He—he got rid of it after I quit watching his house early Sunday morning."

"And what time was that, Jay?"

"His lights went off at two thirty. I waited thirty minutes then left. So three A.M."

"Forensics concluded he'd been dead for over twenty-four hours." Ollie looked at the ceiling and calculated the difference. "He was discovered shortly after eight A.M. Monday."

"Sometime between three and eight—Ed went somewhere—" Ollie suddenly looked his direction and Jay made a mental note to always think of "Ed" as "Johnson" from now on. "*Johnson* must've gone out or maybe someone came by his house. He got rid of the drugs. He felt guilty and shot himself. Or his contact came for the drugs *after* Johnson shot himself. My report says that the police found the door unlocked."

"Possible."

"Possible?" shouted Jay, "Ollie, it's *exactly* what happened! There's no other explanation."

"Bartender claims the package was a shirt. Johnson was returning it to a friend."

"Goddamn, Ollie! Of *course* that's the bartender's story." Sweat slid down Jay's forehead.

"Calm down, Jay." Ollie's concern prompted Jay to regain control of his emotions.

"What friend? What shirt?" Jay asked. "Where's the so-called friend?"

"Won't give the name. Means there *was* no friend or he's in the military," Ollie said. "Jay, the bartender and Johnson don't have any priors." Circling to the front of his desk, he continued in a softer tone. "I don't doubt you. The journalist hasn't seen your report. In fact, only I and a handful of others have looked at it. The reporter doesn't know about the conflicting versions of Johnson's whereabouts Saturday evening—you and I are the *only* ones who know about that."

Ollie leaned forward. From inches away, he said, "I told you Saturday, I retire in six months. Between now and then I don't want *any* problems. Got that?" Jay nodded and Ollie returned to his chair. "We have to be extremely cautious—can't stress that enough—dealing with cases like this." Feeling somewhat better, Jay nodded to let his boss know he understood. Even though he could tell Ollie suspected his story was bogus, at least Ollie wasn't pursuing the discrepancy.

Reverting to his usual officious voice, Ollie said, "As if there weren't enough twists in this case, we got the results back from the lab regarding Johnson's blood test. I'd hoped he had drugs in his blood to back up your story. He didn't."

This was a situation Jay had expected. "Pushers aren't always users."

Ollie's tone was patronizing. "I know that, Jay." Handing Jay copies of medical records, he said, "Johnson was HIV-positive."

The news shouldn't have surprised Jay. Johnson's lover appeared to have died of AIDS. From what Jay knew, statistically that would increase Johnson's chances of having the virus. Still, Jay thought the military discharged HIV-positive people. "How did he stay in the Navy?"

"Although HIV disqualifies someone from *joining* the military, if someone's already in, it's not an automatic discharge—not yet anyway," Ollie explained. "Still, it would've ended—or severely curtailed—Johnson's career. But according to those records, last year he was negative."

Jay's mind raced through all the possibilities this new piece of evidence presented. "So—sometime in the last year, Johnson contracted HIV—and if he'd just discovered it—"

"He'd have a motive for suicide. Or a plausible explanation, at least from the Navy's perspective, independent of his involvement in drug trafficking."

"Good." Jay tried hard not to smile. "Can I keep these copies?" Ollie nodded and Jay asked, "How will you handle the reporter?"

"I'll say that based on the facts, the likeliest cause of death was suicide. Without saying why, I'll try to persuade him that confidential information leads us to this conclusion." Ollie folded his hands. "Then I'll sign and close this investigation, bury it as deep as possible and move on. Doesn't matter what the homosexuals print in their paper as long as that's where it stops. The danger is if the local press picks up the story or, heaven forbid, the national media. If so, we'll play our trump card—Johnson's HIV status. No one's aware of it except the lab and us. No one *will* know unless this reporter digs around the story or they try turning Johnson into a martyr."

"Sounds like the best plan to me."

"It is. Thanks, Jay. Don't want to keep you from your work any longer."

As he hurried out of the office, Jay's emotions were in turmoil. With the gay newspaper's involvement, he faced a tougher adversary than he'd anticipated. On the other hand, he was elated that Johnson's newly discovered HIV status supported NIS's conclusion.

Jay spread several documents on his desk. The evidence analyst's report confirmed that Johnson was HIV-positive at the time of his death. But Johnson's medical records showed that a year earlier, on Friday, January 31, 1992, he'd been tested for HIV and the results were negative. "Exactly a year ago this Sunday." He looked at the date. "Friday. Why does—?"

"Gared," said an agent, popping his head above the wall of the adjacent cubicle. "The station chapel called. Said you'd get this message." He handed Jay a yellow sticky. *Door will be unlocked one hour before service. Naval Station Chapel A/V tech.*

"Thanks," Jay said. "This is perfect."

"What the hell, Don? You said you were wearing civvies. Why'd you change your mind about going in uniform?"

"I never planned on wearing civilian clothes." Don spread his long-sleeved khaki shirt across the ironing board. "I was wearing my service alphas all along."

"You lying bastard," said Karl. "I would've worn my alphas too."

"Why do you think I lied to you?" Smoothing out the wrinkles with his hand, Don ran the hot iron across the material. "Too risky for a Marine corporal to be seen at the funeral of a Navy chief. Especially since everyone knows the chief was gay."

"Fuck that! *You're* wearing a Marine uniform. If you're honoring Eddie that way, I want to." He started for the door. "I'm going back to the barracks to get my alphas."

"Sit down, Karl. We don't have time. Besides, Eddie and I are the equivalent rank and we went on two shipboard deployments together. Our friendship doesn't raise suspicions. Yours would." Don set the iron to the side and paused. "I mean Eddie and I *were*—the—equivalent—"

Karl crossed the room to hug his friend. "Eddie *is* and always *will be* a chief."

Don wiped a tear from his face. "Thanks, buddy. Keep reminding me of that, okay?"

"That's why I'm here." Karl went to the kitchen and grabbed a soda.

Hanging his shirt to cool, Don turned the iron off and sat on the couch to put a final coat of polish on his shoes. "You look *awesome* in that suit, Karl. When did you get it?"

"Um—don't remember. Not long ago. Colonel Spencer makes me wear it when I drive him to official functions in town with civilians." He sat next to Don and popped open the can.

Don reached over to feel the fabric. "Damn! I hope he got the Corps to pay for it."

"He did," Karl said. Don grabbed the coat behind the neck. "Hey! What're you doing?"

"Armani?" Don exclaimed. "The Corps's *never* bought an Armani suit, not even for the commandant. And the Corps never will. Don't lie to me, Karl. Where'd you get the money?"

Leaning forward, Karl clenched his jaw. "None of your goddamned business."

Don's heart sank. He couldn't deal with both Eddie's death and whatever Karl was hiding. "You're right. Not my business." He buffed his shoes in silence and set them to the side.

Changing the subject, Karl asked, "How're the girls?"

"Good as can be expected. Robbi's tough—so is Jeanne—she's been through a lot, so she'll make it through this. Robbi said she couldn't come to the funeral, though."

"Robbi or me have to be in the office at all times. She's the colonel's substitute driver."

"Did he make *her* buy an Armani suit, or whatever it is women wear?" Don immediately regretted the question. "I'm sorry— I've—I've been saying a lot of things I shouldn't this week." Karl looked at the floor and didn't respond. "It's pretty cool of your colonel. Most high-level officers are such chauvinists they wouldn't be caught dead with a female driver." Inspecting the half-dozen spotless khaki neckties in his uniform collection, Don located the newest.

"They're afraid of being accused," Karl explained. "Hear it all the time from the other drivers. Their officers won't hire female aides or drivers. If they hire a woman, then fire her, she might get back at them with sexual harassment charges."

"Their fear sounds worse than their chauvinism. Today's Corps has some valiant leaders," Don said sarcastically. "At least your colonel's not too chicken-shit to be fair."

"He's okay. For a colonel I mean. Speakin' of that—got some good news for you."

Don stopped straightening his tie and looked at Karl. "I could use some good news."

"Promise to quit busting my chops about the suit?"

"For now," Don answered.

"No one else can know—"

A sudden knock surprised them. "Who the hell is that?" Don asked. "You're already here."

"And I haven't knocked since you gave me a key," Karl replied. "Want me to hide?"

"Let's see who it is." Don bent down to look through the peep-hole. "Oh my God! What a great—" He unlocked the door to let his visitor in. "Patrick! What're you doing here? This is—it's so good to see you. Why didn't you say anything about coming over when we talked?"

Patrick stepped inside the living room as Don shut the door. Don gave him a firm hug and they kissed each other on the lips. Karl nodded and looked on with extreme satisfaction. "Didn't say anything 'cause I wasn't sure if I could get away from the squadron," Patrick replied. "But this morning I threw myself on the major's mercy. Said that the squadron CO stuck me with that bullshit escort job, so I rated the rest of today and tomorrow off."

"I should've been an officer," Karl moaned. "Do you guys *ever* work?"

"We work as hard as you did yesterday morning," Patrick retorted. "Remember stuffing croissants down your face at the officers' club?"

"Please, Patrick, sit down. Want some water, or soda, or anything?" Don asked.

"Take it." Leaning across the couch, Karl said, "Been coming here for three years and he's never offered me anything."

"Because Karl raids the refrigerator before I know he's here," Don said. "Didn't think I'd given you my address—yet. How'd you know how to get here?"

"Thank your buddy here," Patrick explained. Karl raised his hands as if acknowledging adulation. "Nice-looking suit, by the way."

"Don't go there," said Karl. "Nice tweed jacket, professor. All your khakis have pleats?"

Patrick looked concerned. "Is—are we being—too flippant? I mean your friend—"

"Eddie would love this." Don handed Patrick a bottle of water. "You two have made me laugh for the first time in days. Some-where—Eddie's laughing with us."

"Back to the good news," Karl said. "Anything I say, you'll tell Patrick anyway, so I'll go ahead and spill the beans now. But you both have to promise that it doesn't leave the room."

The other two men nodded and said, "We promise."

"After I left the O Club, Colonel Watkins rode in the car with Colonel Spencer. He talked your colonel into bringing you up at a Non-Judicial Punishment hearing—"

"That's good news?" Patrick interrupted. "At NJP, Don can lose a rank, be fined a month's pay and/or be locked up in the brig for thirty days. With that on his record, his career is—"

"And the lieutenant gets an A+ on his fucking Marine Corps es-sential subjects test." Karl stared at the newcomer. "I know it's asking the impossible for an officer to go ten seconds without run-ning his mouth, but if you try real hard, we'll get to the good news a lot faster."

"Karl. At ease," Don said firmly. "Colonel Watkins seemed mel-low at my meeting with him yesterday. He scheduled my NJP for February twelfth."

"As I was saying," Karl said impatiently, "Colonel Watkins's plan is to tell the general he's giving you an NJP hearing on charges of disrespect, insubordination, disobedience—you know—all those bullshit things officers need to boost their low self-esteem. At the hearing, he'll drop all the charges and find you not guilty."

"And by waiting two weeks everyone will forget about it." Don said. "Smart move."

"Attention spans are short," Karl said. "It's what your colonel said he's counting on."

"That *is* good news," Patrick said. "And it's a load off our minds as we go to Eddie's—"

"Whoa, whoa," said Don. "Patrick, you've got too much to do up here. You're moving into your apartment tomorrow, you're still trying to find a car—"

"Damn it, Don! He's coming with us. Period. End of story. Now, grab your alpha blouse and cover, and let's hit the road. We're going to be late."

Standing, Patrick smiled and said, "He's the bossiest corporal I ever met. But I agree."

"Okay. I know when I'm outnumbered." Don opened the door. As Patrick walked by, he put his arm around the younger Marine. "I'm glad you're with us. Just wish you'd been able to get to know Eddie. He would've loved you."

"I plan to get to know Eddie very well," Patrick said. "Through all of you."

19

Edward Lamont Johnson, January 15, 1960–January 24, 1993. "Eight days apart," Jay said. He couldn't dwell on his similarities with the Sailor, though. Soon, gay military men would fill the blank pages of the engraved guestbook with their names and addresses, tempting Jay with a trove of information. Borrowing the book or copying it by hand, though, meant he'd have to show his face and that would defeat his long-range goal.

The naval station's chapel was empty. Scouting the building a day earlier, Jay had devised a perfect scheme where he'd arrive early and sneak into place. Fifty-five minutes before the service, a delivery person brought large floral arrangements into the chapel through the lobby. Jay watched but decided against reading the cards attached to the displays identifying the senders. No doubt, most of the bouquets were from military units and family members who couldn't attend the funeral, not from the people Jay was hunting.

Yesterday's reconnaissance had revealed an audiovisual room in the back, separated from the auditorium by a two-way see-through mirror. Jay had finagled his way into the room today by claiming to have a music tape the Johnson family had requested. Not only had the technician shown him how to work the equipment, he'd promised to unlock the door. Funerals were simple—basic amplifiers—and Jay said he could cover for the man. With the lights off,

Jay could see from the AV room into the chapel but no one in the chapel could see into the room. "Fifty minutes," he said, deciding now was a good time to slip in and avoid detection.

As the minutes ticked by, Jay relaxed. Except for three or four hours of restless sleep, his pace over the previous five days had been frenetic, even by his Type A standards. From his solitary position in the musty room, he stared at the flowers, physical evidence that people had loved the dead man. He was unsure why he was upset. Although he was at a funeral, his tension had nothing to do with Johnson's death. "It's the flowers. I need to know who sent them." But as he stepped outside the AV room, a woman and a man entered the auditorium. Jay became terrified when he recognized the man as Johnson's bartender friend. He reentered the room, locked the door and sat in a metal chair.

The floral arrangements represented the dilemma Jay faced with all his work and why he'd adopted extreme methods. Not everyone who'd sent flowers to Johnson's funeral was a queer Sailor and not every attendee at Johnson's funeral would be gay. The problem was that gays could hide too easily. They went to their parades and waved their rainbow flags, but then slid back into normal society where they resembled everyone else. Like chameleons, they were hard to catch. NIS rules requiring proof of homosexuality didn't help. Jay couldn't charge a serviceman with being in a bar, attending a rally or even for going to a bathhouse. Apart from a confession, the only way to ferret out and prosecute a homosexual was to catch him in the act. And the only way Jay knew how to catch him in the act was to commit the act with him. If duty required Jay to go that far, he would, as he had many times. For his country, he'd do it.

Jay heard voices outside the projection room and recognized one as the captain of the USS *Cayuga*. He and thirty or more Sailors walked slowly down the aisle and filed into the church-like pews. More Sailors trickled in, wearing white winter uniforms resembling each other, especially from behind. Fifteen minutes before the service, clusters of men in sports coats, suits or button-down shirts entered. Some appeared nervous, behaving as if this were their first time on a military installation. He recognized the Sailor he'd met at the club Saturday night and tried to recall his name. Jeff? Cary? He'd think of it later. More people streamed through the doors and Jay became agitated, no longer able to tell military from civilian or gay from straight. In two cases, Jay couldn't tell male from female, confusion that almost put him over the edge.

Less than a minute to go, Jay saw the man he'd hoped to see. A tall, muscular Marine escorted a woman, presumably Johnson's mother. Jay recognized him as the Saturday afternoon jeep driver. Jay cursed himself for failing to look up the man's DoD decal number, but he hadn't had time. A small group entered behind the Marine and Mrs. Johnson. Most were African-Americans who Jay assumed were also Johnson's family members. Two, though, were white; the shorter one was the third man who'd been at the park. Walking beside him was a tall and lean blond man with a Marine haircut who Jay didn't recognize. As the procession made its way up the center toward the front row, Jay waited anxiously to see whether the tall uniformed Marine would acknowledge the presence of the obvious homosexuals. "He wouldn't be that stupid."

"Good to see you, Jerry." Leaning over the chapel pew, Don gently squeezed the shoulder of the Sailor who, only six days earlier, had broken his promise to help Eddie with the HIV test. Jerry looked up as Don and Mrs. Johnson passed by, tears streaming down his face.

Leaders of San Diego's gay community sat in the rows ahead of Jerry. A week earlier, Don wouldn't have spoken to them in public while wearing his uniform as that simple act risked his military career. Since then the lesson about life's brevity had sunk in. He considered himself courageous, and he'd done plenty of brave things in his life. But if his fear of discovery meant he couldn't acknowledge people paying their last respects to his best friend, he was a coward.

"Hi, Ricky," Don said to the editor-in-chief of San Diego's *Gay and Lesbian Times*. "Mrs. Johnson, Ricky's a local newspaper editor. A good friend of Eddie's." Ricky offered his condolences and the procession continued.

"My son had a lot of friends, didn't he," said Gloria Johnson. "Important people too."

"Yes, ma'am, he did. But to all the people in here, Eddie was very important."

Karl and Patrick peeled off farther back. Don escorted Gloria to the front row, where the captain of the *Cayuga* greeted her. "Eddie was the most important thing in the world to me," she whispered.

The chaplain stepped forward, beginning Eddie's funeral. Don quietly retrieved his notes where he'd written Eddie's eulogy. At first, he'd declined the chaplain's request to speak. He hadn't felt up to the challenge of selecting the words—if any existed—worthy of Eddie, words that also didn't create suspicions about his and their military friends' sexual orientation.

Don also had another reason for telling the chaplain no. Until he found out what had happened to Eddie, he wasn't ready to give his eulogy. Everyone who knew Eddie well doubted the Navy's conclusion that he'd committed suicide. Likewise, Don was ninety-nine percent certain that something else had caused Eddie's death. But the biggest obstacle to Don's ability to speak at the funeral was the one percent chance that Eddie *had* taken his life. Repeatedly, Don had asked himself the vexing question: *What if Eddie did it? What kind of a friend was I?* When Gloria personally asked him to speak, however, he couldn't say no.

The chaplain followed the standard format for military funerals. He read a few words of scripture then led the mourners in a benedictory hymn. Next, the *Cayuga's* command master chief spoke of Eddie's consistent and reliable nature. He explained that although Eddie had entered the military before graduating high school, he was smart and had a sharp wit. Not only had he earned his GED while in the Navy, but he'd obtained a bachelor's degree in meteorology.

When Eddie's chief finished, it was Don's turn. He stepped forward and raised the microphone. "It was times like this, when the world fell apart, that someone would say, 'Go get Eddie!' We counted on his wisdom, his inner strength, to get us through no matter how bad the situation got. He *always* knew what to do, what to say. One time, when we were on the USS *Coral Sea*, we had a night of liberty in Rota. All that got us out of jail was his fast-talk-ing ability to—let's just say be a little creative with the facts. And he didn't even know Spanish." The anecdote brought out polite but muffled laughter mixed with tears. "So I guess it's one of life's bitter ironies that now, facing the worst situation I've ever faced, my first instinct is the same it's been for the last fifteen years. To call Eddie." Don felt the lump swell up in his throat and he had difficulty with his next words. "Only now, I don't have Eddie to help me get through this."

As Don paused, looking at the crumpled piece of paper in front of him, he tried to compose himself. Friends and family members wept openly and one of Eddie's aunts wailed aloud. Hearing her and the others was almost too heartbreaking. He'd survived so much—Iran, Beirut, Panama, *Desert Storm*—but this was tough. Eddie's friendship had helped him through it all, but losing Eddie meant he had to survive the rest of his life without a vital part of his support. Scanning the audience, he saw Jeanne at the end of a row beside Lance. Her expression told him: *We'll get through this.* "Living the rest of my life without Eddie," he said, departing from his notes, "will be like trying to live with only one lung, or one arm. It can be done but it won't be easy. And every day, from morning, when I wake until I go to sleep, I'll know what I've lost."

Don had planned to speak in vague terms about Eddie's chari-table work, omitting that much of it was for AIDS services organi-zations. Looking at the crowd, though, he saw several men and women Eddie had helped over the years. *Fuck it,* he thought. *I'm not living in fear any longer.* He wadded his notes and tossed the paper in the wastebasket beneath the lectern. "It's not every day you hear a Marine talk about love." Don spoke from his heart. "I don't know why not. Marines like to think we're tough and fear-less—and we are. It's tough to face an enemy shooting real bullets at you. I know, I've been there. In that situation, you do what you're trained—what you get paid—to do. You do what you *have* to do. Love? Love is doing what you *don't* have to do. By watching Eddie, I learned that love, more than anything, takes guts, deter-mination and hard work. Love is consistent and courageous; it's not soft, it's not easy.

"Many of us in here benefited from Eddie's love. Love propelled him to get up at four o'clock many mornings and prepare meals for people with AIDS. Love was his motivation for spending many of his weekends doing laundry for people so sick, they couldn't get out of bed. Love—for people and animals—is why he walked dogs and fed cats—and parakeets—even after some of the owners had died, until he could find a home for the pet."

Don smiled at Mrs. Johnson. "Eddie took the love he learned at home and carried it to others. When Ray was dying—from an AIDS-related illness—Eddie cared for him around the clock. Just before Ray died, I visited them in the hospital where Eddie had been with him for three days and nights. Ray had a fever. Eddie took a damp, cool cloth and gently rubbed it across Ray's forehead. He'd done that for days. He kept a cup of ice water for Ray to sip through a straw to help cool his mouth. He rubbed a balm on Ray's parched lips. Thanks to Eddie, I know what love is. It's not just a vague idea. All I have to do is recall that image, of Eddie with his arms wrapped around Ray's head, in the last hours of his life. That was tough and it took courage, but Eddie did it without a second thought. That, my friends—*Eddie's* friends—is love. In the end, it's the only thing of any real value we can leave behind." When he finished, the auditorium seemed quiet. Maybe his mind was tuning out everything, or maybe people were thinking about what he'd said. Probably both.

The chaplain led the crowd in several verses of "The Navy Hymn," a hymn more commonly known as "Eternal Father, Strong to Save." Don had heard it hundreds of times but today a phrase resonated with him as never before. *Oh, hear us when we cry to Thee, for those in peril on the sea!* Had Eddie known he was in peril? If he had, he didn't let anyone know. Were the rest of them in peril? Throughout Don's adult life, he'd faced every challenge and threat directly and he'd survived. For the first time, though, he realized that the gravest peril was the one he knew nothing about. If unknown dangers lurked out there, was he really in control?

"Gunnery Sergeant Donald A. Hawkins, USMC," Jay whispered, repeating the chaplain's introduction. At last, Jay had the name of the jeep's driver. He'd look up the Marine's unit, research the jeep's license plate number and compare the results. No doubt, they'd be the same.

For now, he had to listen to Hawkins's eulogy over a speaker in the AV room. Jay recognized the voice. "You're everywhere, aren't you, Hawkins?" He was on Johnson's answering machine, in the field being disrespectful to Congressman Coughlin, on the radio, at the park on Saturday—and now at Johnson's funeral service. His eulogy also helped Jay understand how close the two had been. He wondered if Hawkins knew that his friend had HIV.

"Holy shit!"

The air surrounding the mystery suddenly cleared. Of *course* Hawkins knew. . . . *I have to postpone the appointment.* Hawkins was the reason Johnson had passed his HIV test every year and the two friends had made an appointment to switch their blood samples again this year. *Something's come up here* . . . Hawkins was too busy in the field embarrassing Coughlin on Tuesday morning so he'd had to reschedule their blood-swapping arrangement. *Your cutoff isn't until Friday.* According to the guestbook, Johnson was born in January and the military's regulations required every service member to submit a blood sample annually by the last day of their birth month. Tomorrow—Friday—was the last working day of January. It made sense.

"Those two were a pair of blood brothers, weren't they, Junior?"

Jay closed his eyes. "No! Not again." Only one person called him that.

"You've been expecting a visit from your old man, haven't you?" asked the ghost of Jay's father. "Your—*friend*—visited you two days ago—you knew I couldn't be far behind."

"Of course I expected you. You haven't left me alone—"

"After what you and that pervert did? You expect me to leave you alone—after you let *Pastor Stephen* defile your body all those years? Do you?" Jay's father shouted but Jay wasn't concerned. No one else could hear his dad's voice. "Your body is the temple of the Holy—"

"Pa, I told you—back in Washington—I'm doing all I can to

make up for my—my sin." A whisper was all that was necessary for his father to hear his plea.

"Listen to the hedonist, Junior. Talking about love. What does a filthy, godless sodomite know about love?"

"Nothing," Jay whispered, keeping his eyes fixed on Hawkins.

"That's right—*nothing*. Don't forget it. Whatever it is you're doing to atone for your perversions, keep doing it. It's the least God expects from you."

"Yes, Father," Jay said. As suddenly as his dad had appeared, he departed. Jay didn't have to look to be certain. The overwhelming sense of relief he felt told him his dad was gone.

As the Marine droned on about the great things the Sailor had done, Jay's thoughts were filled with a devastating question— more of an admission about a subject he hadn't considered.

Who will tell the world about my good deeds?

"No one," Jay whispered. Sitting in the room by himself at the Sailor's funeral, Jay felt the painful, terrifying truth. He'd die just as he'd lived. *Alone. Always alone.*

Thankfully, the service ended. Jay stood for a better view of the faces filing out of the chapel. Because of the activity in the auditorium, Jay didn't hear the sound of a key in the door. The door swung open and the AV room was flooded with light. Momentarily frozen, Jay stood in place. "Sorry, mister. Didn't know anyone was in here," said a voice. Spinning around, Jay saw a custodian with a vacuum cleaner and cart.

"Turn that light off!" Jay whispered loudly as he lunged for the switch.

Don and Mrs. Johnson were almost down the aisle and out the doorway when a bright light appeared in what had been a dark pane of glass, revealing a man standing in the window. Don assumed the man was a base employee, but their eyes met seconds before the man jumped out of sight and a red flag went up in Don's mind. Scanning his brain's memory for facial images, he realized he'd seen the man before. Unfortunately, his mental and emotional overload prevented him from recalling the details and the image vacated his short-term memory.

Exiting the building, Don escorted Gloria to the limousine waiting to take them to the cemetery. The sun had broken through the morning clouds, causing Don to squint until his eyes could adjust. Gloria said, "I'd like it if you'd ride with me and my family."

"I'd be honored." Don tossed his keys to Karl and told him to follow the family.

As Don slid next to Mrs. Johnson on the plush rear seats of the limo, she said, "Eddie's will gave instructions to bury him next to Ray in his family's plot out here in San Diego." Don nodded but remained silent, hoping Mrs. Johnson didn't want to talk about her son's sexual orientation, at least not now. "You and my son were the closest of friends."

"Yes, ma'am, we were."

"Why did he kill himself, Don? Do you have any idea?"

Don was thankful she hadn't asked if Eddie was gay but the question she *had* asked had kept him awake for two nights. Looking her squarely in the eye, Don saw both tenderness and toughness, a soft resiliency that had carried her through many hardships. But this was the worst time in her life. "No, ma'am, I don't."

"Did he call you? Was he upset? He was such a joy around the house at Christmas. Did I do something to—to—hurt him?"

"No, ma'am, he didn't call me. But I know he wasn't upset with you about anything. He talked a lot about how much he enjoyed being home for the holidays."

"But why would he do this to himself? No matter how down he got—even when his friend Ray died—he never wanted to—to do *this*."

"I know."

"Don, I know there were—things—my boy wouldn't tell me—or didn't think he could say but I always loved him so much. But this is different. He would've *told* me if he'd felt this bad!" Even though they were in the car with close family members, safe from eavesdroppers, Gloria leaned over and whispered, "I *know* there's something the Navy ain't telling us." Her sentiments and the intensity with which she expressed them caught Don off guard. The fierceness in her eyes indicated a resolve that wasn't going away.

"I've—I think something must've happened that we don't know about," Don admitted.

"You do too." Gloria shook her head. Don looked out the car's window as they passed through the front gates of the cemetery. A small number of cars had followed the family for the burial. The pallbearers, Sailors from Eddie's ship, opened the rear of the hearse and carried the casket with Eddie's body to the mound of freshly dug dirt.

Gloria walked ahead with Ray's family, and Karl and Patrick caught up with Don. "That was the most moving thing I've ever heard," Patrick said quietly. "Everyone was touched. They'll never forget Eddie—or what you said." Don placed an arm across Patrick's back and the other across Karl's. Karl was too choked up to say anything. Listening to the chaplain, Don watched in somber silence. The bugler played taps and they lowered the body of his best friend into the earth. To get through this moment, he'd numbed himself to the pain. He'd deal with it later.

Jay was furious with the janitor, but there was nothing he could do now. The Marine had seen him. Jay feared his cover had been blown. The janitor, frightened by Jay's sudden outburst, exited the projection room as quickly as he'd entered. Jay turned the light off and breathed easier once he'd safely returned to the darkness and isolation.

Thirty minutes later, when he felt certain all the attendees were gone from the chapel, he emerged from the projection room and returned to his office. He couldn't wait to find out as much as possible about Marine Corps Gunnery Sergeant Donald Hawkins.

"We're going back to Louisiana, Don. I want you to find out what happened." Gloria looked up at the Marine. "Will you promise me that?"

"Yes, ma'am, I promise."

"You're a good Marine. You won't let an old mother down." Don returned her smile and said good-bye. Patting Don on the arm, she turned to say farewell to the ship's captain.

Riding north on Interstate 805, Don, Patrick and Karl remained silent for almost ten minutes. Suddenly Don exclaimed, "Son of a bitch!"

"What'd you call me?" asked Karl.

"The day we played volleyball—four, no, five days ago. When you and I were driving out of Balboa Park, I saw two men together in a car."

"You're surprised?"

"That's what I thought too, Karl, but that's where I've seen that face—those eyes! That same man was here, behind the two-way mirror—watching Eddie's funeral."

"Okay, buddy, whatever you say," said Karl.

"Are you sure?" Patrick asked. "That would be a really strange coincidence."

"Yes it would," said Don. "But not as strange as Eddie's so-called suicide." Despite Karl's disbelief, Don knew he was right. As the three Marines headed back to Camp Pendleton, Don repeated the promise he'd made to Gloria Johnson. He vowed to learn the truth about what had happened to her son. Don suspected the key to the truth had something to do with the identity of the man behind the two-way mirror.

20

"Colonel Spencer, General and Mrs. Neville have arrived."
Marine officers in their finest uniforms filled the lobby of downtown San Diego's U. S. Grant Hotel Friday evening. The majors, lieutenant colonels and the only colonel, Leonard, wore evening dress uniforms loosely resembling a midnight blue tuxedo with a scarlet cummerbund. Junior officers, the captains and lieutenants, strutted proudly in their dress blues. The form-fitting coats with tightly clasped collars and snug black belts gave every man the frame of a bodybuilder. Smiling, Leonard passed dozens of officers and their companions on his way to welcome the guests of honor. The female guests looked beautiful in their formal evening gowns and the male guests of women officers wore stylish tuxedos.

Leonard complimented the intelligence officer on the brief she'd given a week earlier. She was attractive and slender but she reminded Leonard how poorly the Marine Corps designed women's uniforms. The intent was to diminish the masculinity without emphasizing feminine sexuality, resulting in a professional but unbecoming androgynous look. Perhaps if he were a general, Leonard could influence a new look. "Whoa, Leonard," he mumbled near the hotel's entrance. "Horse first, then cart." Still, the group looked as dazzling as any gathering in America. The excitement penetrating the air indicated his Marines' high level of morale.

"Very well, Mister Vice," Leonard said, addressing his adjutant by his traditional title for the evening's ceremony. "Please ensure the hotel has placed the bottle of wine I brought in the general's suite." Leonard looked through the glass doors as a major escorted the Nevilles inside. "And please do me a favor and get rid of this." He handed his glass of scotch to the captain.

"Sir—you're President of the Mess and I'm Mister Vice. Aren't both of us required to—?"

"You're correct. However, this is a dining in with guests and *not* a mess night with just the officers. We can be somewhat less strict with the formalities." Leonard smiled but his voice was firm. "I'm more concerned about that bottle of cabernet."

"Will do, sir." The captain darted off to accomplish his mission.

"Good evening, General," Leonard said at the entrance. "And good evening to you, Eileen. Kissing her on the cheek, he added, "You look positively stunning."

"You're kind, Leon, but I do *not* look good," said Eileen. "Kenneth gave his driver the night off and decided to drive us here himself. It was the most *harrowing* experience of my life!"

"I'll ensure that the bags are brought up, sir."

"Thank you, Major Burr." To the Nevilles, Leonard said, "Let me show you to your suite."

"A suite? That's too much," said the general.

"I agree," Eileen said. "You should know by now that we don't expect lavish treatment."

As the trio walked down the corridor outside the ballroom, younger officers halted with wide-eyed stares. Many had never seen a general up close before. "Good evening, General. Ma'am." The Nevilles fondly returned the greetings.

"It's my honor, Eileen. After all, you did come all the way down from Orange County."

"And in Friday afternoon traffic too! I'd only do that for you, Leon Spencer." She rolled her eyes. "I told Kenneth this is our absolute *last* tour in California." Leonard recalled similar statements in 1979 and 1986. As if reading his thoughts, she added, "I *mean* it this time. If Kenneth gets orders to California one more time, I'll take the dogs and move back to Savannah."

"As I've told you before, dear," General Neville said, barely masking his exasperation, "the only three places I can go from here are Washington, Hawaii or retirement."

The elevator doors closed. "Take a wild guess which is at the top of my list." Smiling, Leonard chose to remain silent. "Here's a hint: There won't be any grass skirts or politicians."

"Don't think for a minute these officers paid for your suite," Leonard said, hoping to redirect the conversation. "The hotel gave it to us if we booked a certain number of rooms."

Eileen slapped Leonard on the arm. "Good! You always were so practical."

"And honest," said the general. Leonard hoped his smile hid his lie. Not wanting to burden his underpaid officers, he'd paid for the suite. "What did you hear about the Coughlin incident?"

"Read about it in the papers. Saw it on TV." Leonard omitted his chat with Joe Watkins.

"Well, let me tell you. I was standing right there. The gunny had it out for Congressman Coughlin. On the one hand, it was humorous, but—"

"'But' what, Kenneth?" Eileen asked. "I thought it was simply hilarious. I've had to endure five conversations with Mr. Coughlin—*five!* I use 'conversations' loosely because I have yet to say more than three consecutive words to the man. I feel so sorry for his wife."

"The problem is that the infantry has to deal with Coughlin only regarding his power on the Armed Services Committee. What the grunts forget is that *my base is in the man's district!*"

"I see," said Leonard. "But surely, General, Coughlin won't let one minor incident—"

"Who knows *what* a man with his ego thinks? I heard from a reliable source this morning that Congress, in its infinite wisdom, will announce another round of base closures this spring."

"Where will the Marines go if they close El Toro?" Eileen asked.

"The last time," the general said, "they discussed moving us to an old Air Force base out in the Mojave Desert. Either there, or the abandoned Naval air facility at Ridgecrest, California."

"You mean Death Valley?" said Leonard. Eileen gasped and reached for her necklace.

"Quite honestly? *Where* we go isn't the problem. There's no law that says Marine bases have to be in the world's garden spots. Personally I think the fifteen thousand Marines in this Aircraft Wing would do better away from the distractions—and high cost—of California's coast."

"Amen to that!" said Eileen. "But Death Valley? Whatever happened to a happy medium?"

"You're saying that the real problem," Leonard guessed, "is the time and cost of relocation."

"Moving the airwing will cost a fortune and divert us from vital training," said the general. "Congress never allocates enough funds, forcing us to divert our operations budgets. God forbid we have a war in the next ten years. We'll regret wasting time and dollars on a frivolous move."

"And Marines will suffer—and die—because of a bad political decision," said Leonard.

"And who'll be blamed?" asked the general as the elevator approached the penthouse level. "It won't be the 'Base Realignment and Closure Commission.'" Leonard knew. Future generals would be the scapegoats for Congress's failure to do its job today. "That's the urgency. El Toro almost closed five years ago. Whether or not we like Coughlin, he saved us then and he's our only hope now. *We absolutely must have him on our side one hundred percent!*"

"I see," said Leonard. "The politics of command."

"You can't imagine!" declared Eileen.

Leonard hesitated then asked, "General, have you heard what they're doing to the gunny?"

"I believe it's being handled at the regimental level." Leonard was pleased. Joe's plan—*his* plan—had worked. The door opened and Leonard pointed his guests toward their suite.

Fortunately, the bellhop waited in the hallway with the Nevilles' bags. "My compliments on your efficiency." Inside the room, Eileen said, "Gentlemen. Please excuse me, I'm going to rest just a few minutes and freshen up. Don't look at me like that,

I'll be quick, but after that trip down the Interstate 5 speedway with Mario Andretti here, I have to recuperate."

Leonard had orchestrated this moment. Part of the reason he'd arranged a suite for the Nevilles was so that he and the general could have a moment's privacy. Eileen had performed her role brilliantly—knowingly or not—by departing at the opportune time.

General Neville sat in a large overstuffed chair by a window and Leonard poured wine. "Thank you, Leon." Raising his glass, he said, "To the future of Marine Corps aviation."

Leonard tapped his glass against the general's and said, "To the future of the Marine Corps."

"One and the same. Don't forget that. More importantly, don't let the grunts forget it." Setting his glass on a small table, he rubbed his hands. "How is Linda? I've missed her."

"She's well. So are Todd and Sara. Todd graduates from Annapolis a year from May and Sara was just admitted to Cornell. She'll start in the fall."

"Fantastic! You must be so proud." The general paused, a sign for Leonard to have a seat. "We must be downstairs soon. I'll get to the point. No doubt you're aware the list will be out on Monday." General Neville smiled and took a sip of his wine. "This is very good, by the way."

Returning the smile, Leonard tried to seem unaffected. With twenty-eight years in the Corps and his fiftieth birthday looming, he should be past the youthful emotion of nervous anticipation. Moving his hand from the chair's arm, he noticed sweat on the material. "Glad you like it."

"Only four percent of colonels eligible for promotion to brigadier general were selected and one of those names is being withheld—temporarily." Leonard locked his jaw in place. "I don't know who or why, but I'm *dying* to find out." A conciliatory beginning wasn't good. "I tell you these things to remind you that selection to become a general officer is next to impossible."

Leonard set his glass on the table and clasped his hands to hide the shaking.

The general's eyes drifted toward the large windows facing the bay. "And I hate to say it but I can't recall when—the last time an unmarried colonel became a general."

Leonard's heart sank. As he'd feared, his divorce ten years ago had cost him his promotion.

At that moment, General Neville stood and Leonard instinctively followed suit. "You've beaten the odds before and I'm thrilled that you've beaten them again." Setting his wineglass on the table, the general extended his hand. "It's an honor to be the first to congratulate you, Brigadier General-Select Spencer!" He shook Leonard's hand and firmly grasped his upper arm.

"Thank you, sir, thank you." Leonard hoped his knees wouldn't buckle.

The double doors to the bedroom flung open and Eileen ran across the room. "Oh, Leonard! Let me be the second to say how happy I am!" She wrapped her arms around the future general.

"What are we waiting for?" the general asked. "We have a celebration to attend."

"Here comes the bride, here comes the bride!"

The employees and happy hour patrons of The Flame sang to Robbi and Karl as they entered the bar ahead of Don. Robbi said to the small crowd, "You can cut out the singing any day."

"Oh no, that wasn't for you, Robbi. That was for Karl," said Zoe, the bartender, "He's the bride." Everyone laughed. Don thought about how Eddie would've loved that crack at Karl.

"Oh yeah?" asked Karl, "If I'm the bride, I'm wearing a white dress."

"That'll be the day," said a familiar male voice.

"Is that a guy behind the bar?" Don asked. "Or are Jeanne's employees getting butcher?"

"Not possible," said Karl.

Don's eyes slowly adjusted to the dark interior of San Diego's best-known lesbian bar. "Lance? What the fuck are you doing here? Moonlighting? Aren't your tips enough at WC's?"

"Were until yesterday." Lance popped the top off a beer and handed it to Don. "Got fired."

"I always knew you were a lesbian," Karl said to his ex. "'Karl, let's live together!'"

"Fuck you," said Lance. "At least I didn't marry a lesbian."

"Touché," said Karl.

"'Touché'?" asked Don. "Where the hell did you learn that word?"

Ignoring Don, Karl said, "That's right. Tied the knot with the old ball and chain today."

"Damn, Karl," said Don. "Wish Eddie was here to rag you about your language skills."

Karl softened his tone. "That makes two of us, buddy." Looking at Lance he shouted, "A drink, sir! A toast is in order." Lance quickly handed a bottle to Karl, who raised it in the air. "A toast, everyone, a toast!" Within seconds, the bar quieted down. "To Eddie!"

"To Eddie!"

Don felt a lump in his throat. Suddenly, he heard something in the back. "Is that a—?"

"Rocky!" Robbi said. "Come here, boy!" Eddie's dachshund bounded into her arms.

Appearing from the rear hallway, Jeanne said, "Welcome to The Flame and Kennel Club."

"A weenie dog in a dyke bar," Karl said. "Run for your life, Rocky!"

"It's great of you and Robbi to take him in." Pointing to a table of hors d' oeuvres, Don said, "And thanks for planning this last-minute wedding reception for the kids."

"My pleasure on both counts. Just like old times. Like you and Erin, another marriage of convenience—or necessity." She rubbed Rocky behind his ears. "The dogs accepted Rocky as part of the family right away. He feels at home with us already, don't you, boy?"

"I better walk him home soon," Robbi said. "Poor Rocky will get trampled to death in here."

Petting the dog good-bye, Karl said, "Little guy'll get crushed by big feet in Birkenstocks."

Don watched as Lance restocked a beer cooler. "Did I hear Lance right? Did he say—?"

"WC's fired his ass." Before Don could voice his disbelief, Jeanne said, "We need to talk. In the back. Something's goin' on. I don't like it." She motioned for someone to join them.

"I feel it too," Don said. "Eddie didn't commit suicide. And I can't believe Lance got fired."

"Believe this—those two events are related." Another woman approached them. "Do you know Esther?" Don didn't, so Jeanne introduced them. "Before we get to the dirty details—where's this 'Patrick' I've heard so much about? Nothing's official until I give the go ahead."

"I know." Don laughed and said, "He's downtown at a dining in tonight."

"A 'dining in'—sure brings back memories I don't miss. Except when you and Erin made the best-looking couple at the Staff Non-commissioned Officers' dining in. Well, he's coming here later, right? Good." Leaning over the bar, she said, "Zoe, cover for Lance. We've got some business to discuss in my office."

Looking to his left, Jay drove slowly through the green light on Park Boulevard. Although it was only seven o' clock, The Flame was busy, judging from the line of people—mostly women—going inside. Shrugging, he continued another block north and turned right onto University Avenue. Neither lesbians nor their bars interested him.

Ten percent of service members were women but thirty percent of service members discharged for homosexuality were women. This disparity erroneously reinforced the stereotype that female homosexuality was more rampant in the military proportionately than male homosexuality. Taken to its fallacious conclusion, Jay should hunt lesbians rather than gay men. Jay, however, knew better. Logically, the only valid conclusion from the disparity was that the military was better at discharging women for homosexuality than it was at discharging men. Correcting this statistical imbalance was his goal.

Experience had opened Jay's eyes to the Pentagon's dirty little secret. The percentage of gay men in the U.S. military was much *higher* than in the civilian population. The reason was simple: that's who the military recruited. Recruiting ads appealed to lonely boys who felt isolated and excluded from their peers. The slogans—*Be all that you can be,* and *Join the few, the proud*—implicitly appealed to young men who felt less than they could be, *i.e.* neither heterosexual nor part of something in which they felt pride.

Consciously or unconsciously, military recruiters understood this psychological reality and the successful ones were skilled at identifying and targeting kids who yearned, but were unable, to fit into a group. No demographic fit the military's profile better than gay teenage boys. These young men would do anything to aid their denial and to hide their same-sex attraction from the world. Joining the Army or Marines met their needs threefold: the young man became part of a group; the young man carried the title "Soldier" or "Marine" as proof of his manhood; and the young man was surrounded by thousands of men just like himself. The difference between ancient Sparta and the U.S. military was that the Spartans not only accepted reality, they embraced it and built a society of fierce warriors out of it.

Jay suspected the real reason for NIS's abysmal success rate at ferreting out gay men was that the sea services didn't want to know the truth about their extraordinarily high percentage of gay men. Jay, however, wasn't in denial and he intended to fulfill his mission. Sparta and all of ancient Greece had collapsed because they allowed homosexuality to flourish. In time, the same fate would befall America unless Jay, Coughlin and others like them could prevent it.

Driving east along University Avenue, Jay's unfortunate reality lurked everywhere in this part of town. Johnson's face stared at him from newspaper stands. Jay's self-anger at failing to check Johnson's story more closely grew. If only he could go back and change the one flaw in his alibi. Every copy of the paper evidenced a conflict with his version of that night. According to the story, Johnson had dinner in public with friends. If Jay had friends of his own, he might've realized that guys stick together. He didn't have any friends, though, and the report he'd written and filed stated that the suspect had been home, alone with his dog.

Fortunately, Ollie and his superiors realized the matter had devolved into a standoff between San Diego's gay and lesbian community and the Navy. Ollie was right—given the political climate, no one wanted that type of friction. The Navy dropped the matter without responding to the cover story. Friday afternoon, the Navy officially ruled Johnson's death a suicide and closed his case. Permanently. Jay's investigation into a purported Navy "drug ring" had reached a dead end and Ollie had ordered him not to pursue it. "Fine by me," Jay said at his destination.

"Better rest now," Don said. "These women will work you hard the next seven hours."

"Thanks." Don suspected Lance's fearful tone was only half-fake. Lance and Esther took the vacant seats in Jeanne's office. Jeanne sat behind her desk and Don leaned against the wall.

"Seen this week's *Gay and Lesbian Times?*" Jeanne asked. "Hot off the press."

Don and Lance shook their heads. "I'll get a copy from the front," Esther said.

While they waited, Don asked, "Why'd you get fired? You were their best bartender."

"You didn't hear? I'm also a drug dealer." Don was too stunned to speak. "Just wish I knew where I put the drug money. An undercover NIS agent was at the bar Saturday night—"

"Mother-fucking sons of—" Don had hoped NIS agents' practice of trolling through bars looking for gays and lesbians was a shameful part of history. "What happened?"

"NIS agent reported that he saw me hand a package of drugs over the bar to—guess who?"

Don laughed. "This is too ridiculous for me to even—"

"Eddie Johnson."

Hearing his friend's name, Don sat motionless. "Eddie smoked pot, maybe five or six times in the early eighties—before he met Ray. That's *all* he ever did in the way of drugs. He wouldn't know *how* to arrange a drug deal. Neither would you," said Don. "Can't believe they fired you on a false allegation from an NIS agent like that."

"It's tough," Jeanne said. "Bar owners have to take a hard line. I'm on Lance's side, but—"

"I get WC's point of view—they gotta stay in business. Coworker saw me hand Eddie a package so it's my word against a government official's. Manager can't take a chance on charges of drug dealing, proven or not," Lance said. "Don't know what I'll do now, 'cause stripping my shirt off to hand drinks to these women ain't gonna raise my tips like it did there."

Esther returned with the newspaper and Jeanne passed it to Don. An old photograph of Eddie filled the front page. "You took this at a pride festival—1987 or '88?" Don said. Although Eddie was smiling, his eyes betrayed apprehension, which Don attributed to Ray's recent HIV diagnosis. The look matched the magazine's headline. DON'T BELIEVE IT! read the banner at the top of the page in large, bold letters. In smaller print, below Eddie's photograph, a headline blared: NAVY SAYS: GAY = SUICIDAL. WE SAY: NAVY = BULLSHIT!

"Awesome, Jeanne," Don said. "Thanks for making this happen."

"Don't thank me. Esther's the vigilant one." Don and Lance gave the two women puzzled looks. "Tell the guys where you work."

"Southern California's regional NIS headquarters," Esther said. "Here in San Diego."

"Holy shit," Don whispered loudly. "What do you do? You an agent?"

"No. Even better. I'm the assistant to Oliver Tolson, regional director."

Don was shocked and awed. "This is too much, Jeanne, even for you. How'd you find her?"

"Actually, Jeanne got *me* the job," Esther said. "I'm not sure how—" Glancing at Jeanne, she added, "When it comes to Jeanne's connections, I don't ask."

"And I don't tell," Jeanne said. Don and Lance stared open-mouthed at the women and their surreal news. For as long as Don could remember, NIS had been their bitter adversary. NIS had hounded, persecuted and sometimes tortured more of his friends than he could count. NIS had destroyed their careers and, in some cases, their lives. Now, a lesbian protégée of his close friend worked for their enemy leader.

Esther said, "Been there over a year now. I like it—good pay and benefits." She looked down as if ashamed to admit that she enjoyed working for their foes.

"Glad you like it—as long as you stay on our side," Don said.

Nodding, she said, "Hell yeah! I won't forget my brothers and sisters—what I'm there for."

"I'm—I'm amazed!" Don said. "Completely impressed with you, Jeanne! How did you—?"

Jeanne interrupted him by holding up a hand. "Don't ask."

"Right," he said. "Surprised you told Lance and me about your 'mole.'"

"If I can't trust you two, all hope is lost," she said. "But we had to get someone in there, Don. No one should have to endure what I went through—what we all went through in the eighties. Robbi and Karl both have such bright futures in the Corps. Does this sound fucking familiar?" Nodding, Don listened as Jeanne vented. "I said 'no' to some prick who couldn't keep his hands off of me. So I turned this first sergeant in for harassing me, and next thing I knew, I was under investigation! Maybe if Esther had been there, I could've seen it coming."

Jeanne had been down on her luck a few years ago but now she was infiltrating spies into the NIS. Delighted, Don laughed as he marveled at her comeback. "What's so goddamned funny?" Jeanne asked. As if reading Don's thoughts, Jeanne joined his laughter.

"You've come a long way, baby," Don said.

"Thanks for triggering my addiction," said Esther. "Mind if I light up a Virginia Slim?"

"If it's okay with the guys," said Jeanne, placing an ashtray next to her friend.

Don nodded grudgingly and Lance said, "Only if I can bum one." Don shot him a mocking glance. "Hey, when in Rome—" He lit the cigarette and took a drag. "Or when in Lesbos—"

Jeanne said, "We *have* come a long way, haven't we—'Congressman Coughlin, banning gays and lesbians from serving in the military is just plain un-American—it's goddamned undemocratic and a violation of our code of conduct.'"

"Now Jeanne, that's not *exactly* what I said—"

"Oh my God!" screamed Esther. "That was you! I'm so honored to be in a room with a celebrity, and—" Turning to Lance, she said, "Did I hear someone say you got fired from WC's for being a drug dealer?"

Blowing smoke, Lance asked, "Who wants to know?"

As the laughter quieted, Esther brought them back to the serious nature of their meeting. "I know the undercover agent who claimed you were dealing drugs."

21

"I thought you and Karen made, like, the best-looking couple. Seriously, Patrick, that's *so* sad. I didn't know the two of you had broken up. Wow."

Patrick found himself with the wives and dates of his fellow pilots. The men were smoking cigars outside, a tradition Patrick didn't enjoy, although now he wished he'd joined the men.

"What's she doing now?" asked Melanie, Tim Roberts's fiancée from Seattle.

"I don't know," Patrick answered. "I mean, she's graduating in May. Not sure after that."

"Anyone want another drink?" asked one of the wives, turning in the direction of the bar.

"I think I'll take—something," Patrick answered. She walked away, giving him a quizzical look. He answered, "Something with alcohol." Glancing at his watch, he wondered why the doors to the ballroom remained closed. "Seven fifteen. Thought this started at seven."

"You know—Patrick," a third woman said, "hope this doesn't sound *too* tacky." She set her glass of white zinfandel on a small table. Smiling, Patrick pretended to listen but couldn't stop thinking about Don. He hadn't seen Don since they'd returned from Eddie's funeral the day before. Patrick desired to be near him more than he'd craved anything in his life, so much that it tore at his emotions. As fondly as he felt about his fellow officers and as badly as he wanted to enjoy this time with them, he couldn't. He'd attended these dinners for several years, and compared to the way he felt about being with the man who interested him, the formal dinner didn't stand a chance. "But there's a new associate at my firm," the woman continued. "She's *very* pretty and slender. She'd love to meet you, maybe at a party or a dinner or something—you know, low stress, not a hookup. What do you say?"

"I don't know. My breakup was so recent and all." He shook his head and shrugged.

"I hear you, and believe me, I understand. But when you're ready—and I'm sure you'll have no trouble meeting women—but if ya' want, gimme a call. Heck, maybe I'll surprise you someday and show up with my friend." She laughed. "You're young. You'll rebound quickly!"

"I hope so," he said, wishing he could tell this woman about his true feelings.

Tim startled Melanie by putting his arms around her and pressing his lips against the back of her neck. "You oughtta get an award for puttin' up with this shit, Patrick," he said as the guys filed back to the bar from the cigar smoking area. "I don't care how 'attractive' they say their friends are or how great their 'personalities' are, *just say no!*" Melanie punched him in the arm. "Ouch! They haven't opened the doors? Better hit the head now—no more piss breaks till this shit's over!" Several men and women nodded and headed for the restroom to beat the line.

"He's so refined." Melanie rolled her eyes. "How are you enjoying yourself, Patrick?"

"I'm afraid I haven't had a drink yet." Patrick smiled at Melanie and scanned the bar.

"You poor thing!" she said. "I'm sure she'll be back with your drink any minute. Until then, you can finish mine." She handed him her glass of chardonnay. "Do you miss her?"

"Miss who?" He'd assumed Melanie was referring to the woman bringing him a drink. Catching his mistake, he said, "Oh— I'm sorry—Karen. Yes, very much."

Melanie gave him a puzzled look. "Uh-huh," she said as Tim returned from the restroom.

"Oh shit!" Tim said, lowering his voice to a whisper. "Don't look now but here comes—"

"Good evening, gentlemen," Colonel Spencer said as he walked into the lounge area, joining the junior officers and their dates. "Having a good time so far?"

"Yes, sir!" the men answered in unison. Patrick had been closer to more rank this week than he hoped to see in the rest of his career. He prayed Colonel Spencer had forgotten his name.

"Splendid!" Turning to Patrick, he said, "Lieutenant McAbe, I have a question to ask you."

The other lieutenants stared wide-eyed at Patrick. From his position behind Colonel Spencer, Tim silently parroted the commander. "Lieutenant McAbe?" he mouthed and moved his fist and tongue inside his cheek as if he were sucking dick.

Patrick wanted to kick Tim's ass. Instead, he said "Sure, sir. What would you like to ask?"

Suddenly Tim yelled, "There's the six bells! Time to get this party started!" All at once, the doors opened and the other officers and their guests streamed into the ballroom.

"Why don't you come with me, Lieutenant," the colonel said.

Fear suddenly spread throughout his soul. The last phrase a newly "semi-out" gay Marine wanted to hear from a superior was "come with me." "Sure sir. Whatever you need," he said.

The "E-Z Street Bookstore" chain of adult sex shops was notorious among vice officers as a place where queers met and sodomized each other. The stores had private booths in the rear where men watched a wide selection of pornographic videos—straight, gay, bi or fetish. Jay had visited adult bookstores several times since his arrival in San Diego, but had only observed the patrons in the magazine room up front. Before tonight, he hadn't seen any military suspects.

Except for the muffled sex sounds coming from the video booths, the front of the shop was noiseless. Jay glanced around the room, focusing on a straight porn magazine. Long stares drew unwanted attention and aroused the other customers' suspicions. Men who frequented adult bookstores adhered to an unspoken code of conduct and shunned violators.

Jay counted twenty-four men in the store's front section. Although his survey of the area had been brief, years of experience had turned him into a pro at adult bookstores. With a cursory examination, not only could he estimate the number of men within a four percent margin of error, he could also categorize a group as large as fifty. Tonight's two dozen fit the pattern for a town like San Diego. Three or four were homeless and sought relief from the mildly cool winter's night, coming here because adult bookstores were more accepting of odd sorts than most public places. Six other men fit what Jay called the "serial killer" profile, the type of man a person could pass on the street for years without noticing. If police found a stash of decaying corpses under their houses, news broadcasts would interview neighbors stating, "No, I didn't speak to him in twenty years but I never imagined he'd be the type to do something like this."

The largest category was always the "pillars of the community," or more accurately, the "pillars of *another* community." As many as twelve were businessmen, lawyers, politicians, clergymen and others in town from Atlanta, Tulsa and everywhere else. They had wives and grandchildren back home. Although most were interested in the straight porn, some looked at the bi and gay stuff. Jay didn't care about these three groups—they only got in his way.

The men Jay cared about were part of a fourth group he'd labeled the "Curious Blue Collar Guys." Men from America's working classes had more difficulty adjusting to gay life than their better-educated and more affluent service industry counterparts. Factory workers, cops, firemen, mechanics and others faced hostility if coworkers and people in their community discovered their fondness for men. Curious blue-collar guys felt anonymous in the dark backrooms. Ten percent of men in adult bookstores fit this category, although in a military town like San Diego, the ratio skewed higher. Four men fit his preferred category tonight but only one interested him.

Jay moved into position. The young man thumbed through magazines of women having sex with men, with each other and with all kinds of things. He was two shelves away from the gay magazines. Another tacit rule was that all guys trying to meet other guys pretended to be interested in the straight porn, gradually moving toward the gay section.

The young man followed that pattern. Jay walked behind a row of shelves for a better look. He couldn't waste time on a guy pretending to be in the Marines or the Navy, and San Diego had plenty of those. The man was between twenty and twenty-three. His cap said CAT DIESEL POWER, and hid his haircut. Jay didn't rely on haircuts, though, because barbers in San Diego gave military haircuts to anyone who asked for them. The man's backpack had a NO FEAR patch and he wore a military-style jacket, the kind that was easily available at an Army-Navy surplus store. The jacket hung low around his neck, revealing a military dog tag chain, which also wasn't proof of authenticity. The leather bar down the street gave them to customers.

Real Marines had telltale signs of legitimacy that fakers were too lazy or clueless to imitate. If the guy would just take off his— suddenly, the man looked up, making brief but direct eye contact with Jay. Without changing his facial expression, he moved one aisle closer to the gay magazines. He looked down at the "bi" magazines, and as if reading Jay's mind, he raised his arm, removed his cap and scratched his head. Jay almost broke the code by smiling but stopped in time. Standing in front of him was a genuine Marine who, to Jay's delight, cast a backward glance as he made his way to the gay porn.

"Tell him I said he's a fucking moron!"

Esther's news that she knew the NIS agent who'd observed Eddie the last night of his life stopped Don cold and enraged Lance. "The only thing in the paper sack was Karl's sweatshirt," Lance protested. "He left it at the bar—typical, I know. Eddie was taking it to Karl. The goddamned NIS agent didn't even ask me my side of the story. One reason I got out of the Corps was because of those assholes but their stupidity *still* cost me my job!"

"So Lance—you—saw Eddie? Was he by himself? I should've called you this week."

"Almost said something at the funeral but you were with Mrs. Johnson. Figured it could wait till tonight," Lance said. "I saw Eddie but he wasn't alone. He was with a guy I didn't know."

"Did Eddie leave with him?" Jeanne asked.

"I can't believe he did," said Don. "That's not like—"

"They left at the same time," Lance said. "If it was 'together,' I don't know."

"This stranger must be involved in Eddie's death somehow," said Jeanne.

"What'd he look like?" Don asked.

"Looked like a stud, at least across the bar," Lance said. "Had a great body, that's for sure."

"You guys all have one-track minds," said Jeanne. "Did anyone look like an NIS agent?"

"No one who fit the usual profile," said Lance.

"That's funny," Esther said. "What's the 'usual profile' of an NIS agent?"

"Well," said Don, scratching his head, "in the past, NIS agents tried to infiltrate gay bars—but many had huge beer guts, bad haircuts, cheap clothes—"

"—and loud, obnoxious drunken-straight-guy personalities," Jeanne said. "Stood out like Buddhist monks in a Mormon tabernacle, especially when they gawked at the lesbians. Gay guys don't do that for some reason. Thank goodness the agents didn't get it."

Esther laughed. "I'd say you're description is right for ninety percent of them. But this—"

"Jeanne!" shouted Zoe from behind the closed door. "Need someone else up front!"

"Better go help, Lance," Jeanne said. "Karl and Robbi must be a popular bride and groom."

"A hundred lesbians at the end of happy hour." Lance bounded out the door. "And I used to think a bar full of desperate men at last call was a challenge." He closed Jeanne's door.

Don tried to focus and piece the puzzle together, but his mind swirled with old information, new facts and contradictory ideas, like the idea of Eddie leaving a bar with a stranger. Glimpsing the newspaper cover, he asked, "What does the *Times* say?"

"Not much," answered Jeanne. "NIS wouldn't answer Ricky's questions."

Esther said, "We gave the standard 'no comment on an ongoing investigation' response."

"But the article has some interesting information." Jeanne pointed to a paragraph. "Ricky talked to the staff at Hamburger Mary's—" Don tensed and Jeanne reassured him. "No worries. No one at Mary's gave your name or Karl's, even though everyone at the *Times* assumes it was you two. The article says Eddie was there with two unidentified companions."

"Yeah," said Don, "the three of us left the park, went to Eddie's for a quick shower, dropped Rocky off, then went to Mary's and WC's. But what does that tell us?"

"Nothing by itself. But Esther, show Don what you brought."

"This," Esther said, retrieving folded pieces of paper from her pocket.

Opening the pages, Don saw they were copies of the official report of the investigation into Eddie's death. "My God." He read the words, still not believing the papers were real. "According to this, on late Friday afternoon—one week ago—an anonymous person called the NIS and reported that—*Eddie?*—was planning to purchase and distribute two kilos of cocaine sometime after ten o' clock Saturday night." Don looked at the two women. He didn't know whether to laugh, cry or pound his fist into the wall. "Who'd make a call like that?"

Racing through the events of the previous Friday afternoon, Don recalled that he and Eddie had been at the hospital terrorizing Jerry Giles for reneging on his promise to help them with Eddie's HIV test. If Jerry had made the anonymous call, though, Don wondered why he turned on Eddie—who'd been nice to him—and not Don—who'd threatened to beat him to a pulp.

"What is it?" asked Jeanne. "What're you thinking?"

"Nothing." He shook his head. "It's all strange. *Really* strange."

"Keep reading," answered Jeanne. "It gets stranger."

Don read slowly. "The agent said he was in his car outside

Eddie's from nine until after eleven and then followed Eddie to WC's. But he's got the wrong man. Eddie was with us."

"Or," said Jeanne, "the agent's lying."

"Of course." Thinking about this disturbing and conflicting information, Don said, "Know what it sounds like to me?" Esther shook her head.

"Bet I know exactly what you're gonna say," said Jeanne.

"NIS claims they're busting up drug deals in gay bars. Sounds better than a 'witch hunt.' "

"I agree," Jeanne said. "Makes sense considering the proposal Clinton announced today. They're suspending gay discharges for six months so the NIS is trying out a new tactic."

"Know anything about this, Esther?" Don asked. "Is there a 'witch hunt' on? One last hoorah before Clinton lets all of us screaming queens out of the camouflage closet?"

"I don't think so. If there is, it's not official. And I'd know about anything official. But—if one or more of the agents are working on their own—"

"Do you know all the agents?" Don asked. Esther nodded. "Including this—Agent Gared?"

"Oh sure, he works directly out of our office. He's new, so I don't know much about him."

Don went back and forth between the NIS report and the *Times*. "Let's take this report to Ricky! It conflicts with what he's already printed and he can ask the Navy why—"

"Think about it, Don," Jeanne said. "If the *Times* approaches NIS with this report—or let's say the *Times* doesn't mention the report itself, just the *information* in the report, then NIS—"

"—will investigate the source of the leaked information. Which would lead them to Esther."

"And blow her cover," Jeanne said. "She could go to jail. *Not* gonna happen."

"What about a FOIA request?" Don asked. "Can't Ricky use the Freedom of Information Act to demand a copy of the investigation report? It's a government record—"

"—that was filed under seal," Esther said. "An FOIA request

would work—eventually. But it'd take five years of bureaucratic headaches before this report ever saw the light of day."

"Shit!" Don looked around the office's walls, where Jeanne had hung memorabilia. "Damn it, woman! Can't you have *one* bare spot on your walls? I need a place to bang my head."

Jeanne put her arms around Don. "I know. We just talked ourselves into a complete circle."

"The worst part is none of this brings us any closer to finding out what happened to Eddie."

The three sat in silence. In a cheerful voice, Jeanne said, "Look on the bright side."

"What could possibly be the bright side?"

"Patrick will be here in less than two hours."

"I seem to have lost the officers responsible for helping me take care of our guests. Do you mind walking with me to deliver drinks to General Neville and his wife, Lieutenant McAbe?"

"No, sir," Patrick responded as cheerfully as possible. How could his luck swing so wildly in one week? From something awesome, like meeting Don, to being stuck around colonels all the time, his life had never been so volatile. "Don't mind at all."

"Can I get *you* anything?" Colonel Spencer offered. "You haven't had too much, have you?"

"Actually, sir, I've had two sips of chardonnay," Patrick said. "And that's just not working for me tonight. I'll have a beer—or whatever. Makes no difference to me."

"All right then." The colonel laughed and added Patrick's order to the list. "Please put all of these on my tab," he said. Waiting for the bartender, Colonel Spencer said, "You did an admirable job returning the congressman and his staff to Washington on Tuesday."

"Thank you, sir. But all I did was make some phone calls."

"But you made the *right* phone calls. That's the hardest part." The colonel took the drinks off the bar and handed them to Patrick. "Lieutenant McAbe, on behalf of MAG-79, I apologize that you had such a terrible assignment your first week in my group. Who did that to you?"

Patrick hesitated. Ratting out Lieutenant Colonel Hammer would be disloyal. Thinking about it as he followed the colonel across the lobby toward the ballroom, he answered, "You know, sir, being new and all, I don't really know who it was. Besides, checking into a unit is such a whirlwind. And now that it's all over, it really wasn't that bad."

"I see," said Colonel Spencer. "Admirable of you to protect your squadron commander. Don't worry, Lieutenant, I won't say anything to him, if that's what you're afraid of." As they stepped into the noisy and crowded room, a banquet waiter hurried over with a tray to carry the colonel's drinks. "Thank you very much for your help, Lieutenant McAbe," the colonel said, turning toward the front of the room. "But I have to say," he added, laughing, "you're a *terrible* liar!" The colonel's comment shocked Patrick. He couldn't believe he'd been so transparent, a bad trait for a semicloseted gay Marine. As his pulse returned to normal, he scanned the huge ballroom to find the table where Tim and Melanie were saving a seat.

Suddenly a voice that Patrick knew but couldn't place spoke from behind. What the man said startled him far more than Colonel Spencer's comment. "Only one kind of Marine can suck a colonel's dick as good as you did, McAbe. That's a *homosexual* Marine. Can't fool me. I know about you and Gunnery Sergeant Hawkins. You're a homo, aren't you, *Lieutenant?*"

22

The Marine straddled the gap between the straight and gay sections. Returning a straight magazine, his glance over his shoulder signaled interest. He and Jay hadn't made eye contact, but the Marine must've liked what he saw. He reached across the aisle, pulled a magazine from the gay section and thumbed through the pages. Pausing at a picture of two men having anal sex on a rock beside a waterfall, he held it far enough in front of his face for Jay to see the image.

Jay remained still, staring at the Marine's back and the magazine, signaling his own interest. Flipping pages, the Marine stopped at a picture of men performing oral and anal sex in a sailboat. He studied the photo then looked at Jay. Jay returned an emotionless stare so as not to frighten him away. The Marine jerked his head toward the back and headed toward the video booths.

All was according to plan. The Marine knew adult bookstore behavior. Jay waited two minutes and pursued him down the hall. Glancing at Jay, the Marine slipped into a private booth, placing the latch against the doorjamb to prop it open. Men leaning against the walls of the dim passageway ogled the sexy Marine's booth. They weren't threats or military spies and were out of their league—Jay called them the ignorables. He went after the Marine. The Marine's pants were around his ankles and he wasn't wearing scivvies. He flipped through the channels with one hand and beat off with the other. "What d'you like?" he asked in a low voice.

"Whatever you want," Jay answered. "Makes no difference."

The Marine stopped on a video of two men and two women in various sexual positions. "Your mouth better be real wet," he said to Jay. "Take it all the way to the back of your throat. I feel any goddamned teeth, I'll bash your fuckin' head in."

"I don't suck dick," Jay said. "I only get sucked."

The Marine scowled. "What the fuck you take me for? Some kind a faggot?"

"I could ask you the same question," Jay responded.

"What the hell you doin' in here?" The Marine's penis lost some of its rigidity and the video screen went blank. "I'm outta money. You wanna stay in here with me, you gotta feed the machine for another video."

Now Jay was ninety percent sure the man was a Marine. Reaching across the booth so as not to touch his genitals, Jay inserted a dollar bill, which the machine sucked away. The screen showed a video of two women. Frowning, the Marine pushed the button until he found four guys in leather harnesses and hard-ons standing around a blindfolded man tied into a sling. The men took turns pounding the man's hole with their dicks and fists and also dildos of larger and larger sizes. The Marine smiled and his erection returned. He resumed masturbating.

Fortunately, the stores rarely enforced their one-person rule for the booths. With two occupants and a backpack taking up valuable floor space, movement was impossible without some sort of physical contact. Jay unbuckled his belt, unbuttoned his fly and joined the Marine in masturbation. His arm bumped into the other man but the Marine didn't stop his activity. To make the effort worthwhile for his investigatory purposes, the Marine had to fellate him. Angling his body toward the Marine, Jay asked, "Sure you don't wanna suck this?"

His eyes fixed on the video screen, the Marine said, "Only reason your mouth should be open is 'cause it's around my dick. If not, keep your fuckin' mouth shut or go jerk off by yourself."

Jay almost conceded and retreated from the booth, wagering

that a better suspect was up front by now. Something about this Marine stopped him from leaving, though. Any guy who'd mutually masturbate to a gay S&M video would commit other acts. If not, the Marine had discipline regarding his pleasures. Either way, Jay was intrigued.

After a few silent minutes, Jay neared climax. Not wanting to go first, he didn't have to delay for long. Closing his eyes, the Marine stopped the movement of his hand. "Oh fuck," he said. "Goddammit! Watch out! I'm gonna—I'm—" The Marine shot across the room.

Jay let loose of his own load, but without the sound effects, and the Marine handed him a tissue. As they wiped off their wasted semen, they reached a crucial point in their relationship. A strong likelihood existed that they'd silently go their separate ways. Technically, the Marine hadn't violated the UCMJ and there was no way Jay could convict him.

"Wanna get a beer?" asked the Marine.

"Sure."

"Not at a fag bar. I know another place."

"I'll follow," Jay said.

"I was hoping you'd drive," the Marine said. "Ain't got no car."

Jay laughed. "No problem." Now he was one hundred percent sure the Marine was real.

"I proclaim this meat fit for human consumption!"

Leonard's beef-tasting ceremonial declaration commenced the "dining" part of the dining in. Returning to his seat to enjoy the dinner, he watched with amusement as the first-time guests appeared both perplexed and entertained by the rigid, yet humorous, formalities. Laughter and loud voices electrified the room as eight hundred people enjoyed the camaraderie.

"You've got a fantastic group here, Leonard," said Eileen. "Such wonderful energy."

"This is the first dining in or mess night I've attended since Clinton was inaugurated," said the general. "I can't wait to see the reaction to the toasts."

"Oh no," said Leonard. "I hadn't considered that."

At the meal's completion, the stewards removed the dessert plates, replacing them with port decanters. Leonard stood, signaling the start of the traditional ceremony. He charged General and Mrs. Neville's glasses, then his own, passing the decanter to the left as tradition required.

"Mister Vice," Leonard said slowly, projecting his voice to every square foot of the hall. "Her Majesty, Queen Elizabeth the Second!"

The general whispered, "Two Royal Marines are assigned to this group." Eileen nodded.

The adjutant, as Mister Vice, sat alone at a table opposite Leonard. Signifying his role, he wore the Sam Browne belt, a black leather strap that fastened diagonally across the chest, over his dress blues. He stood. "Ladies and Gentlemen, Her Majesty Queen Elizabeth the Second!"

The officers and guests stood as the band played "God Save the Queen." At the end of England's national anthem, they toasted the Queen, sipped their port and returned to their seats. Like the general, Leonard was curious how his officers would respond to the next part of the tradition that was as old as America. On cue, the senior Royal Marine officer stood. In his distinct British accent, he shouted, "Mister President! The President of the United States!"

Everyone looked to Leonard. Ten days into Bill Clinton's presidency, the military's officers despised the man more than they had any commander-in-chief in recent memory. As President of the Mess—as well as commanding officer—Leonard set the example. He was uncertain, though, if his officers would follow, given the strength of their contempt for Mr. Clinton. As loudly and as firmly as possible, he shouted, "Mister Vice, the President of the United States!"

The adjutant followed Leonard's example. He leapt to his feet and in a booming voice declared, "Ladies and Gentlemen, the President of the United States!" Again, everyone stood, and this time, the band played a rousing stanza of "The Star-Spangled Banner." By the conclusion of the national anthem, the officers understood the idea Leonard had hoped to convey. No matter what they thought of the man, the toast was for the office, for freedom, for democracy, for the constitution—and for each other. As long as they remembered that important principle, throughout Mr. Clinton's presidency and all those following, America would be okay.

"The President of the United States!" everyone shouted together.

Sipping his port, the general said. "That may be the loudest toast I've heard in forty years."

"What do you know about this agent?"

"New to NIS," Esther said. "Came from DC. That's about all."

"What does he look like?" asked Jeanne.

"Little shorter than average height—maybe five eight? Short brown hair and big brown eyes. Not the kind of person to stand out in a crowd."

"Is he good looking?" asked Don.

"Is that *all* you boys *ever* think about?" Jeanne asked.

"Got my reasons."

"Not the best judge of that, know what I mean?" Esther laughed. "But he must be all right. Some of the women in the office flipped out over him. He's kind of—weird? Maybe not weird but very serious. No sense of humor. Never talks to anyone unless it's about work, which is all he does besides run and lift weights. Goes to and from the gym a lot. He's in good shape but doesn't seem to have any friends or much of a life. Maybe that's because he's new to town."

"Do you know if he went to Eddie's memorial service on Thursday?" Don asked.

"I never know where he goes. He's in and out all the time. He was gone most of this week."

"You have access to his files?" Jeanne asked. "Or would that be too risky?"

"I can only see what comes across Ollie's desk. Otherwise, it's *way* too risky. This guy—he'd know if I went through his stuff."

"I think I might know who he is," Don said.

"Really?" asked Jeanne. "Think he's involved in Eddie's death?"

"If it's the same guy, he's involved. Both times I've seen him, it's related to Eddie. Esther, can you get as many details as possible—without getting in trouble—on—what's his name?"

"Sure. Name's Jay Gared."

"Jay Gared. If he's somehow responsible for Eddie's death, Jay Gared is a dead man."

"Thought you were outta money."

Neither man had spoken during the ten-minute ride from the bookstore to the pool bar. Inside, the Marine ordered—and paid for—a beer. Jay ordered a bottle of water. Shooting Jay a mischievous grin, the Marine said, "Don't got any *one* dollar bills. Just twenties."

"Video machines take twenties," Jay said, paying for his water.

"They don't give change and it don't take twenty dollars of porn to bust a nut." He took a sip of beer. "You know what you're talkin' about, don't ya'? Come on. Let's play some pool."

Jay briefly weighed his night's agenda—scouring adult bookstores for Sailors and Marines—against pursuing this young man further. "Okay." He followed the Marine to the back, where his new friend put two quarters on the edge of the table, claiming the next game. "What's your name?" Jay asked as they sat on barstools waiting their turn at the pool table.

"Zack," the Marine said, extending his hand. "What's yours?"

"Stephen—I mean Jay," he answered, shaking the Marine's hand.

"Don't even know your own fuckin' name? Which is it? Stephen or Jay?"

"It's Jay—middle name's Stephen. Sometimes go by that."

"Uh-huh." Zack didn't appear to believe him but he also didn't appear to care. He laid his jacket over the stool. "I'll kill anyone that steals this," he said to no one in particular.

Jay studied Zack as he drank his beer. He had light brown hair, and without the oversized jacket, Zack looked small and sinewy. His taut T-shirt had a Camp Pendleton military police unit logo. Up close, a scattering of acne was visible, which only added to his troubled-boy good looks. Some might mistake his thick Southern accent to mean substandard intelligence but Jay had learned not to underestimate the wiles of the country boys from the Southeast's unfamiliar backwaters. Zack had a likable, if unrefined quality that was warmly appealing. The more Jay looked at the laughing, devil-may-care young man brushing against his leg, the more he saw him not as prey, but as a potential ally in his lonely war.

"I gotta piss so bad I can't fucking hold it much longer!" Tim rubbed his groin.

"You're in a world a shit, Roberts," said Jungle, a captain Tim had just introduced to Patrick. They were part of the same ten-person group seated around a banquet table near the back of the ballroom. "The general's gonna start his speech any second."

"Hey! McAbe," Tim whispered loudly, "gimme your empty beer bottle."

Patrick passed the bottle to Tim, but Melanie confiscated it, holding it out of Tim's reach. "No! You will *not* pee in a bottle under the table like you did at the Pensacola dining in."

"Damn it, Melanie! You want me to die from a bladder infection so you can collect my servicemen's life insurance, don't you?"

"Shut up," she said. "Don't even talk—just go to the men's room like a grown-up. You Marines and your traditions, I swear. Go! I'll pay the fine for you."

Tim looked around the table as if seeking advice but Patrick laughed and held up his hands. Jungle said, "You gotta decide this one yourself, buddy. Better hurry if you're gonna piss 'cause you gotta be in your seat before the general starts talking." Glancing nervously toward the podium, Tim dashed out of the room. Mister Vice noted Tim's serious breach of the rules.

"He does this every time we go to one of these things. I say, 'Don't drink too much—your bladder's smaller than mine.' For a Marine, he has no discipline," said Melanie, carrying a ten-dollar bill to Mister Vice. He put it in a cashbox of fines for rule infractions.

"You guys look like you're having a lot of fun," said Chris Ashburn. "That's good."

"I'm not talking to you, Lieutenant," said Patrick, making sure Jungle's attention was on his date and not on himself and Chris.

"Not after you scared the shit out of me, sneaking up from behind and calling me a homo dick sucker. Besides, you could've telephoned to let me know you were transferring from Pensacola to Camp Pendleton. What happened to Pax River?"

"It was a last-minute change. It's no secret Sledge has run off a lot of instructors. Colonel Spencer called up Pensacola and invited me here. Said he needed a mature Navy influence," Chris said. "Besides, what number could I have called? You just got your phone hooked up."

"Coulda called Don," said Patrick. "He knows how to get in touch with me."

"So I've heard." Chris smiled. "Actually, I *did* call Don. Despite the hell he's been through this week, he thought it'd be a nice surprise for you if I just showed up tonight unannounced."

"Really?" Hearing Don's name lightened Patrick's spirits. "You both planned this—Don planned a surprise for me?" Patrick was euphoric. "Very well, Lieutenant. You're forgiven."

Lowering his voice as Melanie returned to the table, Chris said, "Glad you two hit it off. Thought you might."

"Chris, since Tim and Patrick were promoted to first lieutenant, they can call you by your first name now?" Melanie asked. "You military men and your ranks. That's *such* a guy thing."

"Something like that," said Chris. "Squadrons are much more casual with the professional courtesies, at least among us pilots, than flight school is. We've got better things to worry about—like making sure our aircraft is properly maintained and safely flown."

"I see." Melanie stashed her small purse under her chair. "Tim said you and Patrick spent a lot of time together in Pensacola. Did you know each other before flight school?"

Patrick didn't like Melanie's questions and he didn't know how to answer. Chris, however, seemed perfectly at ease. "No, but when I was their instructor, Patrick and I discovered we had a lot of common interests—the same eclectic taste in music, books, movies, you know, shit like that." Nodding his assent, Patrick silently praised Chris for deftly handling the interrogation.

"That's cool," she said, taking a sip of chardonnay. "What music do you both like?"

Chris smiled. "Erasure, Depeche Mode, Pet Shop Boys, Bronski Beat—what else, Patrick?" Patrick couldn't speak as he felt like he might have a coronary. Thankfully, Chris had omitted Madonna and Cher—too obvious, no doubt—but he *had* listed four very gay bands.

Melanie turned to face the two men with a look of amused realization. "I *love* that music! When Tim and I are married—you guys *have* to come to the wedding, by the way—and I move here, I'm hanging out with you—and *your* friends." Leaning closer, she said, "I live on Capitol Hill in Seattle, know what I mean? I've been called a 'something' hag before." She winked and Chris laughed and gave her a hug. Because Patrick hadn't visited Seattle, he wasn't sure what living on "Capitol Hill" meant. He could probably guess, though, and was uncomfortable. He was pretty sure Chris had just outed him to the fiancée of his best straight friend in the Marines.

Bursting into the room from the nearest door, Tim took his seat as quickly as possible. Before the officers around the table had a chance to razz him, though, Colonel Spencer stepped to the microphone and introduced General Neville. Whispering in Chris's ear, Patrick said, "Be ready to bolt 'cause as soon as this speech is over, we're on our way to The Flame."

"Why'd you follow me into that video booth?"

"Why'd you leave the door propped open?" Jay asked.

"To see if you'd follow, dumbass! Any more stupid questions? Or you gonna answer mine?"

"I followed you—to find out why you *wanted* me to follow you," Jay answered.

Zack looked at Jay like Jay was brain dead. "'Wanted to find out—?'" He laughed. "This is the most fucked-up conversation. Why does *anybody* let somebody follow 'em into a booth? 'Cause he wants his dick sucked!" Jay laughed along with his new drinking buddy. Even though he didn't drink, that's how he'd begun thinking of Zack. "What I wanna know is why you didn't blow me. Don't you know the rules? I'm young and good-lookin' and I always get sucked off."

"Like I said," Jay replied, "I'm not gay. I don't suck dick."

Zack exhaled sharply and shook his head. "That don't make no sense! What kind a dumbshit goes after a guy in a booth but then won't give him a blow job? That's just rude."

Jay would have to reveal part of his true motivation to Zack. "Maybe I don't get off on it. Maybe I've got another reason you haven't thought of yet."

"You got next game?" someone asked.

"Go ahead," Zack said to the person. Finishing his beer, he looked directly at Jay. "You trying to catch somebody, ain't ya?" Jay had correctly assumed Zack was smarter than he seemed. Now Jay was at a crossroads. If he told Zack "no," Zack would assume Jay was a gay man who didn't know what he wanted. But if he told Zack "yes," Zack might leave, fearing that Jay was after him. "If you're an undercover cop, why the hell you still hangin' out with me?"

"I'm not an undercover cop, but you're getting warm. Don't worry. You're not in trouble."

"You in the military?" Zack asked.

"No," Jay answered.

"Just 'cause I'm wearin' a military T-shirt, don't mean nothin'. You knew I was the real deal, didn't ya? How could you tell I wasn't one of them military wannabes?"

Jay was happy to show off his cleverness. "When you took your cap off, I could see that distinctive tan line on your shaved head— you know, the dark and light stripes you get because you have to wear a cap—I'm sorry, a *cover*—outdoors in the sun when you're in uniform. Only Marines and Soldiers have that and there aren't any Army bases around here."

"Well, you're pretty fuckin' smart—for a civilian." Zack laughed and punched Jay on the upper arm. "So, you still ain't told me. Who do you work for?" Jay remained silent and looked at the pool game. "Well," Zack answered. "Since you don't seem to wanna tell me anything, I'll tell you something. If you'd gone down on me, I woulda turned you in—after I got my rocks off. Even though your hair's kinda long, I thought you was a Marine—maybe a pilot."

"Well then, Zack," Jay said, relieved that his ally had confessed. "Like I suspected. The two of us are in the same business."

* * *

"And now for those two words everyone loves to hear—*in conclusion*—"

The officers and guests in the ballroom applauded and laughed loudly and a few cheered. When the noise quieted, the general continued. "I'll be rather unconventional. I hope that every one of you young lieutenants and captains, as well as you old majors and lieutenant colonels, leaves from here having learned the lesson that in the Marine Corps, we reward success. If you achieve what is expected of you and more, your success will not go unnoticed."

Leonard had a sinking suspicion that the general was announcing the news of his promotion. He hoped not—junior officers didn't care about the politics of the Corps's upper echelons, a fact the general might've forgotten. As the speech continued, Leonard's fears became more certain. He wanted to remind the general that this evening was about the group, not an individual.

But he couldn't interrupt. "Ladies and gentlemen, as proof, a board met in Washington to select the next round of generals. The president approved that list and headquarters will release it Monday. This afternoon, I received the news: Because of the extraordinary success of Marine Aircraft Group 79, Colonel Spencer has been selected for promotion to Brigadier General!"

The immediate response of the officers was overwhelming. Everyone jumped to their feet, shouting and waving their arms. Some climbed on their chairs while many slapped each other on the back. They displayed genuine exuberance and Leonard was astonished and humbled.

General Neville whispered, "Better have a speech ready. I've never seen junior officers react this way to news about a colonel's selection to general."

Leonard hoped he could talk—he wasn't sure. Slowly, he rose to his feet and stepped up to the microphone. Across the room, the crowd clapped in unison and chanted his callsign. The guests joined in the chorus. The noise became so deafening, the hotel manger peeked into the ballroom. An officer whispered in his ear and the manager joined the jubilation.

"Roy-al! Roy-al! Roy-al!" Waiting for the noise to dip, Leonard gathered his thoughts.

Sensing the right moment, he jumped in. "I want to thank—" He paused after his voice reignited the enthusiastic response. He waited again. "Thank you to General Neville for allowing me to command this group for the last eighteen months. I'll make this quick—I know that some of your bladders are severely over-extended." He waited again for a bout of laughter.

"Selection for promotion means we must reevaluate why we would accept the next level. If it's for the title, or the extra money—and if you joined the Marine Corps to make money, you've no doubt realized your mistake by now—or if it's for the perks that go with being an officer, or for all the pageantry, you need to think about whether you should stay in. We officers exist for only one reason—that is, to *lead* those who follow. America has forgotten that *leadership* doesn't mean celebrity, wealth or privilege. While our nation can revel in its excesses if it wants, it cannot afford for us, the leaders of its military, to forget that *true leadership means service.*

"A brilliant playwright, goes by the name of Shakespeare, wrote in *King Henry V*: 'And what have kings, that privates have not too, save ceremony, save general ceremony? And what art thou, thou idle ceremony?' All of this—the awards, the uniforms, the rank, the traditions, the formalities of this dinner—all of it, while wonderful, is but 'idle ceremony' relative to our actual purpose. For we are to lead, which means we are to sacrifice. We bear a heavy burden. Moreover, we must bear it with courage, integrity and conviction. But most of all, we bear it with joy. Our nation and our Marines deserve nothing less from each of us. Such is our calling."

As Leonard concluded, the officers and guest, applauded and cheered even more enthusiastically than before. "Now, General," Leonard said as he turned to his guest of honor, "it is I who have the privilege to say those wonderful and magical words that every-one longs to hear. Ladies and gentlemen, please join me at the bar!"

23

"I'll talk to you, ma'am. What is it you want to know?" Jeanne pulled Don away from the group. "What're you doing? You don't need to talk to her. *Former* service people can answer her questions just as well—and safer—than you guys."

"A week ago I would've agreed with you." He and Jeanne stepped to a quieter corner of the noisy and crowded bar. "But now—after losing Eddie—life looks different in hindsight."

"Death has a way of changing your perspective. But you shouldn't put yourself at risk."

While Jeanne paused to chat with two frequent customers, Don looked around the smoky room. He recognized at least a dozen patrons as servicewomen. He watched as Patrick, Karl, Chris and Robbi drank their beer and laughed, enjoying each other's company. Suddenly, Eddie's voice interrupted his thoughts. *We've all gotten careless but some have been luckier than others.* "We're already putting ourselves at risk," he said when Jeanne turned back in his direction. "How do we know somebody here's not an NIS agent? We don't."

"Hopefully Esther can—"

"What can she do? She said if an agent's off doing their own thing, she won't know about it until a report crosses her boss's desk. By then it's too late. Our careers are over."

"What's your point, big guy?" Jeanne was used to being the boss and didn't like arguments.

"We think we're safe. We're not. And our lives are never going to be safe until we speak up. Karl said the reporter wants to talk to active duty people—anonymously. To see what it's like for us. I have to believe if most of America knew what we—"

"Get fucking real, Don. America doesn't give a shit about us— hate to say it, Devildog, but you know they don't. Remember Beirut? October 1983? Two hundred and forty-one killed all at one—"

"—stop, Jeanne. Don't—"

"America didn't give a rat's ass then about a bunch of dead Marines so they sure as fuck aren't gonna care what life is like for a few dykes and fags in San Diego." Jeanne had crossed a line with Don and now she realized it. "I'm sorry—I shouldn't have said—"

"No. It's okay. I know you care." Inhaling deeply, he said, "I'm gonna do this interview."

"Yes, you are," Jeanne said. "I support you, even if I don't agree. But Don, don't do this to educate Americans. You'll be dis- appointed. Do it for Eddie, for yourself, for Patrick, for—"

"I know." Don was ready to return to the group. Jeanne had stirred up painful memories and the antidote was the tall, dash- ingly handsome pilot smiling at him from across the room.

When he and Jeanne rejoined the others, Patrick put his arm around Don, who gave him a quick kiss on the lips. Extending her hand, the stranger said, "We weren't properly introduced. My name's Kathryn Angel, from the *Washington Herald*. No doubt you're aware, more than anyone, the topic of gays in the military is the predominant issue in the capital right now—"

"*And* in the military," Chris added.

"—and in the military," Kathryn echoed, seemingly perturbed at the interruption. "I'm writing a story—more of a feature re- ally—about life in the military for gays and lesbians who currently serve. It's interesting to me when people talk about whether to *allow* gays and lesbians to serve, when it's clearly obvious that so many already are."

"You came to the right town for that," said Karl.

"DC has a lot of gays and lesbians in the service, too," Kathryn explained, "but we felt I should get outside the beltway to see what the issue is like in the rest of the country." Don liked her. He sensed—and was impressed—that she grasped their plight. A feature story in her paper would reach millions who'd learn the tragically absurd dark side of America's state-sanctioned discrimination. Jeanne was wrong—Americans historically had done the right thing—eventually. Don's faith in Americans was partly why he'd joined the Marines. "We won't print your names."

"You can count me in," Don said.

Kathryn smiled and nodded. "That's wonderful! I didn't catch your name before."

"Don Hawkins," he said, saying his last name aloud in a gay or lesbian bar for the first time.

Quietly, Kathryn repeated his name as if she should know it. "Oh—my God! You're the Marine who embarrassed Congressman Coughlin this week."

"Very good memory," he said as everyone laughed and gave him high fives.

"I'm *supposed* to be impartial—but I'll say this—you're a hero to almost everyone in DC."

Smiling, Don rolled his eyes. Jeanne said, "I know where I've heard of you. You won a Pulitzer Prize—for breaking that congressional scandal in the early eighties—"

"That was a *long* time ago," said Kathryn. Don looked at Kathryn again. She was attractive and probably could be beautiful, but he guessed her years in journalism had given her look a hard edge. She was tall and thin, with long black hair, and appeared to be his age. "Five years ago I was nominated for a story I like better—even though it didn't win—on women CEOs. Usually I write about women. I came here tonight ostensibly to meet lesbians in the military."

"You're in luck," Karl said. "Don's the biggest woman you'll ever meet."

Don hit his friend over the head with a rolled-up copy of the *Gay and Lesbian Times*. Sensing Jeanne was warming up to Kathryn, he asked, "What do you think now?"

"She seems all right. But don't forget she's a reporter—*not* your friend. Watch your back."

"It doesn't *have* to focus on lesbians. These stories tend to develop on their own. I'd like to include women who are willing to talk." Kathryn looked at Robbi, who smiled but shook her head. "Or not. What do you say—anyone? Besides Don? Who'd like to be interviewed?"

"I'll do it," Patrick said.

"No," said Don and Chris together. They looked disapprovingly at the younger pilot.

"It's just too dangerous," Chris said.

"You're too young and you've got too much to lose," Don said. "No. It's too risky."

"Excuse me?" Patrick's tone was heated. "I've already got a dad in Chicago."

"Aw," said Karl, "how cute! Your first argument."

Jeanne said, "You've got more to lose, Don. Fifty percent lifetime pension—remember?"

Softening, Patrick said, "I mean you've inspired me. We've gotta start saying what this injustice means on a human level. It goes against everything the military claims to be for." Overcome with a feeling of tenderness, "You've inspired me" repeated in Don's head. He planted a long firm kiss on Patrick's lips, a caress that was returned just as warmly.

"Jesus!" said Karl. "Get a room already."

"Leonard, thank you for a wonderful evening but it's time for Eileen and me to turn in."

"Half past midnight. I'm in awe. That's the latest I've ever seen a general remain at one of these events. Except for General Laker, of course. Let me walk you to the elevator."

"Hope we're not in *his* league," General Neville replied. "Sadly, I hear he's not doing well."

"That's so terrible. Paul's an—*interesting* character. Not much older than we are," said Eileen. "Your Marines are delightful and this was the most fun we've had since—since—I can't remember when." As they stopped at the elevators, she asked, "You staying here in the hotel?"

"No, no, I have a fondness for my own bed."

"Oh that's right. You live in that gorgeous house not too far away in La Jolla," she replied.

"Good night to you both and thank you so much for joining us." His guests disappeared into the elevator and he relaxed as the hardest part of the evening was over. Ecstatic about his promotion, only one thing could enhance tonight. He walked to the pay phones, but outside the alcove, a Marine had passed out in a chair. Recognizing the man, Leonard grew disgusted. He grabbed the man's shoulders and shook him. "Wake up, Sledge. You're embarrassing yourself."

Sledge opened his eyes and blinked. "Colonel—good to see you, sir. Havin' a good time?"

"I was having a *splendid* evening until I found one of my squadron commanders passed out in public like a teenaged boy on prom night."

"Is 'at right, sir?" Sledge's words slurred together. "Who? Bet it's Frenchie LeBlanc at seven sixty-three, now *tha's* a lieutenant colonel who never could hold his liquor—"

"It's *you*, Sledge! You were passed out here in the hotel lobby!"

"It was't me. Jus' sittin' here havin' a drink." He rattled his empty glass. "I need anoth—"

"You do *not* need another drink. Where's your wife?"

"She was—she was—right here I thought. Oh. The Burrs took her home hours ago."

"Wonderful," Leonard said quietly. This was his night to celebrate and he wouldn't deal with an inebriated officer. He called out to a major walking by from the group's logistics office. "Would you please do us all a favor and check Lieutenant Colonel Hammer into a room—"

"Oh, no, sir," Sledge protested, "I'm fine. I'll just drive home now."

"You will not drive—where are your keys?" Grudgingly, Sledge surrendered his keys. "Ask the hotel manager to lock his keys in the safe and leave Sledge a note where they are. Use the credit card on file for the general's suite and get Sledge a room. Don't let him out of your sight and *no* minibar." He watched in silence as the major escorted the drunken Marine to reception.

Leonard waited a few minutes, ensuring no one was within hearing range. He placed two dimes in the payphone, pressed the buttons from memory and waited for the tone. "I feel like having some fun tonight. Hope you do too. I'll be home by one." While waiting for his car, he didn't hide his grin. Even Sledge wasn't going to ruin a night of bliss that hadn't even begun.

"I don't need any competition." Zack's tone was serious. "You gotta find another bookstore. Too many guys like us'll scare away the targets."

"What's your authority?" Jay asked. "I mean, how can you turn them in for sodomy?"

"Read my goddamned T-shirt, man! This is for real. I'm a military policeman—an MP."

"So? E-Z Street Bookstore's not on base so you don't have jurisdiction." Jay hadn't planned to disclose his work but Zack had revealed his identity, giving them a bond. "I'm an NIS agent."

Zack laughed. "I gotta get me a beer, man. Want more water?" Jay nodded. Still laughing when he returned, Zack mimicked Jay's Upper Midwest accent and said, "I'll tell you something, Mr. 'I'm-an-NIS-agent.' How long you been at this? Can't be too long 'cause ain't no Marine scared of no goddamned NIS agent. I'm surprised you ain't got the shit beat outta you yet."

"But they're afraid of you?" Jay was upset at Zack's inference that NIS agents were wimps.

"Buddy, every day when I'm on duty, I got a loaded weapon, right here." Zack slapped his right hip. "The perverts that suck my crank know that. The whole time they's goin' down on me, while they got my big gun in their mouth," he said, grabbing his groin, "they thinking about that big piece of steel that I got hangin' right here when I'm at work. Outta plain fear, they do exactly what I tell 'em. After I shoot my load down their throat and make 'em swallow every last drop, I say, 'Listen, you goddamned

pole-smokin' faggot, tomorrow you tellin' your commanding officer that you're a low-life, fudge-packin', cum-suckin' queer! You
gonna tell him you don't belong in my Marine Corps! You understand me, you scum-of-the earth faggot?!' I tell him I'll check the
records to make sure he got outta the Corps. Works every time."

All Jay could do was stare in awe. He'd met his match.

"How d'you do it?" Zack asked.

"Well," Jay said slowly, "I just started over at NIS. Kind of the
same way, I guess. I track them down, fuck them, then tell them to
turn themselves in."

"How far you willin' to go?" Zack asked.

Jay blinked. "What sex acts will I do? Whatever it takes, I
guess—in the line of duty."

"That's a bullshit answer." Zack lit a cigarette he'd obtained at
the bar. "Let me put it to ya this way. You take it up the ass? You
willin' to go that far 'in the line of duty'?"

"No."

"I see how it is then." He guzzled his beer.

"You take it up the ass? Hard to believe you won't suck dick but
you'll let a guy fuck you."

"Never said I didn't suck dick." Zack blew a cloud of smoke.
"You said that." Zack stared.

Jay tried to understand. "So you do give blow jobs?"

"You just a regular Einstein, ain't ya'?" Zack flicked his ashes
onto the floor. "Let me explain somethin' to ya', Jay-man. I do
what I do because I like how it feels. If I'm with a buddy—who's
like me—figure I should give him the same treatment." Zack put
his hand on Jay's thigh. Jay left it there. "But I ain't no fag and fags
don't belong in the Corps."

"But you're just as guilty—of violating Article 125—"

Zack removed his hand and took another drink. "Bein' guilty of
something and gettin' caught—or gettin' in trouble for it—are two
different things. Just like what two men—like us—do together is
different than what two queers do together."

"You aren't afraid of getting caught? Or one of them turning you
in?"

"If they ever say anything to fuck me over, I'll kill 'em. They know it won't be quick or easy and it won't be painless. They have to sense that you got no fear. No fear, man!"

Jay wondered about his new friend's mental stability. Did he want Zack in his life? Guys like him would turn on anyone if they felt the need. Still, since Johnson's funeral, Jay had felt his loneliness. The satisfaction that came from pursuing his goals and helping his cause wasn't what it used to be. What he needed was companionship. Perhaps Zack was the one man who lived up to or exceeded Jay's personal standards. Most of all, Zack understood.

"Tell you what, Jay. I said I didn't need no competition, but maybe you and me could trade secrets of the job. There's a Marine Expeditionary Unit—we call it a MEU, say it like some fucked-up cow goin' 'myoo'—pullin' into port week. Four amphibious ships been at sea for six months. Next weekend, all the bathhouses in San Diego will be full of Marines and Sailors. No way I can catch all of 'em myself. We'll go and I can show you how I do it."

"A bathhouse?" Jay had considered those too risky for military men. "You're on."

The game ended. Zack bummed another cigarette and said it was time to play. Chalking his cue, Jay asked, "Where're you staying? If you don't have a car, how're you getting to the base?"

"I was goin' to a bathhouse till you kinda distracted me. I'll get my backpack outta your car and head over there as soon as I'm done whoopin' your ass at this game."

"Don't stay at a bathhouse." Jay racked their balls. "Crash with me. We can trade ideas."

Zack stopped practicing his shots. "Yeah, right! 'Ideas.' Ain't all we can trade."

Jay laughed. "No, Zack. Unlike you, I don't get any pleasure out of this dirty business. Besides, you never told me for sure what you'll do with guys."

Zack's break shot put two balls in a corner pocket. Grinning, he said, "Let's just say this Marine is willing to do more 'in the line of duty' than the NIS Agent."

"Are you flamers about to leave The Flame and go home together? I'll help you out."

"Oh, really Karl?" asked Don. "Just how're you going to do that?"

"Patrick can drive both of you home in his car and I'll drive your jeep," Karl explained. "That way you can keep feeling each other up all the way up the five. Be a shame if your momentum stopped just 'cause you drove separate cars. Kills the mood."

"No problem here. Chris left with some nineteen-year-old who came here by mistake."

"Fuckin' hilarious," said Karl. "Walked right out of the closet into a lesbian bar."

"Sounds great to me," Don said. "Almost too great. Karl, what do you plan to do with the jeep?"

"Oh, probably going to WC's. I'm over this place. Too much estrogen floating around. If I don't leave soon, I'll start ovulating."

"You guys ready to go now?" Patrick asked. "I am."

"Damn! You're a horny lieutenant. I'll get my coat out of the office before you bust a nut."

Don handed Karl the keys to his jeep. To Patrick, he whispered, "Meet us out front."

Karl opened Jeanne's office door, flipped on the light and found his coat. When he turned around, Don had closed the door. "Um, buddy. Patrick is the one you want. He's outside. This," Karl said, motioning between the two of them, "would be incest. Not into that."

Don frowned. "Tell me what the fuck you're doing."

"What the fuck *I'm* doing?" Karl exploded. "Thought I was borrowing your car to go to WC's! What the fuck is the matter with you?"

Lightening his tone, Don gave Karl a sympathetic look. "I saw you—about twenty minutes ago. You looked at your pager—then you came back here and made a call."

Karl tilted his head toward the floor for a few seconds. When he looked up, he was more defiant than before. "What're you getting at?" he yelled. "What the fuck are you trying to say?"

"Where did you get the money for an Armani suit?" Don shouted. "Why did you have more cash in your wallet than you make in four paychecks? Where did you go last three-day week-

end? Where're you *really* taking my jeep? Who paged you at one
o'clock in the morning? You said that was a military pager you got
when you started driving for the colonel."

"You through?" Karl's laugh was sarcastic. "You think I'm hus-
tling, don't you?"

"What the hell am I *supposed* to think? You won't give me any
believable answers."

The door to the office burst open and Jeanne walked in. "Who's
in—? Oh, hi, guys. Thought I heard—is everything okay?"

"Yeah." Karl brushed past her on his way out. "Everything's
fucking perfect."

Shaking his head, Don watched his friend disappear.

Jeanne was wide-eyed. "If you want to tell me what that's
about, I'll listen, otherwise—"

"Afraid we got a little problem on our hands," he said softly.
Perking up, he added, "But for the next twelve hours—or more—
I'm not giving it another thought."

Alone in her room at San Diego's famous Hotel Del Coronado,
Kathryn Angel was too wired to sleep. Looking over her notes
from the evening, she outlined the words. She grew so excited
about her progress, she had to tell someone. Her editor would be
asleep—everyone in DC would be asleep—and she'd talk to him
over the weekend. Instead, she dialed someone else. The phone
rang five times before a sleepy voice said, "Hello."

"It's Kathryn."

"Kate? What—Jesus! It's four A.M. here. And it's a Saturday."

"What's the problem? Thought you worked seven days a
week."

"I do," answered her contact. "But I still sleep most nights."

"Well, you're up now. Next time you see your people, tell him
that your—operative, or whatever you call me—hit pay dirt." Picking up an emery board from the nightstand beside the phone, she
smoothed her nails and made a mental note to contact the
concierge first thing in the morning to arrange a manicure. "Did
you hear me?"

"Of course," he said. "I can't believe you—even *you* have re-sults this soon."

"That's why I have a Pulitzer, and a year from now, I expect number two will be on its way." She stifled a yawn. "And of course—" She paused for dramatic effect.

"Yes?" her contact said. "What will you be asking for now?"

"I deserve a lot—but you know what a nice girl I am. We'll talk next time I see you."

"Jesus, Kate. I'll see what I can do," he said. "But—this better be good."

"Don't worry, you'll have more on your guy than you ever dreamed of. Just be ready for me when I get back. Good night—or good morning, sunshine!"

"Good night, Kate," said the voice. "My God, how *do* you sleep at night?"

"I sleep *wonderfully* well, thank you very much." After hanging up the phone, she whispered, "Thanks to this new little pill my doctor gave me." She swallowed ten milligrams of Ambien and smiled as she rested her head on the large pillow and happily drifted into dreamland.

24

"It's not much, but it's livable. Gimme your beer. I'll put it in the refrigerator."

Jay put away the six-pack. When he returned to the living room, Zack had dropped his pack and stripped off his shirt. Unlacing his boots, Zack asked, "Where you want me to crash?"

"The couch is comfortable," Jay answered. "Make yourself at home. I'll get your pillow and blanket." As he entered the bedroom to retrieve the items, Jay's emotions clashed. He and Zack were small enough to rest comfortably on his queen-sized mattress. But Jay feared—no, he knew—if he invited Zack into his bed, something sexual would happen. Sex with Zack, a man Jay knew he couldn't—and wouldn't—charge with sodomy, violated his divine pact. His hundreds of male sexual encounters had been part of a larger purpose. *Almost* every encounter.

Reentering the living room, Jay stopped dead in his tracks. Zack's jeans were in a pile by the sofa and Zack was stroking his eight-inch erection. An open bottle of lube sat on the end table. "I brought my own porn tape," Zack declared. With his left hand, he patted the vacant sofa cushion beside him. "I don't mind if you watch it with me."

Without a second's hesitation, Jay dropped the pillow and blanket on the carpet, stripped out of his clothes and hopped over the back of the sofa. "Nice," said Zack, squirting some lube on Jay's half-erect penis. The Marine smiled and looked him in the eye. "Somethin' tells me, Mr. 'NIS Agent,' you're goin' a lot farther in the line of duty tonight than you *ever* gone before. Once you do, buddy, they ain't *no* going back!"

"Hey, Leo! You upstairs?"
The angelic voice was the ideal sound to end a perfect day. "Yes. There's some beer for you in the refrigerator. Take one before you come up." To Leonard's delight, he heard footsteps on the staircase immediately. Within seconds, his handsome young lover appeared in the doorway to the bedroom.

"You kiddin' me?" his visitor asked as he stripped out of his clothes. "Why would I waste time on *beer* when you're up here waiting on me?"

Leonard walked across the room. "Slower! You know how I enjoy watching you undress."

"Yes, Colonel. Your wish is my command." The man began gyrating in a private strip tease for Leonard. "Especially since this is your day." Two minutes later, he slid his shirt over his head, twirling it around before throwing it across Leonard's shoulder. Gently pushing Leonard into the chair, the man faced him and straddled his knees. He rubbed his crotch on Leonard's leg, allowing Leonard to feel his pulsating hard-on. Seated firmly on Leonard's lap, he put his arms around the older Marine's neck, leaned in and kissed him hard and deep. For five minutes, they kissed as passionately as the first time they'd made love six months earlier.

Stopping long enough to converse, Leonard asked, "You heard? How did you—?"

"I ran into—let's just say I heard the good news." The man bent over to remove his shoes.

Leonard admired the man's physique from the edge of the bed. "One of my officers is gay?"

"Is that what I said?" The man dropped his jeans, giving Leonard a tantalizing view of his chiseled body and hard penis.

The man climbed on the bed on top of Leonard and said, "Now, get rid of that robe, mister, 'cause I'm about to give you the ride of your life!"

"Whatever you say, Corporal Steiger. As usual, *your* wish is *my* command."

Don didn't take his eyes off Patrick once during the ride up the freeway. He didn't want to blink because he was so enraptured with the guy. He couldn't stop thinking about what they were about to do. The more he studied Patrick's face in the lights available after one o' clock A.M.—the interior of the car, the moonlight, other cars—the more he wanted to touch it with his hands, to let his tongue wonder over every square inch. He listened as Patrick told him the details of his life. Don loved hearing every word as Patrick described playing soccer in high school, going to mass and his reasons for joining the Marines. Nothing that he said was extraordinary except for the simple fact it was coming from him—such an awesome, giving, understanding soul—and to Don, that made it seem like divine revelation.

Initially, Don's attraction to Patrick had been physical, as he guessed was the case in many human relationships. Within minutes of their meeting at WC's, something unconscious had connected them and they both felt it. The more he learned, the more he realized that Patrick's goodness was what attracted him the most. Patrick was tender and compassionate and he didn't understand the world could be a horrible place. Don had found a priceless treasure. He wanted to be Patrick's protector—to ensure the young man never knew life's dark side.

Don talked about his life. Patrick, keeping his eyes on the road, was at a disadvantage. He looked across his car as much as possible, without risking an accident. This—and dozens of other little things Don noticed—turned him on. They were silent for a while before reaching the exit. Patrick finally asked, "What do you think Eddie would say about talking to that reporter?"

"You won't believe this—I was *just* thinking about that."

Patrick made sure the car was safe on the road, then leaned over and gave Don a quick kiss on the cheek. "Isn't that the third or fourth time we've done that tonight?"

"At least." Don paused. "Eddie? He'd be skeptical. Probably side with Jeanne."

"How so?"

"He was all about doing good for people—but in his own way. Loved helping others face-to-face. He wouldn't see the benefit of someone else's newspaper article that people he didn't know or couldn't see might or might not read. He was very private."

"Do you still wanna do it?" Patrick asked.

"Sure. Do you?"

"With you? Of course I wanna do it."

"Okay," Don said. "Miss Angel's got my number and if she wants to talk to us, she'll—"

"You still talking about that article?" Patrick laughed and put his hand over Don's mouth. "When I said I wanted to do it with you, speaking to a reporter wasn't what I had in mind."

Don grabbed Patrick's hand and put it over his crotch. "*This* what you had in mind?"

"Tell you in about five minutes," Patrick said as he exited from the interstate.

"I don't understand, Karl. You could be with any guy in town tonight. Why an old man?"

Karl rolled over on his side under the satin sheets and faced Leonard. Propping his head on his left hand, his look was one of impatience. "Leo, we've had this conversation before. Like I told you. I've *had* a lot of sex with 'any guy in town' and I'm over it. I've been with guys older than me, or younger, better-looking, worse-looking, you name it." Karl placed his right hand on Leonard's cheek and turned his head so that they looked directly into each other's eyes. "Until I met you—I'd never been with any-one who—I don't know—who—"

"What is it you're trying to say?"

"Fuck it. I'll just say it. I feel like—like you're my soul mate. There. It sounds so fucking stupid when other people say it, but since I've known you, I totally get what they mean."

Leonard was blown away by his lover's admission. "I don't know what to say." He rubbed his hand across his Karl's smooth, tan skin.

"Don't you feel it too?"

Leonard hesitated. As much as he wanted to please the man, he wasn't sure their feelings were the same. "I'm—I've never felt this way about anyone else, Karl, but—things are different for men your age. When I was twenty-three, Christ—what year was that?"

"Nineteen-sixty-seven. I've thought about all this."

"Nineteen-sixty-seven," Leonard repeated, letting his hand wander down to Karl's firmly toned bubble-shaped ass. "Do you know how different things were in 1967 than they are today?"

"Really? Bet they didn't even let gay men join the Marines back then, did they?"

"Now, Karl, you know what I mean—"

"No I don't. Things still suck but I don't see what that's got to do with you and me." Karl gave Leonard his most seductive look. He reached behind and slid Leonard's hand from his buttocks, maneuvering Leonard's finger into his hole, which was still lubed from their earlier lovemaking. Leaning into Leonard's ear, Karl whispered, "I'm tired of talking. You had enough rest? I want you to *punish* me this time."

For half a second, Leonard wasn't sure he had the strength to go another round with the man less than half his age, but all it took was one look at Karl's delicious face and body and Leonard rallied to the cause. "Punish you?" he asked, sliding over on the California king–sized bed. "What do you want me to do?"

Positioning himself on his hands and knees, Karl faced the pillows. "Plow that big forty-nine-year-old cock of yours so far up my ass I have to go to medical first thing in the morning."

"That would be an interesting examination," Leonard said, reaching for lube and the last of the condoms. As he looked at Karl's ass, his dick stiffened even harder, tightening the condom. He squirted lube in his hand and covered his entire shaft, then put some around Karl's rim.

Karl shuddered with joy and said, "About ready to fuck me, Colonel?"

Leonard laughed and rubbed his penis up and down along Karl's crack. The last six months, Karl's youthful zest had made Leonard feel twenty years younger. As he slowly slid into Karl's tight, warm welcoming body, Karl arched his back. "Oh my God, Leo, that feels *awesome!*"

Leonard started pumping in and out, slowly and lightly at first but gradually increasing the speed and force. He preferred making love so that he could see his handsome lover's face, but occasionally, this position was fun. Karl had a stunning V-shaped back and broad shoulders. Leonard grabbed Karl's hips and reveled in the magnificent view.

"I've been a bad Marine!" Karl said. "Punish me!"

Leonard, still thrusting in and out, laughed and said, "I can't do that—"

"Remember the last time we were at the general's house?" Karl raised his face from the pillow and craned his neck around to look at Leonard. "Well—I didn't tell you but—I *accidentally* scratched Mrs. Neville's Mercedes."

"Okay, Corporal, you asked for it!"

Zack's mouth was warm and wet and gave Jay the most incredible sensation as Zack bobbed his head back and forth on his dick. He looked over the top of the Marine's head as a sex scene played on his television. The image gave him an idea. He pulled out of Zack's mouth and lay on the carpet so that his own mouth was inches away from Zack's dangling meat. "Thought you didn't give blow jobs," Zack said, moving closer to Jay's mouth.

"I don't," Jay answered, laughing. "How about we sixty-nine each other?"

As Jay put his mouth around Zack, the younger man said, "Buddy, I like the way you think. We're gonna get along just fine."

Jay pulled his head away from the young Marine's cock and said, "Hey, Devildog, just shut up and blow me!" The two men resumed fucking each other's mouths more furiously than before. Jay hadn't felt this good in at least fifteen years.

* * *

Don and Patrick didn't have to say anything to each other. In a short time, they'd developed an intuition about the other's thoughts. Patrick quietly asked Don to excuse the chaos in his apartment but Don held up his hand. Apologizing for a mess was unnecessary, especially considering that Patrick had moved into the space less than twenty-four hours earlier. Patrick led Don gently by the hand into his bedroom and Don was glad to see that he'd put the bed together.

The two men stopped at the bed's edge. Patrick placed his lips softly against Don's as they put their arms around each other. The kiss was long, slow and passionate. Don slid his tongue around the edge of Patrick's lips and went a little deeper with each motion. Patrick let his hands roam to the top of Don's jeans and his fingers found their way underneath them to Don's ass. Don did the same and the accumulation of sweat in Patrick's crack turned him on even more. The two men laughed at the same time and fell on top of each other on the bed.

They stopped kissing only long enough to kick off their shoes and take off their shirts. Don rolled over on his back and pulled Patrick on top of him. The younger man's tender, smooth skin felt good against his own, and the longer they touched each other, the more it was as if they were merging. Patrick ran his tongue from Don's mouth down his neck and chest, finding his way to Don's nipple, where he played with it and bit it harder and harder. He squeezed Don's other nipple with his hand. The sensation carried Don to a level of ecstasy he hadn't felt in over a decade. He ran his hand through Patrick's short hair. Somehow, their pants and underwear came off and Don felt Patrick's erection against his own. The two men were kissing again. With his large hands, Don raised Patrick's upper body and positioned his dick in front of his mouth. Patrick rose up, giving the older Marine easy access to the full length of his erection.

With his right hand, Don pulled on Patrick's balls, which were large and hung low. He placed his left hand on Patrick's muscular ass and moved it back and forth, controlling the in-and-out motions of Patrick's dick in his mouth. The smell and taste were awesome! Don loved the sweaty, manly odor that rose from the younger man's crotch. Patrick hadn't been part of the gay world long enough to know that most men his age trimmed and shaved. His naturalness delighted Don even more. He didn't like the overly groomed look so many men preferred these days and tomorrow he'd tell Patrick not to change a thing about himself. For now, pressing his face into the thick curly blond mesh at the base of Patrick's cock, Don felt right at home.

Both men had surrendered themselves to the other, and as their bodies moved, their rhythms became the same. Neither was in control of his motions anymore, but together, they controlled the universe. Without removing his mouth from Patrick, Don reached into the top drawer of Patrick's nightstand. Just as he'd hoped, Patrick, anticipating this night, had conveniently pre-positioned condoms and lube. Don found them and brought them over to the bed.

Patrick reached down in the dark, picked up the condom wrapper, opened it with his teeth and put it over Don's erection. Don marveled at Patrick's skill and for a split second wondered if Patrick had been truthful about his gay virginity when he recalled Patrick had probably done this hundreds of—immediately, Don stopped thinking. He banished his negative thoughts and realized that what was happening between the two of them was magic, transcending conscious words. It was better than magic. It was spiritual.

Don put a healthy dose of lube over his dick and then rubbed some on Patrick's erection, which swayed inches in front of his face. Patrick took a handful of lube and put it on his rim. He rested his anus on the tip of Don's erection. Their eyes met and their souls united in pure euphoria. With his eyes, Don asked Patrick if he was sure he wanted to do this, if he was certain he was ready. Patrick's look answered yes, that this exact moment was what he'd waited for his whole life. Don reached up and placed his hands squarely on Patrick's hips, ready to help if his young lover needed it.

Their eyes locked in place. The look on Patrick's face told him more about Patrick's feelings than words could ever express—the joy, anticipation, passion, closeness of spirit—it was all there. They weren't alone and in fact never had been. They'd found each other and were about to unite in the most physical way possible and it would match the emotional unity they already felt. Patrick slid an inch or two, letting the tip of Don's dick enter him. Don felt Patrick suddenly go tense and he helped raise him. Still maintaining eye contact, he mouthed the words "relax" and "take it slow," but he didn't need to; Patrick knew what to do.

Patrick tried again and this time continued sliding until three quarters of Don's dick was inside him. Don hadn't moved a muscle but had simply enjoyed the sight, the feeling and the moment. He experienced the pleasure for the first time again through Patrick. Now that Patrick was more relaxed and confident, Don reached between his lover's legs and massaged Patrick's dick, restoring his erection to his earlier fullness.

Don studied Patrick's leg muscles in awe as they flexed in response to his up-and-down motions, which increased in speed. Don moved his hips in synch with Patrick and was thrilled to see the look of bliss cross his lover's handsome face. Don knew where the look came from because he'd first felt it years ago himself. Patrick had just learned through experience that by letting go of himself, the initial pain gave way to a sense of elation like no other.

Now was the moment for Don to make the move. He reached his hands up and firmly grasped Patrick's back. Slowly and without separating, Don lowered Patrick's back onto the bed and raised himself on his knees. It was his turn and Patrick laughed from sheer joy. Don's eyes said, "Now, my young hard-charging Marine, all you have to do is lay there and let me do the work." Don grabbed Patrick's calves for stability and slowly but steadily pumped his hips so that Patrick took in all of his erection. He rested Patrick's ankles on his shoulders and, with his free hand, felt the ripped muscles of the younger man's abdominals. He let his fingers move slowly up, stopping only to play with Patrick's nipple. He kept thrusting at the same pace until he put his finger in Patrick's mouth. As Patrick sucked hungrily on Don's index finger, he stepped up the speed of his gyrations. Patrick closed his eyes and moaned, causing Don to smile.

Ten minutes later he sensed his lover was about to reach climax.

Just before Patrick did, Don pulled out of Patrick's ass and put his mouth fully over Patrick's cock. He had to taste every ounce of cum that shot out of that dick. Within a second, Don felt the salty-tasting liquid spray the back of his throat. To his delight, it didn't stop and he had to swallow to make room for more. A few seconds later, he tilted his head back, ripped the condom off his own dick, and shot his load all over Patrick's chest. Patrick, who still seemed to be in shock that Don drank him all in, rubbed Don's semen across his own chest and abdomen, a move he finished by licking his fingers clean.

The two men lay side-by-side, arms around each other for an indeterminate amount of time. Don felt as if his mind were floating, along with Patrick's, existing in a state of pure contentment. He knew Patrick felt the same way.

Finally, Patrick rolled over, resting his chin on Don's shoulder. "I didn't ask you before because it, I don't know, just didn't seem relevant. But I take it you're a top?"

Don slid his arm down Patrick's back. "We're a team, stud, and I'm a team player. And like any good team," he said, grinning mischievously, "teammates play multiple positions."

"Sounds like a winning game plan, coach."

"Ready for round two?"

"Devildog, I was *born* ready."

25

Jay was glad Zack fell asleep in his arms. They'd had sex for at least three hours, never once lightening up on the intensity. Despite the exertion, Jay couldn't sleep. He felt too alive and didn't want to lose the thrill. He watched Zack's body rise and fall with the steady rhythm of his breathing and he ran his fingers along the lines of Zack's tattoos. Even the toughest Marine was a harmless baby when he slept.

He refused to feel guilty about what they'd done. A week earlier, in his car outside Johnson's house, he'd been terrified and racked with guilt. He suspected a link between the visits from his ghosts and his guilt over Johnson's death. If he could avoid the guilt, maybe the ghosts would stay away. His emotions this morning were a mixture of sexual gratification and a warm feeling of companionship. Perhaps he could make Zack part of his divine pact. Maybe Zack was a gift for Jay's obedience all these years. Didn't the book of Genesis say it wasn't good for man to be alone? Maybe Jay and Zack could team up against a bitter, cruel and decadent world.

"Mornin'," Zack mumbled, rubbing his eyes and resting his back against the headboard. "I tell ya', Jay-man, I'm impressed. You're the first who's kept up with me the whole time—the first *civilian* I mean." He sat on the edge and looked around. "What'd you do with my clothes?"

"They're where you left them, oh ye paranoid one. On the floor in the other room."

"Oh yeah." Zack laughed as he walked out of the bedroom. "You got anything to eat in this place?" he yelled as he stopped by the bathroom to take a long piss.

"How're you getting back to Camp Pendleton?"

Zack was still in the bathroom. "You throwin' me out already?"

"Not yet. Just thinking logistically. I can't drive you all the—"

"I'll take a cab to the train." Zack stood in the doorway to the bedroom, his fingers laced above the door's frame. As he leaned forward to stretch himself, Jay could see every strand of muscle on his torso as the light of the morning sun streamed in. Zack was also semierect.

"I'll drive you to the train station and buy you some chow at the diner next door."

"Oh you will?" Zack asked playfully. "Don't think that makes me your bitch. I ain't gonna put out just 'cause you're payin' for breakfast."

"I don't expect—"

Zack leapt on top of Jay, waving his hard-on in Jay's face. "Gonna put out 'cause I want to!"

The pleasant aroma of bacon and eggs rose from the kitchen, rousing Leonard from his deep sleep. Putting on his robe, he descended the stairs, pausing halfway to enjoy the view of Karl preparing their breakfast. "Christ!" Leonard exclaimed, "You've already showered and changed—where did you get this food?" Looking up, Karl smiled as he scrambled the eggs. Leonard rubbed his hand across his lover's prickly face. "Like our weekend at Lake Arrowhead two weeks ago. I love it when you don't shave." He stepped behind Karl and put his arms around him. Leonard kissed the back of Karl's neck while he scooped the eggs onto two plates.

"Walked down the hill to the corner store. Seriously, Leo, you need to keep this place stocked better—or maybe you need someone to stock it for you." Karl turned his head and raised his eyebrows. Leonard kissed him on the lips.

"That store is overpriced—and the manager is rude. I hope you didn't spend your money—"

"Don't worry. I had some left over from the suit money you gave me, which, by the way, got me in trouble with one of my buddies." Karl poured two tall glasses of freshly squeezed orange juice. "I wanted to bring you breakfast in bed."

"Let's eat on the terrace. It's too beautiful to stay inside." He pulled several pieces of sizzling bacon off the pan as two slices of bread popped out of the toaster. "You are incredible."

"I know I am. Don't forget it." Karl carried their plates to the sun-drenched patio high in the La Jolla hills. Facing the ocean, they sat with the sun behind them. Although the morning breeze was cool, Leonard felt as comfortable as ever.

"What do you mean you got in trouble with a friend?" Leonard asked as he buttered his toast.

"I was a fucking moron. The suit was gonna be ready the next day, you know, and I wanted to count how much cash I'd have left over—"

"Which is your money, Karl. I'm also going to repay you for this breakfast."

Karl held up his hand. "You don't have to—" Leonard gave his young lover a stern look. They'd had this conversation before. "Okay, fine," Karl said. "I wanted to pay for his dinner, like, to repay him for the thousands of dinners he's bought me. He saw me with all the cash."

Leonard refrained from telling Karl he shouldn't keep that much cash in his wallet. As a grown man, Karl could decide these things for himself. Instead, Leonard said, "Why did that upset your friend?" He sprinkled a dash of pepper on his eggs and took a bite. "Delicious, my handsome chef." With a wink, he added, "So is the food."

"I wore the suit to—that event I went to this week—"

"And he wondered how a corporal could afford Armani."

"Exactly," said Karl. "But it's the only suit I have—and, well, let's just say the event was—it was the kind where you have to wear a suit, even though I *should've* worn my uniform." Karl looked down at his plate and played with his bacon. "After that, I guess, he started wondering about things, you know, putting shit together. Like, he got suspicious about where I was over Martin Luther King Day weekend. Last night was the kicker, though, oh man! He saw me get your page and return your call."

Putting down his silverware, Leonard stared. "What exactly is it he thinks you're doing?"

"You'll never believe this, but he thinks I'm a hustler, you know, a prostitute."

"Yes, my sweet prince, I *know* what a hustler is. Why would a friend think that about you?"

"Because," Karl explained, "he's seen it happen—hell, *I've* seen it happen—too many times. A young, good-looking military dude like me comes here." Karl grinned, feigning modesty. "Next thing you know—" Instead of finishing his sentence, he bit off a piece of toast.

"Marines? Prostitutes? You're joking! How long has this been going on?"

"Jesus, Leo. I don't know, like forty years. I've seen pictures from the 1950s, soft-core porn shots of Marines and Sailors who'd go up to L.A. every weekend. Guys would give them rides up there. Pimp them out to movie producers, businessmen, you name it."

Leonard pondered this news while staring at the ocean below the quaint village north of San Diego's beaches. Even though he'd fought in wars and had survived more combat missions than he could count, he'd never felt so naïve. To think that all this was happening in his backyard! "Why do Marines and Sailors do this?"

"Why? Fuck if I know. A hundred reasons." Karl laughed. "For starters, Brigadier General–select, if you bastards paid us enough money, we wouldn't *have* to moonlight."

"Something tells me they're not in it completely for the dollars. Money's a problem a general has no control over. To fix the problem of low pay—for *all* of us—we look to Congress."

"For *all* of us?" Karl asked. "Looks like you're doing pretty well, Colonel Spencer."

"None of this—" Leonard decided against trying to explain

why a colonel's salary couldn't pay for his possessions. Given Karl's poor background, he wouldn't understand the tremendous privileges and responsibilities that came with having enormous wealth. Someday Leonard would discuss it, but not now. Instead, he asked, "Did you tell me the Marine who embarrassed Congressman Coughlin was from the fourth Marine regiment?"

"Maybe," Karl said. "I mean, word got around base pretty quick what unit he was from."

"I think you told me Wednesday morning on the way to the conference. At the time, it wasn't common knowledge, at least not among the colonels or the media."

"And you let it slip to Colonel Watkins that you know D—the gunny—was from his regiment." Karl laughed and said, "So *that's* why he ended up in our car on Wednesday."

"Exactly," said Leonard. "Do you know him?"

"Colonel Watkins? Of course. I drove him to his office on Wednesday, remember?"

"Don't be a smart ass, Corporal," Leonard said, smiling. "Gunnery Sergeant Hawkins."

Finishing his breakfast, Karl placed his knife and fork across his plate. "Leo, I don't tell any of my friends about you to protect you *and* them. But I also don't tell you about any of them. Please don't ask me about gay military people." Softening his tone, he added, "I don't mind bein' caught in the middle. For you—for what we have—I'd do anything."

Leonard was touched almost to the point of tears. Clasping Karl's hands, he said, "What I find so remarkable about you is that you're not even aware of how wonderful you are."

"Are you kidding? My friends would argue with you on that if they ever stopped laughing."

"I don't think so," Leonard said. "This—persona of yours—maybe I've been around long enough that I can see right through it. Don't misunderstand me. I think your larger-than-life machismo is cute and adorable—probably *not* the effect you were going for—but I can see underneath all that bravado, you have a core of pure goodness."

Now it was Karl's turn to look at the ocean and the waves hitting the rocks. "Leo, this is what I was talkin' about last night. We're *soul mates*. I feel it. I just wish you did."

For a reason Leonard didn't understand, the term "soul mate" frightened him. "My son is barely younger than you are," Leonard protested. "I can't—"

Karl slammed his fist down on the table. "This has *nothing* to do with your son, okay? I'm your lover. I'm twenty-three. I'm a grown man and I can do whatever I want, with who I want. And I *want* you, Leo." Karl stood and grabbed the empty dishes off the table. "I just wish you'd get over your hang-ups."

"Do you want any coffee?" Leonard asked when Karl was in the kitchen.

Instead of answering, Karl returned with his jacket. "Can't. Gotta go to Oceanside and return the car." Leaning over, he looked closely in Leonard's eyes. "You're pure goodness too, Leo. You're the handsome, studly one. I mean it. You're gonna realize that and I hope I'm the one who helps you see it." He kissed his lover on the forehead. "Have to run. See you bright and early Monday morning." Heading out the back door, Karl said, "Your coffee's brewing."

"Hi, Jay. Table for one?"

"No, actually, table for two."

"Oh," said Jay's usual server when Zack entered the diner. "Who's your friend?" She led them to a corner booth. Jay introduced Zack to the server he'd met his first Sunday in San Diego. She sat them on opposite sides and gave them dirty menus. "Bring you coffee? Juice?"

"Coffee," Zack said. "A whole pot." Jay ordered juice and the woman disappeared.

"Hangovers *suck*!" Zack said. "Why don't you drink? Was your old man a drunk?"

"Nope. He was a God-fearing man who never drank a drop of liquor in his life."

"Shit," said Zack, flipping through the menu's multicolored laminated pages. "What the fuck is *that* like? Mine—my *real* dad— was a drunk. Disappeared when I was ten."

"I wish my dad had disappeared." Jay knew what he wanted and didn't look at his menu.

"Why? He fuck you?" asked Zack. "Or make you go down on him?"

"No, nothing like that." The server set a tall glass of juice in front of Jay and poured a cup of coffee for Zack. "Thanks." Jay ordered his usual and Zack said he'd have the same. "A lot of—really rough spankings," Jay admitted when she left. "Nothing sexual."

"Then why're you so pissed at him?" Sipping from the cup, Zack said, "This coffee tastes like radiator fluid, but it ain't as bad as that horse diarrhea they have on base." Setting the mug down, he looked at Jay through his bloodshot eyes. "Where do *your* scars come from?"

"My 'scars'?" Jay asked. "I don't have any—"

"I mean scars *inside*. You got 'em. I can tell. Like me. My mom moved me and her in with this guy when I was thirteen. For years he fucked me every chance he got."

"He should die for what he did," Jay said. "Where is he now?"

"If I saw him, I'd kill him. When I was sixteen, I ran away. Turned him in. He went to jail and they say child molesters get special treatment in prison. For all I know, he might be dead."

"Hopefully the other prisoners took care of him and made it as slow and painful as possible."

"Hope so." Zack refilled his cup. "Social workers said he 'scarred me emotionally' and I 'needed professional help,'" he said in a nasally Northern accent. "I'll help myself." He changed to a fragile, even vulnerable, tone. "As much as I hated him—and wanted to kill him—"

"What?"

Zack raised his head and, to Jay's amazement, looked like he was about to cry. "To get through it, I'd close my eyes. Pretend it was somebody else doin' it to me. Yeah, it hurt like hell, but after a while, I didn't mind it so much. In a way, I started to like how it felt."

No one had opened up like this to Jay in over a decade and he was clueless about what to think, feel or say. He sat stone-faced then asked, "Who did you pretend like it was?"

"Sebastian. He lived upstairs from us. He was nice to me, you know? Even though I was just a kid, he respected me." A hint of a smile flashed across Zack's face. "He was twenty-four. Just got outta the Marines. He's the reason I enlisted."

"Did you and Sebastian ever—?"

"Hell no! I done told you, I ain't no faggot. I don't wanna be a woman, I don't dress up like one, I don't fix people's hair and I ain't no goddamned florist. I'm a man—a Marine MP. I was honor man in my platoon at boot camp and I killed two motherfuckin' ragheads in Kuwait."

Jay leaned a few inches back in the booth. "Quiet down, buddy. I get you, Zack. Okay?" Patting Zack on the shoulder, he said, "I didn't say you were gay. I know you're not."

Jay expected Zack to reassume his hypermacho defensive aura, but to his surprise, Zack said quietly, "I bared my soul to you, Jay-man. Now it's your turn. You gotta bare your soul to me."

Jay smiled and said, "Oh? Is that how it is? We take turns—doing everything?"

Now it was Zack who squeezed Jay's shoulder. "We're a team, now 'member? One thing I learned in the Marines is how to act like a team. So—now—what's *your* story?"

"Here you go, boys," the server said as she set their breakfast on the table in front of them. "Be careful, those hot plates'll burn ya!"

"Ready for another one of my favorite acts of man-on-man de-bauchery?"

"My God, Don, what else—what else is there to do?" Patrick pulled Don's arm tighter around his naked shoulders. "Can't wait to find out."

"Patrick, we just got started! You barely got initiated into the world of homo action. There's so much I can't wait to do with you." Don kissed him tenderly on the top of his head. Sliding to the edge of the bed, he said, "but what I'm talking about now is—*showering together!*" With a quick motion, Don stood up and scooped Patrick's nude body in his arms. The two laughed as he carried his lover into the bathroom. "Glad you rented an apart-ment with a big shower." He tilted Patrick gently onto his feet in the tub.

"I am too. It wasn't something I'd thought to look for."

"That's when you find the best things in life," Don said, adjusting the water. "When you're not looking for them." Feeling the right temperature, he soaped up his hands and whispered, "Turn around and I'll clean your backside like you never had it cleaned before."

Patrick spun around, leaned forward and placed his hands on the rear wall. Don lathered his shoulders and back before slowly moving toward his ass. "You can go there," Patrick said, "but only if you promise me one thing."

"What's that?"

"That neither of us puts on our clothes the rest of the day."

"Deal," Don said as his soapy fingers slipped between the younger man's cheeks and massaged the rim of his hole. "For once I won't mind if Karl doesn't return my jeep on time."

"All my life we went to this Baptist church in Michigan," Jay explained as Zack shoveled eggs into his mouth. "When I was fifteen, the church hired a new guy to be the youth pastor and music director." Although he'd begun sharing the tale, he wasn't sure how far he'd go.

"How old was he?" Zack asked. Most people who talked with a mouth filled with half-chewed food looked disgusting, but with Zack, it just made him seem like a wayward little boy who needed his rough edges smoothed out a little bit. "Was he a nasty old perv'?"

"No." Jay shook his head. "Twenty-one, I think. Just graduated from a Bible college in one of the Carolinas. They brought him up that summer. All the kids loved him. He didn't yell and he let us do things—nothing bad, but he let us listen to music that none of the other grown-ups liked, and he let the guys and girls hold hands, and if they kissed a little, he never said anything."

"Shit! Where the fuck did you grow up?" Zack poured ketchup on his hash browns.

"A different world." Jay left it at that. "One weekend in July, Pastor Stephen—that's what we called him—took just the boys camping to the U.P., that's Michigan's Upper Peninsula."

"Uh-huh," Zack said. "Mind if I have some of your pancakes?"

Jay passed his food across the table. If he continued, he'd be sharing more with Zack than he'd ever shared with anyone. "There were eleven boys. And I was the odd man out."

"Let me guess. Pastor Stephen said, 'Come here, little Jay. I'll let you share my tent.'"

"Well, hell, Zack, it's just like you was there," Jay said, imitating Zack's thick accent. In his normal voice, Jay said, "But yeah, I woke up and told him I heard a noise outside the tent."

"Did you?" Zack asked with smirk on his face.

"As far as I can remember, I did. But who the fuck knows. Pastor Stephen asked if I was scared. Of course I was. So he said, 'Climb inside my sleeping bag if you want', and of course, I did. Well, so, I get inside Pastor Stephen's sleeping bag—and he didn't have any clothes on."

"Hell no, he didn't!" Zack laughed. "Why would he? He's got eleven teenage boys sleepin' all around him. He's like a fat chick at an all-you-can eat buffet!"

"Only he—he wasn't a fat chick, that's for sure," Jay said quietly, remembering how good the older man's body had felt against his own. "So right away I said, 'I'm hot', which I was, you know, even the U.P. gets hot in July. So he said, 'You can take your clothes off too.' And he helped me get undressed. Next thing I knew, the two of us were lying there, buck naked, skin-to-skin, inside his sleeping bag."

"He grab your dick?" Zack asked, finishing the extra pancakes.

"No—not right away. The first thing he did was put his arms around me and pull me in close. I rested my head on his hairy chest and put my arms around him and felt that small part of his back. And then I went to sleep."

"That's it?" Zack asked. "That's your 'scar'?"

"You know what, Zack? I've got some work to do today, so I'm going to pay for this and head out." Jay motioned for the bill and reached for his wallet. "Here's my number. Call anytime." Before the Marine could protest, Jay was at the register and out the door. He couldn't handle any more sharing today. Zack would have to understand.

26

"Good flying, Lieutenant Ashburn. I haven't flown with a Navy pilot in a long time."

"Thanks, Royal," said Chris. "Means a lot, coming from a legendary aviator like you."

After shutting the Cobra down, Leonard opened the canopy and the two men stepped from the cockpit onto the flight line near the Aircraft Wing's headquarters building at El Toro. "Now that the tower's not listening to our conversation—about our time at Central Command, I—"

"No need to say anything, Leonard. Didn't work out for us in Tampa. It happens."

Walking toward the gate in the perimeter fence, Leonard said, "I can't be open, not like young men are these days. I'm glad the world is different. You can go to—to gay bars and parties and beaches—and parades. Soon, you may be able to bring your boyfriend to the ball."

"If—when—I have a boyfriend," Chris said. "Not looking right now, though. I've got an unfortunate attraction to the early twenty-something crowd—my time with you being the deviation from my habit." Chris winked. "Best to take it slow and easy with the young men."

Leonard was late, but his opportunities for helpful dating advice were rare. "Really? Why is that?" He stopped walking to prevent a pilot on the other side of the fence from overhearing.

Chris paused. "Oh my God, Leon, you found yourself a boy toy, didn't you? That's—!"

"I don't like that expression. He's—a man. And his—his spirit is much older than mine."

"I see. One of *those*. The wisdom of the ages in a youthful, energetic body. Pure heaven."

"So you've experienced it." Leonard laughed. "You understand why I'm hooked."

"Yes, I do. I'm thrilled for you. Enjoy it," Chris waved to the other pilot. "Just don't forget—his soul may be twenty thousand years old, but his body and mind are—twenty-two?"

"Twenty-three," said Leonard. "Who is that standing there?"

"Captain Pfeiffer." Chris laughed. "After lunch, he says he's going to teach me how to fly."

Realizing the time, Leonard resumed walking. "Damn. I was hoping to convince you to take my place at this godforsaken meeting." Opening the gate, he said, "Good to see you, Jungle."

"You too, sir," Jungle said enthusiastically. "Hope you don't mind me borrowing your bird for a few hours, sir. Figured I'd fly Chris around Saddleback Mountain this beautiful Friday afternoon." Nearing the headquarters, he asked, "This building gonna be yours someday, sir?"

"The odds are slim. But I can dream," he said. "Lieutenant Ashburn, let's be optimistic and try to return to Camp Pendleton no later than sixteen hundred." The men separated with Leonard hurrying to General Neville's private entrance. He bounded up the stairs to the second-story suite.

Passing the general's office, he heard the familiar voice call out. "Good afternoon, Leonard." General Neville motioned for him to step inside before they joined the meeting with a dozen or so other commanders and staff officers. To his surprise, the general closed the door. "Have a seat."

"Thank you," Leonard said as the general handed him an ice-cold bottle of water.

"We have only a minute. You're friends with Colonel Joseph Watkins, correct?"

"We met at Quantico thirty years ago. Then Vietnam. We've been close friends ever since."

"You're aware his name wasn't on the selection list for promotion to general."

"I am," Leonard said. "We had dinner Tuesday night—and quite a few drinks afterward."

"At the dining in a week ago, I told you a name had been withheld for an unknown reason. I've just learned that it was your friend, Joe, who was selected—but whose name was taken off."

Leonard let the news settle. "Taken off. By whom? Why?"

"No one knows," the general said. "Has he upset anyone high in Clinton's administration?"

"I don't think he *knows* anyone in the Clinton administration," Leonard said. "Or *any* administration. He's not a political officer. He's a Marine's Marine all the way."

"As his record shows. Unfortunately, the atmosphere in the capital has never been so acrimonious. Even during Watergate, it wasn't this bitter. Republicans are completely shut out of power for the first time since Jimmy Carter and they're in a 'scorched earth' mode. Congressional Democrats aren't accustomed to having one of their own in the Oval Office and don't intend to defer to the young Mr. Clinton at all. It's *really* bad. Guess who pays the price?"

"I'll take a stab at it and say it's *not* the Russians," Leonard said dryly. "Or Saddam."

General Neville laughed. "Good guesses. As always, we—and our Marines—pay the price."

Leonard hesitated. "General, I hate to interject race into this—because I'm sure we both believe it has no place. No matter what skin color he has, Joe's the most qualified colonel in the Corps as far as I'm concerned. But it's inconceivable that Clinton would halt the promotion—"

"—of the only African-American colonel selected for general in the Marines? Race *shouldn't* have any place in these decisions. Unfortunately, race has a lot to do with these decisions. I agree with your intuition—his name hasn't been withheld by the White House."

"Then by whom?" Leonard asked. "Does Joe know about this?"

"Anyone with power and a vendetta could have their hand in this. Joe doesn't know and the few Marines who do aren't talking. I found out using my back channels in Congress. You can't tell him or anyone about this. I told you so we can try to put his name back on the promotion list." The general stood, signifying the end of their private meeting. "And Colonel Spencer," he said, "don't lose your sense of humor. As a general, you'll need it more than ever."

As Leonard walked down the short hallway from the general's office to the conference room, he suspected Coughlin had held up Joe's promotion because of the incident with Hawkins. As a member of the minority party, though, he wouldn't have the power for something this drastic. However, if true, it was a disgusting and vindictive act of pettiness, even for Coughlin.

"Attention on deck!" yelled the chief of staff as the general entered the room.

"You never do miss a chance to suck up, do you, Leon?" whispered Pete as Leonard sat beside him. "Congratulations, General Spencer, but to be honest, I don't envy you, not one bit!"

Two o'clock Friday afternoon.

Before this week, Jay hadn't grasped what "living for the weekend" meant but he'd been counting the minutes until tonight. Although they hadn't spoken since Jay had left Zack so abruptly at the diner, Zack had left two messages on his machine.

Jay didn't use his work phone for personal calls—he didn't have any to make. But he *had* to know if Zack had phoned him with tonight's instructions. The office was mostly vacant—only Esther and a couple of assistants remained. He dialed his home number and was elated when his machine indicated he had a message. "Hey, Jay-man. It's me." Grabbing a pen, Jay scribbled the information. He pressed the code to delete the message, hung up and studied the words. Folding the note neatly, he stuck it in his wallet. He smiled in anticipation of a great weekend.

* * *

"Gotta question for you, Judge," said Pete. "Can you tell us what the hell is going on with Clinton and the homosexuals? What're we supposed to do if any queers turn up in our squadrons? The news says something different every day." The others murmured in agreement.

"Don't pay attention to the news," said "Judge," El Toro's senior member of the Judge Advocate General's corps. "It's wrong half the time. More importantly, because of our location—in Southern California, 'land of fruits and nuts'—we face a unique situation." He passed around summaries of recent court decisions. "One week ago, a federal district judge ruled—"

"No good news *ever* began with *that* phrase," Pete mumbled to the others' amusement.

"—that the Pentagon's ban on homosexuals was unconstitutional. As of last week the military isn't allowed to discharge or refuse enlistment because of homosexuality."

"That applies only to the one Sailor, correct?" asked the general. "Not to the military."

The JAG colonel shook his head. "No, General—it's a lot more complicated than that. Judge Terry Hatter's ruling applies to the Central District of California." Leonard listened attentively as the JAG attorney adopted a patronizing tone. "And to answer your next question, the Central District of California, for our purposes, consists of Orange County and San Bernardino County."

"So, out of the entire military, I have just about the only command barred from discharging people for being gay?" the general asked, trying to comprehend the JAG officer's announcement.

"Right now, yes, but only partly. His ruling applies to Marines stationed at El Toro, or to the field squadron out in the Mojave Desert at Twentynine Palms. It does *not* apply to Colonel Spencer's squadrons because Camp Pendleton is in San Diego County, *i.e.* the Southern District of California, and of course, the harriers are in Yuma, which is Arizona, a different state."

The room devolved into a dull roar. "This is absurd," the general said. "If a Marine just happens to check into a squadron here—at *this* base—he can simply declare he's homosexual?"

"There's nothing that we can do about it, unless and until Judge Hatter's ruling is overturned by the Ninth Circuit or nullified by Congress," said the JAG. "But if they check into a squadron at Camp Pendleton or Yuma, then the same rules apply that govern the rest of the nation now."

"I'm afraid to ask what those are," the general sighed. "But why don't you tell us."

"This is why you must call me as soon as a Marine says, 'I'm gay.' The temporary policy is: 'New recruits won't be asked if they're gay. Questions about homosexuality will be removed from the entry questionnaire. Homosexuality isn't grounds for discharge. Court proceedings against those discharged for being gay will be delayed. Rules on conduct will be explained to recruits. The Pentagon will draft an executive order banning discrimination.' Now for what's unchanged: 'Service members who are gay remain subject to discharge proceedings. Homosexuals can still be removed from active duty, those who have reached the point of—' "

"This is bullshit!" said Pete. "You just said, 'Homosexuality was not outright grounds for discharge,' and then you say, 'Homosexuals are still subject to discharge proceedings.' I hate to tell you, Judge, your explanation is only makin' things a hell of a lot worse."

"I'll tell you *precisely* what's going on!" Leonard threw his handout on the table. The room became silent, partially out of respect for the new brigadier general–select but mainly because they'd never seen Leonard erupt like this. "President Clinton refused to give Sam Nunn a cabinet position, which hurt the Georgia senator's feelings. If Clinton had chosen him to be Secretary of Defense, this discussion wouldn't be necessary. Instead, we'd be learning a special welcome order to read to gay and lesbian recruits. Nunn is chairman of the Senate Armed Services Committee and he's a very powerful Democrat from a conservative state. What the Judge just read is nothing more than a standoff between two Democrats with clashing egos. And our Marines are pawns in their ridiculous game of chess. It's simply pathetic."

"I think this would be a good time for a break," said the general as everyone nodded.

* * *

"Welcome to my humble little apartment, ladies! Oh—and you too, Lance," Patrick said.

"Yo! What the fuck am I?" asked Karl. "Just a piece of meat?"

Patrick smiled mischievously. "I said 'ladies.'"

Karl took off his jacket. "Lieutenant, you ain't been here long enough to get fresh with me."

"Don't listen to him," Robbi said. "You're as much a part of this family as anyone."

"You have such an amazing ocean view!" Esther handed Patrick a white orchid. "We brought you this as a housewarming gift."

"I wanted to get you a mirror," Karl said. "All you officers love to admire yourselves."

Thanking his friends, Patrick placed the flower in the center of his small dining table. "One day, Corporal Steiger, you're gonna fall in love with an officer. That'll be the definition of poetic justice." Surprisingly, Karl didn't have a comeback. "Hey, stud, help me get drinks for everybody." As he and Karl served the others, Patrick asked, "Lance, how goes the job hunt?"

"Good news." Lance twisted the cap off a beer. "WC's called me back. Since everything's calmed down, they say it's not a problem for them. And the raise isn't a problem for me."

"That's great," said Patrick, raising his bottle. "To Lance getting his job back!" The small group tapped their drinks together and took the first of what Patrick hoped would be many drinks with his wonderful new friends this Friday evening. "*Has* everything calmed down?"

They looked at Esther. "From NIS's perspective, yes, Eddie's case is closed. Nothing else happened this week regarding Agent Gared, either. That is, until this afternoon."

"Shouldn't we wait until Don gets here," Robbi asked. "Esther won't have to tell it again."

"I disagree," Karl said. "I think we need to leave Don out of this. For now, at least."

"What?" Robbi voiced the question that was on Patrick's mind. "Eddie and Don were best friends and he promised Eddie's mom—"

"Never thought I'd say this," Jeanne said, "but Karl may have a point. What's up?"

"Thanks, Jeanne—I think. I'm the dumb jock here, but I gotta say something." Karl looked at Lance, Jeanne and Esther and asked, "Didn't you three talk about this last Friday at Jeanne's tribal elders' council?" They looked confused but nodded. "You missed something. Kind of important too. Don told me Esther's news about this NIS Agent Gared—"

"—who Don says is the mystery man from Balboa Park who was also at Eddie's funeral."

"Yes, ma'am," Karl said to Jeanne. "Agent Gared claims he was at WC's the night—the night—" Karl's voice choked up and Patrick put his arms around Karl's shoulders. "The last night we saw Eddie alive. *However*, Lance didn't see an NIS agent—"

"Didn't see anyone who *looked* like an NIS agent," Lance said.

"Now we're gettin' to my point." Karl looked at Lance for confirmation. "Lance saw Eddie leave with a guy who was short, dark and muscular. Esther, how would you describe Agent—?"

"Holy shit!" Slapping her forehead, Jeanne said, "Of course! Oh my God, Don and I were too blinded by our own anti-NIS prejudices to see what should've been fucking obvious!"

Karl looked smug. Lance, Robbi and Esther looked puzzled. Patrick asked, "What—?"

"Eddie left WC's with a good-looking, well-built guy—who happened to be Agent Gared."

Patrick let Jeanne's declaration sink in. Although he hadn't known Eddie, Don had described him as being too perceptive and cautious to be duped by an undercover investigator. "If that's true," Patrick said, "and this Agent Gared was the last person to see Eddie alive, then—"

"Don will fucking kill him," Karl said. "That, my dear Watson, is why Don can't know."

"Again—things I thought I'd never say—Karl *definitely* has a point," Jeanne said. "Let's hear Esther's news. If it's something Don should know, we'll tell him." Catching Patrick's eye, she said, "I mean, if it's something *Patrick* thinks Don should know, *he* can tell him."

"They record our telephone calls at work," Esther said. "They don't listen to the tapes much but they keep them for seven days then record over them. I listened to Agent Gared's phone calls this week. Until today, there wasn't anything interesting. It was strange, but he seemed more cheerful this week than since he started working there."

"Fucking bastard." Karl clenched his teeth. "He killed Eddie and now he's cheerful?"

"Let's be careful what we say," Jeanne said. "We don't know for sure what happened."

"Agent Gared worked only on his assigned cases this week, from what I could tell," Esther said. "I was about to give up and report to you guys that the trail had gone cold."

"What happened today?" asked Lance as Esther looked in the bottom of her bag.

"I made a copy of the tape." Esther showed them a microcassette recorder. "This afternoon he called his home answering machine. Surprising, because he's usually so secretive and he knows they record these calls." She pressed PLAY. "Maybe you guys know what this means."

Esther turned up the volume. A voice with a heavy Southern accent said, "Hey Jay-man. Guess who? You ain't returned my calls this week but no hard feelin's. I told you that MEU got back this week. You won't miss this opportunity to go fag huntin' tonight. Here's—I want you to pick me up, but just in case ya' don't, here's the address. Ya' ready to copy? It's 125 El Cajon Boulevard. I say again, that's one-two-five El Cajon Boulevard." The tape went silent.

"What's '125 El Cajon Boulevard'?" Jeanne asked. "*Where* is that?"

Robbi shrugged. "Don't know, but hearing that asshole say 'fag hunting' gives me chills."

Karl and Lance smirked, prompting Patrick to ask, "The boys know that address, don't you?"

"Well, gang, looks like Lance and me are going on a fact-finding mission tonight," Karl said.

"What gives?" Jeanne asked. "Where're you going? Whatever you're doing, be careful."

Karl put his hand on Lance's shoulder. "Don't get the wrong idea, ex-boyfriend, 'cause I know you still think about me when you jack off. But me and you are goin' to a bathhouse."

Leonard was afraid his outburst would result in a lecture from the general about the proper way for a brigadier general–select to conduct himself in front of other colonels. General Neville, though, didn't say anything and used the break to return messages. Leonard tried to de-stress. He stared out the window facing the massive dual opposing runways surrounded by aircraft hangars. Thinking of Karl and his mysterious group of gay military friends, Leonard wondered how many Marines working in those hangars right this minute were gay. In keeping with that thought, Chris and Jungle returned with his Cobra. "Ten till four," he said. "Perfect."

"We have one item left on our agenda," said the general, reconvening the meeting. "More accurately, there are two items, but unfortunately, they've merged. The future of this base—and Congressman Edward Coughlin." A loud groan went around the room, prompting the general to raise his hands. "That's *precisely* the type of attitude we cannot afford. I learned this week that Marine Corps Air Station El Toro is at the top of the short list for closure when they make the announcement in May. We cannot let that happen and we must be able to depend on Coughlin."

The situation made Leonard nauseous. The general was emphatic. "Whatever Coughlin wants from this Aircraft Wing, he gets. Is that understood?" Everyone nodded, including Leonard. Like a good Marine, he'd followed orders for almost thirty years and he would follow them—*most* of them—into the near future. But it didn't get any easier.

"Secretary Aspin gave a profound statement during his testimony before the Senate. He said 'the current situation in Congress right now is not a split between hawks and doves, between liberals and conservatives, between Democrats and Republicans. It's between those people that have military bases and facilities in their districts and those who don't.' He's right, and that's a tragedy! Our job is to train these Marines to wage, win and survive war. Unfortunately, the people who pay our bills and make our rules are playing politics with our bases, and ultimately our lives. We must keep this base open *at all costs*! There are 435 members of Congress, but only one is ours and his name is Coughlin. If he's not on our side, we'll be fed to the wolves. Hate to end on such a dire note, but I've said enough. Let's adjourn to the officers' club."

"Hop in."

Throwing his duffel bag in the back seat of Jay's car, Zack climbed in the front. "It's good to see ya' again, there, Jay-man. I was gettin' worried you'd turned chicken shit." He gave Jay a good-natured jab on the shoulder.

Jay pulled away from the train station. "Not a chance," he said, smiling. "I was just—busy this week. Had a lot of catching up to do. Where do you want to go now?"

"Get somethin' to eat. Hell, I'll even buy this time since today was payday. After that, we need to go back to your house and take a nap."

"A nap?" Jay asked. "That's all, right? A nap."

Zack laughed. "Look at you, you horny fuckin' bastard! Yeah, we need to sleep 'cause we got a long night of catchin' queers ahead of us."

27

"What photographer? No one said anything about a photographer."

"Jeanne, don't worry about it," Don said. "Kathryn Angel said our faces will be blurry."

Jeanne scowled and stormed into the kitchen. "I guess she doesn't approve," Patrick said.

"She had a rough time after they booted her out. She doesn't want us to have to endure it."

Kathryn arrived ten minutes later with a *Washington Herald* photographer. Patrick escorted them into the living room, where Kathryn introduced the man, impressing Don that she remembered everyone's name. She pointed to large glass doors that opened to the balcony. "There? Incredible shot with the sunset over the ocean. Can you squeeze in the pier? Perfect." She paused. "I apologize for rushing. When the pictures are taken—with the little sunlight that's left—the photographer can leave. Then we'll sit down for a nice long chat." She turned to the photographer. "Get some shots with their arms around each other." The rest of the group moved safely away from the camera. "Is it ready? Good. Don—stand right—perfect. Patrick, you're a little taller, stand behind Don and put your arms—oh my God. Such a *shame* we can't use your faces! You're a great-looking couple. Seriously, you could be models. Okay, how's that?"

"Right on," said the photographer. Kathryn stepped back, letting him go to work. After twenty minutes of shooting the men in various poses, he said, "Think that's got it. Kate?"

Kathryn rubbed her chin, looking at the couple with a thoughtful expression. Slowly, she asked, "You guys ever had your picture taken by an award-winning world-renowned photographer before today? Well, now's your chance—while he's here—and it's on the *Herald's* dime. What do you say to a couple more shots—but without your shirts?"

"No way!" shouted Jeanne. "I thought you wrote for the *Washington Herald*, not *Playgirl*."

Kathryn kept her eyes on Don and Patrick. "It's up to the boys. What do you think?"

Don looked at Patrick. "Will we get copies of these pictures?"

"Oh—these prints will *only* be for you two," Kathryn said. "I promise you the *Herald* won't use any pictures you don't approve of. These are our gift to you for being so helpful."

"What do you say, handsome?" Don asked Patrick. "Wanna do it?"

"With you?" asked Patrick. "Of course I want to do it!"

Don stripped off his T-shirt, and as Patrick unbuttoned his striped flannel shirt, Don said, "Here, sexy. Let me do that for you."

"*Oh my God!* That is *so* hot!" shouted Kathryn. "Get that picture! Are you getting that shot?" The photographer went into action, taking numerous "action" photos of the dark Marine with the bulging arms and huge pecs, taking off the shirt of the slightly taller, leaner, fairer-skinned blond man. Robbi, Karl, Esther and Lance made catcalls while Jeanne's face exuded displeasure. The photographer snapped a few more shots of the shirtless men in varying poses. Minutes later, he packed up his equipment and departed.

As the guys put their shirts back on, Jeanne said, "This isn't a game, Don."

"I know." He hoped his voice sounded soft and comforting, as he'd angered his friend enough. "We won't let them use those pictures. They're just for Patrick and me to enjoy. When we're old, we can look back and say, 'Damn! Look at how hot we used to be!'"

"Then get a Polaroid camera like everyone else. Or borrow mine and Robbi's."

Kathryn returned to the apartment after walking the photographer out. "Ready to interview?"

"Yes," said Don. He smiled reassuringly at Jeanne then grabbed Patrick's hand and followed the reporter to the sofa. As she set up a tape recorder, Don asked Patrick, "Are you sure—?"

Patrick put his hand over Don's mouth. "Stop asking me. With you, I'm ready for anything."

"Ya' liked it, didn't ya'?"

Jay shook the plastic bottle, squirting mayonnaise on his hamburger bun. "Liked what?"

"The young pastor at your church. You. The tent in the woods." Zack took a huge bite of his cheeseburger, never breaking eye contact with his dinner companion.

Jay hesitated. Zack had reacted angrily when Jay had asked him if he and the former Marine in his building, Sebastian, had ever had sex. He didn't want another outburst. "I was young."

Their eyes remained locked. "Ain't what I asked." Neither man blinked.

"I didn't know what I was doing," Jay finally responded. "But yeah, I liked it."

Zack smiled. "Was that so hard?" Downing some beer, he added, "But that's bullshit. You knew *exactly* what you was doin'. How long did you do it?"

"Almost two years." Jay looked at his plate. "I liked having a person be nice to me at that age. Pastor Stephen was the only one. He respected me."

"Where was your mom? Wasn't she nice to ya'?"

"She was there," Jay said. "But that's about all. She was more afraid of my dad than I was. But she didn't do anything to stop Dad from—"

"Stop what? Thought all your dad ever did was spank ya'," Zack said, wolfing down a couple of thick French fries. "It was more than just spankin's, wasn't it."

"Yeah. More like beatings. Hell, it *was* a beating. Black eyes, bruises on my legs."

"That's good, let it all out," said Zack, using his mock–social worker voice. Reverting to his usual accent, he asked, "When's the last time you saw Pastor Stephen?"

"Fifteen years ago."

"What'd you do if you saw him today?" Zack asked. "Kill him? Ignore him? Fuck him?" He licked some ketchup off his fingertips. "Kiss him tenderly?"

"Kinda hard to kill a man who's already dead."

"Holy shit!" Zack's eyes had never looked wider. "What happened? How'd he die?"

Jay cleaned the remnants of his meal from his hands, wadded up the napkin and threw it on his plate. "I'm through talking about the past. Tell me what's in store for tonight."

"Sounds good to me," said Zack. "How much I owe you for this dinner? Only got a ten."

Jay laughed as he slid his plate across the table. "Forget about it."

"I'm sure you both know more than I do about President Clinton's proposal—or rather his campaign promise—to lift the ban on gay men and lesbians in the military."

"Probably not," said Patrick. "You're the one in the news business. I hate politics—it distracts me from my focus: learning to fly the Cobra. When I'm not doing that, I spend as much time as possible on positive things, like doing stuff with Don and our friends."

"Life's thrown us some curveballs," said Don. "My ruckus with that asshole Coughlin—"

"Your sudden notoriety." Kathryn laughed. "Has that caused any problems?"

Patrick looked at Don and Don looked at the microcassette tape spinning around, recording every word. "My disciplinary hearing is in seven days. Haven't heard anything else about it."

"That's—February 12." Kathryn adjusted the notepad on her lap and tucked her hair behind her ears. "This issue has been going *crazy* in Washington. On one side, there's the President and a minority in Congress who want to lift the ban and let gays and lesbians serve in the military. The other side is the military—you know Colin Powell and the Joint Chiefs of Staff—and a majority of Congress who want to keep the status quo, *i.e.* the DoD Directive barring gays and lesbians. Then there's a *third* side—mostly Republicans—who want to pass a federal law forbidding gays and lesbians from serving in the military under any circumstances."

"That's bullshit!" Don said. "Don't they get it? They debate *if* we can serve while I've *served* for fifteen years. The fact I'm gay doesn't make a bit of difference."

"Very good point," said Kathryn. "The capital has reached a stalemate—a six-month ceasefire then they'll revisit the issue." She raised her eyes and smiled. "You're right, Don. They're missing the big picture." Patrick leaned forward and grabbed Don's hand. "You guys are already serving in the Marines. I look at you two—so obviously in love—" Kathryn paused.

Don blushed. Kathryn said, "You two just met, but I can tell what I see in front of me." Don gave Patrick a quick kiss on the lips. "My editor loved my idea. It might seem cheesy, but trust me, it'll be great. The first part will be in the Sunday, February 14 issue—Valentine's! What a great coincidence. Three months later, in May, we'll do a follow-up story. We'll show what it's like for two men trying to build a relationship in a hostile environment."

Don paused to absorb the concept and then looked at Patrick, who said, "That's a *great* idea. You've really hit on something that everyone else involved in this debate seems to be missing. We're Marines, but we're human beings and this is a human story. What do you think, Don?"

Don agreed and Kathryn said, "Super! Let's move along to the questions." They told her about coming out, meeting each other and forming their group of friends. Next, she queried them about their activities as a couple. "For example, can you go to the movies together?"

"Besides the ban," Don said, "there's the military's code against fraternization. Patrick's an officer and I'm from the senior enlisted ranks."

"But when you go to a movie theater," she said, "you're in civilian clothes, right? So no one knows your rank. What's the problem?"

"Oceanside's a Marine town," Don explained. "Whenever I go out, I run into someone from my battalion or a Marine I've worked with who knows my rank. If I'm with another senior enlisted Marine, it's no big deal." Don smiled affectionately at his lover. "But Patrick looks just like a lieutenant. Not sure why but any Marine would know he's an officer. Technically, it's a violation of the UCMJ for a gunny, an E-7, to hang out with a first lieutenant, an O-2."

"To answer your question," Patrick said, "no. We can't go to the movies together, we can't work out together, we can't even go running along the beach in front of my apartment together. Couldn't take him with me to a Super Bowl party my buddy Tim threw. We can't eat out together, at least not around the base. Although—a few nights ago—"

"—a few nights ago we did something stupid." Don put his arm around Patrick's shoulders. "We walked out to the end of the pier and ate dinner at that restaurant."

"It was Monday night. The place was empty," Patrick said, shaking his head. "Hopefully we'll be fine. If he were another pilot, it wouldn't be a problem—to a point. But even then, if two officers of the same rank are seen out together too many times, it looks suspicious."

"Especially when you hit thirty," said Don. "If you're not married, people wonder why."

Kathryn looked at Don. "You're—are you? Over thirty?"

"Yes," said Don. "But I'm married. To a woman. Another Marine—my rank—in Japan."

Kathryn stared open-mouthed. "I don't get this. Feels like I'm in an episode of the *Twilight Zone*. You've explained it to me and

I'll listen to the tape later, but it's another world for me—as I'm sure it will be for most of my readers. So what *do* you two do together? Stay inside?"

"If I had my way, we would." Don raised his eyebrows. "Fortunately in Southern California we have options. We go out together in San Diego. We feel safe in the Hillcrest area. Well—we *used* to feel safe," he added softly.

"Before Eddie," Patrick said, comforting Don.

Kathryn was looking at her notes and didn't comment. Instead, she said, "Not only are you breaking the military's ban against homosexuality by being who you are and in the military—"

"And by having gay sex, which is still a crime under the code," Don said.

"—and that, you're also breaking the rule against fraternization." She looked up from her notes. "Does it bother you that you're breaking all these laws?"

"No," Patrick answered. "If the law is unjust, I break it with a clean conscience. Call it the 'Oliver North' defense. It was okay for him to break the law and lie to Congress about illegal arms sales because he didn't like the law or Congress. Just following Colonel North's example."

"Never thought of it that way." Don laughed. "The ban and the UCMJ article against sodomy are double standards. If they were serious about throwing people out of the military for sexual misconduct, we wouldn't have a military. They ignore most heterosexual misconduct."

"That's—that's very good," said Kathryn as she wrote. "Last weekend in North Carolina, three Marines went to a gay bar and beat up a gay man pretty badly. They screamed, 'Clinton must pay.' Do you worry that might happen to you?"

"It could happen," Don said. "It's something we think about."

"It's patronizing and hypocritical for so-called leaders to say that the ban is for our protection." Patrick's sudden passionate display turned Don on. "That's like the mayor of a Southern town keeping African-Americans out of a public swimming pool, saying 'it's 'cause they might drown.' It's bullshit. He doesn't care about blacks, just like the generals don't care about us. Don't discriminate against us, and let us take care of ourselves. Besides, someone who lives their life paralyzed by fear isn't the type who joins the Marines."

"The rules against us," Don said, "are like a green light for some Marines to be violent."

"To make sure I'm following you—you're saying that if the military allowed gays and lesbians to serve, other people in the military would be less inclined to commit gay bashing?"

"Don's saying that officially sanctioned discrimination reinforces personal prejudices."

"Wow, thanks, Patrick," said Kathryn as she wrote. "This is going to be a great story."

Jay closed the door to his bedroom and sat on his sofa to watch television. Zack was asleep but Jay wasn't one for naps. He picked up the remote control, but before he could turn on the news, he had a visitor. "What's going on, Jay?" Pastor Stephen's ghost sat beside him and smiled. "You've never told anyone about us. Why the Marine?"

"I don't know," Jay answered quietly. "No, Pastor Stephen, that's not true. Being with him reminds me of when I was with you. It feels—I'm not alone again. It feels good."

"I'm glad," said the ghost. "It's okay if you want to tell him what happened."

"But—it's not just—" Jay said, but Pastor Stephen disappeared as quickly as he'd arrived. "It's not you I'm worried about," Jay whispered. His body tensed because he knew who'd visit him next. He didn't know when, but he was certain it would happen.

"We'll walk you to your car," Patrick said as he and Don followed Kathryn outside.

"You Marines are such gentlemen," she said. "I'm sure I'll have some follow-up questions as I work on the story. But I'll call you with those next week." She agreed to send them copies of the best photographs, especially the shirtless ones, and to update them on any developments.

"I hope we've made the right decision," Patrick said as she drove away.

"We have," said Don. "That's my gut reaction."

Patrick put his hand on the doorknob to reenter his apartment but froze when a familiar voice shouted his name. "McAbe! You dirt bag!"

"Who's that?" asked Don.

"Fuck! It's my worst nightmare. Tim Roberts is crashing my gay housewarming party."

"Locker number one twenty-five, your room is ready."

Zack checked the number attached to his springy plastic bracelet. "Fuckin' A, Jay-man, that's us." Drops of water poured from his naked body as he climbed out of the hot tub. "What're you lookin' at?" he barked at three men seated in the far corner. He dried himself and wrapped the towel around his waist. They looked at the water and pretended not to hear.

After Zack left the area, one of them said, "Your friend doesn't *have* to be such an asshole."

"I know," Jay replied. "It's a choice." Deciding he'd had enough of the hot tub, he walked to the front to find Zack. Jay navigated the darkly lit corridors where men hovered in the doorways to their little rooms. Four or five showed him their erections, enlarged by leather or rubber cock rings affixed to the base of their penises. The San Diego bathhouse reminded him of the ones he'd visited in other cities. The odor resulted from the ongoing battle between bleach and mold, but Jay suspected mold was winning. Sex also permeated every corner of the facility, mixing the smells of semen and lube with poppers, pot and other drugs.

In case the bathhouse customers weren't sure what to do, TV sets located throughout the club provided round-the-clock demonstrations of man-on-man action. The background music was a house-techno-trance hybrid heard only in this environment. Because the building had no windows, its interior had never seen sunlight. The place was mostly vacant by day, springing to life at night, giving it a vampire-like atmosphere. Being here made Jay one of the vampires.

"Here ya' are," said Zack. "We got a great room. Follow me."

"Wanna get our clothes out of the locker?" Jay asked.

Frowning, Zack shook his head and motioned for Jay to follow him to their room in a back corner. It had its own television set with clear images of orgies. Zack locked the door. "We're havin' guys in here, but we ain't lettin' 'em rob us blind." Zack set a small black bag on a short wooden shelf by the bed frame. He slapped the mattress. "Sit here." His towel was open, reminding Jay of the fun they'd had a week earlier, except tonight Zack wore a leather cock ring.

Jay hadn't felt comfortable since arriving at the sex club. He'd hoped that familiarizing himself with the place would ease his anxiety. It didn't and Zack's odd behavior increased his apprehension. "Thought we were here to catch Marines and Sailors."

"Chill the fuck out, man." Zack grabbed the bag. "We will. It's early. The military fags will get here later." As Jay's eyes adjusted to the darkness in the room, he saw Zack pull out a lighter and a small glass vial. In a low voice, he asked, "Ever done tina? You know—crystal?"

"I know what tina is. I've never done it." Suddenly Jay felt sick. He was angry with himself for trusting Zack and he was angry with Zack for betraying him with an illegal drug. Sadness also weighed him down because this new revelation about Zack had just ended their friendship.

"Wanna try it?" Zack put a small amount of the compound in one end of the glass pipe.

"No," said Jay. "Can't really have a good time—or do my job— if I'm out of control."

"You're funny." Zack put the other end of the glass tube to his lips. "Bein' outta control is the *only* way I can have fun." He flicked the lighter and held the flame under the pipe.

Jay stood up. "I'm going to walk around."

"Suit yourself. You know where I'll be—or not."

Jay didn't look behind. "I'll be back." But he knew he wouldn't.

* * *

"Tim! What's—what—? Hi, Melanie."

Don knew what he needed to do. "Hey, man, I'll go inside to see what the women are up to."

"Sure," said Patrick. It saddened Don to see Patrick so petrified. He wanted to fix it.

Entering the apartment, Don motioned for the others to listen. "There's a problem. Patrick has a straight Marine friend outside. Guys butch it up. Girls do—whatever it is you need to do."

"Shit," said Karl. "Is he a helicopter pilot? He'll recognize Robbi and me from the colonel's office." He glanced at Lance. "Me and Lance will leave now. Let's climb down the balcony and go around the building." Sliding the glass doors open, Karl stepped onto the patio.

"Fuck it," said Lance, racing into the bedroom to grab his and Karl's jackets. "'Let's climb down the balcony' my ass! Thought I was done with obstacle courses." He threw a good night kiss to everyone. "Tell Patrick we said 'thanks'!" He followed his ex-boyfriend outside.

Karl was halfway down. "Shit! Forgot my—Lance, can you get—?"

"One step ahead of ya'!" Lance whispered loudly, tossing Karl's jacket to him.

When the boys were out of sight, Don looked at Robbi. "Robbi—can you—?"

"Back in the closet." She grabbed some water and opened the door. "Glad it's a walk-in."

Through the door, Don overheard the exchange between Patrick and Tim. "We had dinner at the restaurant on the pier," Tim said. "You said we could stop by anytime, so here we are."

"I *told* him we should call first," the woman said.

"I didn't have your number," Tim said. "Man, that was a hot babe who left. Who's she?"

"Oh, a friend," Patrick said, his voice filled with tension. "Um, she's visiting from DC."

"Did you meet her at Quantico? Why didn't you—?" Pausing briefly, Tim exclaimed, "Patrick! You're a dog. You saw her in DC while Karen was back in Chicago? Is she the reason you ditched Karen? Now it's all startin' to make sense."

"Tim, maybe we should go now," said the woman.

"Um—" Patrick said. Don desperately wanted to rescue Patrick from his discomfort but he wasn't sure how. Maybe he could step outside the door, say he was taking the girls home, and then come back when the pilot left—

"Melanie, it's Chris Ashburn!" said Tim. "Have a good flight with the group commander?"

"Holy shit. As if things couldn't get more complicated," Don said, "Chris just showed up."

Jeanne shook her head in frustration. "This is ridiculous." Pushing Don gently to the side, she opened the door. "Why is everyone standing out here in the chilly night air? Come inside."

Tim and Melanie looked surprised to see two strangers in Patrick's doorway. Chris looked like a deer caught in headlights and Patrick looked terrified. Don, unsure what to do, put his hand on Jeanne's shoulder. "Patrick, invite your friends in for a drink. Jeanne and I would love to meet them." As the group filed in, Don whispered to Chris, "You're Esther's boyfriend, okay?"

"Who's Esther? She the one with the T-shirt that says, 'i'm constantly craving k.d. lang'?"

"Shit," Don said as the two men laughed together. "That's Esther."

"This is gonna be fun," said Chris. "Too bad your reporter wasn't here to see it."

28

Jay navigated the bathhouse's labyrinthine passageways alone for at least half an hour. Finding a seat in a dark corner with a view of the front, he observed a steadily increasing number of men enter the club. He was glad some looked like servicemen, justifying his presence in this den of iniquity. He preferred the quickness of hunting for military gays in the bookstores but the bathhouse had its advantages. Nakedness helped sort military men from fakers. In addition to the striped-scalp tan lines caused by military caps and haircuts, Marines and Soldiers had indentations on their legs three-and-a-half to four inches above their ankles. The mark was because servicemen tied the bottom of their camouflage trousers tightly against their boots with either strings or elastic bands. These inevitably slid off the boot leather and onto their lower calves, leaving a mark. If a man had the haircut, the tattoo, the striped tan-line around his scalp and the ring around his upper ankle, Jay gave him a ninety-nine percent chance of being the real thing.

Zack hurried by without noticing Jay. Two men—not military—pursued the Marine MP. Jay cursed himself for believing that unstable Zack could be his ally in this fight. Like gay men, Zack was a slave to his physical pleasures—a quintessential hedonist. The good feelings Jay had felt last weekend and his anticipation for tonight had tempted him away from his calling. He was frustrated, lonely and about to leave when a man arrived whom Jay recognized as a friend of Johnson's. He was the short Sailor or Marine at the park who'd been at Johnson's funeral. Jay's spirits lifted—now he understood his purpose for being here tonight. Waiting a safe distance, he followed the man into the locker room. Tonight had just become much more interesting.

The last hour had begun awkwardly but Patrick's friends quickly warmed to each other. Alcohol helped grease the conversation and Don, Jeanne and Chris were old pros at what they called "heteroception"—pretending to be heterosexual by active deception. Tim bought all their lies about how Chris met Esther, Jeanne's old friend who was with Don. Patrick stood alone on the balcony, listening to the waves and watching his friends through the glass. Although Chris and Esther were laughably mismatched, Don and Jeanne easily passed as a couple who'd been together a long time. In a way, Patrick realized, they were. His jealousy surprised him.

The doors slid open and shut and Melanie joined him. She took a sip of wine and they turned to face the ocean. "Tim doesn't get why you'd invite Chris and his friends but exclude us."

"Thank you for not telling him." He turned to face her. "You know, about Chris and me."

"Not my place." Melanie put her hand on Patrick's sleeve. "I've known Tim since high school. You've known him almost as long. He's a good guy. He's met my gay friends in Seattle. He doesn't have a problem with it."

Patrick was amazed how easily the "G" word had passed between them, as if he'd just crossed a major hurdle only to discover it was the easiest thing he'd ever done. "He's my best friend in the Corps. But your friends aren't Cobra pilots. A huge difference in our world."

"I know. I've thought about that." She rubbed the rim of her glass with her finger and added, "It's your decision. But you can trust him."

Patrick and Melanie looked over their shoulders into the living room, where Tim laughed along with the others. "I want to believe you're right. But it's a risk and it's not just me."

Melanie let out a little laugh. "Last week at the dining in, I wondered if you and Chris were a couple but, as Tim said earlier, 'it all starts to make some sense.' Don and Jeanne make a fine-looking pair but not nearly as fine as Don and *Patrick*." Looking at her fiancé, she said, "Straight guys are so—" She sighed. "Tim could spot an enemy target fifty miles away. Any sport he plays or watches, his intuition about the game is perfect. But when it comes to people, the man doesn't have a clue what's going on right under his nose. For goodness' sake, Esther has 'k. d. lang' stretched across her tits." Patrick laughed so hard he almost choked.

"Gay Marines depend on that inconsistency for our survival. Like you said—he's a good guy. Takes people at face value. He's not cynical—looking for what others might be hiding."

"But, Patrick, this is just my opinion so please take it for what it's worth. Forgive me if I'm overstepping the bounds of our friendship."

"Bounds?" He leaned against the railing. "As long as we've been friends? What bounds?"

She smiled and nodded. "I've known gay men who are angry at the world because the world shuts them out," she said slowly. "It's understandable. But they react by shutting out the people who love them. That, I don't understand. Tim loves you. He doesn't have any brothers of his own—he thinks of you as his brother." She put her chin on Patrick's shoulder and looked up.

The heavy glass doors slid open. "Hey, what're you doing out here, bro'?" Tim asked in a joking voice. "Scammin' on my woman?"

"I tried to seduce him," Melanie said, "but he said he couldn't betray his best friend."

"What?" Tim asked in mock indignation. "My girl ain't pretty enough for you?"

"I'm feeling a little cold," said Melanie. "I'll step back inside and you men can work this out between yourselves." Patrick winked at Melanie as she disappeared from the balcony.

Tim put his arm around Patrick's shoulder and sipped his beer. "You got a fun group of friends. Jeanne even owns a bar! Now *that's* my kinda gal! You should've invited us over."

Patrick turned his head and looked into his friend's eyes. "You're right. I'll grab another round. Stay right here, okay? There's— there's something I need to tell you."

"I could get fired for doing this, ya' know."

Lance slipped the attendant a twenty. "Karl tell you about the undercover agent?" The man nodded as he secured the bathhouse's rear emergency exit. "Motherfucker will recognize me."

"Hope you catch 'em. Assholes down at vice wanna run us outta business. Hate all those bastards." The attendant gave Lance a towel. "Karl's room is two doors down on the right."

"Thanks. Next time you're at WC's, drinks are on me." Lance counted doors and knocked. "It's Lance." Karl opened the door wearing only a thin, small towel. "Damn."

"Get in here." Karl looked at Lance's crotch. "Glad I still got that effect on you."

"Don't flatter yourself, Don Juan." Stripping out of his clothes, Lance wrapped the towel around his waist. "Been so long since I got laid, a stiff breeze could make my dick hard."

"Ready for your five-paragraph order?" Karl asked in a quiet but forceful voice.

"Cut out that Marine Corps bullshit," Lance said, folding his clothes and hiding them under the bed. "'Five-paragraph order' my ass. You ain't no grunt—you're a driver for a pilot."

"SMEAC—'S'—Situation—"

"The 'situation' is we're in a goddamned bathhouse," Lance said. "In scratchy towels."

"'M'—Mission," said Karl, clearly intent on following standard operating procedures. "My mission will be: To lure person most likely to be NIS agent into the steam room."

Lance had no choice but to play along. "My mission is to hide in the steam room and confirm if the person you lure in is the same guy who left WC's with Eddie. If he is, I'll come back here. Now quit fucking around—we gotta get busy."

"'E'—Execution. Let's execute this motherfucker."

"Don't think that's what they mean by execution, Devildog." Lance opened the door.

"We got two more paragraphs!" Karl protested.

Stepping into the hallway, Lance kissed his ex-boyfriend. "See ya' in the steam room."

"Why so serious?" Tim took a beer from Patrick. "You upset I found out about your babe? Bro', that's your business. I liked Karen, but if you were gettin' some on the sly in DC, then—"

"Tim!" Patrick said. "It's—it's not like that. I never cheated on Karen."

"Woulda been surprised, but either way it's cool. Who you sleep with is your business."

"I hope—hope you mean that." Tim looked puzzled. "Because—Tim, buddy—I'm—" Patrick looked over Tim's shoulder and stared across the Pacific. For the first time, he was about to come out to a straight friend. The way he felt right now reminded him of the first time he'd jumped off the rappelling tower at Officer Candidate School, secured only by his grip on a rope. Postponing the leap never make it easier. He took a large gulp of beer. "I'm gay."

Tim blinked a couple of times but his expression didn't change. He smiled and a few seconds later said, "That's cool." Patrick waited while his friend absorbed the full impact of this news. "Wow. Never—I never saw this coming." Now it was Tim's turn to take a big drink. "But it's totally cool. I mean—wait—was that babe a *dude*? Holy shit, I couldn't—"

"Jesus, Roberts! No, the babe was a babe—I mean, a *woman*. I'll—I'll explain that later."

As if on cue, Melanie returned to the balcony. Tim asked, "Do—is it okay—if we tell—?"

"Honey," Melanie said sweetly, "I already know."

"You know?" Tim looked through the glass doors. "Do they know?" Patrick observed as a wave of awareness crossed Tim's face. "I'll be damned. Chris Ashburn—?"

Patrick shook his head. "Tim, don't assume anything about the

others. You're *my* friend. I trust you with my career and my liveli-
hood because, well, we have this bond between us."

Melanie smiled as her fiancé slowly grasped the full impact of
Patrick's revelation. "Wow," he said. "You really *do* trust me. Man,
that—that means so much!" Tim gave Patrick a big hug. When
Patrick got over his initial shock, he returned his friend's embrace.

"Oh my God, this is so sweet!" Melanie said. "Wish I had my
camera."

"From now on, bro'," said Tim, "please don't shut me out of
your life. Promise?"

"I won't. That's a promise."

Jay stood in the shadowy corridor leading to the wet area—the
pool, hot tub and steam room. Johnson's friend circled twice. Men
stood along the halls, in corners, or in open doorways lusting after
Johnson's friend, the bathhouse's most desirable occupant tonight.
Not surprisingly, the man strolled by with an air of confident dis-
dain for those less-worthy, taunting them to look and admire, but
only from a distance.

Zack's room was around the corner. Jay lost count of the men
who'd gone in, some for brief periods but others for longer
amounts of time. Zack, however, hadn't emerged. As Jay was trying to forget about him, Johnson's buddy passed by a third time.
He walked more deliberately than before, slowing almost to a stop.
He looked at Jay. Without speaking, he jerked his head in the direction of the wet area. Jay followed ten feet behind, pursuing him
into the steam room. After Jay's bad experience with Zack, he felt
good returning to his original mission.

The steam reduced visibility to less than four feet. Tile-covered
benches lined each wall. As Jay fumbled past, a man to his right
was on his knees burrowing his face in a guy's crotch. To Jay's left, a
naked man sat alone, his towel draped over his head. Jay couldn't
see his face and the man left the steam room as Jay walked by, but
Jay didn't care. His prey was just ahead.

Sweat beaded and dripped from every pore in Jay's body as he
walked toward the back. Johnson's friend sat on the bench, his
back slouched against the wall. Jay sat beside him, careful not to

touch him too soon. When the man glanced in Jay's direction, Jay dropped his right hand from his lap into the empty space between their legs. He touched the man's thigh, which the man pressed firmly against Jay's hand. The man opened his towel and Jay moved his hand toward the man's crotch. As Jay was about to touch the guy's dick, he grabbed Jay's wrist. "Not here. Too many pervs. Follow me."

"Sure." Jay was glad the man had a room as Jay could learn more about him in private. They'd also go farther sexually, and the more acts the serviceman performed, the more violations Jay could bring against him on Monday morning.

Don watched with amusement as Tim hugged Patrick, curious about what they were discussing. "While Tim and Melanie are outside," he said to Esther, "any news about Eddie?"

"Sorry, Don. Nothing crossed Director Tolson's desk," Esther said. "The only good news—if you wanna call it that—they ruled inconclusive evidence on the drug-dealing allegations."

"No shit," said Don. "Even after Ricky's article, they're still gonna say it was a suicide?"

"'Fraid so," she said. Don shook his head in anger. Unbeknownst to his friends, he'd also approached Giles, who'd convincingly denied making the anonymous call about a drug deal.

"Maybe I'm misreading the balcony scene," Chris said, offering a distraction from the impasse, "but I think Patrick's housewarming party just became his 'coming out' party."

"Serious? Think that's what going on out there?" It was a great next step for Patrick.

Esther said, "He makes a cute debutante."

"He's gotta be careful," said Jeanne. "He'll get in trouble if he tells too many people."

"I trust Patrick's judgment," said Don. "If he just came out to Tim, I will too."

"I've known Patrick over a year," said Chris. "He's cautious. I'm sure he told you Melanie figured us out a week ago." Don nodded and Chris changed the subject again. "Where's Karl?"

"Took off with Lance. Not sure where," said Don. Jeanne and

Esther looked at each other and shrugged. "Oh no, Chris. Don't tell me you're interested in Karl. He's a heartbreaker."

"Hmmm, a young Marine who looks like he stepped off the cover of *Muscle and Fitness*. And he's a desirable heartbreaker." Chris laughed and took a drink. "Mother of all shockers."

Don scratched his head. "Yeah—but lately, I don't know. He's been actin' weird."

"We take it up the ass, Don. That by itself is weird in most people's opinions."

Everyone laughed and Don said, "Karl disappears for long periods. Doesn't say where he is. Hasn't hooked up in months. Lately he's got lots of cash—designer clothes. Paged at all hours."

"Think he's a rent-boy?" No one answered. "Does he have time? What's his Marine job?"

"That's a funny story," said Don. "He's supposed to be in aviation logistics. But midway through last year, some colonel handpicked Karl to be his personal driver."

"Aviation colonel at Camp Pendleton?" Chris asked. "Has to be helicopters. Which one?"

"Think the name's Spencer."

Chris had the best poker face Don had ever seen, but for a moment, he thought he detected a crack. "*Leonard* Spencer?" Chris's poker face returned. The women didn't seem to notice.

Don shrugged. Laughing, Jeanne said, "Marines don't call colonels by their first names."

"How old is Karl?"

"Forget about Karl, okay?" Don said. "I *hate* it when my friends date—or trick—with each other. Complicates my life. But if you insist, he's twenty-three—your preferred age bracket."

Chris smiled and looked at the floor. Looking up, he said, "Karl's gonna be okay. *Better* than okay. Can't say how I know, but trust your buddy and back off about his business."

Before Don could question Chris further, the glass doors slid open. "Everyone," Patrick said. "Got something to—to share. Um, you all know this about me already, but I just told Tim—"

"What the—!" Tim shouted. "Is that—? Corporal Reynolds! Is that you?"

Everyone looked to the back as Robbi low-crawled across the carpet from Patrick's bedroom toward the bathroom. Standing up, she said, "Can I come out of the closet now? I gotta pee!"

"Wanna fuck me?"

Jay nodded. Johnson's friend put his key in the lock. "Good. We get inside, lay on your back. I'll sit on your dick. You hard?" He felt Jay's erection. "Good." Opening the door, the man led Jay to the thin mattress. "Gimme your towel." Jay did and lay down on his back. Closing the door, Johnson's friend removed his towel, exposing his firm body and hard penis. He stepped onto the sides of the small bed and straddled Jay from above. "Nice cock."

"Thanks," said Jay. "Got condoms? I'm always safe." Jay reached down to stroke himself. Suddenly, the man grabbed Jay's wrists, pinning them against the bed over his head. The man, using his body weight, dropped his torso on Jay, trapping him in place. "What the fuck are you doing?" Jay asked. "What kind of—?" The man plowed his knee into Jay's groin, causing him to moan in pain. The man's free hand muffled Jay's cries for help. Another guy emerged from the shadows but Jay couldn't see him well enough to identify him, although he wasn't big enough to be Hawkins. The guy blindfolded Jay, grabbing his wrists from the first man. To Jay's horror, he felt a cold steel blade against his neck. He tried to scream as the knife sliced through his skin but the man's hand over his mouth muted his pleas.

"Make another sound and I'll slice your fucking head off, you worthless piece of shit," the man whispered loudly in Jay's ear. "We'll have your corpse out the back door on its way to an unmarked grave in Baja in a heartbeat. 'Course it won't be *your* heartbeat 'cause you'll be *dead*." Jay's predicament was as bad as anything he'd ever experienced. Johnson's friends were serious about killing him. He had to think faster than ever before. "We know who you are, *Agent Jay Gared*." Jay felt paralyzed. They knew his name. They meant business. The man rubbed the cut on Jay's neck and stuck his fingers in Jay's mouth, causing him to taste the warm metallic-flavored liquid. "How's your blood taste, asshole?

Don't answer our questions—with the truth—it'll be the last thing in your mouth." The man drove his knee harder into Jay's groin.

"Ahhh," Jay said into the man's hand. He nodded and felt the hand move away from his mouth. He had an idea. "I'll tell you anything you want. But I know who you are."

"That right, motherfucker. Who are we?"

"Friends—friends of the Marine, Gunnery Sergeant Hawkins," Jay whispered between labored breaths. The blindfold prevented him from seeing their reaction but the silence and stillness told him he'd caught the men off guard. "Got a complete file on Hawkins. Anything happens to me—I don't show up Monday—another agent will find out Hawkins's name. He's a grunt at Camp Pendleton. Got his address, number, sworn statements from guys about sexual encounters. Got enough in that file on Hawkins to put him away at hard labor for years." Jay prayed they'd fall for his bluff—he didn't have any statements and hadn't yet opened the file.

The man paused. Jay's scheme might be working. Every cell in his brain focused on escaping from these two crazy men. As the nanoseconds slowly ticked by, he felt like he might be gaining some advantage. The man finally said, "What d'you know about Eddie Johnson?"

Jay had guessed this was what they wanted to know. "Killed himself. Gunshot to the head."

"Bullshit," the man snarled, putting more pressure on Jay's groin with his knee. "Eddie wouldn't kill himself. Not in a million years."

"Sure he did," Jay protested. "Lover died a year ago. Johnson found out he had HIV. Chose the quick way instead—ahhhhh!" Jay screamed in agony as the knee went deeper than ever.

"Fuck you!"

The occupant of the next room yelled, "Yeah! Fuck him harder!"

"Fuck you," Johnson's friend repeated, this time in a whisper. "Eddie was *not* HIV-positive. He woulda got kicked out of the Navy."

Jay had won. Johnson's HIV status had been his and Hawkins's dirty little secret for years and now it would be their Achilles' heel. Jay couldn't prove it—not yet—and he'd have to bluff his way now, but he believed his theory about Hawkins and Johnson switching blood samples was right. Not even Hawkins's closest friends knew what he'd done—hell, they didn't even know Johnson had HIV. "Not lyin' to ya', man," Jay said. "Autopsy showed he was positive."

Jay felt the heat of the man's breath on his face. "You left WC's with Eddie." Jay felt the blade leave his neck. Before he could feel relief, though, the man wedged the steel blade between the base of Jay's dick and his scrotum. Revving up his intensity, he lowered his voice and moved his mouth centimeters away from Jay's right ear. "So help me God. I'll cut your dick off real slow you don't tell me the truth about what happened at Eddie's house."

Tears rushed down Jay's face involuntarily. "I didn't kill him. I swear to God."

"What happened?"

"An accident," Jay managed to say between sobs. "I didn't mean—it wasn't supposed to—Ed—*Eddie* invited me. But he got suspicious. Pulled the gun on me. I got scared and jumped at him. Don't know why I jumped—just did." Jay gasped for air. The man eased back slightly and Jay continued. "He fell. Gun went off and the bullet went up through his head. I'm not bullshittin' ya'." Jay lost all concept of time. The man didn't say anything and Jay went into a hypnotic trance. His mind melded with the music and the orgies on the other sides of the thin walls. Jay wondered if he'd died and this was his hell, to spend the rest of eternity with these insane men, as they slowly and excruciatingly cut his body into thin slivers, kneeing his groin while all around him but out of sight, nasty men fucked every available orifice.

As suddenly as he'd gone into the trance, a voice inside said: *Save yourself.*

"Something else you don't know." Jay's voice was barely audible.

"Waitin'."

"Your buddy—Hawkins—switched his blood with Johnson's. That's how Johnson passed his HIV test every year."

The unknown man in the corner whispered, "Bullshit! Don wouldn't be that stupid."

"You're right." The man on top of Jay hesitated. "But he'd be that loyal."

"Anything happens to me," Jay said, gaining confidence, "the military will find out Johnson was HIV-positive *and* Hawkins broke the law, switching his own blood for Johnson's. Let me go— I'll make sure nothing happens to you, or to Hawkins or to any of your friends. If you hurt me, the military will find out."

"I'm the only one makin' deals around here, fucking asshole!" said the man, putting the knife back at Jay's throat. "Here's what's gonna happen. Thirty seconds, I'm kickin' you outta my room. You're gonna destroy that file you claim you got on Hawkins. If me or any of my friends *ever* sees you again, we'll fuckin' kill you. If any of us ever gets reported, we'll kill you. We know where you work, we know where you live, we know every move you make. Fuck with us, we'll kill you. Clear?" Jay's tears had stopped but his throat was clogged. "Am I clear?"

"Yes. It's clear," Jay gasped. A second later, the door opened and two pairs of hands threw him into the hallway. Removing the blindfold, he saw he was standing in front of horny men without his towel. He hurried to the locker rooms, his nakedness drawing plenty of unwelcome stares and a few uninvited physical advances. He passed Zack's room but the drug-using Marine was the last thing on his mind.

"Hey, get your towel on or get out," shouted one of the attendants. "You pay to get in?"

"I'm going." In forty-five seconds, Jay dressed, checked out and was in his car. Partly, he wanted to learn the identity of his attackers. But he realized he'd risked fate too many times recently. Instead of staying, he went home and lay awake in his bed.

29

"Did you plan a special treat for a nice lady, sir? Valentine's is Sunday—in just two days."

"Not this year," Patrick said. "What did you need me to sign, Corporal Delarosa?"

"Two things," said the squadron's personnel clerk, riffling through the filing cabinet for Patrick's Officer Qualification Record. "Commanding general's inspection is next month. All officers must review their OQR for accuracy." Opening the folder, she turned it upside down on the counter for Patrick's perusal. "Too bad you don't have a Valentine. Looks like perfect weather for a romantic picnic. But you've only been here a month—you'll find someone, sir."

"What am I reviewing, Corporal?" Patrick hoped his irritation didn't show. Her well-intentioned pleasantries reminded him of the lies he had to tell. The truth was that he hoped the man he'd fallen for had planned a special treat for *him*. Patrick laughed, recalling the saying: "The truth shall set you free." *Bullshit*, he thought. The truth would end life as he knew it.

Dropping the subject, the corporal switched to her bureaucratic voice. "First is your Record of Emergency Data. Your primary next of kin on your RED are Sean and Carol McAbe of Park Ridge, Illinois." Confirming the information, Patrick initialed beside his parents' names. "Next is your Servicemen's Group Life Insurance. The gov-

ernment increased the SGLI benefit to $150,000. You've desig-
nated 'Sean and Carol McAbe' as your beneficiaries. Correct, sir?"

*Carol, your son doesn't want to work with a bunch of queers. If that
president of yours has his way, fairies will be all over the place.*

"Actually, Corporal, does the SGLI beneficiary have to be the
same as the next of kin?"

"No sir. You can designate anyone you want. Would you like to
do that?"

"Yes I would. Thank you."

As the corporal searched for a blank form, Patrick confirmed in
his mind that this was what he wanted to do. Despite his dad's insensitive remarks, he wasn't doing this out of anger or spite. His
parents had plenty of money and Don didn't. Patrick loved his dad
and mom, but based on practical need, if something happened to
him, he'd rather Don have the money.

"Here you go, sir. Make sure you sign the bottom."

In bold letters, Patrick wrote "Hawkins, D. A." and Don's address. "I get a copy of this?"

Finishing his report for the week, Jay carried it to Ollie's office
for his review.

"You can go on in," said Esther. "He just finished a phone call."

"Thanks." Jay stuck his head in the door. "Ollie? Want to see
the Point Loma report?"

Ollie took off his reading glasses. "That wasn't due till next
week, but I'll look at it over the weekend. Nice to get ahead." He
held up his hand and motioned for Jay to bring it in to him. "I
looked over the work you did on the USS *Tripoli* matter. Very good
work, Jay. I'm impressed. You asked the right questions, took care
of all the details and your report's outstanding." He took the folder
from Jay and set it in his in box. "You've worked hard. Take a few
days off."

"Don't need to do that—but it's four now—how 'bout I just
knock off early and take it easy this weekend?" Ollie said all right
and Jay smiled faintly and closed the door.

"Glad to see that shaving cut on your neck healed," said Esther.
"Looked bad on Monday."

"Yeah. It did," said Jay as he ran his hand over the scar. "Have a good weekend, Esther."

"You do the same, Agent Gared."

Jay put on his sports coat. Two hours at the gym and then a long weekend at home. Alone. Dreading the arrival of his uninvited guest.

"How did the Non-Judicial Punishment hearing go?"

"Just like Karl's colonel said it would," Don said, entering Patrick's apartment. "No punishment, charges dropped."

"Awesome!" Patrick said as Don lifted him off his feet.

"To celebrate that," Don added, kissing his lover, "but mostly to celebrate our first Valentine's together, I've got a huge weekend planned for you."

Patrick looked surprised. "You didn't have to do that."

"I know, but you deserve it," Don said. "Pack a bag for three nights and two days, we're goin' for a drive up the coast. Won't need many clothes 'cause we'll be inside most of the weekend. I'm gonna ravish every square inch of your naked body." The two men began kissing passionately, and before either realized what was happening, all of their clothes were on the floor.

"Good morning, Kate. It's—let's see—it's Saturday morning, February 13. Shit. Gotta get my wife a card and some flowers. Anyway, just calling to see if you're back—"

"It's me," Kathryn said, still half asleep.

"Welcome home," said her contact. "You sound bright and cheery today."

"I'm still on Pacific Standard Time, asshole." She dragged herself and her cordless phone to the window. "Got home last night." As she opened the blinds, she heard a noise downstairs and remembered her coffeemaker came on automatically at nine. *Thank God*, she thought.

"Thought you wrapped up everything in San Diego midweek."

"I did." Kate descended the stairs in her Georgetown townhouse. "Wednesday I went to L.A. An entertainment exec wanted to seduce me. I thought, 'Why not stay and support the arts'?"

"Why not indeed," he said. "What film can now expect a glowing review from the *Herald*?"

"You know it's nothing like that." Pouring a cup of the magic liquid, Kathryn reminded herself that, in this town, any phone conversation might be recorded. "Old friends, that's all."

"Well, good." His tone signaled a change of subject. "Were you successful?"

"I'm waking up now," she said. "Meet me at one. The deli on Connecticut above the circle."

"Look at it this way," said Don. "You only gotta pack for *two* nights and two days." He and Patrick awoke wrapped in each other's arms, happy and content in the moment. Unfortunately for Don's surprise plans, they were still at Patrick's Oceanside apartment, naked and in bed. "We need to hit the road. I'm gonna treat you better than you've been treated in your life."

Patrick played with Don's curly chest hairs. "You've already accomplished that mission."

"Speaking of accomplishing missions, this would've been a perfect week—if only—"

"Only what?"

"If we coulda learned what happened to Eddie." Don ran his hand along the small of Patrick's back. "Esther said she'd call the second she found anything new. But I guess the trail's gone cold." Patrick's body tensed. "What's the matter?"

"Get in the shower," Patrick said, sitting up. "I'll make a quick breakfast and we'll talk."

Don became concerned. "I don't like the sound—"

"Don't worry." Patrick slipped on some shorts. "Let's move! I'm ready for my surprise."

"Now you're talkin'." Don headed for the shower. "Wanna shower with me?"

"Of course. But sometimes delayed gratification is better." Patrick went to the kitchen. "Looks like eggs, toast and, I guess, yogurt. Oh, and some melon."

Fifteen minutes later, they were at the table. "Enough suspense," Don said. "What gives?"

Patrick seemed anxious. "Karl and Lance found out some—information about what really happened to Eddie. Jeanne asked me to tell you."

Don smiled. The fact that Jeanne had asked Patrick to relay news was a sign of her approval. Still, he wondered what could've happened. "How'd they find out?"

"Didn't ask. Not so sure their 'interrogation tactics' were totally legal."

"Those two? I'm *sure* they weren't." Don refrained from asking the questions swirling in his head. He trusted his boyfriend—as he thought of Patrick—to explain things.

"Lance told you Eddie left WC's with a guy the night he died. Esther told you there was an NIS agent named Jay Gared at WC's the same night." Patrick spoke slowly. "As it turns out—"

"Eddie left WC's with NIS agent Jay Gared." Don paused, putting his head in his hands.

"Lance confirmed he was the same guy."

"Holy motherfucking—NIS wised up and recruited agents who fit in at a gay bar. Scary."

"Gared told the boys that he went home with Eddie, but just to talk. Gared must've said something that made Eddie suspect he was an undercover agent. Eddie pulled the gun. Gared jumped. Eddie fell backward." Patrick paused. "The gun went off. Says it was an accident."

"That's Gared's story?" Patrick nodded. "Were they positive Gared told the truth?"

"Yep. Both Karl and Lance seemed pretty sure he wasn't lying."

Don hesitated, wiping a tear from his eye. "They're reckless, but those two are wise beyond their years about shit like this." Rubbing his temples, Don laughed, sadly recalling a memory. "Eddie was so goddamned clumsy. I taught him and Ray how to shoot that gun at a pistol range in Escondido. Ray was fine, but Eddie—one of the scariest things in my life—and I've been in five combat zones." Biting his lip, Don clenched and unclenched his fists. "This is fucking bullshit! Agent Jay fucking Gared just happens to be in charge of the investigation—?"

Don paced the short distance between Patrick's dining table

and living room. As he spat out the words, the picture cleared. "There was no anonymous caller. I saw Gared at the park—he saw us. He saw Eddie—probably all of us—at WC's. He made up that bullshit about the drugs. Put the investigation under NIS's— under *his*—control. Motherfucking son-of-a-bitch!" Don shouted as he pounded his right fist into his left palm. "His whole report was a lie! We gotta demand the Navy reopen the investigation. I gotta call Jeanne about this—she'll know—"

Patrick gently took Don's wrist. "Already talked to Jeanne. Can you sit down—please?"

Don grew calmer and rubbed Patrick's forearm. "Anything you want."

Patrick stared as if searching for words. "Did you know Eddie was—was HIV-positive?"

"Yeah. I knew." Don put his head down. "Didn't think they'd check—what does HIV have to do with a bullet through the head?"

"According to what Karl and Lance—coerced—from Gared, Eddie tested negative exactly a year ago but his autopsy showed he was positive. Esther covertly verified this. NIS's theory is that Eddie recently learned he was HIV-positive. Not only was that a death sentence, it also meant his career was over. Considering that Ray died a year ago—"

"To them, it's obviously a suicide." Don couldn't believe this was happening. The scheme he and Eddie had pulled off every year to save Eddie's career prevented him from saving Eddie's postmortem reputation. "It's my turn to tell you something."

"Eddie actually tested positive years ago, didn't he?"

"How did you—?"

"Gared thinks you substituted your blood for Eddie's." Don thought nothing could shock him anymore but this stunned him speechless. "That's the most admirable thing I've ever heard, Don. You're a loyal person. You'd do anything for your friends. Only the bravest of men would risk everything for the people they love."

Don felt defeated but the growing connection he felt with

Patrick sustained him. "So now, if we demand another investigation, they'll publicize Eddie's recent HIV status. If we say that being HIV-positive had nothing to do with his death, the Navy will wonder why. When they investigate further, they'll find out I—and others who helped us—was involved. Fuck!"

"You'd go to jail for a long time," Patrick said. "I ain't letting that happen."

"So it ends in a goddamned stalemate? Between us—and this asshole Gared."

"Don't wanna sound like I'm minimizing the importance of Eddie's life and memory—but since *we* know what really happened—does it matter?"

"What am I supposed to tell Gloria? I promised her I'd get to the bottom of this. But she didn't know Eddie was either gay *or* positive. How do I explain to her what happened?"

Patrick shook his head. "Can it wait? Do you have to tell her right now?"

"It has to wait." Don sighed. "Hate leavin' her in the dark—but she'll understand. I hope."

Scratching his head, Patrick said, "The only difference I can think of—God! I hate to bring up money—but it matters. Does SGLI pay if a death is ruled a suicide? Some policies don't."

"Yeah. SGLI doesn't have a suicide or war—what's the term?—exclusion. But good point."

"If we know the truth and Mrs. Johnson gets the money Eddie wanted her to have—it's not really a stalemate. The people Eddie loved know the truth about what happened."

Don smiled. "You're even more of an optimist than me."

"Well—got something to confess." Patrick crossed the room. "SGLI was on my mind." He fumbled through the papers in his bag and brought something to Don. "This is for you. It's not as romantic as a weekend getaway, but—I want you to have it. If something happens to me, you get my SGLI money."

As he looked at the forms, Don felt sickened and then horrified. "Nothing's going to happen to you." Crumpling the paper, he tossed it across the room, where it hit the wall and fell behind

Patrick's entertainment system. "Hear me? I appreciate the thought, more than I can say, but that form is worthless because *nothing's gonna happen to you.*"

"You're right," Patrick said, smiling.

Staring out Patrick's window at the ocean, Don said, "I don't understand." He looked at his boyfriend. "All of you discussed this—why am I finding out now—in the past tense?"

"Um—this is the last discussion, then I want my surprise, okay? Everyone seemed concerned that if you—you were in on the plan to—*approach* Gared . . ."

Don waited as Patrick's words trailed off, unfinished. "What were they concerned about?"

"Everyone tells me you have this temper," Patrick said, "but I haven't seen it."

"And you won't. I promise. But I couldn't make the same promise to Agent Gared. My friends—guess they're looking out for me. Yeah, I might've done something I'd later regret." He leaned over and kissed Patrick on the lips. "And you're still here. With me, I mean. My temper didn't scare you away?"

"Yeah, I'm still here! Your so-called temper comes from the same part of your soul as your passion. And Don, that passion I met three weeks ago—that's when I came alive."

Jay lifted weights for two hours Saturday morning. At sunset, he planned to go for a six-mile run on Pacific Beach. Between the physical exertions, he consoled himself by reading *The Closing of the American Mind*, a text reinforcing his fears and convictions that moral relativism—especially regarding homosexuality—was destroying America.

While Jay was at the gym, Zack had left another message on his answering machine, the third since Jay had left the Marine to his drug-induced orgy at the bathhouse.

As Jay turned the pages in the book, he wondered when the ghost would return. "Hurry up, Pa," he said. "Tell me how I got what I deserved for having sex with the Marine—and for finding pleasure in it. Come on, please? I'd like to get on with my life."

30

"Fantastic, Kate. Photographs, dates, names, places." He gave her a look she could only interpret as awe. "How did you obtain so much information so fast?"

"Check the front page of the *Herald* tomorrow," Kathryn said. Anticipating his reaction, she added, "Don't worry. I didn't spoil whatever use you might have for this information." Kathryn waved her hand, motioning for the server to refill her cup. "I went to San Diego two weeks ago for a legitimate human-interest story. Originally, I wanted to focus on military life for lesbians. By sheer coincidence, my first day there, I met your Marine."

"Gosh, it sounds too easy. Maybe we should cut your—"

"Bullshit," Kathryn said. "You better have double what—"

"Kate. I'm kidding. I don't care *how* you got the information. All I care about is that you did. Your money is right here. Twice the original amount, in hundreds." He pushed a red box toward her, wrapped like a present. "Happy Valentine's—a day early."

Kathryn shook it and was satisfied. "I hope your wife doesn't have a spy following you."

"She'd be so glad if I had an affair. I should put an investigator on *her*," the man said. Returning to the topic, he asked, "What's in the paper tomorrow?"

"When I came across your Marine," Kathryn explained, "I also met his new boyfriend, another Marine. I realized I could save myself a lot of trouble and do the human-interest story on the same man. I did and it worked out perfectly! Tomorrow's story doesn't report their names or faces. It's more of a fluff piece about the challenges gay Marines encounter in building a relationship." Kate gave her contact a look of smug satisfaction and bit into her sandwich.

He looked down at his plate. "I didn't pay you all this money so I can stick these documents in my scrapbook. We *will* use this information and it *will* end their military careers."

Kathryn wiped crumbs from the corners of her mouth. "Of course I realize that. I feel bad about it too. Don't look at me as if I'm some kind of monster. Yes, I developed a fondness for them and I hate to see anything bad happen." Looking out at the weather, she was glad she'd remembered her umbrella. "But business is business. I'm not treating them any worse than I've been treated. Besides, they're young and smart. And *resilient*. They'll bounce back."

"It's not *them* I'm worried about," said her contact. "Ever hear of Lee Harvey Oswald?"

"Of course."

"Ever hear of Charles Whitman?" Kathryn wasn't sure. "Climbed up in the clock tower at the University of Texas thirty years ago carrying a bunch of firearms. Killed fifteen people."

"Is there a moral to this parable?"

"He wounded thirty others. I'm worried about what Oswald and Whitman have in common with Hawkins—*and* his boyfriend. They're all Marines, not the soft-bellied politicians and bureaucrats you're used to screwing over. They're professional trained killers. Marines have a history of going psycho. Geez," he said, pulling the photograph of the two shirtless men from the envelope. "Look at that. Hawkins looks like the love child of Arnold-fucking-Schwarzenegger and Sylvester Stallone for crying out loud. And the other guy's got muscles of his own. You get too personal with these guys, it could seriously come back to haunt you."

Indignant, Kathryn put the box of money in a large bag. "I never knew you were so concerned with my well-being. How thoughtful of you."

"Don't kid yourself," he said. This is our fifth 'transaction.' You've got as much access as anybody in this town. Makes you too valuable. Our little deals put my girl through college and now they have to put her through law school."

"You said Don would never know the information came from me. You promised."

"I said I'd do my best. But that was before I knew you'd be— *daring*—enough to write an exposé on the same guy. Besides, once I pass this information on, it's out of my control."

Kathryn was through with her half-eaten sandwich. "You plan to use it before May 16?"

"What's May 16?"

"I'm doing a three-month follow-up interview with Don and Patrick in the Sunday *Herald*."

"Damn, you are one heartless bitch, you know that?" he said. "As despicable as my clients are, at least they don't enjoy cozying up to the people they're about to destroy."

Kathryn stood to leave. "I've never asked you this before," she said angrily, "because I usually don't care. Who exactly *is* your client on this matter?"

"You know I can't tell—"

"It's Coughlin, isn't it? He's so mad at Don, he'll do anything to destroy him, won't he?"

"Does it matter?"

Kathryn had debated that question in her mind dozens of times. "I hate that chauvinist pig Coughlin as much as anyone. But ultimately? No, it doesn't matter." Walking toward the exit, she said, "You'll pick up the tab, won't you, dear? Thanks for lunch. It was *fabulous*."

"Oh my God, Don! Whose house is this?"

"Two good friends Eddie and I met at a place called The Little Shrimp. It was here in Laguna Beach about six years ago." Don set their bags on the floor. "They're in Puerto Vallarta. Said we could use it as our little love nest this weekend." Don followed his lover onto the patio overlooking the canyon, the village and the cliffs plunging into the Pacific. "All we have to do is water the plants and have lots of sex. And give the usual dog sitter the day off. Speaking of—where—?" Don walked across the large living room and opened a door to the garage. "Hi, DJ!" He introduced his friends' pet to Patrick. "Let me give you a tour."

"You mean two *guys* live here? Like—a couple?"

Don laughed. "Sure. Been together twenty-five years. You'll meet them if we can catch them between their world travels."

"Wow." Patrick admired the beautiful interior and furnishings. They stepped outside onto the small but well-landscaped back-yard. "It's a whole different world than anything I've ever known." Patrick took Don's arms and wrapped them around his chest. "I fell for the religious propaganda that gay men are doomed to lead lonely, miserable lives as the 'town queer.' When I came out, I didn't imagine *all this* was a possibility."

"You ain't seen *nothing* yet!" Don kissed his lover on the neck and whispered in his ear, "Stick with me, baby, and this is just a sample of what I plan to do for you."

"Thought you shut off your phone," Karl said as he flipped the steaks on Leonard's grill.

"I wish." Leonard went inside the house. "With two teens, that would be irresponsible."

"Isn't Todd twenty?" Karl asked.

"Touché," Leonard yelled. "Thanks for the reminder."

"Bring the phone outside. You should be next to me every second this weekend."

"Yes, sir!" Leonard replied playfully. Following Karl's order, he brought the phone into the backyard. "Hello."

"Hello, Leonard," said one of his friends. "How is everything on the left coast?"

"It's the middle of February. I'm wearing shorts, standing in my backyard, smoking a cigar—won't say which Caribbean country it comes from—while watching the sunset over the Pacific Ocean." Leonard set the cigar on an ashtray and put his arm around Karl.

"So what you're trying to say is that life really sucks and you want to come back to DC."

"Coming back to DC." Leonard picked up his scotch. "Is that an attempt at a clever segue?"

"Ha! Listen to you. Let's just say I'm calling with news. First bit may be bad, may be good, depends on how you feel about it. But then I've got some *definite* bad news."

"Wait. Let me sit down." Leonard remained standing and winked at Karl. "Go ahead."

"They want you here at the Pentagon. Aviation procurement. Early as July."

Leonard sighed at this expected news. The position was a prerequisite for the role he coveted—commanding general of a Marine Aircraft Wing. "Is that your 'definite bad news'?" he joked.

"Ha. Afraid not," his friend said. "The commandant's office received an advance copy of tomorrow's *Washington Herald*. Front-page story, with photograph. A couple of your Marines out there in 'la-la land' are butt pirates and they talked to the press."

"Only a couple?" Leonard rattled his glass and took a drink. "Who?"

"Story doesn't say and we can't tell from the photos because their faces are blurred."

"What does the commandant plan to do about it?" Leonard chomped on the cigar.

"Compared to all the other stories about gays and lesbians right now, this one's not that bad. As long as it doesn't get any bigger, the commandant prefers to let this story die."

"Sounds to me like his instincts are correct." Leonard watched Karl season the filets.

"Just thought you'd want to know in case they're your Marines. Have a happy Valentine's Day and see you in DC this summer. It'll be good to have some personality back in this town."

Leonard grinned as he set the phone down on a patio table. "What was that about?" Karl asked, sliding their twelve-ounce steaks onto plates.

"You aren't on the front page of the *Washington Herald* tomorrow, are you?"

"No." Karl hesitated as he turned the gas off. "Let's eat. I'm starving." At the patio table, Karl said, "They wanted to interview me. For once in my life I didn't wanna risk it."

"Why not?"

Karl grasped Leonard's hand. "I wouldn't risk what you and I have together for anything in the world. Nothing's this important."

Sunday morning, Jay's routine was similar to Saturday's. Instead of working out his chest and triceps, though, he pumped up his legs and shoulders. This afternoon, he'd see how far he could push himself on his run after a tough morning of squats and dead lifts. As Jay stepped out of his shower, his telephone rang. He knew who it was. Just like before, the machine took the call.

"Good mornin' Jay-man," said Zack. "I'm gonna overlook the fact that you ain't answered the other three calls I left 'cause you wanna take this one." Jay stood next to the phone. "You know about the newspaper article that came out this morning? Everybody on base is talking about it. It's about two queer Marines—"

"What is it, Zack?" Jay asked, picking up his phone.

"Well, well. He's alive. It's a fuckin' miracle. What the hell happened to you?"

"What's this about a newspaper article and gay Marines? What're you talking about?"

"Hold on one goddamned minute. You left me at that bathhouse. You *abandoned* me—"

"Bullshit. You weren't in any pain when I left. Tell me about the article or I'm hanging up."

"Ha ha! You right about the 'no pain,' part, brotha'! The sergeant on duty at my barracks told me about this article when I came in this morning. Said there's a story in the paper about two fags at Camp Pendleton in love. Thought you might wanna know in case they was some of the queers you been chasin'."

"What newspaper?"

"Hell if I know!" Zack said. "You think I read the paper?"

"No," said Jay. "Is that it?"

"Why you gotta be such a dick, man? I didn't mean to scare you away. I just wanted to help you have a good time, that's all."

"You should've known better." Although it felt good to hear

Zack say these words, Jay couldn't let his feelings for Zack soften his resolve. "I need to find this newspaper."

"Okay," said Zack. "I was just wantin' to see if you might—"

"I gotta run, Zack. Bye."

"'We're tired of living in fear that our gay lives and straight lives are on a collision course.'"

Patrick listened as Don read Kathryn Angel's article. "I'd say she nailed it."

Don folded the newspaper and set it under his chair. "I agree. She really got what we told her." Don's head was spinning. The article, Valentine's Dinner with Patrick, being here in beautiful Laguna. His emotions were in overdrive. "Nervous they'll find out who we are?"

"Based on what you read, I don't think they can. That picture could be anybody." Patrick laughed. "As exceptional as I think we are," he said, "we look like generic Marines."

Reaching across the table, Don took Patrick's hands. Patrick anxiously looked around the restaurant. "We're safe," Don said. "The ratio here is ninety percent gay, ten percent straight."

"This has been an incredible weekend, my Marine Valentine."

MARINES FIND FORBIDDEN LOVE REGARDLESS OF THE RULES.

Jay read the headline and the article a second time and stared at the picture. He was positive the featured Marine was Gunnery Sergeant Don Hawkins. Someday soon, he'd prove it. He cut the article and photograph out of the paper and set it aside.

Jay had accumulated volumes of information over the years—including the pages he'd photocopied from Johnson's address book. He kept the notes and documents stashed in boxes under his bed. Rummaging through an old box from DC, he hoped he had what he needed. If so, maybe this was his reward for refusing Zack's advances on the telephone earlier today. The Marine who'd threatened him and cut his neck had been his punishment but this new and wonderful development was his reward. Underneath piles of clippings, articles and other things, he found what he was looking for.

"Perfect." Jay placed the folder on his table. He wouldn't use the information today, next week or even this month, but in the near future, when the time was right, it would be useful.

Feeling devilish, he said, "I look forward to working with you again, Kathryn Angel."

So far, the weekend had gone according to Don's plan. They finished dinner at the optimal time. Rather than return to the jeep, Don led Patrick by the hand across Pacific Coast Highway. They climbed rickety and weathered steps down to the beach as the sun set over the ocean.

Don was ready to say what he'd said to only one other person. With the sun a semicircle to their side, he stopped walking and faced Patrick in the sand, taking Patrick's hands in his own. "Patrick, I—I don't know what—" He returned his young lover's sweet smile. "I've never been good at sorting out feelings. But to me—what I feel for you—"

"Don," Patrick said, "I love you."

Breathing in deeply, Don felt a tear roll down his cheek. "I love you too."

Part Two

May Gray

31

"Damn, McAbe! You got a *sweet* ass."

"Oh yeah? You're a *smart* ass," Patrick said, lathering his body with Irish Spring.

"Share your soap?" Tim asked. Patrick passed him the bar.

Having completed practice flights for the upcoming air show, Chris and Jungle—the lead pilots—joined Patrick and Tim in the showers. "Good flight today, men," Jungle said to the two copilots. "I'd say we're ready to do three shows this weekend. Chris, you agree?"

"Absolutely. Just hope the fog's not as bad at El Toro as it was over the coast today."

Chris rubbed shampoo in his hair, prompting Tim to say, "'*GI beans and GI gravy, Gee I wished we'd joined the Navy.*' Patrick, then we could grow our hair long enough to style too."

"I'm sure you would've made a good hair stylist, Roberts," said Chris.

"Ouch!" said Jungle. "Roberts, Melanie coming down this weekend?"

"Yep. Her last exam is May 5—shit, that's today! She'll meet me at the El Toro guesthouse tomorrow night. Means I'll be gettin' some before the weekend!" He gave Patrick a high five.

Thirty minutes later, Patrick and Tim went to a fast-food place outside Camp Pendleton's main gate. "Don coming up to the air show?" Tim asked, unwrapping his cheeseburger.

"Yep. The whole Scooby Doo gang's coming up on Sunday."

"Cool. Been meanin' to tell you, bro'—you seem a lot happier now. Glad you met Don."

Patrick smiled. "Thanks, buddy. Still seems crazy, how scared I was to tell you." Patrick lifted his bun as Tim reached over and took his tomatoes. "With Don it's like a whole new life, you know? I finally get it—what was missing with Karen."

"Mel noticed you were on edge—at times—around Karen. Now even I can tell how much you've changed. You're relaxed, you smile all the time. Hell, you've become just like—"

"I've become just like you? Is that what you were gonna say?" Patrick wadded up his napkin and threw it at Tim's face. Winking, he added, "Guess that's not such a bad thing." Taking a bite of his lunch, he thought about the difference. "With Karen, I had to work so hard all the time, playing the role of boyfriend and fiancé. At the end of the day, I was worn out. Didn't know why. With Don, it's just so—natural. We know we're supposed to be together."

"Wow. That's awesome. Melanie and I are so happy for you— for both of you. Oh, she'll wanna hang out with Don and your friends on Sunday, especially after spending all day Saturday with the officers' wives' club. Will this be the first time Don sees you fly?" Patrick nodded. "Have you ever seen him—do whatever it is a gunny does on the ground?"

"Yeah," said Patrick. "Didn't I tell you? When I met Don three months ago, we were both part of that stupid dog-and-pony for that congressman. It was fuckin' hilarious too. I saw him lead his Marines in the field. That's what he does."

"Now I remember," said Tim, stuffing fries in his mouth. "He get busted for that?"

"Nope. He had NJP, but they dropped the charges. Let it quietly fade away."

"No fallout from the newspaper article?"

Patrick shook his head. Quietly, he said, "No. The story was kinda tame. Think the powers that be let it go. Come to think of it, she's supposed to call us back soon for a follow-up."

"Don was so great. He sure told that guy where to go. Damn, he's sure got a huge set of balls." Tim stopped and laughed. "Of course, you'd know that better than anyone."

"You're havin' a lot of fun with this, aren't you?"

"What's the benefit of having a gay best friend if I can't talk about this stuff?"

"I gotta ask you something," Patrick said, ripping the top off a ketchup packet. "After our flight today—how did you feel, showering with two homos?"

"Before you told me, you know, that you're a rump ranger, I probably woulda said the same thing all the guys say. 'I don't want some faggot starin' at my ass in the shower.' Honestly? Like today—now that I know who you are, at least you and Chris, it's like—" Tim looked out the large plate glass window as if searching for words in the sky. "How do I say this without giving you the wrong idea?"

"Fuck it, man. Just say it."

"I would be *more* offended if you *didn't* check out my ass, know what I'm sayin'? I mean, if I'm standing there, bare ass nekkid, with two guys who've got the same ability to crave me the way I lust after women—and you *didn't* want me, I don't know if my fragile ego could handle it. My opinion? That's what the guys are *really* afraid of." Tim bit into his cheeseburger. "Here's a question. Say you weren't with Don, and you could have any pilot in the squadron. Who—?"

"Jesus, man! I don't think of the guys like that. I can't, that'd be—"

"Bullshit, McAbe. I was honest with you, you gotta level with me. Make it easier for you—don't name any names, gimme a number. How many pilots in our squadron you're attracted to."

"Damn, Tim. You're persistent. Maybe—seven or eight. Couple more on a good day."

"See what I mean? There are dozens more you're *not* attracted to." Tim wiped mustard from his face. "What scares these guys, even though none of 'em would admit it, is that they're standing there in their birthday suit taking a shower—and *no one* wants them. Seriously, a quarter of those guys couldn't get laid in a Filipino whorehouse with a fistful of pesos and a plateful of lumpia. Their worst nightmare is that even the fagg—shit! Sorry, bro'. Old habits."

"Tim—no offense taken. Loyalty and friendship are in deeds, not words."

"These guys' worst nightmare is that even gay guys wouldn't be attracted to them. What then? They're stuck bein' sexless worker drones in the beehive of humanity."

"Wow. That's deep," Patrick said sarcastically. "Slaving away so the queen can breed?"

"Hysterical." Tim laughed. "I mean it. Guys that vocalize anti-gay comments the loudest—*they're* the ones who're the most afraid. *Not* being desired is a primeval human fear. We're afraid the herd will leave us to rot." Tim leaned back, crossed his arms and gave Patrick a self-satisfied smile. "Wanna know how I know so much about all this shit? I was a psych minor."

"What'd you say? You just admit you're psycho? You crack me up, buddy. Hmmm. Interesting theories. Never thought of it that way but maybe on some level, guess you're right."

"Me personally? I'd rather *know* which guys are gay. Right now, for all I know, Sledge could be checking me out."

"Oooh." Patrick shuddered. "Hello! Eating lunch now."

Tim waved his hand, motioning for Patrick to say something. "Come on. Tell me."

"Tell you what?"

"You know." Tim flashed a mischievous grin. "I got a hot ass, don't I?"

"Oh my God, Tim! I'm through with your questions."

"Tell me! We're like brothers. We can say anything to each other."

"That's just it," said Patrick. "You *are* just like my brother. Not into sex with my brothers."

"All right. I see your point."

"But if it's any consolation, and your ego obviously needs it right now, my friends—including the lesbians—say that you're a very good-looking man. And a—comment or two has been made about—you know, that you do have—a—hot ass."

"You just made my day, bro'!" said Tim, finishing his cheese-burger. "Gay guys think I'm a hottie! *And* lesbians. Wait till I tell Melanie."

For three months, Jay's emotions overwhelmed his mind. At first, he'd felt enough terror to stay away from anything related to homosexuality. He imagined the crazy knife-wielding man every-where. The guy who delivered the bottled water to the office looked like him. Half the guys at the gym looked like him and the UPS man looked like him from a distance. His image dominated Jay's nightmares, dozens, sometimes hundreds, all naked, brandish-ing long knives with razor-sharp edges. In every vision, Jay felt the sudden, excruciating pain of his skin being sliced apart. Some nights he gagged on his own blood while, all around, men sodomized each other. Sleep was hell. Being awake was hell. Life was hell.

The visit he'd feared more than anything didn't occur. For two months, the dread Jay felt about seeing his father's ghost con-sumed him. Ollie asked if he was losing weight and getting enough sleep. The answers were "yes" and "no."

Jay had an epiphany. His father hadn't visited because a visit was unnecessary. Jay had punished himself far worse than his fa-ther could ever punish him. His inner turmoil was worse than pur-gatory. After the epiphany, punishment time was over. He began eating and sleeping and now he looked as good as ever. With one exception.

Jay rubbed the thin scar on his neck, the lone physical reminder of his night of horror. When his fear subsided, shame took its place. He was ashamed that two faggots had frightened him, di-verting him from his original path. The shame was there, but each day it transformed slowly into a more productive feeling. Jay's rage—his simmering and inexhaustible fuel—had returned.

Jay had followed Ollie's instructions, concentrating only on as-signed investigations, and Ollie had showered him with praise. He was bored and anxious, though, because he wasn't doing the job he'd been called to do but he was unsure how to revert to his orig-inal plan. His steps had to be smarter next time.

Half an hour after arriving home from his daily workout, his phone, which hadn't rung in weeks, startled him. "Jay-man, it's Zack—I'm baaack." The Marine imitated the little girl in *Poltergeist II*. Jay listened, but didn't budge from his reading chair. "It's Cinco de Mayo, amigo, and I'm gettin' on the train to San Diego. Heh, that fuckin' rhymes. I miss you, you slack-ass civilian. Pick me up at the train station at nineteen thirty-eight, or seven thirty-eight P.M. for you civilian shitheads. I know you gonna be there 'cause I got some information for ya'—about those two Marines in that newspaper article from a while back. Somethin' tells me you just itchin' to get back in the game. Okay, Jay-man, see you in a little while. Adios!"

Jay walked to his desk. In a corner, he'd placed the folder where he'd written "Kathryn Angel." Beside it was the *Washington Herald* article. Opening the folder, he looked at the photographs and read the old stories. His time had come. Putting the folder in a bag, he slipped on a shirt. Zack's train would arrive in an hour and Jay had heard enough to whet his appetite. The Marine was right. He was itchin' to get back in the game.

"Who's in for another pitcher of Margaritas?" asked Jeanne.

"I'll drive us home, lover boy," said Don. "You indulge since your weekend will be busy."

"You tryin' to get me drunk? You wanna take advantage of me?" Patrick asked. "'Cause if ya' are, I'll definitely have another." He kissed his boyfriend on the lips.

"I don't understand why you have to go up to El Toro tomorrow," Don said. "This little weekend event has turned into a four-day production."

"We fly the helicopters up tomorrow afternoon," Chris said, "then a dress rehearsal Friday. Show's Saturday and Sunday. They expect half a million people this weekend at the air station."

"Rumor is El Toro might close," said Robbi. "Could be the last air show in Orange County."

"Then we have to leave early Sunday," said Don. "Traffic on and off base will be brutal."

"Back to your point," Patrick said. "That's why I have to stay on base each night."

"You realize the next four days will be the longest we've been apart since we met?"

"I know." Patrick sighed. "I'm gonna miss not waking up next to you." The waiter arrived to take their order. "I'll take a Greek salad—"

"A salad?" said Karl. "Hey, Mary. This is Hamburger Mary's. Get a hamburger."

"Same for me," Don said. "But no onions on mine and no tomatoes on his."

"No burger. Tim Roberts talked me into lunch at Burger King today." Patrick took a sip of his frozen drink. "Melanie wants to spend Sunday with you guys. It's not fair, though. Tim can bring her into the officers' quarters for the weekend. I should be able to do the same with you."

"Too dangerous. We've tempted fate too many times this year. Speaking of that, Miss Angel called. Wants to do the follow-up interview by phone Monday night. Still wanna do it?"

"Sure. The first article was fine. It had a lot of good feedback in the gay community."

"But the Marine community was strangely quiet," Don said aloud.

"Guys," Karl said, "they might not be so nice for round two."

"Decision's up to you," Patrick said. "I'll do it if you will."

"Hi, Kate, guess who?"

"Haven't heard from you in a while," said Kathryn. "Listen. Got a massage in half an hour. I wouldn't have taken this call but I thought you might be the spa rescheduling."

"Just a quick question. When we last met in February, you gave me a date. I don't recall what it was. Something about a follow-up to your story on the two Marines at Camp Pendleton."

"Oh that. Funny you should ask. I'm interviewing Don and Patrick on the tenth, by phone. The story will be in the *Herald* on Sunday the sixteenth."

"We're using the information you provided next Tuesday, the eleventh. It'll take a few days or a week before it has an impact on the two Marines. You can run your story on Wednesday or any date after that. But not Tuesday or before."

"The timing couldn't be more perfect. All I care about is getting the interview from them Monday night. Whatever happens after that isn't my concern.

"Sounds great," said her contact. "Enjoy your massage, Kate. Good night."

"Good to see you again, Jay-man."

"Good to see you again too, Zack." Jay meant it. Zack was a kindred soul, albeit a disturbed one. Jay held out hope that he might be able to reform the Marine's out-of-control behavior. For now, though, he had a specific mission. "What new information do you have?"

"Can you drive me to a party in Chula Vista?" Zack asked. "You can come too if you want. I'll explain on the way."

"Is this a drug party?" Jay asked.

"Damn, Jay, I don't do drugs all the time. It's not like you think. But it might be."

"I'll drop you off." Putting his car in gear, Jay headed for I-5 south. "What's the news?"

"Couple a weeks ago, I was down at the Oceanside pier. All kinda cocksuckers down there. I thought of that picture in the newspaper 'cause my roommate brought a copy to the barracks. You know, the one I told you about with the two queer Marines? I remembered the pier in the background so I thought 'Wonder why the Corps didn't just figure the angle of the pier in that picture and see whose apartment that was.'"

"They probably thought about it," Jay said. "But aren't there a lot of apartments with that view? Just because the *Herald* took the picture there doesn't mean whoever lives there is gay."

"Who the fuck is Harold?"

Jay laughed. "I missed you, Zack."

"All I'm sayin' is that the Corps shoulda done what I did. That's be patient and disciplined. I went down there every night I was off work and staked out those apartments."

"Sounds like you just wanted an excuse to cruise the pier for dick."

"I don't need no fuckin' excuse to do *anything* I wanna do,"

Zack protested. "But yeah, it helped me kill two birds if you know what I mean. Finally, one night after dark, I saw two guys standin' on a balcony. Both of 'em looked like Marines. Get this! They *kissed* each other. Those fuckin' faggots *kissed* each other, right there in broad—well, broad moonlight."

"That's good work." Jay was impressed. "The apartment was the right angle for the photo?"

"Yes! That's what I'm saying! Oh, you need to take this exit." Jay put his blinkers on. "I couldn't be sure because I ain't been in the apartment, but from where I saw it—outside the gate—it was the same angle. So I went around to the back of the apartments, where the street is. A few days later, I saw one of 'em get in a jeep, then I saw the other. One's an officer, the other's a gunny. If you can't bust 'em for fucking each other, you got 'em on fraterniza- tion."

"You get their names?"

"Of course. You think I'm some kinda dumbass, don't you? I got their vehicle numbers. Since I'm an MP—turn right on this street— since I'm an MP, I looked 'em up on the system."

Jay turned onto a narrow street crowded with small houses. "One of them D. A. Hawkins?"

"Damn, you're good! It's this house with all the cars in front." Jay pulled over the curb. "That's him. And the other guy is a first lieutenant. Name's McAbe, Patrick S."

"Zack, before you go, I want us to work together. But you've got to promise me—*no drugs*—not in my car and not in my house."

Zack sounded irritated but he promised. "Okay, no drugs in your car or house." He opened the door. "Thanks for the ride. When will I see you again?"

"Can you show me which apartment is McAbe's this weekend?"

"I'm on duty Friday and Saturday nights. But we can meet in Oceanside on Sunday afternoon. I'll call ya'."

"Sounds good, Zack. Thanks for keeping in touch with me." Zack waved and went into the house. As Jay pulled away, he felt better than he'd felt in months, the kind of elation that can only come from doing the right thing.

32

"Here's one for you. How is flying a helicopter just like jackin' off?"

"This is a joke I haven't heard before," Tim said sarcastically.

"It's fun while you're doin' it, but you sure as hell wouldn't want your friends to see you!" The jet pilot and his buddies erupted into raucous laughter.

"That's so goddamned original," Patrick said. "You guys need some new material."

"Aren't you guys fighter pilots?" asked one of the men. "You *look* just like we do."

"It's too loud in here," Patrick said in Tim's ear. "Melanie! Wanna go outside?"

"You kidding me? I *love* being felt up by drunk pilots."

"That does it," said Tim, "we're goin' outside."

Searching the club for the nearest exit, Patrick said, "Over here!" One thousand people had crammed into the El Toro Officers' Club after Saturday's air show. Patrick took Melanie's hand, who grabbed her fiancé's, and they formed a chain to navigate their way through the vast crowd.

"Thank God I can still breathe!" said Tim. "Tell me who felt you up."

"So many guys I lost count," said Patrick. "I'm sorry. Were you talking to Melanie?"

"Seriously, Patrick," said Melanie. "A few of those jet pilots were checking you out."

"What? Wasn't anybody checkin' *me* out?" Tim asked, taking a drink of beer.

"Does your ego *ever* go on vacation?" Melanie asked.

The threesome migrated to a grassy spot near the club's corner as dozens of other patrons spilled onto the patio. Patrick asked, "How was your day with the officers' wives club?"

"Actually," Melanie said, pulling her hair back, "not that bad. I shouldn't have stereotyped them as—how did Hillary Clinton put it? Women who just stay at home, bake cookies and have teas, or who stand by their man-pilots. They're smart and dedicated just like you guys are. Just the same, I'm looking forward to standing by *your* man tomorrow."

Patrick nervously looked around to make sure no one overheard Melanie's slip.

"Shit," said Tim. "Don't look now but here comes your buddy." Patrick turned around. "What did I say? Don't look!"

"Lieutenant McAbe, you and your team did a fantastic job today," said Colonel Spencer, rounding the corner. To Patrick's surprise, he wasn't alone. "General Neville, I'd like you to meet two of our newest and finest Cobra pilots. Lieutenants McAbe and—Roberts, isn't it?"

"Yes, sir. And gentlemen, my fiancée Melanie."

"It's wonderful to meet all of you, especially you, Melanie. Congratulations on your engagement," said General Neville. "When is the big day?"

"June nineteenth," Melanie said.

"Congratulations, and best wishes to you both," said Colonel Spencer. "And Lieutenant McAbe, Lieutenant Roberts, over 500,000 attended today—at least 50,000 saw your flight. New estimates for tomorrow are we're expecting close to 750,000. If you put on a show tomorrow half as good as today, this weekend will have been a complete success."

When the colonel and the general were out of earshot, Tim jabbed Patrick on the shoulder. "Thanks, McAbe, now he knows *my* name too!"

"Well," said Melanie. "At least he didn't put any pressure on you guys."

"They get younger and younger," said the General as he and Leonard walked toward the club.

"Those lieutenants are at least twenty-five, general. You and I were younger than that when we started flying. And we flew in combat," said Leonard as he looked into the club. "On second thought, if you don't mind, let's stay out here—assuming they set up an outdoor bar."

"I don't recall looking that young as a pilot. Lieutenant McAbe doesn't even look like he shaves yet. Colonel, I'm afraid that while we weren't watching, you and I both grew old."

"There's the bar—and no line," Leonard said, gently coaxing the general to follow him. "I have to disagree, sir. I've been painfully aware of every step of Father Time's encroachment into my life." He looked back over the mob scene. "There's the buffet table, General. They've thought of everything." The air station's band had put together a jazz ensemble as background music for the occasion. "This is quite a celebration." Leonard ordered a scotch for himself and a rum and Coke for the general. "I especially like the ice sculptures. An F-4 and an A-6—what a coincidence. The jets you used to fly."

"Nice touch, isn't it? I'll have to thank whoever came up with that idea."

"I assume the ice sculptures of the helicopters melted already," Leonard joked.

"Your turn will come, Leonard. Be patient." He thanked Leonard for the drink. "Here's to having another successful air show tomorrow." The general and Leonard touched glasses and sipped their drinks. "Because it could very well be the last air show at this base."

"Any updates? Seems like news of the base closures has been very quiet."

"It's been extremely secretive," said the general. "But in six days, the commission will release the closure list. Washington geniuses believe that if they present bad news to the media late on a Friday afternoon, no one will pay attention. Well, when Congress talks about billions of dollars flowing out of some local economies into others, people pay attention, I don't care *when* they publish it." The general walked toward other groups of people and Leonard followed. "Missed you at the VIP tent today."

"I visited the squadron displays around the base and said hello to the Marines. Don't worry. I'll be at your tent tomorrow."

"Then you might not have heard the news. General Laker died this morning."

"That's a shame. But I can't believe he held on till now. How long was he on life support?"

"Four months. His situation prompted Eileen and me to sign something called a living will. I certainly don't want to end as he did. Paul Laker might have lived life in the fast lane, but he sure dragged out the final act." The two men milled about, greeting old friends and acquaintances as well as professional enemies. "Coughlin will be at the tent tomorrow."

"I assumed as much," Leonard said.

"Your enthusiasm is contagious. Believe me, I'm just as excited as you are. But if El Toro is on the list of base closures, he's our only hope. I know everyone is tired of hearing me say it—"

"No, General. I understand why it's necessary for you to repeat that point. It's only human to let our opinions and feelings get in the way. But if Coughlin has the power to help us, we should be reminded not to let our personal dislike of the man prevent us from getting what we need from him. Telling people only what they want to hear is for politicians, not leaders."

"Couldn't have said it better myself. Anyway, Coughlin will be thrilled to meet a rising star in the Marine Corps's general officer ranks." Leonard nodded as Lieutenants McAbe, Roberts and Roberts's fiancée walked by to reenter the building. "Which squadron are they in?"

"Seven-oh-seven," Leonard answered.

The general changed to a sober tone. "Seven-oh-seven? Let's go inside, Leonard. We need to talk."

Leonard followed the general through the club into a small private conference room. "The results of the colonels' selection board have been released for publication on Monday."

Leonard was confused. "Thought DC gave us a week to notify the officers in person."

"The message was supposed to be held until Friday but someone at the Pentagon accidentally sent it to the communications center yesterday, once again proving my theory that the world is run by idiots. By Monday, everyone will know who was—and was *not*—selected for colonel."

Only one of Leonard's lieutenant colonels was up for promotion this round. "Sledge?"

The general shook his head. "Didn't make it." Leonard was surprised, even though he shouldn't have been. Despite his poor opinion of Sledge, the man was well connected. "Leonard, if you want to succeed as a general, you mustn't show your thoughts on your face."

Leonard smiled. "You're the only one who can see through my poker face, General."

"You're wondering how a man who's kissed the ass of every general since the Revolutionary War was passed over for promotion, aren't you." The general's eyes twinkled as he took a sip of his rum. "All the retired three-stars in the world aren't a match for this active-duty two-star."

"I don't know how you did it or how many people you upset to block his promotion, but you did it based on my reports. It means a lot that you trust my judgment."

"Of course I do. You're like—not a son, I'm not *that* old, but like a younger brother to me—*and* to Eileen. If Sledge was half as bad as you said, it was worth all the political capital I had to burn in order to put him out of the Corps. Of course, blocking him wasn't as difficult as it might have been if Laker had been conscious. But Laker wasn't—and never will be again." Looking Leonard directly in the eye, the general said, "The hard part, I'm afraid, is now. It doesn't sadden me to pass the buck to you. Okinawa will receive the list by noon tomorrow—Monday over there—and they will post it immediately."

"Shit," said Leonard. "That means I have to tell him. I have to tell him *tonight*."

"Unless you want him to learn about it by an overseas telephone call from God knows who."

"Damn that international date line," Leonard said. "General MacArthur learned President Truman had fired him when he saw it in a press release."

"If you want to go that route, the station public affairs officer is in the next room. We can—"

"I was joking, well—*half*-joking. No, I can't let him find out that way." Leonard wasn't looking forward to this. "He'll be at the Blue Angels' reception in an hour. I'll tell him then."

"Some party he'll have. Let's go back into the club and make sure my wife hasn't had too much to drink," the general joked. He opened the door and the noise from the main bar was deafening. "Relish the joys of command, Leonard. They don't last long."

"Talked to the missus today?"

"No," said Patrick. "I'll call at ten. From the privacy of my room." Across the reception area, Patrick observed Sledge follow the colonel down the hall into a side office.

"Your honey gonna read you a bedtime story?" Chris asked. "Or will it be phone sex?"

Patrick smiled, but in a low voice asked, "You ever get over the paranoia?"

"What do you mean?" asked Chris, dipping a piece of shrimp in cocktail sauce.

"Just saw our squadron commander leave the reception with Colonel Spencer. Looks like a private conference. My heart skips a beat. I'm afraid they've discovered one of their pilots, say, oh, I don't know, First Lieutenant McAbe, likes getting fucked. They're discussing how to prosecute me. It's crazy, but for a second, that thought crosses my mind."

"Patrick, that's normal. I felt that way too when I was—at your stage. Not to sound patronizing but I hope it helps. Just recite a simple phrase—'It's not about me'—because guess what? Usually it's not. At this point in your career, you can't imagine how hard it is to run a squadron. Try running an airline with obsolete equipment, no money and underpaid employees."

"Guess you're right." Patrick took a drink of water. "But we can't ever know for certain."

"I'm sure they're talking about maintenance, or trying to get new equipment or a change in operations." Chris put a hand on Patrick's shoulder. "Colonel Spencer—soon-to-be Brigadier General Spencer—knows you're an outstanding pilot. Trust me. If anything, they'd be in there talking about how to *save* your career, not end it. Quit worrying. Let's rejoin the gang."

"How many did you say?" Jungle asked Melanie when Chris and Patrick rejoined the group.

"750,000," said Melanie. "That's what the corporal—"

"Colonel, honey. He's a 'colonel,' not a 'corporal,' " said Tim.

"Whatever. Some old guy said 500,000 today and 750,000 tomorrow." Tim rolled his eyes.

"Speaking of tomorrow, men," Jungle said. "Chris and I agree. It's time. Tim and Patrick will fly lead and Chris and I'll copilot. How's that sound?" Tim and Patrick stared at each other in amazement and gave each other a high-five. Patrick couldn't believe his luck. The day Don would see him fly, he'd be the lead pilot! "I don't give a shit if there's only two people there tomorrow, men," Jungle said. "We're gonna put on the best show yet!"

"Sir, with all due respect, you picked one hell of a time to give me this news."

"Mel, I explained why it was necessary to tell you now. Did you want every message clerk in Okinawa to know before you did? How about their squadron commanders?"

"You hear General Laker died this morning?"

"I just heard the terrible news. I'm very sorry, Sledge. He was your mentor—"

"I learned everything I know about flying from that man!" Sledge put his head down and Leonard thought he might cry until he looked up with a defiant expression. "Who made it?"

"Don't know. All General Neville told me was that your name was not on the list."

"I bet that made you two happy, didn't it?" He spat the words. "Fuck this, I need a drink."

"You *have* a drink, and from the way you're behaving, I suspect you've had a lot more."

Sledge guzzled the last of his beer. "*Now* I need another drink. I want some vodka."

"Did it ever occur to you, Lieutenant Colonel Hammer, that the reason you'll never be a colonel is that you drink too much?"

Sledge stood up and squared off against Leonard. "I guess it doesn't make any difference now, does it, General Spencer?" Leonard wanted to beat Sledge to a bloody pulp. He couldn't recall the last time he'd tried so hard to restrain his temper. "Used to be that real Marines weren't afraid to drink a little, like General Laker. With all this 'politically correct' bullshit, the only Marines they keep around are limp-wristed pansies. Guys like me—the old Corps, the 'tough breed'—they put out to pasture. Fine, sir, they can put me out to pasture. I don't want to be around this—this—spineless clusterfuck they call a Marine Corps anymore!"

Leonard neared his breaking point. "You can repeat that line of bullshit, Sledge, but saying it won't make it true. What *is* true is that you're the most worthless squadron commander I've ever known. I rated you six out of six, even behind a lieutenant colonel I promoted less than a year ago. You're a drunk and a failure as a leader. I can't believe my predecessor gave you the training squadron. Your pilots' quality ratings have decreased dramatically since you took over and you've done nothing to correct it. None of this comes as a surprise to you—we've discussed it countless times. I was shocked you weren't selected because you've sucked up to more general officers than any field grade officer I've ever met, and believe me, that's some stiff competition! I actually looked forward to your promotion so I could get rid of you.

"This is wonderful, though, because now I'm justified in what I'm about to do. I have the concurrence of a board convened at Headquarters Marine Corps. Their actions validate what I've felt for a long time. You, Lieutenant Colonel Melvin Hammer, are not fit for service!" In almost thirty years, Leonard hadn't spoken this harshly to another Marine. No one had ever pushed him this far.

Sledge's failure should've convinced him to seek help, but instead, he blamed everyone and everything but himself.

"I'm doing what I should've done a long time ago. As of this moment, you are no longer commanding officer of 707. Effective immediately, Major Burr, your executive officer, is now the acting squadron commander. I will notify him and General Neville right away."

Sledge was speechless. Opening the door, he stormed down the crowded hall, knocking several men and women out of his way. "Hey, motherfucker!" someone shouted. "Watch where the fuck you're going!" Leonard stared at Sledge's back and let him go. Monday morning, he'd be someone else's problem. For now, Leonard had to notify a major that he was a commander.

Leonard reentered the reception area. Across the room, the Blue Angel pilots autographed posters where Major Burr waited in line with his daughter. Leonard approached and the major introduced Leonard to his child. "I need to speak with you in private," Leonard said.

"Let me get my wife." The major motioned for his wife to watch the girl, then followed Leonard into the room where Leonard had just fired Sledge.

"Major Burr, you're the acting CO of 707. Sledge failed promotion. I felt it wasn't in the best interests of either your squadron or the Marine Corps to keep him on as the CO."

"Colonel Spencer, I'm honored that you've placed this much faith in me, sir, and I promise I'll do my best not to let you down. But—"

"But what?" asked Leonard. "Kevin, what's the matter?"

"It's about Sledge, sir. It doesn't make any difference, but the timing just sucks, pardon my French. His wife left him yesterday. She took the kids *and* served him with divorce papers."

"Oh my God. Well, you're correct. It doesn't really make any difference."

33

"Why is Karl riding shotgun," asked Jeanne, "while the three of us are stuck back here?"

"Same reason he doesn't have on a shirt," said Robbi.

"Same reason we don't have the top on the jeep," said Don.

Smiling broadly, Karl tilted his body back to catch some rays. "It's all about the tan, ladies."

"Not about being seen and admired?" asked Don as a minivan full of teenage girls crawled beside them on the interstate. Karl flexed, reveling in the attention while the girls made catcalls. "Ignore them. Daddy might have a gun. He doesn't know you're a big ol' girl yourself."

"That'd be ironic." Jeanne put sunscreen on Robbi's shoulders. "Can't believe this traffic."

"I knew it'd be bad, but thought we left Vista early enough to beat the air show crowd." Don propelled the jeep slowly up Orange County's most congested freeway. "I was wrong."

"All this construction doesn't help," Karl said, pointing to closed lanes. "It's why I can never guess the drive time when I bring the colonel up here."

"Why aren't you chauffeuring your boss around the air show this weekend?" asked Jeanne.

"You kiddin' me?" Robbi asked. "Karl has the old man wrapped around his little finger. Tell them how many hours you worked last week."

"Thirty," Karl answered, laughing. "But my free ride on easy street's almost over. Colonel Spencer gets promoted to general and leaves in June. We get a new group commander."

"Aren't you getting orders soon?" Don asked Karl.

"Have to ask the missus. We're married now, so they're supposed to transfer us together."

"Colonel Spencer's pulling some strings," Robbi said. "Might have an answer tomorrow."

"Oh my God, Jeanne!" said Esther. "What're you gonna do when Robbi leaves?"

"Yeah, Jeanne," Don said. "What if the kids get shipped to someplace like Adak, Alaska?"

Don caught Jeanne's eyes in the mirror. "I'll resort to that time-tested coping mechanism gays and lesbians have relied on forever—denial. Pretend it ain't happening and I don't have to think about it." Looking at her watch, Jeanne asked, "What time is Patrick's flight?"

"One," Don answered. "We'll be there. But we gotta meet Melanie before that."

"Melanie? I remember her," said Esther. "She's a fox!"

"Take it easy, girl!" Robbi said. "She's straight—and engaged—to Patrick's best friend. And I'm still not happy that, because of her, you made me hide in Patrick's closet for an *hour*."

"What?" Karl turned around to face the three women crammed in the backseat. "My wife was forced back into the closet? How'd I miss that?"

"Um—you and Lance were on a little mission, remember?" Jeanne said.

"Oh yeah," Karl replied. "Never mind."

Don gave his friends a puzzled look. He hadn't brought up Agent Gared or the NIS issue since his conversation with Patrick three months ago. This was the first mention of it, at least in front of him, but he decided against pursuing the matter. "Where's Lance? Why isn't he here?"

"Work. And studying for final exams," said Karl. "He dealt with the military enough this year to last him the rest of his life."

They rode in silence until Don exited off the freeway onto Sand Canyon Road. "Glad the morning fog finally cleared," said Esther. "How's that tan coming along, Karl?"

"Welcome to Coastal California," Don said, "where 'May Gray' leads to 'June Gloom.' "

"But the sun always shines sooner or later," said Karl, inspecting his bronze torso.

"Gotta hit the head. Catch up with you guys outside," Patrick said to Jungle, Chris and Tim. Pushing open the heavy steel door, Patrick flipped on the lights. He was startled to see Sledge wearing a flight suit, seated on the bench outside the showers. "Sir! You surprised me."

"Good, McAbe. I surprise myself sometimes." Slowly, he stood. Sledge looked disheveled and unshaven. "Colonel Hammer, you all right?" Patrick walked toward his commanding officer.

"Get the fuck away from me, McAbe!" Sledge ordered. "I'm as all right as I've ever been."

Dozens of thoughts sped through Patrick's mind. Why was his commanding officer alone in the men's locker room of another squadron's hangar at a different base on Sunday morning? Patrick couldn't tell if Sledge was drunk. He didn't slur his speech and his walk was steady. But he recalled that some people with a high tolerance for alcohol could function normally after consuming a lot. Maybe that was the case with Sledge. Deciding he couldn't do anything about it, Patrick stepped to the urinal to take care of the business he'd come here for.

"I'm flying today!" barked Sledge. Patrick's discomfort was partly because he didn't like to talk while he was urinating but mostly because he didn't know how to reply. What did Sledge mean when he said he was flying? In the air show? What aircraft? "You hear me, McAbe? I'm flying your bird today. You're my copilot."

Patrick became livid. Of all flights for Sledge to cut in, why did it have to be the one where Patrick was flying lead? He finished quickly and zipped up his flight suit. "Sir, Captain Pfeiffer signed for the aircraft. He said I could fly lead—"

"I don't give a fuck about Jungle or who signed for what." Sledge raised his voice several decibels. "I'm flying that bird today and you're my copilot." He stopped a foot-and-a-half from Patrick. "You got a problem with that, Lieutenant?"

Sledge's breath stank like halitosis, not the beer odor Patrick was familiar with. He'd heard that some liquors didn't leave an alcohol smell, but he wasn't sure. "No—no, sir. But—"

"But what?" He jabbed a finger into Patrick's chest. "You got something against me?"

"No sir, but please don't touch me again. It's just the aircraft belongs to Jungle and he—"

"Bullshit! All these aircraft belong to me—I'm the squadron commander. Where's Jungle? I need his gear." Without waiting for a response, Sledge stormed out of the locker room. Patrick washed his hands and hoped that Captain Pfeiffer and Lieutenant Ashburn would be able to talk some sense into the crazed lieutenant colonel.

"Melanie!" Don yelled over the heads of dozens of strangers. Melanie's face brightened when she recognized Don. "Think you've met everyone except Karl."

"Damn," Melanie said, stopping in front of the two shirtless Marines. "Good to meet you, Karl." She gave them all hugs and she kissed Don. "Patrick has the *best* taste in men!"

Don laughed. "Thanks. I'd say Tim's taste in women is right on."

"I wouldn't argue with that," said Esther. Melanie thanked her for the compliment.

Don reverted to his role as a gunnery sergeant. "Not much time until the flight. They'll be pissed if we don't get some decent photographs. Karl, you got the camera?"

"Check."

"Don't lose it. Jeanne's got the backup camera? Good." Leading the group toward the stands, he asked, "Patrick said he and Tim are flying lead today. Is that still true?"

"Yep," Melanie said, swinging her long ponytail as she walked. "Otherwise the Marines will have to deal with two very pissed-off lieutenants."

"With all due respect, sir, these are my aircraft and I don't see why—"

"'All due respect' my ass!" shouted Sledge. "There's no respect from you, Captain Pfeiffer. Don't think I forgot how you *conspired* behind my back with the colonel to end my career."

"What? What're you talking—?"

"Remember our ill-fated flight this winter against the Stingers—with Colonel Spencer?"

"Sir?" Jungle asked. "I was just following Royal's—"

"'Royal,' huh? I guess you and 'Royal' are drinkin' buddies now, aren't you, *Jungle*." Sledge stopped inches away from Jungle's face. "That's right. You thought I'd forget all about that faulty machine gun. Gimme your gear or I'll court-martial you for direct disobedience."

Jungle looked at Patrick. "Do it," Patrick said. "It's not worth risking a court-martial."

"Sir," Jungle said. "You can fly, but as my copilot. Leave McAbe here."

"Fuck no! Let's get one thing straight, *Captain!* I'm flyin' this bird—with McAbe—not because you 'let' me, but because I say so. And I won't be anyone's copilot, you get that?"

"That's—that's—good, sir." Jungle's face showed the terror that Patrick felt. Chris and Tim had the same look. "Then I'll be your copilot, okay, sir? Leave McAbe here."

"Fuck no, Captain Pfeiffer! You think I'd fly with you, you goddamned backstabber?"

"Sir," Jungle protested, "I don't know what you're talking about. No one stabbed—"

Sledge grabbed Jungle's flight vest and helmet away from him. "Get in, McAbe," the lieutenant colonel ordered. "We're going for a ride."

Nothing in the four officers' training had prepared them for this situation. Their mutual indecision paralyzed them. Patrick recognized it as a classic Hobbesian choice—they could choose to stop Sledge by force, but physical violence against a superior officer would result in confinement at hard labor for many years. The alternative was acquiescence. Sledge had flown thousands of hours, although not in this condition. As Sledge squeezed his large body into Jungle's flight vest, Jungle huddled with the other three. "Chris, fly lead. Tim, take the copilot's seat. Patrick, try to slow him down. I'll call the MPs and hope they get here before you break skids."

"Should we let him go up by himself?" Chris asked. "He doesn't need a copilot to fly."

Jungle looked nervously at Sledge. "But if anything happens to him or the bird, we're responsible. One of us should go. That way at least someone sane will be at the controls."

"I agree," said Patrick. "I'm the only one he'll fly with. I should go."

"If you fly, we're going with ya', bro'," said Tim. "Right, Chris?"

"Abso-fuckin'-lutely," said Chris. "Let's go!"

Jungle patted Patrick on the shoulder and ran inside. Patrick returned to his aircraft, where Sledge prepared to climb into the cockpit. "Where the fuck did Jungle go?" Without waiting for a response, Sledge said, "Doesn't surprise me he'd turn and run. You heard me, McAbe. Get in front." Putting on his helmet, Patrick climbed into the small attack helicopter as Sledge squirmed into his seat, three feet behind Patrick. "Let's get her started, McAbe." The squadron commander closed the glass canopy over their heads. "We need to give you a callsign."

Unfortunately, the mechanical crew they'd brought with them from Camp Pendleton was the best in the squadron and everything checked out quickly. Looking through the glass at Tim and Chris, Patrick shrugged. He didn't know how else to delay the flight except pray the MPs arrived soon. "I know what we'll call you," Sledge said. "'Honest Abe' McAbe."

"I told Sam Nunn I don't care about his six-month truce with 'Billary.' A deal between Democrats is like honor among thieves— meaningless. While we're on the subject of Democrats, my bill to turn the military's existing ban on homosexuals into federal law is ready to go. I need one Democratic cosponsor and I can bring it to the full House as early as this week."

"That soon?" asked the mayor of the town of El Toro. "Well, Congressman Coughlin, do you think you can find a Democrat willing to break ranks with Clinton?"

"More Democrats have broken ranks than are standing by him," replied Coughlin. "Look at Nunn in the Senate. The problem in the House is getting one of them to mutiny by sponsoring a bill directly opposing their president. It'll be tough, but there are Democrats I can persuade."

"Or perhaps bribe." Leonard and Pete had been standing silently off to one side.

The politicians laughed. "Not a bad idea. I like your sense of humor, Colonel Spencer," said Coughlin. "Mayor, meet the Marine Corps's newest aviation general." Coughlin introduced Leonard to the mayor and continued with his legislative report. "When I get it out of committee, it'll pass by a wider margin than predicted. They can thank Edward Coughlin for ridding the United States military of homosexuals. The mothers and fathers of America can once again feel secure when they send their sons off to fight for freedom. Isn't that right, Colonel?"

"Thank *you* for their freedom? Yes, Congressman. I'm—*certain* that will happen." Leonard hoped his sarcasm was only slightly obvious. "If you'll excuse us, gentlemen, I believe Eileen Neville is trying to get our attention."

"Keep the boss's wife happy, right, Colonel?" said Coughlin. "You're a smart man."

With fake smiles, Leonard and Pete backed away. Crossing the general's tent, Pete said, "I've met that prick a dozen times, but ever since I got passed over for promotion, I'm invisible."

"Count your blessings," Leonard said. As they sided up to Eileen, he whispered, "Help!"

"Oh, you poor things! Thank you for taking him away from me. As a reward, here, have some of my homemade banana pudding."

Leonard and Pete thanked her and took a serving while Leonard checked his watch. Fifteen minutes until the Marine Air-Ground

Task Force demonstration where his Cobras would be flying. He was confident it would be as smooth today as it had been the previous two days.

General Neville returned to his seat at the front of the tent between Leonard and Eileen. "Thank God the mayor arrived. If I hear Coughlin tell the story of how he survived that F-86 crash one more time—" Changing subjects, he said, "We need to set the date for your promotion and change of command ceremony, Leonard. The commandant has given the green light. We can do it anytime." Leonard sighed and didn't say anything. "Giving up your command is the hardest thing a Marine officer can do, but it is a prerequisite for your promotion. This Aircraft Wing is only big enough for one general—and I'm not going anywhere for another year."

"I assume my replacement is ready to go?" Leonard asked.

"Every day he asks if we've set the date. So yes, it's up to us," the general explained. "When do you have to report to your new assignment in Washington?"

"Who wants another hot dog?"

"How old are you, Karl?" asked Jeanne. "Twenty-three? I give you two more years before all that nasty food you put in your body shows up on your gut."

"Two years," said Robbi, patting the taut skin on Karl's abdomen. "That's forever."

"Says the other twenty-three-year-old," said Esther.

"You can't leave the stands now," said Melanie. "You'll miss Tim and Patrick's flight." She glanced at her watch. "They're starting any second."

"And you're the cameraman." Don shook his head at Karl's irresponsibility. "You got the rest of the afternoon to get people to look at you."

"All right, I guess I can wait. They should have people walk around and sell that shit like they do at the baseball stadium," Karl moaned, returning to his spot in the stands. "Hey! There they are. I see the Cobras." Don looked as Karl pointed toward the southern end of the air station. A feeling of warmth and happiness overcame

Don as he watched his boyfriend doing what he loved to do. Don had never felt prouder to be a gay U.S. Marine than at that moment.

"It's settled then," said General Neville. "I'll have my aide put it on my schedule and the protocol officer will begin making the arrangements."

"Thank you, General." Leonard checked the program and his watch. Almost time.

"Eileen, Leonard's ceremony will be the Friday of Memorial Day weekend." The general turned around. "Can you remind me of that, Eileen? Eileen? Now where did she—?" The general stood to find his wife.

"Would you like me to toss your plate?" Leonard asked Pete. "I'm going forward for a closer look." Pete thanked him and Leonard threw the plastic away as he walked in front of the tent for a better view of the activities on the flight line.

"That bastard has stabbed me in the back before," Coughlin said loudly. "No, he hasn't committed to my bill, but mark my words—"

No longer paying attention to the congressman, Leonard stared into the distance. The helicopters had taken off from a hangar on the far side of the air station and he could see them now. The plan was for them to turn as the announcer introduced the squadron and the pilots' names to the vast crowd of spectators, as they'd done the previous two days. Today, however, the flight seemed off-kilter. Perhaps the pilots had adjusted their route for an unknown reason, but right now, they were too far away. The flights were timed so that the helicopters would immediately precede the troops on the ground. From where the birds were flying, Leonard didn't see how they could maneuver in time.

Suddenly, instead of crossing north in front of Saddleback Mountain, the Cobra in front turned, rapidly accelerating toward the viewing area. The second helicopter followed. Leonard wondered if the show's coordinator had changed the plan. He turned to ask. Minutes before she'd stood a few feet away, but now she was nowhere in sight.

"Eileen! Eileen, where are my aide and protocol officer?" asked the general. "I need you to write something down. Colonel Spencer's ceremony will be—"

"Then I told that faggot-loving son of a bitch from New York to—"

The helicopters picked up more speed. Something had gone seriously wrong. No one on the West Coast knew the capabilities of the AH-1W Super Cobra better than Leonard, and from the trajectory the birds were now on, he knew that if they didn't bank sharply to the left and to the right or pull up in just a few seconds, they'd hit the stands. The helicopters flew faster and faster and thousands of people could die. Leonard's mind instantly went into command mode. The coordinator had walkie-talkies. If only he could find her, he could call the tower and—and do what? All at once, he realized his powerlessness. Whatever happened was now up to those men flying the helicopters.

"Sledge! What the fuck are you doing?" Patrick screamed into his headset.

Thirty seconds after the two Cobras broke skids—departed the hangar—MPs arrived. Sledge laughed at his narrow escape. Otherwise, he'd remained eerily silent during the flight despite Chris and Patrick's instructions to change course. Because the pilot's seat was in the rear, Patrick couldn't see Sledge's actions or his face. In Patrick's line of sight were hundreds of thousands of people on the ground growing closer by the second.

"Sledge, break right!" Chris screamed over the radio. "McAbe, what the hell's going on?"

Patrick had been on the highest alert during the flight and Sledge's sudden turn toward the stands sent him into overdrive. Unfortunately, the cockpit configuration put the copilot at a disadvantage. Sledge controlled the aircraft with a center collective—a large stick—between his legs, allowing him to use most of his muscles to control the aircraft. The copilot's power control was a simple throttle on the armrest. Realizing Sledge's sinister intentions, Patrick fought for his life to gain control. The interior of the Cobra became a battle of leverage between the two men. As hard as

Patrick tried, though, his wrist was no match for Sledge's massive body power. Sledge was driving the helicopter faster and faster toward the center of the stands.

"I'm tryin', man! I can't—can't get control—!"

"We can't radio the tower!" Chris shouted. "Sledge must've fucked with the comm!"

"What the fuck are we supposed to do?" Tim screamed. "What the—?"

"He's gonna kill himself and thousands of others," Patrick said, continuing to struggle against his commander. *Including me.* He was surprised at his calmness because he knew what was about to happen. Maybe the certainty of his fate was the cause of his serenity. At first there'd been a momentary shock, which had been replaced by sheer, absolute terror unlike anything he'd ever felt. But just as suddenly, he was at peace. He was about to die, and as hard as he fought against the monster in the back, nothing he could do would change his fate.

Chris could do something, however, but the thought of it was so terrible, only he and Tim could make that decision. Patrick couldn't even suggest it, even though his heart ached for Don and their friends in danger below, along with thousands of other people.

"Oh my God, Chris! Melanie's in those stands." Tim was crying. "Melanie's—Chris—we gotta do it, bro'! We just gotta—"

Patrick closed his eyes and clenched his jaws. Tears streamed down his face.

"Motherfuck!" Chris shouted into his microphone. "Goddamn motherfucking son-of-a-bitch! I'm not—I'm not—"

"Chris! Chris," said Patrick. Chris had the same idea. "I can't stop him—we're outta time."

"Hey, fellas, what do you say?" Chris's voice sounded like he'd reached the same level of tranquility as Patrick.

"Do it," said Patrick. "Do it!"

"We gotta save 'em! Do it!" Tim cried. "I love you, Melanie!"

"I love you, Don," Patrick said quietly.

"Let's send this motherfucker to hell!" Chris screamed.

The last sound Patrick heard was the ear-shattering noise of metal slicing metal as Chris flew his and Tim's Cobra into Sledge and Patrick's. The two sets of rotor blades slashed into each other, shredding the helicopters—and their occupants—into pieces. The impact caused an immediate explosion and sent small and large chunks of debris in thousands of directions.

They felt no pain.

34

"Don, what's happening?" asked Melanie.

Seconds before the explosion, spectators were in one of two categories—those who believed the helicopters' rapid approach was part of the program and those who knew better.

Don was in the latter group. "I'm not sure but it doesn't look good." The horrifying sound of metal hitting metal followed by the sight of the tremendous explosion caused mass hysteria in the stands. The fireball billowed until Don felt the blast's heat on his face, chest and arms. The air filled with black smoke and smelled of fuel. Small burning pieces of the aircraft sprayed viewers. The helicopters had collided far enough in front so that none of the larger pieces seriously injured anyone on the ground. Unfortunately, people panicked and climbed over each other to flee from the flight line. Some fell, others were pushed and many were trampled.

Don stood with one arm around Melanie and the other around Karl. Robbi, Jeanne and Esther stood one row down. The six huddled for protection from the screaming stampede. Chaos surrounded them but their little band held together. Remaining in place, Don felt as if his mind had frozen in time. The scene replayed in his head. The helicopters flew toward the stands, one turned in to the other and they both exploded. The helicopters flew toward the—

"Tim! Oh my God, no!" Screaming, Melanie broke away from Don. She pushed through the throng and ran onto the tarmac. Don was a step behind and the others followed. With the crowd scrambling to escape the crash, Don had an unobstructed view of the apocalyptic scene. The smoldering rubble resembled post-bombing pictures of Hiroshima, not two helicopters.

The realization hit him hard. Patrick was dead. Don felt as if he might go into convulsions, but he continued running. Melanie must've had the same realization about Tim because she crumpled to the ground. Robbi and Esther ran to help her while inertia carried Don toward the nightmarish scene. Jeanne and Karl were a few yards away.

"Leonard! Where are you going?"

For the first time in his life, Leonard ignored a general. The staff could take the Nevilles and their guests to safety. Leonard had other more important duties.

The tent was located fifty yards from the center of the flight line. Running toward the middle, everywhere he looked, all he saw was pandemonium. The military police and their reinforcements tried to control the crowd but their efforts were futile. Like a giant herd of buffalo, hundreds of thousands of spectators charged away from the stands. Thousands of air show attendees had spent the afternoon milling about the acres of military exhibits scattered elsewhere on the base. They hadn't seen the show and weren't aware of the cause of the bedlam. When they saw the crowd rushing away from the stands, their instincts took over and they joined in the mad dash. Leonard wondered how many people would die.

The entire area was an exercise in sensory overload. The smell of the crash was so thick he could taste it. The sight was gruesome and the screams and other sounds made by people panicking were overwhelming. The air station's CFR—crash, fire, and rescue—Team was already at the site. Emergency medical technicians pried the charred and unrecognizable remains of the pilots from what was left of the cockpits. An MP tried ushering him away, but a Camp Pendleton firefighter recognized him and told the MP to let him onto the scene. Staring at the gruesome image, Leonard felt like a captain whose ship had sunk without him or a father witnessing the death of his children. When he recalled one of the pilots was Chris Ashburn, a former lover and one of the few men he trusted completely, his agony became unbearable.

"Patrick! Patrick!"

Leonard turned to see whose voice sounded so painful. To his astonishment, Karl had his arms around a friend, a man suffering agony worse than Leonard's anguish. Behind Karl was the pilot's fiancée Leonard had met the night before. When the MPs tried to remove Karl and his friends, Karl and Leonard's eyes locked. Karl's face pleaded for help. Leonard understood the situation and he knew what he needed to do, to hell with the risks to his career. He ran to the group. "They're with me." Putting his arm around Karl's friend, he guided him from the debris.

As they approached the pilot's fiancée, medical vans sped across the flight line. An MP ran to them, shouting, "Colonel, want to ride to the regional hospital in one of the vans?"

"How much space do you have?" he asked.

The MP spoke into his radio then put it to his ear. "Four can go!"

Leonard said to Karl, "Ride with your friend."

Karl nodded. "Thank you." He reached into Don's pocket, grabbed the keys and threw them to another member of his group. "El Toro Regional!"

Leonard recognized her. "Corporal Reynolds. Do you want to ride with your friend to the—?"

"Her name's Melanie, sir! No thank you, but Jeanne will go with her if that's okay."

"That's right—Melanie." Leonard motioned for Melanie and Jeanne to get into the van.

As the vans sped away, Corporal Reynolds said, "Colonel, you're welcome to ride with us."

"It will be impossible to get there with this traffic. A million people are leaving at once."

"Trust me, sir," said the corporal. "We've got the right vehicle and you know how I drive."

"You're right, let's go." Running toward the parking area with the corporal and her friend, Leonard was struck with the pointlessness of going to the hospital. No one survived the crash. The families, though, not knowing where to go, would be at the hospital. So would the media. He thought about what could've caused today's collision. Whatever it was, it hadn't been an accident. Hundreds of thousands of people were witnesses. The news channels would replay the collision many times in the coming weeks for an audience of millions. From what he'd seen, the only conclusion was that someone had a death wish. Despite his pain over the death of his men—especially Chris—slowly he grasped what was coming. This wasn't an ordinary accident. He didn't know what lay ahead, but he was certain of one thing—there would be surprises.

"Breaking news from Orange County, California."

When Kathryn worked close to a deadline, she tuned her television to cable news as background noise, blocking the more bothersome sounds from the street in front of her house. She didn't pay attention to the shows, but the broadcaster's reference to California reminded her to prepare for tomorrow night's interview with the Marines. The visual caught her attention. Grabbing the remote, she turned up the volume and walked across the room for a better view. "Holy shit!" The news channel replayed actual footage of a midair collision. "Oh my God!"

"The collision occurred minutes ago during an air show at the Marine Corps Air Station El Toro, California. Our local Orange County affiliate was recording the air show's event for later broadcast." The station cut back to the footage, this time in slow motion.

Kathryn shook her head and lowered the volume. "Thank God my Marines are at Camp Pendleton," she said, returning to a story that was due to her editor in three hours.

"Classy joint."

"Ya' like The Red Rooster?" Zack asked, chalking the tip of his pool cue. "Reminds me of back home." The MP sent the three-ball into the side pocket of a well-worn table. "Nothin' like cigarette smoke in a pool bar to add flavor to a cheeseburger. Best in town. Just ordered me one. You should get you one, too, Jay-man. You look skinnier than the last time I saw you. Meant to tell you that on Cinco de Mayo. You missed a good party by the way."

"I'm sure I did." Jay passed on ordering any food. "How far are we from the apartment?"

"Less than a mile. Don't worry, we got plenty of time. Wanna know how I know?" Zack didn't wait for a response. "'Cause I called that lieutenant's unit on Thursday." Zack paused to line up his next shot. "I said I'd wait before I did anything but I couldn't hold off four days. I'm a man of action—like I thought you were. I even figured out how we can get inside if we want."

"We need to be more careful this time. No mistakes. You talk to McAbe?"

"No. They said he was at El Toro, flyin' in the air show. Won't get back till late tonight."

"Good. You shouldn't be talking with him directly, Zack. What the fuck were you gonna say? 'Hey, sir, I saw you with your tongue down another Marine's throat on your balcony'?"

"I'll tell him what I tell all of 'em. Turn themselves in or I'm comin' after 'em." Zack won his game. "Grab a stick, Jay-man. I'll let you break."

Jay pulled a cue off the wall. "If we do this right, we can snare a large group of homosexuals at once. That's better than cruising bookstores, the pier and bars, catching them one at a time."

Zack frowned. "I like doin' it my way. Appeals to my 'predator instincts.'"

"My goal is to help you evolve past that. Here's how we proceed with Lieutenant McAbe. I like this case because we can easily involve his command, thanks to the fraternization charge. During that investigation we'll uncover what's obvious—McAbe and Gunnery Sergeant Hawkins are fuck-buddies."

"Heh, heh. I like the way you think."

"We get McAbe's command to request NIS do a full investigation. Tolson assigns me—"

"Even though you ain't up here at Pendleton?"

"That's where you come in," Jay said, his ball missing the hole.

"You report the fraternization up here and I'll report sightings of the two of them together in San Diego. When both reports are in the system, I'll convince Ollie to merge the files and put me on the case. Once I get my hooks into the investigation, I intend to uncover everything."

"Including your buddy Karl?" Zack asked. The bartender yelled that his food was ready.

Jay waited impatiently. "Who the hell is Karl?" he asked when Zack came back to the table.

"'Who's *Karl*?' Well, well, Jay-man." Zack walked around the table, stopping in front of him. Leaning over, Zack looked at his neck. "Let me ask *you* a question. How'd you get that pretty little scar on your neck? You have some kind of operation you didn't tell me about?"

"The name of the guy who did this to me is Karl?" Jay asked. "How do you know?"

"I've known about Marine Corporal Karl Steiger for two years. *Everybody* knows Karl—this town ain't that big. He's one motherfucker so crazy even *I* stay the hell away from him."

"How do you know he's the one who assaulted me?"

"Jay-man." Zack sat on top of pool table. "You think I'm fuckin' stupid, don't you?"

"What you did that night wasn't too smart."

"Aw, shit. I was just havin' a little fun. If people can't use crystal responsibly, they just shouldn't use it at all, that's what I say." Someone across the bar lit a cigarette and Zack ran over to bum one. When he came back, he inhaled the smoke and leaned against the table by Jay.

Jay put his hand on a bulge in Zack's jeans. "What the hell— you always carry this shit?"

"Heh, heh, it's a little early to be gettin' fresh, ain't it?" Zack reached into his pocket. "No, this ain't what you think it is. It's a Leatherman tool—no good Marine should be without one."

Jay opened the pouch and took out a combination wrench, pliers, knife, etc. "Hell, looks like a Swiss Army knife on steroids." Retuning it to the pouch, he put it in Zack's pocket. "Sorry."

"Apology accepted," Zack said smugly. "Back to your buddy

Karl, if you didn't know that every swingin' dick in that bathhouse was tryin' to get into his room that night, then you're the one who's stupid." He blew a long puff of smoke into Jay's eyes. "After you ditched me—"

"I didn't 'ditch' you." Jay fanned the smoke away as Zack bit into his cheeseburger.

"Whatever. I asked what'd happened to you and everyone said you went into Karl's room but came out real quick, without your towel and bleedin' pretty bad."

"If you knew who it was, you should've called."

"I *did* call! You didn't pick up the damn phone."

"Okay. You got a point. Good. We know more than I thought we did. I was saying—"

"Jesus, Mary and Joseph!" shouted the guy Zack had bummed the cigarette from. "Look at that!" The Red Rooster's other three patrons were watching a television across the bar.

Jay and Zack turned to see where the man was pointing. "Motherfuck!" Zack exclaimed. "Those were Cobras." Jay and Zack moved closer to the television.

The newscaster described the crash, concluding, "The pilots' names have not been released."

"What kind of airplane does Lieutenant McAbe fly?" Jay asked.

Zack stared open-mouthed. "A Cobra. If I was a bettin' man—and I am—my money would be our First Lieutenant McAbe looks like a piece of burnt toast 'bout now."

There was only one thing for them to do. "Ready to go?" Jay asked.

"El Toro?"

"You bet, bettin' man!" Jay said as the two men started out of the Red Rooster.

"Hey!" screamed the cocktail waitress. "You goddamned sons-of-bitches didn't pay!"

"Can you get that? Gotta get something." Jay threw a twenty-dollar bill at the woman. As they hurried into Jay's car, Zack said, "It's good to have you back, Jay-man!"

* * *

"But I want to ride in the van with Tim," Melanie said through her tears. "Don't you want to ride to the hospital with Patrick?" Don put his arm around Melanie as she cried on his shoulder.

The EMTs had ushered Don, Melanie, Jeanne and Karl into the back of an ambulance along with four rescue and medical personnel. Melanie had asked Don why the medical people didn't ride in the ambulances with the pilots. Even though he knew the answer, Don hadn't replied. There was nothing left to save. Patrick, Tim, Chris and the other guy—Jungle, if he remembered the last conversation with Patrick correctly—weren't there anymore. In their place were four mangled corpses—if that. Nothing more than charred and decaying biological matter. The men they'd known had vanished to the mystical domain mortals couldn't comprehend.

Karl had handed Don his shirt, which he'd dropped somewhere along the way, and Don had put it on. He didn't remember it, though, and when he stepped out of the ambulance at the hospital, he was surprised to find himself wearing it. "Where are my keys?" he asked, wondering how he could ask such a mundane question.

"Gave 'em to Robbi." Karl said. "She's driving your jeep over."

Don thanked Karl for being so thoughtful, and with his left arm around Karl and his right around Melanie, they walked toward the hospital's emergency entrance. Jeanne was on the other side of Melanie. Within a few steps, Don felt himself slip into his familiar "robot mode." He'd been here before, too many times. Kuwait, Panama—Beirut. Only this time, it was a civilian hospital, civilian medical staff, and most of the injured were civilians whom the crowds had stampeded. Still, the parking lot and ER entrance looked a lot like a combat zone, the occasional military uniform adding to the resemblance.

Thousands of people from the air show had found their way to the medical center. Don assumed thousands more were on their way. The hospital's interior was overwhelmed and every available medical person helped. They'd employed advanced triage, a combat and mass casualty practice Don knew painfully well. Doctors dismissed victims who would survive without assistance. The most difficult and controversial part of triage was turning away those who were very likely to die even with assistance. Patients receiving the most advanced care fell into the last category—those who would live only if they received immediate medical attention.

Police tried to clear the driveways but there weren't enough officers to control the crowds. Fortunately, the ambulance's sirens had cleared a path close to the large sliding glass doors leading into the ER. Television news crews had been among the first to arrive. The reporters assumed that Don, Melanie, Karl and Jeanne were important enough to question because they'd ridden over in the ambulance. One reporter stuck a microphone in Karl's face.

"Sir! Sir, can you tell us the cause of the collision?"

Shaking his head, Karl pointed to the rescuers. "You need to ask one of those guys."

"Are you a relative of one of the pilots?" the reporter asked.

Karl looked into the camera and spoke clearly into the microphone. "I'm a friend of the family." Police prevented the media from following them into the hospital.

"You handled that well, buddy." Don leaned his head down and buried his face against Karl. "I wouldn't make it through this without you."

"Woo hoo, yeah, man, now *this* is what I'm talkin' about!" Zack shouted as Jay raced up Interstate 5 at over ninety miles per hour. They'd made it through the border control checkpoint south of San Clemente, hopefully their last hurdle. "But I'm confused. What's the plan?"

"It's so simple, it's brilliant. We just said we needed a reason to investigate McAbe, right?" Zack nodded. "You're sure he's one of the pilots?"

"Some WM corporal said he's flying a Cobra at the El Toro air show."

"There's a good chance he was in the collision. If it turns out he was the pilot who *caused* the collision, I can dig into every aspect of his life."

"Fuckin' A, man! Then we can find out the name of every faggot in the Corps!"

"That's the idea. Shhh!" Jay increased the volume as the radio announcer gave new details.

"We're reporting to you live from the El Toro Regional Medical Center," the woman said, "where the four pilots involved in the collision have been brought."

"What a coincidence," Jay said sarcastically. "We're on our way there. You know the way?"

"Exit onto 405 at all the construction. We can bypass the traffic coming out of the air station," Zack said. "See what a good team we make? Jay and Zack's excellent adventure!"

"You're right, buddy. We make a great team."

"Thank you for driving me over here and for dropping me off at the entrance, Corporal Reynolds." Leonard jumped out of the jeep. "It would've taken me another hour on my own."

"Sir, it really means a lot to Corporal Steiger and to me how you helped our friends." Leonard waved to the corporal and her friend as he turned toward the ER.

"Leonard!" General Neville and Eileen stepped out of the sedan. "You made it here quickly."

The reporters mobbing the entrance surrounded the general's sedan. "Congressman Coughlin!" they screamed. "Congressman! What can you say about—?"

"He *insisted* on coming over here with us," Eileen said.

Leonard stepped to Eileen's left. With the general on her right, the three of them fought their way into the hospital. "I would do the same thing if I were in his position," Leonard said.

"We both would," said the general. "But his presence makes the situation more difficult."

"Didn't think that was possible," Leonard said quietly as they stepped inside the building. In his heart, though, he knew better. The most awful situation could always be worse. Somehow, he knew this nightmare was about to grow much more dire before it started getting better.

35

"You'd think this was Dallas and they just shot Kennedy," Jay said, pulling into the hospital's parking lot. Luckily, a car at the far end of the lot left. As he and Zack jumped out, he spotted Hawkins's vehicle. "They're here." The jeep's presence in the lot linked everything—the park, Johnson, Hawkins, Johnson's funeral, Karl and the bathhouse and now McAbe. Jay's reward for his months of patient suffering was just around the corner.

"Come on!" Zack shouted. "Action's inside."

Jay was back on top. His old drive had returned and he was in control. His mind raced through all the possibilities and factors these circumstances presented. "Zack! Hawkins and Karl will recognize me. I'll enter from the back and find out what I can from the hospital staff. You go in the lobby. See who's there and learn what you can."

"Aye, aye, sir!" Zack laughed, giving Jay a mock salute as he ran toward the ER's entrance.

"Excuse me, ladies. Are either of you married to one of the pilots?"

Jeanne shook her head. Melanie said, "I'm—Tim's—Lieutenant Roberts's—fiancée. We—we're getting married in six weeks."

"Please come with me, ma'am," the orderly said. "The doctor would like to speak with you."

Melanie had been clinging to Don and Jeanne's arms. She gave Don a fearful look. "Don needs to come too," she said. "I want him to come with—"

"Are you related to one of the pilots, sir?" the orderly asked Don.

Don didn't know what to say. His relationship with Patrick had been personal and spiritual; labels weren't adequate. Why couldn't the orderly see that he and Patrick were the same person?

"Yes, he is," said Karl.

"I'm sorry," the man said, "right now the doctor insists that only spouses—or fiancées—"

"Wait here," Karl said. "Be right back."

"General," said the hospital's chief physician, "I've asked to see the spouses of the pilots who are here, and your chaplain will also be present. Would you and your wife like to join us?"

"Yes, certainly," the general said. "May I ask you to turn off the televisions in the waiting area? Every station shows the crash and the panicked crowds. That doesn't help these people."

"Sure, General Neville. I'll take care of that right away."

"Colonel Spencer should join us for this meeting," the general added.

Leonard felt a tap on his shoulder. Still paying attention to the doctor, he slowly turned his head. "Sir," said the voice of his lover, "we need your help."

He turned around and put his hand on Karl's shoulder. "Whatever you need."

As Karl motioned for him to cross the waiting area, General Neville said, "Leonard, you should really come with—"

For the second time in his life, Leonard refused a general's directive. "I'll be a moment."

He and Karl pried their way through the crowded waiting area. Some people cried uncontrollably while others looked relieved. Most, though, had the unmistakable look of anxious confusion that comes from fearing the worst while hoping for the best. Karl halted near his friends and a member of the hospital's staff. "What's the problem?" Leonard asked.

"I wasn't aware there was a problem," the orderly said. "I was told to assemble—"

"Don is next of kin and should be part of this group," Karl explained.

"My name is Colonel Leonard Spencer and this man," he said, placing a hand on Don's shoulder, "will join us in the room with the chief physician."

"Okay," the orderly said. "Please follow me."

With one hand on Don and the other on Melanie, Leonard gently moved them toward the door behind the orderly. As he stepped away, the sweetest voice in the world whispered in his ear, "Thank you for this, sir. You're the greatest man I've ever known."

"Can't believe the military has already put an investigator on this. Talk about efficient." The harried doctor shook his head. "You get two minutes. What do you need to know?"

"Can you tell me anything about the pilots?" Jay asked, preparing to take notes.

"They're dead," the man said impatiently. "What else?"

"From what you've seen of the corpses, is there any indication of the cause of the collision?"

"Corpses? You realize what happened out there? These guys are in pieces. What caused it? Hell if I know. I saw the same news footage you did. One chopper plowed into the other."

"Any reason that might've happened?" Jay asked.

"I'd be speculating at this point, but one of the pilots might've had a seizure—or a blackout."

Jay stopped writing and looked at the doctor. "A blackout? Alcohol related?"

"Not necessarily," the doctor said, "but a possibility. I've examined the pilots' remains—at least what's been brought in so far. One has extensive signs of acute alcohol toxicity. But there's no evidence at this point that his condition is related to the cause of the collision." The doctor looked through the small window in his office door into the hallway.

Another member of the staff motioned for the physician. "Just one more minute, Doctor," Jay said. "What evidence of alcohol toxicity do you mean?"

The doctor nodded, indicating he was on his way. "Their bodies suffered severe trauma in the explosion, which actually facilitated an examination of the inner regions." He paused briefly, giving Jay a chance to catch up. "Even given the condition of the remains, one pilot had visible signs of extreme accelerated oxidative stress throughout his body, *i.e.* excessive fatty tissues around the brain, increased evidence of cell death and the like. His liver showed signs of cirrhosis. Oh, and pancreatitis. Prolonged alcohol abuse eventually affects almost every organ in the body." The doctor stood to attend to the patients. "If you'll excuse me, Agent—"

"Before you go—" Jay processed this information rapidly. "This damage—could it occur in the body of a man in his mid-twenties?"

"Not unless his mother nursed him with tequila," the doctor said, opening the door. "It's impossible to tell the exact age, but this pilot was mid-forties at the youngest. The other three were much younger. The level of extreme alcohol damage that I described generally occurs after two or three decades of heavy drinking. If that pilot hadn't been killed today, his end wasn't too far off." The doctor stepped into the hallway and motioned for another hospital staff member. "If you have any more questions, Agent, our technician can assist you."

"Thank you for your time, Doctor," Jay said as the man walked quickly down the corridor. Turning to the technician, he said, "I definitely have more questions."

As Leonard escorted Melanie and Karl's friend toward the private room with the hospital's chief physician, his mind assembled some pieces of the puzzle. The man in front of him was Gunnery Sergeant Hawkins, the Marine who'd embarrassed Congressman Coughlin on television. Thankfully, Coughlin was outside talking to the reporters. As Leonard had suspected, Hawkins was friends with Karl. Was Hawkins Chris's lover? Chris had said he was single. Thinking of Chris, Leonard recalled another image. Chris was with First Lieutenant McAbe at the dining in, something Leonard hadn't considered significant because Chris was friendly with most of his student pilots. But now, it seemed more relevant.

Another scene slowly returned. In the back of the officers' club a few months ago, Karl had also been talking to McAbe. The memory had stuck because lieutenants and corporals generally don't engage in idle chitchat. Was McAbe gay? Was Hawkins his lover? Leonard's fears were becoming reality. The only thing worse than hell was a complicated hell.

General Neville and Eileen waited with the head physician at a large set of double doors. The general looked puzzled. "Where are the other wives?"

"General, Eileen, this is Melanie. You and I met her last night. She's engaged—"

"Oh yes, to Lieutenant Roberts." He hugged Melanie and introduced her to his wife. Leonard introduced Hawkins as a friend of the family Melanie had requested to be with her.

"Captain Pfeiffer was divorced," Leonard said, looking at Hawkins.

"Lieutenants Ashburn—and McAbe—were single." Hawkins was stoic.

Leonard placed a sympathetic arm around the Marine. Leaning in, he whispered, "I understand—and sympathize—with what you're going through. You have my total support."

Major Burr—in his first sad duty as commanding officer—and his wife joined the group. The general pulled Leonard aside. "I realize you fired Sledge last night, but he should still be here out of respect for his men."

"My guess is that he returned home to Oceanside, General. Either that or—"

"Leonard? What's wrong?" the general asked. "Where are you going this time?"

"General, can you go to the room? I'll be right behind you." What Leonard didn't add as he moved across the lobby was that he was looking directly at a ghost.

* * *

"The doctor suspects that alcohol may have played a factor in the cause of today's collision," Jay explained to the technician. "How will you determine for certain if that's the case?"

"It wasn't easy," the lab technician said, "but I collected these." The technician pointed to a metal container holding four vials filled with blood. A scream in the lobby caused the technician to jerk his head. He looked through the glass in the doors holding back the noisy crowd. Terrified, he said, "I've never seen it like this. Never seen *anything* like this."

"You're doing a fantastic job," Jay said, nodding reassuringly. "What can you tell me about the blood samples? What do you do with them now?"

"Store them in the refrigerator." He pointed to a small cabinet in the room behind him. "They'll be tested tonight for alcohol and other substances."

"How do you know which vial of blood came from which pilot?"

"From this chart." The nervous man handed Jay a folder.

Jay was dismayed he didn't see any names. Instead, someone had written four cursory descriptions of the remains. Three were in their mid-twenties or early thirties and the fourth was a large man in his mid-fifties, although someone had written "forties" with a question mark. "What's the purpose of the labels with the numbers?" Jay pointed beside the descriptions.

"The numbers match the label I affixed to the vial with the blood sample. That way—"

A nurse opened the hall door. Sternly, she said, "The doctor needs you—*stat!*"

She disappeared, but her tone caused the technician to panic. "I—I—I've got—"

"Go on," Jay said. "Help the doctor. I'll put these in the refrigerator for you."

"Thank you, Agent. Thank you." The technician hurried out of the room.

Jay had to act fast. He carried the chart and the blood vials into the room, closing the door. Boxes of empty vials and clean needles sat on a counter against the wall. He scanned the chart for the number identifying the alcoholic, matching it with a number on the blood vial. Slowly, Jay peeled the label off the vial, keeping it intact. He affixed the label to an empty vial.

Now for the painful part. He'd watched as nurses had done this to him many times. He inserted the empty vial into the hypodermic needle, held out his left arm and flexed until he could see his vein. Gritting his teeth, he pricked his skin. To his delight, blood spurted out of his arm, through the needle and into the vial. "Hurry," he said. A minute later, the vial was full. He sealed it with a rubber cap, set it in the container with the other three vials of pilots' blood and put the container in the refrigerator. He tossed the needle into a red biowaste bin and put a cotton swab on his arm. "Better not leave this," Jay said, picking up the sample he'd substituted with his own. Inserting the vial in his pocket, he grabbed his notebook and exited the building.

"It's all my fault, sir! It's all my fault!" Captain Pfeiffer sobbed. "I shouldn't have let—I tried to tell—it was my aircraft! I should've done more to stop—!" Leonard hugged the distraught pilot and let him cry as much he needed to before asking questions.

Leonard had assumed Jungle had died in the collision and was stunned when the captain entered the hospital. When shock passed, they stepped inside the men's room near the entrance. "Tried to tell whom?" Leonard asked. "What happened? I thought you were flight leader."

Within minutes, Jungle regained his composure and dried his eyes on a tissue. "We were beginning our preflight when—I shoulda been on that flight, sir! It's all my fault! I shoulda—"

"Jungle, whose remains are lying in the other room?"

"It's the squadron commander, sir. It's Lieutenant Colonel Hammer. Sledge is in there."

"Oh, dear God in heaven." The picture cleared. It was ugly and horrible but at least what had happened today made sense—gruesome, grotesque, tragic sense, but sense nonetheless. Leonard hugged Jungle again. "Go home and get some rest, Captain Pfeiffer. Don't blame yourself for what happened today. This wasn't your fault. Please hear me—*this wasn't your fault.*"

* * *

"Where is the first set of samples?" the doctor asked the nervous technician.

"They're—they're in the refrigerator." The technician prayed the agent had kept his word. To his great relief, when he opened the door, he saw the container with four vials of blood on the top shelf. The chart identifying the blood was on the counter.

"Good," said the doctor. "Those samples will be kept here for overnight analysis."

"I don't understand why you just had me draw a second set of samples. Where do they go?"

"New California law," the doctor explained. "A second blood sample must be shipped to the county crime lab for testing and storage in all DUI arrests or incidents where alcohol definitely was or might have been a factor."

"Even military accidents?" the technician asked.

"Who knows? If it happened in Orange County, courier it to the crime lab."

"Okay, Doctor, if you say so," the technician said, not happy he had another task to track.

"Nothin' happened out in the waitin' room. The doctor took McAbe's *boy*friend—"

"Gunnery Sergeant Hawkins?" Jay asked.

"Fuck yeah—a *gunny!* Simply disgustin'," Zack said. "The doctor took him and a woman in the back, along with some other high-rankin' fuck wads. Then they turned off the televisions so all I had left to do was watch all the people get the bad news. Heh, heh, it was just terrible!"

"Sometimes you're one scary motherfucker, Zack." Jay had to admit, though—he was more thrilled about today's turn of events than Zack was.

As they exited onto the 405 freeway south, Jay tuned the radio to news of today's collision. "All four helicopter pilots were killed in the explosion but their names aren't being released until next of kin have been notified." The radio broadcaster cut to an unidentified woman's voice. "'Those helicopters were headed directly for the crowds of spectators. If one of them had hit the stands, I don't want to think what would've happened.' Can you estimate how many people would've died? 'They were headed toward the largest section of stands in the center. I'd say at least five thousand factoring in the initial impact and the explosion. Maybe more. Depends on where the wreckage blew.' The hospital reports that twenty-three others died from falling or trampling. In one case, a man died in traffic in the mad rush to leave the air station. As terrible as the news has been, as you heard from the air show coordinator, if the helicopters had reached the stands, the news would be far more devastating than it already is."

Zack lowered the volume. "You ain't told me what happened. Doctors know anything?"

"Not much. Likeliest conclusion is that a pilot was intoxicated at the time of the crash."

"Our boy?"

"No," Jay answered. "Definitely not."

"That sucks," Zack said. "I thought you wanted to blame the accident on McAbe."

"We'll try to. You and I are the only two who know—or who ever *will* know—the real blood alcohol content of the fourth pilot." Jay pulled a vial of blood out of his pocket.

"Holy fuckin' shit!" Zack said. "What'd you do?"

"If *I* were a betting man—and unlike you I'm not—I'd bet that this vial contains almost as much alcohol as blood. It belonged to one of the pilots—the one suspected of being drunk."

"Won't the people at the hospital know it's missin'?" Zack asked.

"No. It was replaced with blood drawn from a man who's never tasted alcohol in his life."

Zack was wide-eyed. "You stuck yourself and switched your blood with one of the pilots? People don't usually impress me much, Jay-man, but I gotta admit I am in *awe*!" Jay anticipated Zack's next question. "But I don't get it. How does that show McAbe caused the crash?"

"We don't give a shit about this crash, okay? Some old geezer got drunk and decided to fly a helicopter in an air show today—for some reason, I don't get 'cause I've never been drunk—"

"Heh, heh! I bet flyin' those things drunk—or high—would be a shitload of fun," Zack said.

"—and he blacked out, or had a seizure, or just rammed the helicopters. I don't know but I'm sure that's what happened and the Marine Corps will figure it out sooner or later. We wanna ensure it's *much* later. Our goal is a long investigation. That's how we'll find evidence on Karl, McAbe, Hawkins and their sick circle of military queers. But if the geezer's blood showed he'd had a lot of alcohol, the military would blame him right away, without an investigation."

"I getcha now, Jay-man. As long as all four pilots was sober, the Corps ain't got no choice but investigate the cause of the crash. I'm sure you'll think of how to get your ass—with me as your helper—assigned to the case. You're a fuckin' genius. Where to now, boss?"

"Only one logical place to go, Zack my man. Patrick McAbe's apartment."

36

"Colonel Spencer, have you seen the Nevilles?" Leonard stopped just in time. Congressman Coughlin almost followed him into the room where his nemesis, Hawkins, was grieving the loss of the man he loved. Leonard turned, blocking Coughlin's path. "There's a chance they returned to headquarters." Technically, it was a true statement. "He really should be near the communications center at a time like this."

"You're right," said Coughlin. "Tell him I have to catch a redeye to DC. Things are moving this week on military issues—base closures and the gay ban. I've got to shepherd the process but this collision is my top priority. Tell the general to call me for anything you need."

"I will," Leonard said, thankful for the man's imminent departure, "and I wish you Godspeed, Congressman." Coughlin exited, walking two feet from Karl, who was leaning against a wall by the entrance. Leonard had never seen a more striking contrast between two men. Coughlin embodied America's ugly underbelly of hatred. Karl represented what America was supposed to be about—strength through adversity, hard work, talent and loyalty. Best of all, Coughlin, though powerful, was a dinosaur. Karl was the future and that gave Leonard hope. Maybe that was the reason his mind was racing—he was searching for anything that offered a glimmer of hope. His eyes locked with Karl's, signaling that they were together in spirit. Soon they'd be together in person, but for now, they had to survive this tragedy, charades and all.

As Leonard pushed on the large door, he took a deep breath. He felt drained of energy but dropping on the floor wasn't an option. "What did you find out?" General Neville asked. Leonard looked at the faces. Besides General Neville, there was Eileen, the doctor, the acting squadron commander and his wife, Lieutenant Roberts's fiancée Melanie, and Gunny Hawkins.

"The—the doctor should go ahead with what he has to say," Leonard said. "We shouldn't keep anyone here any longer than necessary." The general had questions but Leonard's tone and demeanor implied the answers would have to wait.

Melanie sat between Don and Eileen. "I'm terribly sorry," the doctor said, "but Tim was killed in the explosion, as were the others. From the nature of the injuries, though, we know they died immediately. They didn't feel any pain." Melanie's face was puffy from crying. Leonard studied Don's expression and identified with what he must be feeling. Hawkins probably occupied his conscious thoughts with all the tasks required of loved ones at times like this, allowing him to get through this moment. In a week, a month or next year, today's events would catch up with him and demand a reckoning. Now, though, he'd become a survival machine.

As the doctor explained what to expect, Leonard's mind wandered to the ugly reality magnifying this tragedy. No doubt Hawkins's love for McAbe was just as real as Melanie's love for Roberts, yet she'd receive support and counseling and would be encouraged to grieve openly, as she should. But Hawkins couldn't let others know of his relationship with McAbe. His loss was his secret and his grieving must be in private or restricted to his most trusted friends.

Everyone stood, jerking Leonard out of his reverie. The level of activity in the waiting area had subsided as the hospital released patients to loved ones who carried them home. "Kenneth," Eileen said, "Melanie was planning to return to Seattle tomorrow. Her things are in the officers' quarters but I've asked her to stay at our house tonight. I'll go with her to get their bags."

"That's a good idea," the general said.

Leonard looked at Hawkins and then across the lobby at Karl who, along with their other friends, came to his side. "Can you take him home?" Karl took Hawkins by the arm.

"Isn't that your driver?" the general asked as Karl and his friends walked away.

"Yes. Corporal Steiger has—has volunteered to help out."

"That's the spirit that will see us through this tragedy. Marines taking care of Marines."

Eileen led Melanie outside, where the general's driver waited to give them a ride to the base, leaving Leonard alone with the general for the first time today. "Is there some confusion?" the general asked. "According to the chief physician, the pilots' descriptions don't match the profiles of four young officers. Who was flying those helicopters?"

"First Lieutenant Roberts, who we met last night—"

"Melanie's fiancé, Tim?"

"Yes. He was the copilot for a Navy lieutenant, Chris Ashburn. Chris was—Chris was a fine young officer I had the privilege of working with before *Desert Storm* at CentCom. Both of those pilots perished in the collision today. In the other helicopter, First Lieutenant McAbe was the copilot—we met him last night. You said he was the one—"

"—who didn't look old enough to shave." The general winced at the reminder of lost youth.

Leonard took a deep breath as he looked around to make sure no one was listening. "The section leader was supposed to have been Captain Pfeiffer."

"'Supposed to have been'? What does that mean?"

"Captain Pfeiffer was here a half hour ago. Sledge was at the hangar this morning and bumped him out of the flight. The fourth pilot killed in today's collision was Sledge." General Neville reacted as if Leonard had hit him with a steel rod. He fell into a chair a few feet away. Leonard sat beside him. "Sledge ordered Jungle out of the helicopter. He demanded to fly."

General Neville absorbed the information. "Firing him was the right thing to do." He looked around the lobby. "Where are his wife and children? Were they at the air show? Do they know?" He looked directly at Leonard, his eyes pleading for answers.

"There's—there's something else. Telling you this last night seemed unnecessary. After I relieved Sledge of his command, Major Burr informed me that Sledge's wife left him on Friday. She took their children with her. I assume she and the boys returned to Pittsburgh."

The general held up his hand. "I've heard all the bad news I can handle in one day." He pointed to a military policeman standing in the hospital's entranceway. "He's here to give me a ride back to the base. You can ride with me if your car's still parked at the air station."

"I hadn't even thought about that—but I do need a ride. Thank you."

Before they stood, the general said softly, "Let's not discuss this in front of anyone else at this point. We don't know what caused this collision. I mean that. This incident was in your Aircraft Group. You will be the officer in charge of the investigation and I will defer to your findings. Until you reach a conclusion, however, you must keep an open mind." The general spoke to the MP and Leonard followed them both to the waiting police car.

They rode in silence for a couple of miles when Leonard recalled a distant memory and applied it to the present. "Did you just laugh?" the general asked.

"Before Todd and Sara were old enough to consider anything 'cliché'—or as they would call it, 'cheesy'—whenever they felt overwhelmed, I'd quote an old song's lyrics to them. You know, "Look for the Silver Lining." It was all I could think of to say but it seemed to do the trick. For some reason it popped into my head just now."

"What 'silver lining' could you possibly think of at a time like this?"

"Not much of one, I'm afraid, but I forgot to give you a message. Congressman Coughlin said to tell you that he's on a flight back to Washington, but to call him if you need anything."

"Thank you, my friend. I'll hold that thought as well."

* * *

A concrete barrier separated the south and northbound lanes of Interstate 5 along the route between El Toro and Oceanside. It also represented a dividing line in Don's life. This morning, on the other side, he and his friends had traveled north sharing joy and hope. The sun had broken through and their expectation of happiness had been so real, bad thoughts hadn't stood a chance in the jeep's cab. Now, as Karl drove them south, Don shivered in the backseat between Jeanne and Robbi while Esther rode up front. The fog had rolled in, casting a grayish pall over the coast, causing the temperature to plummet. Without the jeep's top, they were cold and windblown. Don's drop in body temperature, though, was the result of his mental state as much as the atmosphere. Emotionally and physically, he'd numbed himself to the world.

"We're setting up a round-the-clock schedule," Jeanne said when they reached Don's condo.

"No," Don said. "It's too much to ask. I'll be okay."

"Yes, you *will* be okay because we're going to help," Jeanne said, picking up Don's phone. "Robbi, can you bring me my address book, please? I'll find out Lance's schedule—"

"He's got finals," Don said.

"He'll bring his books and study on your dining room table. Many people will help us, Don. Ricky can contact other friends— hell, even Jerry Giles will help. Thanks, hon," she said to Robbi, flipping the pages in her contact list. Jeanne turned her attention to scheduling friends.

Karl sat on the sofa next to Don. "One thing I should do," Karl said softly, "is check out Patrick's apartment. Make sure nothing would let the military, you know—know about you."

Don looked up. "You're right. I'll go with you." Karl's comment stirred something inside him. It was a terrible but familiar feeling. He'd been through this before and it had shut him down emotionally for a decade. He wouldn't let that happen this time. Instead, he'd let his emotions do what they needed to do and trust his friends to protect him.

"Is that a good idea?" Robbi asked. "Why don't you stay here? Let us go with Karl."

"No," Karl said. "I'll go alone. You should stay here with Don."

Don felt his tears return and this time he didn't stop them. "Do you see how fucked up this is? The man I care about most in this world—is *dead!* All we can talk about is hiding. How can I keep Patrick alive if I have to keep him a secret?"

Esther crossed the room and sat on Don's other side. "Oh, Don! But don't you see? Patrick wants you to take care of yourself. He loved you—wherever he is he *still* loves you. He knows you'll keep him alive. I'm sure he's protecting you too. For the rest of your life he'll be your guardian angel. He'll always be here." Don sobbed uncontrollably on Esther's shoulder.

"I better go before anyone from the squadron gets there," Karl said. "Anything in Patrick's apartment I should look for?" Don shook his head as Robbi handed him a tissue. "No photographs? Letters from you? Underwear with your name? Gunny chevrons? Gay porn?"

"Porn? We're talking about Patrick, not you or me," Don said, smiling faintly. "I left some skivvies in his top right drawer. Don't think he had any pictures of us yet and we weren't apart—I never wrote him a letter. But check the bottom shelf of his entertainment system. He has a photograph album or two. If he took any pictures of us, that's where they'd be."

"Sure." Karl hugged Don and took Patrick's apartment key. "I'll be back as quick as I can."

"That's the apartment," Zack said. "Door's probably locked. Want me to check?"

"Yep. Look under the mat. See if he had a key stashed somewhere. Don't leave any prints."

"I swear you think I'm a fuckin' moron."

While Zack was checking the door, Jay reached down to the floor of the backseat where he'd stashed a bag after the incident with Johnson. He carried some things that would've helped him, including a box of surgical gloves. Grabbing two pairs, he stuffed them in his pocket and surveyed McAbe's apartment complex. The building consisted of fifty or sixty condominiums, each with a private rear entrance from the street opposite the ocean. Military officers—especially pilots with their flight pay—apparently made a lot more money than Jay did. The fact that an officer could get away with such an openly gay life—or *former* life—was disgusting.

"Everything's locked up," Zack said, returning to the car. "If we go around to the beach side, I think we can get in from there." Jay jumped out and followed the Marine around the complex, turning down a small side street onto the beach. A gate and high fence separated McAbe's complex from the sand. Zack stood on the sidewalk outside the gate, pointing to the balcony of a second-story apartment. "That's McAbe's and that's where I saw him kissin' the gunny. And—heh, heh, we're in luck, Jay-man! Look, next to the balcony door is the window to his bedroom. It's cracked open a little bit to let air in. He's thinkin' nobody can get to it. But if we jump this gate and climb up the balcony, you can hold me while I go in through the bedroom window."

"What's the chance we'll get caught?" Jay asked.

"Most of these apartments are vacation rentals. They're empty until Memorial Day. I know 'cause I been plannin' this night for a long time." His eyes gleamed with anticipation. "Let's go!" With one leap, he was over the gate. "I can open it for you from this side."

By the time Jay walked through the open gate into the courtyard, Zack had climbed onto McAbe's balcony from the railing of the one below. Jay followed the Marine's lead, and within minutes, he balanced Zack as he stretched his lithe body from the balcony to the partially open bedroom window. "See what I mean?" Zack asked, whipping out his Leatherman pocket tool. He pried open the screen, handing it to Jay. "Bring this in—we'll put it back in place."

"Sure, but when you get inside, put these on." Jay whispered, handing him some gloves.

He was amazed how quickly he and Zack were in the apartment. "Look for anything gay," he instructed, "or for any evidence linking the two men together."

Jay scanned the living room while Zack turned left into the kitchen, where he turned on a faint light above the oven. "The faggot's got matchin' plates and bowls with pretty little designs," Zack said. "Ain't that queer enough?"

"No," said Jay. "Why don't you check—?"

"Jay! Look where you just walked in. Don't this look like that picture?" Zack pointed to the sliding glass doors to the balcony. Although the sun had set hours earlier, the moon, the stars and the streetlamps provided ample brightness. Jay removed the carefully folded newspaper clipping from his wallet. "Shit, man," Zack said, "And I thought *I* came prepared."

Jay held up the photograph of the two Marines with their faces blurred. The view was of the same window, plant, balcony, pier, and angle of the ocean. Without a doubt, they were in the right apartment. "Check the bedroom for any clothes that could be Hawkins's."

"Good thinkin', Jay-man. Or I know! Any uniform shit only a gunny'd have!"

Unfortunately for Jay's purposes tonight, McAbe kept a relatively clean and empty apartment. The few pieces of furniture looked comfortable and generic. Two plants sat on stands under the windows. He feared the place might not contain any clues. Searching a row of books on the bottom shelf of a small entertainment center, Jay hoped to find some titles by gay authors. Instead, he found *On War* by Carl von Clausewitz, *War and Peace* by Leo Tolstoy, *The Prince* by Niccolo Machiavelli, *Plato: The Republic* and twenty other similar books in the Marine officer's collection. Jay opened the cover of Sun Tzu's *The Art of War*. In crude but bold black ink, McAbe's father had inscribed a message: *To my one and only son, a man who makes me the proudest man alive. Congratulations. Love, Dad. 2nd Lt Patrick Sean McAbe, USMC, 1990.*

Jay quickly replaced the book. His emotions boiled. He felt sadness that a man's son had died today and shame that he and Zack relished the tragedy. Jay also felt anger at McAbe for having been so brazen in his homosexuality and envy that he'd lived such a privileged life with loving parents, a partner, a career, friends and a bright future—or who'd *had* a bright future.

The last two books were photograph albums. Jay hoped these contained evidence of McAbe's homosexuality and pictures of gay military friends, as had Johnson's. Instead, there were pages of family photos, high school basketball games, summers at the lake, weddings, ski trips, Christmas dinners and so on. The second book had more of the same, including images of Patrick with a beautiful dark-haired woman, images damaging to Jay's case.

Frustrated, Jay knelt to return the second album to the shelf. Behind the entertainment center, he saw a crumpled piece of paper on the floor wedged between the entertainment center and the wall. The shelves had no backing and he retrieved the paper by removing more books, creating a space where he could reach. Grabbing the paper, he smoothed out the wrinkles as he carried it into the kitchen. He held it under the light and tried to understand what he was reading.

"Hope you had better luck than me." Zack entered the living room. "McAbe must be the most boring goddamned officer in the whole fuckin' Marine Corps. *That's* sayin' a lot!"

"Zack," Jay said, "Take a look at this?"

"You found somethin'?" Stepping aside, Jay let the Marine study the paper under the dim light. Zack's initial look of confusion changed to euphoria. "Jay, you realize what this is?"

"No, shithead, that's why I asked for your help."

"Oh my God! This is an 'SGLI Change Form.' This means that on—on the twelfth of February—*this* year—McAbe changed the person he wanted to get his life insurance money."

"How much is that?" Jay asked. "Is it a lot?"

"For a Marine? Fuck yeah! One hundred and fifty thousand dollars, that's all! He changed it to go to 'Hawkins, D. A.' and he put Hawkins's address in Vista, California." The two men stared at each other in silence for a few seconds as the relevance of their discovery sank in.

"I was trying so hard to think of a way to pin this on the lieutenant," Jay said slowly.

"Little did you know that Lieutenant McAbe had a death wish. I don't care what you said in the car, Jay-man. I think McAbe caused this collision. He wanted to make his boyfriend rich."

For a brief moment, Jay allowed himself to consider the possibility that perhaps McAbe *had* caused the crash today. "No. This collision was caused by a drunken pilot a lot older than McAbe. But, Zack man, you and I are the only two people who need to know that."

"Well, whatever you say, but let's get the fuck out of here. This is all the evidence we need."

"How do we get out of the apartment?" Jay asked.

"The way we came in. Or since you're a lazy civilian, bet you wanna go out the front door."

"You can go out whichever way you want," Jay said, barely able to contain his enthusiasm. "But I'm in a hurry to place an urgent phone call I've waited a *very* long time to make."

"Oh no. You got that evil sound in your voice that scares me. But I like it!" Zack laughed as he opened the door. "How long you been waitin' to make this 'urgent' phone call?"

"Ten years," Jay said. "Ten long fuckin' years."

"Spencer." Leonard answered the phone in his sleep.

"Good evening, sir. Sorry to wake you—but—"

"What?" Slowly waking, Leonard rubbed his eyes. This wasn't the first nighttime phone call he'd received from his executive officer, but given the circumstances, it was the most alarming.

"I'm afraid this couldn't wait until morning, sir."

"Go ahead." Leonard braced for another dose of tragedy.

"There was a suicide," the lieutenant colonel explained. "An instructor in 707. He put a bullet through his skull about an hour ago." At a time when Leonard felt nothing more could render him speechless, fate had disproved that belief. "Sir? Colonel Spencer? You still—?"

"Oh—yes, I'm sorry. Who—who was the instructor?"

"Captain Pfeiffer, sir."

"Jungle," Leonard said softly.

"Yes, sir, it was Jungle. The duty officer didn't know why Jungle would—"

"I'm afraid that I know *exactly* why he did it. Thank you. Please try to get some rest. It's going to be one of the worst weeks of our lives."

More than anything, Leonard wanted to call Karl but right now, his lover was taking care of a friend who needed him more than Leonard did. Instead, he hung up the phone, and for the first time in years, he cried.

37

"What."

The voice was too groggy to be recognizable but the nasty tone was unmistakably hers. "Kathryn Angel. Is that any way to greet an old friend?"

"Who the fuck is this? I'm hanging up—"

"It's Jay Gared."

If she'd recognized his name immediately, Jay would've been surprised. If he waited long enough, though, she'd—"What—on earth—could *you* possibly want from me?"

"Kate," he said, recalling her nickname, "I *loved* your article about the two homosexual Marines. That was *so* inspirational. It really warmed—"

"It warmed a lot of hearts, asshole," she said. "You didn't call after ten years to say how much you enjoyed one of my stories, you fucking prick."

Through the phone, Jay heard a faint but familiar sound. "Need a second to light your cigarette? Thought you'd quit that disgusting habit."

"I did. What gives? Have you got another Pulitzer-prize-winning story for me?"

"Perhaps. I mean, come on. Considering the thanks I got in your acceptance speech last time, who wouldn't be knocking down your door to help out again."

"Oh, come off it," Kathryn said. "How was I supposed to thank you?"

"Just kidding. God, lighten up. You were always too uptight." Covering the mouthpiece with his hand, he ordered a homeless person away from the phone. No one could overhear this.

"What've you got now?"

"I'm sure you heard about that midair helicopter collision yesterday in California."

"I saw it on television a dozen times, just like everyone else in the free world," she said. "Why? You have something related? What do you do now, by the way?"

Kathryn's question indicated she was waking up. "Been a military investigator for a while," he said, stretching the truth. "Until yesterday, I was pursuing a pilot killed in the crash. Now I suspect he might've *caused* the crash. You're the first person who came to mind for this scoop."

"Hold on," she said. "I'm gonna record—"

"No. Do this the old-fashioned way—paper and ink." She agreed to his terms and excused herself. Although Jay knew she'd record the call, without his consent on tape, she couldn't use it against him. While he waited, Jay peered around the ice machine blocking his view of the car where he'd left Zack. Everything looked peaceful down the street by McAbe's apartment.

Kathryn returned to her phone. "How do I identify you?"

"You don't, except as an 'unnamed source within the Department of Defense.' "

"What is—was the name of the pilot you were investigating?"

In his clearest voice, he enunciated the words slowly. "Lieutenant Patrick Sean McAbe."

When Jay was out of sight, Zack reached over the seat and grabbed his backpack. They'd left The Red Rooster in such a hurry, Jay hadn't noticed when Zack had picked it up. Zack removed the glass pipe and small bag of methamphetamine. Tonight was going to be a long one and he needed some help. Maybe he could even get Jay to try it this time and they could have some fun celebrating their success. He rolled down the window of the car far enough to give any smoke he didn't inhale a way to escape. A minute later, he breathed the bitter chemicals into his lungs. He waited with nervous anticipation for the power coming his way. Each breath brought him closer to that feeling he craved.

Zack looked up in time to see a man enter McAbe's apartment. The chance to nab someone enhanced Zack's euphoria. "Damn, that's some good shit," he said as he began to fidget.

"Patrick—Patrick McAbe?" Kathryn asked. "That's impossible."

"Impossible?" Jay asked. "Did you *know* Lieutenant McAbe?"

Another long pause. "I—the news said that the collision was at El Toro."

He'd cornered the *Washington Herald*'s star reporter. "El Toro doesn't have Cobras. The helicopters in the crash came from squadrons at Camp Pendleton, forty miles to the south."

Silence, then a quick drag. "What were you investigating First Lieutenant McAbe for?"

"How did you know he was a *first* lieutenant, and not a *second* lieuten—?"

"Lucky guess, smart-ass. I had a fifty-fifty chance."

"He was under investigation for homosexuality, among other things," Jay said.

"You? *Ha!* You're investigating Marines for being gay? This has gotta be a joke."

"Fuck you." Jay was letting Kathryn get to him. "Getting to the point. In your Valentine's story, you interviewed McAbe and another Marine named Hawkins. The photograph you ran was of the two of them together, taken in McAbe's apartment. Their faces were blurred. McAbe was one of four pilots killed in the collision. Now, here's what I want you to do."

"What you want me to do? You gotta be kidding me with this."

"No joke. You'll do it. Wanna know why?"

"Dying to know," she said dryly. "Tell me."

"Last time I brought you a story, you learned a lot of information—"

"Newsflash, Sherlock. I'm a reporter. That's what we do. We gather information—"

"Reporters *report* the facts they learn, not sell them on the black market. True, you reported enough facts to win yourself an award, but what about the information you sold—?"

"Fuck you."

Jay heard a noise. "What'd you do? Stop the recording device I didn't authorize?"

"You can't prove any of it."

"How stupid did you think I was? I've got pictures, recordings, receipts, statements, you name it, honey. I kept it all 'cause I knew this day would come. The last thing you want is your newspaper to know that its star reporter is a freelance informant." He spat the words out quickly, pausing to let her grasp his meaning. "I bet the congressional scandal of 1983 wasn't the last time you engaged in self-indulgent double-dealing, was it?" Silence. "Didn't think so. If the feds investigate you, you'll lose your job, be stripped of your prizes, and my personal favorite—go to jail for years. A beautiful woman like you? You'd be *real* popular in a women's prison."

Jay savored every second that ticked by. "What do you want?" She was shaken.

"Front page. Same photo as Valentine's, except *without* the faces blurred. Storyline: McAbe recently changed his servicemen's life insurance benefit to go to Gunnery Sergeant Hawkins."

"Is this true?"

"Not only is it true, Kate, gimme an hour and I'll fax you proof—a copy of the form," Jay said. "Go on—turn your recorder back on 'cause I don't want you to fuck this up. You'll write: 'According to an unnamed source within the Department of Defense, the military is operating under the theory that Lieutenant McAbe was despondent because he believed that an investigation into his homosexuality was closing in on him. Military investigators suspect that McAbe killed himself and three other pilots so that his lover, Gunnery Sergeant Donald A. Hawkins, could collect one hundred and fifty thousand dollars.'"

"The earliest it can run is Thursday," she said.

"Bullshit," Jay said. "I better see it on the front page of Tuesday's paper or I'll send every piece of evidence I have on you to the editor-in-chief of the *Herald* overnight. Is that clear?"

"I'll do what I can, but this is out of my control. Let me give you my fax number."

Zack couldn't sit still. "Heh, heh, this is comin' in *real* handy tonight!" he said, pulling out his Leatherman pocket tool again. He also kept handcuffs in his backpack for a variety of reasons and he took those out as well. He waited excitedly to see who'd emerge from McAbe's apartment. Minutes seemed like days. The door opened and a short guy walked down the sidewalk. Zack opened the car door stealthily and stepped outside. Crouching low, he crossed the street. The man went toward a jeep, the same one Jay had pointed out at the hospital. Zack scurried ahead, using another car's tire as a cover. When the man stepped between Zack and the jeep, Zack jumped, catching him by surprise. Zack wrapped his right arm around the man's neck, putting the knife's point to his throat. With his free hand, he cuffed the man's wrist.

"Well, well, if it ain't Corporal Karl Steiger," Zack said. "We meet at last."

"How the fuck do—?"

"Shhh," Zack said, placing his knife hand over Karl's mouth. "I'll slit your throat, motherfucker, if you make one goddamned sound. Gimme your right hand, nice and slow—that's it." Zack cuffed Karl's other wrist and led him to Jay's car. Karl was several inches smaller, and with his hands in cuffs, his superior strength was useless. Zack opened the trunk and, with a little difficulty, forced Karl inside. "I hear one sound outta you, I'll open this trunk and slice you to pieces." He slammed the trunk lid, returning to his spot in the passenger's seat. Just to be safe, he pulled an extra sock out of his bag, reopened the trunk and gagged his victim.

"Ready to roll?" Jay asked, returning to his car.

"You bet, Jay-man! Where we rollin' to?"

"My house in San Diego. First I need to swing by the office for a few minutes. Okay with you?" He took the keys from Zack and started the ignition.

"You the man in charge."

"Anything to report?"

"Nope," Zack said, "not yet anyway."

Because they sped away in the opposite direction from the jeep, neither Jay nor Zack noticed the pair of boxers Karl had dropped on the street.

"What's the emergency?"

"The military helicopter collision in California—one of the pilots was Patrick McAbe."

"How do you know?" asked Kathryn's contact. "The military hasn't released the names."

"My contact in the DoD," Kathryn answered. "Preliminary conclusion is that Patrick knew the military was investigating him. He used the crash to commit suicide."

"Seems a bit premature for a conclusion," the man said, stirring cream in his coffee. "Preliminary or otherwise. They have proof?"

"He'd just made Don the beneficiary of his life insurance policy. My source faxed me a copy of the form. Here's a copy for you."

Looking at the paper, the man said, "He wanted his gay lover to receive his insurance benefit. Wow. Interesting theory. We can use this." He folded the form and put it in his lapel pocket. "Military investigations take months. Why're we meeting at eight thirty A.M.—on a Monday?"

Even though she'd had only one cup of coffee, Kathryn felt her pulse approaching its maximum rate. "I'm telling you now because the *Herald* is running a front-page story identifying both Patrick McAbe *and* his lover, Gunnery Sergeant Hawkins."

He took a sip of his drink. "When? Better not be before Wed—"

"Tomorrow."

"No!" He slammed his fist on the small coffee shop table, rattling a container of artificial sweeteners. "Not on your life, Kate, absolutely not! You've got to kill—or delay—that story."

The ferocity of her contact's reaction startled her. "I—I don't have a choice—"

He leaned forward and spoke quietly. "I'm executing a plan this week that has two dozen variables. They've all got to be synchronized. If not, everything falls apart and powerful people will be mad as hell. If you don't delay that story, I'll expose you as the fraud you are."

Throughout her fourteen-year journalistic career, Kathryn had never been in a bind as bad as this one. She wanted to cry but she couldn't let this man see her tears. Perhaps venting her rage would block them. "It's out of my hands, don't you see that? Four pilots died and dozens of people were trampled to death and—and you think I give a shit about Coughlin's wounded ego? When this story runs, the world will know Don is gay. Won't *that* satisfy Coughlin?"

Her contact ran his hands through his hair and closed his eyes. When he opened them, his look terrified her. "I don't work for Coughlin, you stupid bitch! You think you've got it all figured out. Well, Miss Angel, you don't have a fucking clue what you're dealing with!"

Kathryn was shocked. The employee who'd opened the coffee shop looked at them with deep concern on her face. In a low voice, Kathryn asked, "You don't work for Coughlin? Then—who else—who else would care about information proving Don Hawkins is gay?"

He matched her subdued demeanor. "I've already said too much." He stood to leave. "Kate, this is way over your head." She stared at his back as he left the shop.

The employee asked, "Can I get you something, miss?"

"A large latte to go," she said. "And while you make that, I'll step outside for a cigarette."

"You better tell me the name of every faggot in my Marine Corps, you filthy cocksucker!"

"The United States Military—Code of Conduct—is the moral guide for the behavior of U.S. military members who are evading or captured by hostile forces."

Jay's alarm clock told him it was 6 A.M. He wondered if he was dreaming. He could've sworn someone yelled "faggot" and "cocksucker" as a weaker voice recited the Armed Forces' Code of Conduct. Slowly, his memory returned. He'd slept just a few hours. Before that, he'd been at the NIS office sending a fax to Kathryn Angel in Washington. Before that, he'd driven from Oceanside to San Diego—with Zack.

Jay sat up, rubbing his eyes. He'd made a bed for Zack on the sofa. Before Jay had closed—and locked—his bedroom door, Zack said he'd left his bag in the car. He'd taken the keys.

"I *know* what the Code of Conduct is, you worthless piece a shit. It don't apply here 'cause I ain't the enemy!" Zack said.

"Article One: I am—an American—fighting in the forces that guard my country and our way of life," the barely audible voice said. "I am prepared to give up my life in their defense."

"Shit!" Jay said. Swinging his legs over the edge of his bed, he threw on a pair of briefs.

"You *better* be prepared to give up your life!" Zack said. Jay opened his bedroom door in time to witness Zack strike a bare-knuckled blow across someone's bloody face.

Zack was stripped to the waist. He'd shoved Jay's table to the side of the dining alcove and positioned a chair directly under the brightest light in the house. A naked young man sat handcuffed and tied to the chair. Recovering from the blow, the man said, "Article two: I will *never* surrender—of my own free will. If in command, I will never surrender the members of my command—while they still have the—the *means to resist*." He spat the last three words at Zack.

"Zack!" Jay said. He ran across the room and grabbed Zack's wrist before he could strike the man again. "What the fuck are you doing?"

Zack's victim continued. "Article three: If I am captured I—I will continue to resist by all means available. I will make every effort to escape—"

"Jay!" Zack said, "I'm helpin' you out, buddy. Don't you know who this is?"

"—and aid others to escape. I will accept neither parole nor special favors from the enemy."

"Was gonna slice his neck like he did to you but thought I'd wait and give you the honor."

Jay looked at the man again. Zack had bruised the guy's face badly and one eye was swollen shut. But sitting here, with his body on display, Jay recognized him. "Karl Steiger."

Hearing his name, Karl raised his head. Through his good eye, he gave Jay a sinister glare. "Article four," Karl said through gritted teeth, "If I become a prisoner of war, I will keep faith—keep faith with my fellow prisoners. I will give no information nor take part in any action which might be harmful to my comrades."

"That's right, Jay-man." Zack bounced around the room in obvious delight. "This is the corporal who gave you that scar on your neck. I knew you'd be proud of me for this."

Jay flashed back to the night in the bathhouse. Staring at the exposed and vulnerable form in the chair, he felt the metal blade slice the skin covering his artery. Tasting his blood, Jay relived the terror and shame this man had put him through. Jay folded his arms. "What's he said?"

"Article five," Karl said slowly, "When questioned—should I become a prisoner of war, I am required to give name, rank, service number, and date of birth."

"Nothing yet," Zack said, looking back at Karl, " 'cause he keeps givin' me the code of conduct. Must think he's in the Hanoi Hilton." He raised his arm to hit Karl again. Karl flinched. This time Jay didn't stop Zack.

Zack's fist landed hard across Karl's left cheekbone, causing their prisoner to rock back in the chair. He dropped his head for thirty or forty seconds then resumed his recitation. "I will e—evade answering further questions to—to the utmost of my ability."

"Hey, Corporal! This ain't no goddamned meritorious promotion board." Zack got down in Karl's face. "I bet you the biggest ass-kisser in your unit, ain't ya', pretty boy? Got the goddamned code of conduct memorized like you're still at boot camp."

Karl grew weaker. "I w—w—will make—no oral or w—w—written statements disloyal to my country and its allies or ha—harmful to their cause."

Zack turned to Jay. "Been workin' him over all night. Watch him, will ya'? Gotta piss."

Zack slammed the door to the bathroom, leaving Jay alone with the man who'd threatened him, cut him, humiliated him and haunted his sleep for months. Even though Karl's energy was depleted, he returned Jay's stare. Jay pounded his fist into his palm as he circled the unprotected body. He relished the thought of pummeling this man. More than bodily satisfaction, though, he wanted answers. Grabbing a chair, Jay placed it inches in front of Karl. Karl looked pitiful with his hands cuffed behind the chair and his ankles tied to the chair's legs. Yet he also looked erotic with his rock-hard muscles glistening with sweat and blood and his genitals exposed.

Jay put his hands gently on Karl's thighs. Quietly, he asked, "Why do you do it?"

"Article six: I will never forget that I am an American fighting for freedom—"

Jay put his hand over Karl's mouth, careful not to let the man bite him, though Jay doubted Karl had the strength to inflict physical pain. When he had Karl's attention, Jay continued. "Save the rote memorization for your fellow Marine. What *I* want to know is—when you attacked me at the bathhouse, you—and whoever your friend was—put yourselves at risk. *For a dead guy!* And now, tonight, or this morning, all you had to do was give up a few names—not even names of your best buddies, just acquaintances—of other military gays. He woulda let you go. Why didn't you? Why take this punishment for other people?"

Karl didn't resort to his memorized response. Instead, he looked Jay in the eye and mustered the will to answer. "It's okay, ya' know, if you wanna hate *yourself*—'cause a' who you are. Your life, man. It's when you take your hatred out on other people—*especially* my friends and me—buddy, you crossed a line. I *will* make you pay."

You're not on your time now, Agent Gared. You're on my time. You can be certain—when the time is right, my friends will avenge me. Jay shook his head, hoping to lose the voice of Johnson's ghost that had followed. "What're you talking about? I don't hate—"

"Who're you kiddin'?" Karl asked. Jay had to strain to understand the man's words. "You're a fag too, only the worst—" Jay's rage fired up inside and he coiled his arm, preparing to hit Karl. "Figures NIS would side with a crack-smokin' tweaker against an honorable gay Marine." Karl's statement stopped Jay's arm. "You didn't know he's doin' this to me, did you?" Karl raised his head and, incredibly, managed a trace of a smile. "Your psycho friend's a lost cause. You're smart. You get help—*professional* help—you *might* still be worth something. But it's probably too late for you too."

"Ha, ha! Good thinkin', Jay-man, you be good cop," Zack said, stepping out of the bathroom. "But know what, faggot? The bad cop's back!"

Karl braced when he heard Zack's voice. "I am responsible for my actions, and dedicated to the principles which made my country free."

"He still sayin' that shit?"

"Zack," Jay said. "Why'd you take your bag in the bathroom?" Jay stood, positioning his body between Karl and the torturer. "You have to change your tampon? Maxi-pad? What?"

"Jay-man, why're you turnin' against *me*? He's the one that cut your—"

Jay shoved Zack hard against the far wall of the room. He grabbed the backpack out of Zack's hand and opened it. "What the fuck is this, Zack? Huh? A chemistry experiment? You *promised* you wouldn't bring this shit into my house!"

"Don't know how that got in there. I promise I ain't *used* any of it."

"Put on your shirt, give me my keys and give me the keys to the handcuffs. Go back to your barracks, get cleaned up and get some rest. I need help tomorrow and you're the only one I can count on. But if you look one bit tweaked out, Zack, forget it. Get out. Give me a call tonight!"

Zack looked hurt but did as he was told. As he pulled his shirt over his head, he looked at Karl and yelled, "I'm comin' after you, faggot! This won't be the last you see of me!"

"I will trust—in my God—and in the United States of America."

38

"Honey, come here. What's the matter?"

"I'm so scared, Jeanne. I found these." Robbi handed her a pair of white boxers with HAWKINS, D. A. printed inside the band. Don, like every Marine deployed on ship for six months, had stenciled his name in his uniform items, including his T-shirts and underwear.

After yesterday's traumatic events and a night without sleep, Jeanne's mind was operating in first gear. "Why—? You put Esther on the train to San Diego?"

"Then I drove down the street to Patrick's apartment. The door was locked, Don's jeep was there—and these were laying in the street beside the jeep."

Jeanne was worried. "No sign of Karl?" Despite the fancy beachfront condominiums and apartments, two blocks inland, downtown Oceanside became a sketchy neighborhood.

"No. I'm so worried about him."

"Oh doll, I'm sure he's okay," Jeanne said, although she wasn't sure of anything right now. Don needed to sleep as long as the pill Esther had given him would last. With Karl missing, she realized more than ever—Don was right. *I really need Eddie,* she thought.

"Can't go to a hospital," Karl said. "You'd have to take me to Balboa. Too many questions. 'Where'd you get beat up, Corporal?'

'At an NIS agent's house, sir.' *You'd* get in trouble. Then they'd ask, 'Why'd you get beat up, Corporal?' ''Cause I suck dick, sir.' *I'd* get in trouble. The way I see it, Jay, we're kind of in this shit together—back to our old stalemate."

Jay cleaned the blood off Karl's shoulders and neck gently with a sponge. After several minutes, he asked, "Why'd you say what you did?" Karl looked puzzled, so Jay added, "You said I 'might still be worth something.' What made you say that?"

Karl moved the icepack Jay had given him from his swollen eye. "That's a fucking good question." Karl closed his good eye. Opening it, he said, "Let me ask *you* something—why'd you put me in a tub of warm water? Why are you cleaning my wounds, giving me a bath?"

Jay rinsed the blood from the sponge in the sink and knelt beside the man. "No matter what you think of me, I'm still human." He cleaned Karl's upper arms. "You're right. I didn't know Zack kidnapped you. I sure as hell didn't know he was going to do *this* to you."

"There's your answer. There's still some good left inside you—somewhere."

"You ready for me to clean these cuts on your face with alcohol again?" Jay asked.

"Sure. Pain's just weakness leaving the body."

"Three months ago you slit my throat with a knife and threatened to kill me." Jay applied rubbing alcohol to a cotton ball. "You and I are sworn enemies. But out there, you were nice to me even though my 'partner' was beating you. Why the sudden change?" Jay removed the ice pack from Karl's head and rubbed the alcohol-soaked cotton lightly across his facial cuts.

"Ahhh!" Karl said. "*Fuck!* That burns."

As Jay paused, letting Karl's pain subside, he studied the contours of his face. Without thinking, he said, "Zack is a fool, doing this to such a beautiful face." Karl looked at him. An understanding passed between the two men—their similarities far outweighed their differences.

"You let Zack hit me. You almost hit me yourself. Now we're in here like you're some kind of Florence fucking Nightingale.

Seems like your change is more sudden than mine." Karl managed
a weak smile, splashing water on Jay's bare chest. He took Jay's
hand, saying, "I'm ready. Do me again." His playful comment
caught Jay off guard. "I mean put some more alcohol on my cuts,
Clara Barton." Karl didn't break eye contact or remove his hand
from Jay's wrist. Instead, he guided Jay's arm to his wounds where
they cleaned his cuts together. Jay rose up on his knees, stretching
around Karl's head. As he leaned across, Karl raised his head and
their lips met. The touch lasted no more than five seconds, but it
was a kiss. "Jay, don't take this wrong, but I woulda said—or
done—*anything* to stop that fucker from beating me—except give
him my friends' names. The only way to stop him was to get *you* to
do it for me."

"You *don't* think I'm worth anything? You just said what you did
to stop Zack?"

"No. What I said is true. It wouldn't have worked if you were as
bad as I used to think."

"'*Used* to think'?" Jay washed Karl's chest and stomach. "You
don't think I'm bad now?"

"I been around a lot of wisdom lately. I see things different. You
think you're doin' the right thing with your life. You're wrong."
Karl took the sponge from Jay, saying, "I can wash my balls myself." Slowly, he sat up in the bathtub and soaped his groin. "Me
and you are complicated men. You're not the only one who had a
rough childhood. The difference between us is I always knew I
liked guys. I never had a problem with it."

Karl's inference that Jay was a homosexual caused him to retreat
from their tender discussion. He stood and opened a towel for the
Marine. "I'll dry you. Get dressed and I'll drop you off at the train
station on my way to work. You can catch the Coaster up to Oceanside." He picked up the Marine carefully so that he didn't slip in the
tub. Karl put his arms around Jay's neck, leaning against Jay's body
while Jay dried his skin. Toweling close to Karl's hips, Jay became
aroused. His erection was obvious through his briefs and he didn't
try to hide it.

"Bein' a homo's not that bad, Jay," Karl said. "Not as bad as
tryin' to run away from it. Why're you hiding?" Ignoring the ques-

tion, Jay dried the remaining drops from Karl's legs. He couldn't expect this Marine to understand he was hiding and running from a dead father who was never far away. "I need to borrow some clothes," Karl said. "Your buddy cut mine off of me."

"Sorry," Jay said. Staring at each other again, Jay felt the kinship return. He'd read a World War II story where German and American soldiers stopped fighting on Christmas Day in 1944 to have Christmas together outside a French village. This moment with Karl was like that, only more personal and intimate, and he knew Karl felt it too. "You can borrow—I mean *have*—something to wear." Jay wrapped the towel around Karl's waist and helped him to the bed.

Karl said, "I'm sorry—for this." He ran his finger gently along Jay's scar. "I shouldn't have cut you." Karl turned his head and kissed the mark he'd made. "I went too far."

The last time Jay cried was in Karl's presence. A tear escaped his eye again, this time for a far different reason. Despite Karl's homosexuality—maybe because of it—Jay admired his courage and loyalty to his friends. "Thank you." He pulled some shorts and sweatpants from his closet, tossing them to Karl. "Looks like a cool morning. I'll give you a—" Jay suddenly remembered his souvenir from January. He looked back at Karl, who was struggling to get dressed. "You okay to go back by yourself?"

"Yeah." Karl pulled the sweats around his waist. "Can I have a shirt?"

"I told you the truth about your friend, Eddie. You believe me?"

"Yes. Why?" Jay tossed Karl the sweatshirt he'd left at WC's, the one that Eddie was supposed to have returned to him. "The bag of drugs." Karl unfolded the sweatshirt, slowly putting it on. Now it was Karl's turn to shed a tear. "You saved me from the psycho," Karl said, his expression becoming more serious. "So I don't hate you as much as I did before. But Eddie would be alive today if it wasn't for you. I'll never forgive you for that."

"I know," Jay said. "I'll get ready fast so we can get you home."

"Why have the memorial service here at El Toro? The pilots were from Camp Pendleton."

"It was an aircraft collision, at an air show, at this air station. What happened yesterday will affect Marine aviation years into the future. The investigation, the publicity—it *all* must remain under our control. You know better than any aviator that Camp Pendleton is an infantry base."

"Why tomorrow?" Leonard asked. "Isn't that too soon?"

"Two reasons." General Neville stirred packets of sweetener into a cup of coffee. "The families have requested it. They want to return to their respective hometowns and have the funerals by the end of the week. More importantly, we must move beyond this as quickly as possible." He took a sip. "Speaking of the families, all four—five counting Captain Pfeiffer's—will begin arriving this afternoon at two. We need the best Marines—like Corporal Steiger— helping us with transportation. He didn't drive you here this morning?"

"He's taking care of things at Camp Pendleton." Although Leonard assumed Karl was aiding Hawkins, he was worried Karl hadn't called him. "He'll be here as soon as possible."

The general left the small table and walked to his desk. "About the investigation. The NIS director has already put someone on the file—they're on hold on my phone. Come over here and I'll put them on conference." Leonard crossed the office as the general pressed a button under a flashing light. He shouted into a speakerphone. "Director Tolson, are you there?"

"Yes, General Neville. I'm with Agent Jay Gared,who I've assigned to this case."

"Good morning, gentlemen." After introductions and greetings, the general said, "It's terrible to be communicating with you under these circumstances but I assume it's necessary. Can you tell us why NIS is involved? Particularly, why has Agent Gared been assigned?"

"This is Agent Gared. I was at the air show yesterday. Immediately after the collision, I went to the hospital and spoke with a physician and a laboratory technician."

"You were at the hospital?" Leonard asked. "Why didn't you introduce yourself to General Neville and me? We were there for hours."

"As you know, the scene was chaotic. I needed to question the doctors—in private—about the remains of the deceased pilots. Or more specifically, one of the deceased pilots."

"That wouldn't be Lieutenant Colonel Melvin Hammer, would it?" the general asked.

"Actually, no. I was at the air show, pursuing a lead about another officer."

"What officer?" the general asked. "Pursuing what lead?"

"Military police at Camp Pendleton informed us on Saturday they suspected that First Lieutenant Patrick Sean McAbe was one of two Marines anonymously featured on the cover of the *Washington Herald* about three months ago. The story about two *homosexual* Marines."

Leonard remained stone-faced even though he felt as if he'd been kicked in the ribs. "Our understanding was the commandant's office opted not to investigate that matter."

"Well, sir," said Director Tolson, "when NIS is made aware of criminal activity, we have no choice but to follow it up. Apparently, the MPs figured out it was McAbe's apartment in the photograph. They observed McAbe engaging in homosexual activity with another Marine—"

"Was it on Camp Pendleton?" the general asked. "Off-base jurisdiction is a dicey matter."

After a moment's hesitation, Director Tolson said, "It was at McAbe's off-base apartment. As it turns out, that's no longer germane. My secretary faxed you a form where McAbe changed his SGLI beneficiary to the other Marine we suspect, Gunnery Sergeant D. A. Hawkins."

"Wait one minute, Director Tolson, while I see if it's here."

You aren't on the front page of the Washington Herald *tomorrow, are you?*

No. They wanted to interview me. For once in my life, I didn't wanna risk it.

Recalling his brief conversation with Karl about the *Herald*, as well as Karl's closeness to McAbe and Hawkins, Tolson might be right about McAbe and Hawkins being the two Marines. If McAbe changed his SGLI to Hawkins, NIS might try to use that to show they were gay.

"It's here." The general showed the form to Leonard. "It looks authentic to me."

"I spoke with Corporal Delarosa, a personnel clerk at McAbe's squadron. She recalls that the lieutenant changed his beneficiary. She can authenticate this form."

Leonard exchanged glances with the general. Although his mentor had decades of experience hiding his expressions, the strain was beginning to show.

Agent Gared continued. "We also confirmed with the air show coordinator that Lieutenant McAbe had been scheduled to fly as the lead pilot in yesterday's show."

"I thought Captain Pfeiffer was the lead," Leonard said.

"She—the coordinator I mean—spoke with Captain Pfeiffer at a reception Saturday evening. He informed her that Lieutenants McAbe and Roberts did such outstanding jobs on Friday and Saturday, he was rewarding them with the privilege of flying lead on Sunday. That would explain why Lieutenant McAbe waited until Sunday to crash his helicopter."

"Now wait just one goddamned minute here, Agent!" Leonard shouted. "What are you saying? That NIS is operating under the theory that—that—a homosexual lieutenant committed suicide—and in the process killed three others with him? That's the most preposterous—"

"It's gotta be hard to learn one of your men is a homosexual," said Director Tolson, "and that he might've committed this terrible deed. But you're the senior officer for this investigation. Keep an open mind while we carry out our fact-finding duties. The facts point in this direction."

Leonard couldn't believe this was happening. Sledge caused this collision. McAbe had been an innocent victim. His mind raced, looking for a way to make NIS see that without giving himself away. "Agent Gared, when you spoke to the doctor yesterday, what did he say?"

"Based on his examination of the remains, he couldn't see anything that might've caused—"

"No sign of—" The general hit MUTE before Leonard could finish. "—alcohol abuse?"

The general held up his hand, indicating for Leonard to remain silent. Hitting MUTE again, he said, "Did the doctor indicate whether the hospital would run blood tests for alcohol or other substances that might have impaired the pilots' abilities to fly?"

"Yes. They drew blood samples from all four pilots and tested them overnight in the hospital's laboratory," said Agent Gared. "I spoke with the lab tech this morning. He promised to fax the results to us—and to you as well, gentlemen—as soon as the doctor has signed them."

"Thank you, Agent Gared," the general said. "We should have another conference call—"

"Actually, I'd like to meet with you and the colonel in person tomorrow morning."

"That will be difficult," said the general. "The memorial service for the pilots is at ten."

"I'll attend the service," said Agent Gared. "Can we meet at your office immediately after?"

"Yes, that sounds best," said the general. "Thank you for your time, Director Tolson, Agent Gared." Leonard returned to his seat at the table and was disappointed that his coffee had grown cold. As the general joined him, someone knocked at the door. "What now?"

His aide stuck his head in the door. "Congressman Coughlin is on line two."

"Captain, if you don't mind," said Leonard. "I'll need a fresh cup."

"What was that about? Why do they sound so worried about blood tests and alcohol?"

"This is pure speculation on my part, Ollie," Jay said, "but the squadron's personnel clerk said that the commanding officer was a last-minute change to the air show's schedule. I talked to some pilots hanging out in the ready room. No one's sure why the lieutenant colonel switched places with the flight leader, but 'why' is irrelevant. He's the CO—it's his prerogative."

He paused. His plan required him to keep the focus away from Lieutenant Colonel Hammer as long as possible, but he had to do it in a credible manner. "Seems the squadron commander had a reputation for being a heavy drinker," Jay said, airing the unpleasant facts. "The general and the colonel are worried that the collision was the result of an intoxicated lieutenant colonel."

"I see. If this lieutenant colonel was a known drunk and they let him command a squadron and fly helicopters, their heads will roll if he killed all these people. Gotcha now, Jay."

"This is going to be a tough investigation," Jay said, preempting his enemy's arguments. "Gay activists and McAbe's friends will say the cause of the collision was a drunken squadron commander. Bet they've already started a propaganda campaign."

"If his blood test comes back negative, they don't have much of an argument."

"That's right. From what the doctor said yesterday, I'd be surprised if any of the pilots had been drinking before the flight. When the general and the colonel discuss this new evidence pointing to McAbe, they'll see it's a lot better for them and the Corps if it turns out a young suicidal gay pilot caused the collision rather than a commanding officer." He stood and smiled. "If you'll excuse me, Ollie, I have a lot of work to do before tomorrow's meeting."

"Sure, Jay, keep me posted okay?"

Jay closed his boss's door slowly behind him. As he turned, he smiled at Esther. "You look almost as tired as I feel this morning."

She didn't give him her usual smile. "Looks like it was a rough weekend all around."

"I'll give him the message but I'm telling you he won't be coming in today." Jeanne slammed the phone. "Fucking pricks." Suddenly she heard the key in the lock to Don's front door. Lance was on his way but he didn't have a key and Don was still asleep. "Stop! Who are—Karl! Oh my God! What happened to you?" she said, dashing across the room. She hugged her friend and led him to the sofa. "What can I get you? A cold compress—that's what I'll get."

"Don't worry about it, Jeanne," Karl said, but she was already at the freezer putting ice cubes in a plastic bag. Returning with the bag wrapped in a towel, she placed it on his head. "Thanks."

"We've been worried out of our minds. Don's asleep."

"Where's Robbi?" Karl asked.

"At your office," Jeanne said. "Sit down, Karl. What are you doing on your feet?"

"Gotta call her. Have to get a message to Colonel Spencer."

"With all that was happening yesterday, I didn't give you proper condolences, General, and I apologize. You either, Colonel Spencer. I'm sorry for what you Marines are going through."

"No need to apologize, Congressman," General Neville said. "We know your sympathies are sincere." On a notepad, the general wrote, *Quiet re: gay pilot!* Leonard nodded.

"I had to catch one of those God-awful redeyes back to DC last night. A lot's happening this week. I may have a Democratic cosponsor for my bill to codify the existing ban that prevents homosexuals from serving in the armed services. If I'm successful—and I think I will be—I plan to introduce that on Friday." The general rolled his eyes and wrote, *Humor him.* Leonard smiled. "Also on Friday, the commission's announcing the bases it's recommending for closure. I'm still fighting like the dickens to keep El Toro off that list, but it's a tough fight."

"We appreciate your efforts, sir," the general said. "More than we can adequately express."

"And General, I want to personally thank you for moving the memorial service to El Toro so that I could attend. I've just been confirmed on a seven A.M. flight out of Dulles that will put me there just in the nick of time." Leonard was confused. The general hadn't mentioned Coughlin's attendance as a factor in his decision to move the service. Coughlin continued. "I've taken the liberty of scheduling a press conference for noon tomorrow at the air station. I want to announce the preliminary results of the investigation into the cause of the collision."

Leonard grabbed the general's notepad and pencil and wrote, *TOO SOON!* He shook his head vigorously. The general said,

"You're welcome to hold the press conference here at my building. We'll give you the information we have. At the present time, however, I can't make any promises about conclusions." Coughlin thanked the general and ended the call.

"Leonard, Coughlin misspoke. I didn't move the memorial service to El Toro *just* for him."

"Your reasons are valid, General, and I accept them at face value. But why didn't you tell me Coughlin was part of your decision to move the service? I don't like it, but I understand."

The general sighed. Folding his hands on his desk, he said, "Because I'm not proud of my decision. The service should be at Camp Pendleton. We'll provide buses to transport all of the Marines who need a ride, but in a perfect world, I would tell Coughlin to go fuck himself. I'd also tell him to forget about a press conference. But what do I do? You heard me—I'm rolling out the red carpet for him tomorrow, allowing him to turn a solemn occasion into a grandstand for his personal agenda right here in my very own building. Why? Because I've racked my brain but I see no other way to save this base, and ultimately save lives down the road."

Someone knocked on the door. "I'm beginning to hate that knock," said Leonard.

"I hear it in my sleep," the general muttered. "Maybe it's something routine."

This time, the knocker wasn't the aide; it was the general's much higher-ranking chief of staff. "General, a fact checker from the *Washington Herald* telephoned HMT-707 half an hour ago. They're running a front-page story tomorrow with evidence the collision was caused by a gay suicidal pilot. And a photograph showing Lieutenant McAbe with another male Marine."

"Good heavens," the general said. "Chief, I want the public affairs officer in here now. We must prevent this story."

39

"This is Corporal Steiger, Colonel Spencer's driver. I need to speak to him right away."

Lowering the game show's volume, Don sipped water from a glass Lance had given him. "Want anything to eat?" Lance asked. "Make you a sandwich? I'll go get whatever you want."

Don put his arm around Lance's shoulders. "No thanks. I want you to stay here with me."

"I know that, sir." Karl's impatience was apparent. Don looked at his battered friend with an expression that asked, *What's wrong?* Pointing to the phone, Karl rolled his eyes. "Major, I can't be at El Toro. Corporal Reynolds will be there in the colonel's sedan. I'm honored the general specifically requested me—okay, *'ordered'* me—can you get Colonel Spencer?"

"I don't miss all that rank structure bullshit," Lance said. "Where's Jeanne?"

"Sleeping," Don said. "She didn't sleep at all last night."

"Can you knock on the general's door?" Karl asked. "*This* is an emergency too!" Karl banged the receiver against Don's counter. "Sorry 'bout that, sir. Accidentally dropped the phone." Suddenly the game show cut to a news commercial showing the collision. Lance was a few seconds late changing the channel. "Will you tell Corporal Reynolds to call me at this number?"

"Did—did they just show the crash?" Don asked. "Or was that in my head again?"

"The major's a damn jerk. I'm just a corporal. I'm not important enough to interrupt a closed-door meeting with the general." Grabbing a soda, Karl joined his friends.

"Don't know why they call it the 'news.' Nothin' 'new' about it—they just keep showin' the same old footage," Lance said. "A Marine MP did this to you? You sure he's for real?"

"Yeah. Seen him at the front gate lots a' times. He wasn't on duty last night, though."

"He was working with the NIS agent? The one responsible for Eddie?" Don asked. He took another sip and set the glass on a coaster. "If this had happened to you any other time, I'd bust someone's head open. But right now—" Don's tears choked his words.

"I'm okay," Karl said. "These cuts and bruises will heal in a few days. Besides, the agent didn't know the MP had kidnapped me."

"Don't matter," Lance said. "The MP pulled a knife on you, threw you in Gared's trunk and took you to his house, so Gared's responsible. Now we know where the motherfucker lives."

The phone rang, causing the three men to turn their heads at the same time. "Maybe it's Robbi with the colonel," Karl said, limping across the room. "Hello? Oh, hi, Esther. Jeanne's asleep. Okay, I'll wake her—but I wanna talk to you about you-know-who." Karl knocked on the bedroom door. "Jeanne! Esther's on the phone. Says it's urgent." Karl returned to the living room. "How're you doing, Don? You sleep?"

"Esther gave me something that knocked me out." Don finished the glass of water. "How am I? I always thought that if someone lost their spouse after twenty or thirty years, that was a real heartbreaker, you know? And I don't mean to—mean to say it's not 'cause that's gotta be its own kind of hell. But at least they got twenty or thirty years' worth of memories with the other person to get them through. There's pictures, and—and stuff they bought together, and kids and grandkids. But with Patrick—" Don stopped to wipe his eyes. "With Patrick, we had three months. Within a week of meeting him, I knew—I *knew* I would spend the rest of my life with him. What—what we lost was the opportunity, you know? I mean the hopes and plans—and dreams. I wanted to retire from the Corps in four years and start a contracting business here, build a life with him. None of that will happen." The three sat in silence. "But I'm sorry, guys—you've lost so much this year too. Patrick was your friend. So were Eddie and Chris."

"Don, we'll make it," Lance said. "We're here with you—for you."

"But it's gonna get worse," Don said. "I know it."

Jeanne emerged from the bedroom. "Karl, Esther said you wanted to talk to her?" Karl went to the bedroom and Jeanne took his place on the chair. "There's a problem," she said. "Don, were you aware Patrick had signed his SGLI over to you?"

"I'm not going anywhere until I speak to Colonel Spencer—sir."

"What's with you and Steiger today? I'll tell you one more time, Corporal. You'll drive the sedan to the airport—*now*—with the chief of staff to pick up Mr. and Mrs. Pfeiffer and their—"

"Major, before she goes anywhere, I need to see Corporal Reynolds." Leonard said, stepping out of the general's office to look for Karl.

"Sir, can I talk to you—in private?" Corporal Reynolds asked quietly.

The general was on the phone with his superior in Hawaii briefing her on the collision's aftermath. "Sure," he said, motioning for her to follow him into the vacant conference room.

She handed him a folded slip of paper. "Corporal Steiger needs you to call him at this number. As soon as possible, sir. He's tried to reach you all day but they wouldn't put him through. He's got information he can give only to you, only in private."

"Thank you," Leonard said. "You should help the general's staff with whatever they need." Her mission complete, Corporal Reynolds hurried to her next assignment. The Colonel closed the door, using the conference room's outside line to call Karl. A woman answered. Seconds later, he heard the best sound in the world. "Hey. It's me."

"It's so good to hear your voice. How's your friend?"

"Are you calling from a secure phone?"

"I—I'm not sure. But right now, I don't care. Are you all right?"

Karl hesitated. "Um, we're hanging in there. There's a small group of us here. But—"

"But what? What is it?"

"I was kidnapped last night in Oceanside—at Lieutenant McAbe's apartment. By an MP."

The news angered Leonard, making him feel even more helpless. "Are you okay?"

"I was thrown in the trunk of a car and taken to an NIS agent's house. Agent Jay Gared."

"Holy mother of—! General Neville and I just spoke to him. He's assigned to this case."

To Leonard's surprise, Karl replied calmly, "We know. We also know NIS is claiming Patrick was suicidal so Don could have his SGLI. That's bullshit, Leo. Don't believe it."

"I don't," Leonard said. "I know better than to ask you how you knew about NIS's theory, although I suspect that by now the news is leaking like a sieve. Are you aware that the *Washington Herald* is running a front page story with NIS's theory?"

Karl was silent. "No," he said. "I'll have to tell everyone here 'bout that as gentle as I can."

"I'm sorry to have to tell you that," Leonard said. "But I'm more concerned about what that agent did to you. I'll personally strangle the son of a—"

"Agent Gared actually might've saved my life. Me and him have a little history so I was shocked. He stopped the MP from beating me to death. Then he threw him out of his house." Leonard felt intense physical pain at the thought of someone abusing Karl. "Gared's a snake, though. You can't trust him, Leo, not at all. He's just like every other closet case. He'll say and do anything to hide who he really is—even from himself."

"Afraid that's something I know very well," Leonard said reflectively. "I'm so angry and—and terrified. I want to be with you, to hold you and do anything I can to make this better—"

"I want to be with you but can't right now. I'm outta danger, I'm bruised but healing. It helps me just knowin' you're there. I need to be with Don. But there is one thing you could do."

Someone knocked at the conference room door. Without waiting for Leonard to respond, the major stuck his head in the door. "What is it?" Leonard asked Karl.

"Colonel Spencer, the general needs you back in his office," the major said.

Karl said, "It'd really help Don a lot right now—if I could tell him—you know—"

"Go ahead," Leonard said without hesitation. "You may tell him."

"Sir?" the major asked. "What do you want me to tell him?"

Hanging up the phone, Leonard said, "Nothing, Major. I'm on my way."

"I'm a former Marine. I understand the rank system," Jeanne shouted into Don's phone. "Quite honestly I don't give a fuck who you are, he's not doing it!"

Don listened as Jeanne fielded the calls. Obviously this one was from his battalion. By now, they knew. It was everywhere: Esther's office suspected Patrick of suicide based on the SGLI form; the commanding general of the Aircraft Wing knew Don was gay; and the *Herald* was fact-checking a story. Don was certain every echelon of his command knew he was gay. That's how it was in the military—wartime communication must flow smoothly so Marines practiced it that way in peacetime. Especially when the communicated information was scandalous.

"Put the battalion commander on the phone, I don't care! I'll tell him the same goddamned thing. Don's *not* coming in to the battalion today, do you understand me?"

"Jeanne." Walking to the phone, Don felt like he'd strapped one-hundred-pound weights to his ankles. "If they put Lieutenant Colonel Ritter on the phone, I should speak to him."

"No, Don! Absolutely not. Yes, Colonel. No, his wife isn't here, I'm a family friend."

Don motioned for the phone, which Jeanne surrendered reluctantly. "Yes, sir. On my way."

"What're you doing?" Jeanne, followed by Karl and Lance, pursued Don into his bedroom.

"Putting on my cammies and going to talk to my battalion commander," Don said, opening his closet. "It's over. With the *Washington Herald* running the story tomorrow, I'm done for. And to tell you the truth, I don't give a fuck." Don pulled his shirt off and grabbed a dark green T-shirt out of a drawer. "You three are welcome to watch me strip, I'm not shy."

As Jeanne closed the bedroom door, she said, "Don, don't do this. Don't be rash; don't make any life-changing decisions right now. I know a great lawyer in San Diego. She'll—"

"As always, Jeanne, I appreciate your advice, but I've never seen things better than I see them right now. Maybe death clears things up. This isn't the life I wanna live anymore." She said she understood and closed the door, leaving him alone. He and Patrick had been so paranoid about being caught, they hadn't taken any photographs together. The only picture he had of the two of them was from the *Herald*'s photographer. Don kept it in the drawer by his bed and he pulled it out now. He cried as he put on his uniform, staring at the image from that night. Don was bare-chested unbuttoning Patrick's shirt. They'd felt so carefree and invincible.

Karl burst into the room. "Let me go with you." He sat on the bed and hugged his friend. "You know how much I love you, right? We never say that to each other, but from now on, I'm sayin' it—a lot."

"I love you too—my little buddy with the giant heart." Don laced up his combat boots and said, "I wouldn't think of doing this without you. I'd like for you to go with me, as long as you don't mind waiting in the jeep."

"At last, some good news." The general hurried across his office, closing the door. "Please have a seat." Motioning toward the table, he said, "Look at this."

Leonard put on his reading glasses and studied the faxed report. "It's from a lab? What—?"

"It's the report of the pilots' blood test." The general pointed to a column on the left with four ten-digit numbers. "Each of these numbers represents a pilot. If you follow the chart across to this column," he said, moving his finger right along the page, "all four pilots had blood alcohol contents of zero. There's no evidence of any illegal or behavior-altering substances."

"Even Sledge?"

"Yes! Even Sledge," the general said. "What's the matter? This is fantastic news!"

"General," Leonard said, removing his glasses, "the last time Melvin 'Sledge' Hammer had a blood alcohol content of zero, he rode a bicycle with training wheels." Leonard returned the fax to the general. "Sledge was drunk at nine o' clock Saturday night. You're trying to tell me that sixteen hours later, he was completely sober?"

"I'm not trying to tell you anything," the general said, returning to his desk. "I'm simply showing you the lab results from the hospital." Leonard attributed the general's testy tone partially to the solemn nature of the day's events. Mostly, though, he suspected the general had mixed feelings. He knew as well as Leonard did that Sledge was a drunk—he was the one who'd blocked Sledge's promotion primarily for that reason. Yet here he was, clinging to a document with obviously false information because it supported a conclusion he wanted.

"Shouldn't we at least confirm—?"

"The staff secretary has already called the hospital and verified the report's authenticity." The general looked away from his computer and at Leonard. "I spoke with the Commandant earlier and I'm sending him a follow-up message. At Coughlin's noontime press conference tomorrow, you'll give the preliminary results of the investigation. And Leonard," he said, returning to his computer, "you know what's at stake."

"Yes, I do." Leonard stood to leave. "I'll be in the vicinity if you need me." As Leonard left the office, the general picked up his phone and didn't respond. In the outer space, he asked quietly, "Major, can you give me the number to the lab at El Toro Regional?"

"Still think I'm a hooker?" Karl asked as the guard at Camp Pendleton's main gate waved Don and him onto the base. "You gave me such a hard time about it but then you let it drop." He feigned a pouting expression. "Thought you didn't care about me anymore."

Don smiled for the first time in over twenty-four hours. "I don't know what you are. I mean, I don't *care* what you are—escort, porn star, circuit boy—you're my friend. I love you no matter what. Being with Patrick—I felt loved and, once again, I knew *how* to love, you know, unconditionally. If you want to fuck nasty people for money, that's your business. I just don't want to see you get hurt or get burned. But you know I care about you. And always will."

"I know."

They rode in silence for several miles between the scrubby hills and cliffs and the Pacific Ocean. Suddenly a memory made the leap from Don's unconscious mind into his active thoughts. *Karl's gonna be okay. Better than okay. Can't say how I know, but trust your buddy and back off about his business.* "What did Chris know about you?"

"What? I didn't even know Chris until you introduced us a few months ago."

"That's what I thought," Don said, "but he knew something about you. I told him you were keeping secrets from me. He said not to worry, that you're gonna be okay. He didn't say why."

Karl looked thoughtful. "Oh my God, Don. This is such bullshit! Why can't we—we all love each other, right? But we gotta keep these fuckin' secrets. It all makes sense now."

"What are you talking about? How did Chris know something about you I didn't?"

"I'm not sure—but it's time I leveled with you about something."

Don patted his friend's shoulder. "You don't have to—"

"I know—but I want to. I wanna end all this lying. What I have to say might make you feel, well, not better, but it helps. I've had a—a boyfriend, I guess you could say, for almost a year. Chris must've figured that out, because I think several years ago, he dated the same man."

Almost any piece of news would've been less shocking. Changing lanes, Don stopped at one of the base's few traffic lights. He looked at Karl. "Why don't I know this? Who?" The left turn arrow flashed green and he pressed the accelerator, taking them away from the main part of the base and into the more secluded regions.

"Colonel Spencer."

Don had reached emotional overload and this news required extra time to process. "That's why he was so kind to me yesterday. He really did understand what I was going through."

"More than understand." Karl wiped a tear from his cheek. "A month ago Leo let it slip that another officer was here he'd dated before, that they were still friends. I was a little jealous—a new emotion for me. He never said who it was but I bet it was Chris. It's so sad. We've all got each other—but he lost his only other gay military friend."

"You'll have to let him know," Don said, "now he's got all of us too."

"Were you able to kill your story?"

"Meet me at—"

"I don't have time to meet," said her contact. "Just tell me. Don't worry—and don't flatter yourself. I'm not recording this call."

Kathryn rattled her glass of gin. "No, I couldn't kill it." She omitted the fact that she hadn't tried to kill the story. Jay Gared's threat to her career was real; her contact's threat was vague. She braced for the onslaught.

To her surprise, he remained calm. "You're in luck." He waited for her response but she was too exhausted to react. "I swam a couple of oceans and moved a mountain or two today for you. Everything's been taken care of. By tomorrow, it won't matter what's in your paper."

"Good." Kathryn attributed her wonderful drowsy feeling to the relief she felt at the unexpected news mixed with the booze and Xanax she'd taken earlier. "Now, I've been sitting here all day in terror of something—or someone—I don't even know. Tell me who you work for. Who's using this information? You owe me at least that much."

"I already paid you everything I owe you. You're an investigative reporter, sweetheart. Follow the money trail."

After hanging up the phone, Kathryn switched off the television. She had nothing to fear from her contact and nothing to fear from Jay Gared. Tomorrow she'd take off for the rest of the week to her favorite spa in the hills of Virginia. Tonight she was free to pass out in peace.

40

"Rumors are flyin' all over the battalion—hell, all over the base. I don't know what to say."

"You don't have to say anything, sir," Don said to Captain Bruce. "There's not—"

"Yes, I do." The captain strained for words. "I want to—I *want* to know what to say. I really do. If the rumors *aren't* true, it doesn't matter. Somebody will apologize to you and everyone will know it was all bullshit. Life goes on."

The captain paused. His next word would be "but"—a conjunction as symbolic of the "before" and "after" in Don's life as the divider between the north and southbound lanes of Interstate 5. On one side was the optimistic, hope-filled world of promise—the "before" world, the world of "*If the rumors aren't true, it doesn't matter.*"

"But if the rumors *are* true—" Shaking his head, the captain looked at his office floor.

The rumors *were* true—undeniably true. He was in the southbound lane, representing the grim realities of grief, death and loss. Life had pushed him into the "after" phase, where the compartments he'd designed as protection—walls between people and places—had vanished. Don had awakened to discover his nakedness and vulnerability. "Sir, I can—"

"Don't—don't say anything." Captain Bruce held up his hand, speaking gently but firmly. "This is outta my league. We'll be in front of the battalion commander soon—everyone's workin' late tonight. He'll explain things. Save your thoughts for him. Gunny Hawkins, even though I don't understand, or—hell if I know—can accept—regardless of how I feel about certain things, if these rumors are true, you've suffered a great deal in the last twenty-four hours. No matter what happens, no matter who says what, you've got my sympathy—and respect."

"Thank you, sir. That means more to me than I could ever express."

"I wasn't aware Corporal Steiger was married. How long has it been?"

"Three and a half months, sir," said Corporal Reynolds as she drove the van to the airport.

"Belated congratulations," said General Neville. "My wife says, 'Being a Marine is difficult; being a married Marine is more difficult; being married *to* a Marine is the most difficult.' Following her logic, being a Marine married to another Marine must be *exponentially* difficult."

"We like it. Colonel Spencer helped us get orders together. Today we found out we're on our way to Washington, DC next month. Corporal Steiger will be on the silent drill team at the Marine Barracks at 8th and Eye. I'll be at Headquarters Marine Corps."

As he observed the attractive young woman driving the van, Leonard realized he knew little about her, yet she was legally married to his lover. He'd accepted the constraints on his life so readily, until now he hadn't seen how ludicrous they could be. He hadn't asked Karl, but Leonard had wondered if Corporal Reynolds might be a lesbian. After seeing her at the air show with Karl and the others, he assumed she was. If not, she was friendly to gay Marines. But now, he couldn't ask her a simple question about herself. Their present situation—with its requisite secrecy and deception—was dehumanizing.

"Speaking of today's orders," the general said quietly, "I saw they posted the colonel's selection list. Everyone will know soon that Sledge didn't make it."

"Soon? You were trapped in your office all day. Everyone in the Corps already knows as much as you and I—hell, maybe more. You should read some of the conspiracy theories."

"Conspiracy theories? Like what?"

"The two lieutenants were secretly lovers. The Navy officer was jealous so *he* caused it."

"Good heavens!"

"Here's one you'll love: The Marines at El Toro—all the way up to the top, which would be you, General—are involved with a drug cartel, allowing military and civilian aircraft with illicit cargo from Mexico to land at odd hours. The theory goes that Sledge had threatened to expose you and the whole operation so someone tampered with the Cobras, causing them to crash in such a way that it would look like a midair collision." General Neville was speechless.

"My personal favorite," Leonard said, "is that Bill and Hillary Clinton hired the lieutenants to assassinate Coughlin but Sledge sacrificed himself to thwart the attempt."

"My God, Leonard. Please tell me you're making this up." The general was visibly upset by the preposterous allegations. Calming down, he said, "Wouldn't surprise me, though, if that last theory could be traced back to Coughlin himself." He shook his head. "It amazes me how these situations bring out the best in some people—like Corporal Steiger volunteering to help out that Marine at the hospital yesterday—and Corporal Reynolds working late tonight."

"Thank you, General, but we're honored to be able to help out."

"But in others, like these conspiracy theorists, it brings out the worst. E-mail doesn't help. Everyone in the country will soon have an e-mail address. They'll communicate all kinds of garbage to each other instantly. Lies will spread like viruses. Glad I'll be retired by then."

They rode in silence for a few miles when the general asked Corporal Reynolds to turn on the news. Merging onto the 405 north, she turned on the radio. "Seven P.M. news time."

The announcer said, "Breaking news out of Washington DC, affecting Orange County."

"What now?" said the general.

"This just in. The *Washington Herald* will run a shocking front-page story tomorrow about a possible cause of yesterday's collision at the El Toro Marine Corps Air Station," the man said. "According to the *Herald,* there is evidence that one of the pilots, Marine First Lieutenant Patrick McAbe, was a homosexual and that he had recently designated his male lover, a Marine Corps gunnery sergeant at Camp Pendleton, as the beneficiary on his Armed Forces life insurance policy. The air station's public affairs officer wouldn't comment on the investigation but said a press conference will be held tomorrow. Now for traffic, let's go high-in-the-sky with—"

"Do you think the story broke before Mr. and Mrs. McAbe departed Chicago?"

"We're about to find out," Leonard said grimly.

Corporal Reynolds hadn't reacted to the news at first, but as she turned the van into Orange County's John Wayne Airport, Leonard saw her quickly wipe a tear away from her cheek.

Don stood at attention in front of Lieutenant Colonel Ritter's desk. "Base legal—"

"Sir, if I may. I think I can save all of us a lot of time and energy." As despondent as Don felt, he'd never been as focused and resolute as at that moment. His love for Patrick had helped him see how life could be, not just as it was. The other Marines in the room were good men, but trying to explain his new life's vision to them would be futile. "I'd like to propose a deal—"

"A deal?" Don's battalion commander pounded his fist on his desk and leapt to his feet. "Where the fuck do you think you are, Gunny Hawkins? Wall Street? This is the United States Marine Corps. There are no 'deals' here. There are orders and there are those who obey them."

"Sir—please. Hear me out." Anticipating the commanding officer's outburst, Don held his ground. "I suspect the Marine Corps will like this deal." Lieutenant Colonel Ritter returned to his seat and Don continued. "I submitted a reenlistment package in February."

"I know. I'm the one who signed it."

"It would carry me to retirement in April 1998. I understand the package has been approved." The battalion commander nodded. "I'm volunteering to pull that package." Don's announcement shocked everyone in the room. Sixteen-year military veterans didn't refuse reenlistment four years before beginning their lifetime pensions. Not only would Don forgo half his pay for the rest of his life, he wouldn't be entitled to any benefits.

"What do you get out of this deal?"

"An honorable discharge. And I want it no later than Friday afternoon."

"What?" barked the sergeant major. "You've gotta be fuckin' with me, Gunny Hawkins! You're in deep shit right now. You can't just run away from—"

"You sure about this?" asked Lieutenant Colonel Ritter.

"Never been more sure about anything in my life. I won't confirm or deny anything that's been said about me—to you or to the press. I want an honorable discharge. Seventy-two hours."

"Given the nature of my discussions with regiment, I think that can be arranged. Dismissed."

"Gunny," said the sergeant major, "Get in my office!"

"If it's all the same with you," Don said, "I would prefer not to."

As Don turned an about-face and exited the office, he was grateful Karl was waiting for him in the jeep. Enduring this in isolation would've been impossible.

"FYI, General, Mr. Roberts is a high-powered attorney in Seattle."

"Just when the day couldn't grow any darker," General Neville said as he and Leonard walked through John Wayne Airport to Sean and Carol McAbe's gate. Their uniforms drew stares from passengers but Leonard focused on his unpleasant task and didn't notice.

"Good evening, Melanie," Leonard said solemnly, hugging the young woman. The general greeted her and they introduced themselves to her mother and Tim Roberts's parents.

"The McAbes' plane just landed." Melanie's eyes were red and tears streaked her face.

"General Neville, we have a lot of questions for you," said Mr. Roberts.

"We'll provide the best answers we have, sir. First we'll go to your accommodations at the air station, where your casualty assistance officer awaits your arrival. She'll take care of any—"

"We appreciate that, General. But my questions relate to the proximate cause of the collision. We've seen the footage like hundreds of millions of people. It's clear that one of those helicopters turned in toward the other. Was it an equipment malfunction? Was it deliberate? Pilot error? We want to know which helicopter our son was in and who was actually flying it."

"Sir, I am the presiding officer of the investigation." Leonard spoke compassionately, but also forcefully. "You will receive a copy of the comprehensive report—if you'd like—but that won't be completed for another six months. Now, before then, I can—"

"Six months!" Mrs. Roberts interjected, "What's this we've heard about a—a press conference tomorrow? Why are you telling the press more than you're telling the families?"

"Ladies, sir, addressing the media this soon was *not* our idea," the general said. "Congressman Edward Coughlin represents this district in the House of Representatives. He felt a press conference was necessary. Twenty-five civilians have died in the aftermath—many of them his constituents. Whether or not we agree with Coughlin's timing, he has the right to—"

"Coughlin? Isn't he that asshole you told me about?" asked Melanie's mom.

"Yes," said her daughter. "That's the one."

An agent opened the door to the Jetway. Passengers streamed from the plane into the airport, where most were greeted with smiles and hugs. Minutes later, a couple emerged who appeared about Leonard's age. From their sad expressions, he assumed they were Patrick McAbe's parents. Mrs. Roberts confirmed his assumption when she cried and hugged the woman.

"Tim and Patrick were rack mates at Officer Candidate School. They were nineteen and became best friends," Melanie said. "After six years of OCS graduations, college graduations, ceremonies at The Basic School, flight school wingings, you name it, their families are close." They watched as Mrs. Roberts gave Mrs. McAbe a tissue. "Such happier times."

Leonard thought he'd prepared for this moment as best he could but there really *was* no way to prepare. He tried to empathize, but his mind wouldn't let him consider the possibility of losing Todd or Sara. Maybe he'd blame the military, always an easy target for grieving families. Parents didn't grasp that he was also grieving. Each of the 3,000 Marines in his command was his responsibility and he had no one to blame but himself. He shouldn't have let Sledge out of his sight Saturday night. He should've known Sledge's wife had left him the day before. He should've respected the grief Sledge felt over General Laker's death. He shouldn't have fired Sledge so quickly. Alternatively, he should've fired him much sooner.

As a leader of Marines, though, he was also concerned about the good of the Corps. Right now, the Marine Corps was in danger from many unknown ramifications. For almost thirty years, Leonard had maintained the proper balance between the needs of his individual Marines and the needs of the Corps. Looking at these parents tonight, he wasn't so sure.

After brief introductions, General Neville guided the group to baggage claim and out to the van. Corporal Reynolds saluted smartly and closed the door. As they drove away, Mr. McAbe said, "We've heard some terrible accusations, gentlemen." His speech was slow but clear. "And we want to know how the Marine Corps plans to refute these lies."

General Neville repeated what he'd said to Mr. and Mrs. Roberts. Leonard remained quiet but wondered how they could rebut facts unfolding at such a rapid rate. He also wanted to know how Karl was faring. By the time they reentered the air station, he'd been away for almost two hours and he was worried. He wanted to know why the investigator assigned to this case had kidnapped and beaten Karl. He wanted to know exactly why Karl said not to trust the man. As they assisted the families to the base's VIP lodging facility, introducing them to the casualty assistance officers, Leonard wondered how the situation, and consequently his career and his command, had spiraled out of control so quickly.

"You aren't driving all the way to La Jolla tonight, are you, Leonard?" General Neville asked as Corporal Reynolds carried them back to the headquarters building.

"Your wife said I could use your guestroom."

"Good. We can strategize for tomorrow. Coughlin will be here in fourteen hours."

Melanie's mom was in the bathroom of their double-occupancy room. No sense telling her mom this was the same room where she and Tim had spent their last night together. Not even forty-eight hours had passed and already Melanie felt far along on a much less joyful life. She tried reading a novel but couldn't concentrate on the words. Maybe she needed a simpler and funnier story although nothing would seem humorous. The knock on her door was a welcome distraction. "Mrs. McAbe, please—come in."

"Who is it, Melanie?" her mom asked from behind the bathroom door.

"It's Mrs. McAbe—"

"Please call me Carol."

"Carol McAbe, Mom."

"Tell her I'll be right out!"

Melanie smiled weakly. "As you probably heard, she'll be right out." Looking in the hallway, asked, "Where's Mr. McAbe?" Carol entered the room and Melanie closed the door. Pointing Carol to a small loveseat, Melanie returned to the adjacent reading chair.

"Sean's in bed already." Carol sighed and pointed to the furnishings. "Can you believe the Marines call this VIP quarters? At best it's a two-star hotel."

"That's exactly what I said. Know what Tim's response was?

'You know, Melanie, in the Marine Corps, "two stars" means major general!' Guess that was his way of saying it's relative."

"I suppose so. It's nice enough. That new sports car Sean bought Patrick is in the parking lot here. I guess this is where he stayed. Makes me feel a little closer to him to know that he was here so recently, although I can't explain why. We're driving it to Patrick's apartment tomorrow afternoon." Melanie handed her a box of tissues as her eyes welled up with tears. "I don't think we can stay there, though. We'll come back here."

Carol clasped her hands in her lap. "But that's not what I came here to ask you tonight." She looked around the room and her eyes welled up. "I need to know who my son really was. Something tells me you knew him better than I did." She looked at Melanie and pleaded. "Please, Melanie. Tell me who he was. I *need* to know."

41

Don wasn't sure if he looked okay. Patrick would've known. So would Eddie. Even though Karl had teased Patrick for his conservative clothes, he and Eddie had fit the gay stereotype by having fashion sense, a trait Don considered useless without the means to afford it. Besides, who needed fashion sense when the Marine Corps published a two-hundred-page uniform regulation? Don would've known from memory exactly how he should look, if only he were wearing the same green service uniform he'd worn to Eddie's funeral. Service coats were semi-form-fitting. The chest could have two inches of freedom; the waist one. The coat extended between one and two inches below the crotch. The hem on the trousers was two to three inches wide. *Et cetera.*

No more. As he inserted his arms through the sleeves of his charcoal-gray suit, he couldn't remember the last time he'd worn it. Fortunately, his chest had grown only an inch or two larger, making the coat snug but wearable. But was it fashionable? How had Patrick and Eddie known what was proper wear? Was there a published fashion regulation? If so, who authorized it? Was there a gay commandant or Pope who approved these things? Who chose him? Or her?

Don wasn't walking away from just a paycheck or a job. Neither was he running away from a life he'd messed up beyond repair, something people did every day. Instead, he was leaving the only

way of life he'd ever known. Chris had coined an expression—
"Mil-Tao," short for "The Military Tao." He'd said a lot of guys
needed Mil-Tao to get them through life. Don and Chris probably
had been drunk at the time because that's when Chris became
philosophical. Don hadn't understood what his better-educated
friend had meant, but this morning, it made sense.

The Marine Corps was tough because Marines had orders to follow regarding every aspect of their lives—on and off duty—and
their jobs. Staring in the mirror, Don saw that the greater challenge
would be living with*out* orders. Worst of all, he'd have to do it without Patrick, Eddie and Chris. He was terrified and felt deep excruciating pain. He'd survive. For the rest of his life he'd carry a piece
of Patrick's spirit with him. Same with Eddie and Chris. These
men had shaped his life, and by surviving, he'd keep them alive as
well.

"Whenever you're ready, Don, we can go." Karl stepped into his
bedroom and smoothed the back of his coat. "This is a great suit.
You look good." Karl winked. "We just need to have it taken out a
little here—and here—other than that, you could be on the cover
of *GQ*."

"I can count on you to give me fashion advice from now on, little buddy?" Tears streamed down Don's face as he hugged Karl
tightly, not wanting to let him—or any of his friends—out of his
sight. He thanked God for all of them. "You're wearing your uniform today?"

"Yeah. I spoke with Colonel Spen—Leo—this morning. He's
got an off-base errand for me as soon as we get to El Toro," Karl
said. "But after that I might have to drive the families."

Don shook his head. "A corporal calling a colonel by his first
name—"

"*Pet* name. I'm the only one he lets call him that. Actually, he
doesn't *let* me. I just do it."

"Another thing I have to get used to—life without a rank structure." Don looked at Karl's face as Karl straightened his tie. "You
okay to drive? You've got swelling around one eye."

"I can see fine. It hurts when tears get in the cuts." Karl sighed
and look up at Don. "I can't be at the service. Leo says this errand

is important. Might help him solve the mystery of what happened. The timing sucks but I have to do this. Jeanne will be with you and so will Lance."

"I'll be okay, Karl. I'm sure if your—your boyfriend says it's necessary, it is."

"Man! You look sharp."

"Borrowed this goddamned coat from my sergeant." Zack slid into Jay's passenger seat. "Ain't looked this respectable since my granddaddy's funeral. Will I blend with the mourners?"

"Yeah." Jay pulled away from Zack's barracks. "What did you tell your sergeant?"

"Told him I was goin' to mass. He said, 'Oh! That's—that's good, Lance Corporal Schein. You goin' to confession too?' I said, 'Naw. Ain't got nothin' to confess.'"

Jay glanced across the car. "That's your last name? How'd you spell it?"

"S-C-H-E-I-N. Don't ask me why the spellin's so fucked up, I don't know," Zack said. "You gonna put me on the FBI's most wanted? I'll be right next to you, brotha'!"

"The FBI wouldn't know what to do with you," Jay said. "Glad you didn't bring your pack."

"Clean as a whistle." Zack held up his arms. "Wanna search me?"

"Should I? No. Call me crazy, but I trust you. Besides, I'm impressed. You clean up well."

"What the fuck d'you mean? You bet I clean up good—I'm a good-lookin' guy." Silently, Jay agreed with him. "What's this? Holy shit, Jay-man! Now *I'm* awe-struck." Picking up the morning's *Washington Herald* Jay had wedged between the seats, Zack opened the front page, holding it out for a better view. This time, McAbe and Hawkins's faces were clearly visible. "'Marine pilot in collision signed life insurance to gay lover.' How'd you get this in print?"

"Kathryn Angel and I go *way* back."

"Who's that? She the bitch that wrote it? Let's see what it says—'A lance corporal at the squadron confirmed it before the captain could say "no comment."' Ha ha! Gotta love us lance corporals! 'McAbe and Hawkins were the subjects of a Valentine's Day cover story about gay relationships under the ban.' Aw, ain't that sweet? Proves your case, Jay-man. What next?"

Jay exited out the base's main gate, merging north onto Interstate 5. "I'm worried we were *too* good. The investigation gives us a green light to look into every part of McAbe's life. But if the colonel decides McAbe's suicide was the definite cause, they might halt the investigation."

"Shit." Zack tossed the *Herald* in back. "Think they'll try 'n' stop us?"

"No. The military drags out investigations as long as it can. Especially high-profile ones."

"Good," Zack said, " 'cause we havin' too much fun to stop now."

The two men rode in silence up the eighteen-mile stretch of coastal highway slicing through Camp Pendleton's western edge. Drivers in the southbound lanes pulled into a small vista point to enjoy the dramatic ocean view while large CH-46 and gigantic CH-53 helicopters ferried Marines between the 200-square-mile base and the amphibious ships offshore.

"You never did answer my question," Zack said. "How did Pastor Stephen die?"

"Whoa. Where'd that come from?"

"Since you usually don't like to talk, figured I'd ask now since you're in a good mood."

"I'm in a good mood?" Jay asked. "What're you talking about? I don't have moods."

"Bullshit! You're about the moodiest human who ever swung a dick," Zack said. "Back to the question. You wanna answer it or not?"

Brake lights popped on just ahead. "Fuck!" They'd have to wait at the border control checkpoint. Slowing to a crawl, Jay looked across the car at his young friend. "When we got home after the camping trip to the Upper Peninsula, Pastor Stephen started asking me to help him out with projects. We'd meet at the church once or twice a month—usually on a Friday evening—and I'd put together bulletin boards or copy Sunday School lessons, you know, shit like that. As a reward, he'd take me out for dinner. After a couple of months, he started inviting me to his apartment to watch TV. Before long we—um, we—we had a sexual relationship."

"How sexual?"

"*Very* sexual." Jay nodded as the agent quickly waved them through. "Pastor Stephen lived in the same neighborhood as my grandma, so the next summer, I begged my dad to let me stay with her. He thought it was weird—no sixteen-year-old boy wants to spend a summer with his grandma. But Mom thought it'd be great to give Grandma—her mom—some company, 'cause it wasn't too long after Grandpa died. So Dad let me stay. That was the most awesome time of my life, Zack. I'll *never* forget it—it was the bicentennial summer of 1976. Let's just say I saw fireworks almost every night. I'd walk my grandma's dog, Porky, over to his house—"

"Porky? You gotta be shittin' me. That's fuckin' hilarious!"

"Never thought of it that way. I'd walk Porky over to Pastor Stephen's and he'd pork me." Jay laughed along with Zack. "No, it wasn't like that. The sex was only a part of it. But the kids in the youth group eventually figured out what was going on. The rumors started. The guys called me Pastor Stephen's 'bitch.' By Christmas, my dad heard people talk. Dad never asked me about it. He just said I couldn't go over to Pastor Stephen's anymore."

"I bet that was rough, wasn't it?"

"It was the hardest thing in the world. One night after my parents went to bed, I sneaked out of the house and hitched a ride over to Pastor Stephen's. A few hours later, we were lying in bed, naked of course, and I was crying. I didn't know how I could see him. And—" Jay had relived this scene in his mind hundreds or thousands of times but he'd never told it to anyone. He wasn't sure why he was telling Zack, other than the Marine's persistent questions. Maybe he needed to get it out and Zack was the first person he'd bonded with since Pastor Stephen.

Jay was startled when Zack gently put his hand on his shoulder. "Buddy, you can stop if you want. I'm pretty sure I know how this story ends."

"I was asleep when my dad burst into the bedroom waving his

shotgun. He threw me into a corner—jerked my arm so hard he almost dislocated my shoulder. Then—then he blew a hole in Pastor Stephen. It was as big as a grapefruit." Jay glanced at Zack. "I saw the whole thing."

"Holy shit," Zack said. "Did your old man go to jail?"

"The jury found him not guilty."

"Not guilty? Even with you as an eye—?" Zack paused. "Jay. Oh my God. You didn't testify against him, did you? You were too scared of your old man to tell a jury what you saw."

"Didn't stick around for the trial. The night Pa killed him, the neighbors called the police and they came and took him away. But I went home, packed my clothes, stole some money my dad had hidden and left. He must've been pissed because I don't know where Ma got the bail money." Jay looked at Zack. "I've never been back."

"What about your old man?"

"I kept in touch with my mom over the years, by phone. Dad died six or seven years ago. Heart attack. It was strange because he was still relatively young and healthy."

"Wow, Jay. I thought *I* had a fucked-up childhood." Zack paused, then asked, "Why're you so eager to chase homos outta the military? This is a lot more than just a job to you, ain't it."

"What Pastor Stephen did to me was wrong." Jay was glad their conversation had moved beyond the nightmare of that awful night. "My dad was an abusive prick. What I needed was a friend, not someone to fuck me. Maybe if Pastor Stephen hadn't come along, I would've developed normally, you know? I could've dated girls and who knows? Maybe I could've found a woman to marry. Had kids, lived a normal life."

"What stopped you after that?" Zack asked. "Why don't you fuck women now?"

"Rather insightful questions for a Georgia redneck."

"Most people don't give rednecks enough credit. I use that to my advantage."

"What's stopping me now? I'll never find anything that came close to what I had with Pastor Stephen. No woman—no man—could ever make me feel as good as he did. And that's just wrong. It shouldn't have happened. It wasn't natural. He warped me for life."

Zack was silent for a few minutes. "What it sounds like to me is you're blamin' Pastor Stephen for somethin' that ain't his fault. He might've fucked you in the ass but your daddy fucked with your head. Pastor Stephen took care of you. What'd he get for it? His chest blowed wide open with a shotgun, that's what. So what if you fucked each other? Sounds to me like you were in love with him."

"I've never used that word to describe it. I never will."

"Oh hell, Jay-man! You used the 'n' word. Ain't you never heard? Never say never."

They were five miles from the air station. "Zack, my man, you're a completely different person when you're not on drugs. Without crystal, you're actually a decent human being."

"I know."

Jay had expected a retort and was surprised at the young man's admission. Maybe this was a sign he could be a positive influence in Zack's life. He mentally noted to revisit this subject when they had more time. If he could keep Zack off methamphetamines, Jay was certain the two of them could achieve great things. Today, though, their agenda was set.

"Okay buddy," Jay said. "Get ready for a crazy morning. Here's the plan."

"Here are detailed instructions for you but I'll briefly explain it." Leonard handed Karl a sheet of paper. "The doctor informed me that another sample of blood was taken from the pilots after the crash, but it's at the Orange County Crime Lab in Santa Ana. Someone is waiting there to give you a portion of Lieutenant Colonel Hammer's blood specimen. You must take it to the lab at the El Toro Regional Hospital, where we were on Sunday. Someone will be waiting in the ER lobby to receive it from you. That's all you need to do. They'll compare the samples immediately and telephone the results to me. You don't need to be concerned with that. Just get the sample from the crime lab to the hospital. It's extremely important that you do that in the next hour. And Karl, you're the only one I can trust."

"Yes, sir." Karl had an intense look on his face that was irresistible, despite the bruises that had only begun to heal. Leonard glanced around the empty conference room, making sure the door was closed, and kissed his lover. Karl was shocked, but smiled. "Thank you, sir. May I have another?" Regaining his composure, Karl opened the door, ready to embark on his mission.

Down the short hallway, Leonard heard General Neville call his name. As he joined the general for the ride to the service at the station chapel, he prayed for Karl's safety and success.

"Jay! Jay!" Zack shouted, "There's Karl Steiger! He's leaving the air station!"

Driving though the main gate, Jay turned his head sharply to the left, looking past the guardhouse. To his astonishment, Karl, the same Marine he'd cared for in his bathtub just over twenty-four hours earlier, was leaving the base in uniform in a government sedan. "He see us?"

"I don't think so," Zack said. "Should I follow him?"

Jay's mind raced through all the possibilities. He expected Hawkins would attend the service. If Karl was Hawkins's best friend, perhaps he was driving to pick up other gay Marines to join them. But Karl looked official, like he might be on an errand for someone high-ranking. Maybe he was picking up family members at a hotel or the airport, in which case Jay wasn't interested in pursuing him. Still, maybe the wise thing would be for him and Zack to split up. He had to make a quick decision. Veering into a small lot just inside the gate, he hopped out of the car and told Zack to slide over. "Follow Karl and don't lose him. Don't be gone more than two hours. I'll meet you at the general's headquarters building."

"You got it, Jay-man!" Zack slid over the console into the driver's seat. He made a U-turn, squealing the tires. The MPs at the gate were oblivious to the car speeding off base.

Jay walked the short distance across the air station toward the chapel and the headquarters. Along the way, he'd pass through the exchange, commissary and food court to learn whether the average Marine knew about the revelation in the *Washington Herald*. As the story picked up steam, he'd have free rein with this investigation.

To his delight, four Marines on a break in the food court huddled around a copy of the *Herald*. They had wide-eyed disbelieving expressions as one read the article to the other three.

"This is going to be a very good day," Jay said.

Karl was off on his errands while Robbi acted as chauffeur. Don had Jeanne and Lance with him. The unstated truth was that, on or around military bases, Don couldn't be in public with Karl and Robbi. They had promising careers ahead of them; association with him was toxic.

Jeanne parked far from the chapel because closer spaces weren't available. Walking to the chapel, Don asked, "Is it just me, or are people staring?"

"It's not you," Lance said. "People are staring."

Jeanne added, "Thanks to Kathryn Angel."

"Maybe the story wasn't her fault," Don said. "Maybe the *Herald* didn't give her a choice."

"Don, you're a good person," Jeanne said. "You accused Eddie of being a softie, but so are you. You want to think the best about Angel. I love the quality in you that looks for the good in people. But she stabbed you in the back at the worst possible time of your life."

"Jeanne's right, Don. She should've at least called and warned you."

Lance was right but Don was too low on energy to care about the reporter. Besides, it was irrelevant. "She may have done me the biggest favor of my life, indirectly. I needed to get out but wouldn't have done it on my own." Approaching the chapel, he said to Jeanne, "Would you mind, miss, taking my right arm in yours?" She smiled at her old friend and locked arms with him. "And you, sir," Don said to Lance, "would you do me the honor of escorting me on my left?"

Lance locked arms with Don. "Welcome to the First Civ Div, Don. Glad to have you aboard."

Marines in dress blues escorted the families to the front two rows of the chapel. General and Mrs. Neville, Leonard and Major and Mrs. Burr followed, sitting in the third row. Mercifully, Congressman Coughlin's flight out of Dulles departed too late for him to attend the service.

Friends, squadron mates and family members had created small shrines to the pilots out of photographs, spare flight helmets, boots and other items. Just before the service, Leonard heard a small commotion throughout the standing-room-only chapel. Turning, he glimpsed Hawkins, dressed in a suit, entering the building with a woman Leonard recognized from Sunday as well as another young man. Neither the general nor the McAbes indicated whether they noticed his presence. Soon afterward, the air station's chaplain stepped to the front to begin the memorial.

Leonard tried to focus on the service but his thoughts ran wildly along several paths, none reaching a conclusion. Men and women had always died in the service of their nations. This memorial represented a link in a chain that had begun thousands of years earlier and—barring a sudden spurt in humankind's evolution—would continue thousands of years into the future. But *these* men hadn't died fighting the Germans, the Japanese, the Viet Cong or Saddam Hussein. They'd perished in an air show. From the viewpoint of senior aviation officers, air shows were necessary in a democracy. Citizens who saw the fruits of their tax dollars were far less likely to complain to their legislators about visually impressive projects than they were about intangibles such as welfare. Nonetheless, an air show was an exhibition and these men—as brave and fearless as they'd been—had died as needlessly as tightrope walkers falling under a circus tent.

His professional dilemma also weighed on his mind. Was Coughlin so spiteful and narrow-minded that he'd close a military base and move an entire Aircraft Wing, even if the evidence indicated that a gay pilot probably had nothing to do with the collision?

Since last night, a more basic question had been nagging at him. Was El Toro worth saving? He'd blindly followed and preached the general's doctrine that El Toro must be saved. Should it? Was the price of closing it and moving the Aircraft Wing really so high? Leonard hadn't seen any studies either way. Why *was* General

Neville so obsessed with keeping the base open? When Leonard was in General Neville's position, he'd rather not be in Coughlin's district.

The most pressing—and haunting—question, though, was what had happened in those helicopters on Sunday. Before Sledge's blood sample came back with an alcohol count of zero, Leonard assumed he knew the horrible truth about Sunday's crash. Now, he wasn't so sure. Or what if Sledge *had* been sober? Was he in such a sad state that he could've done this with*out* the influence of alcohol? Leonard's announcement in two hours partly depended on Karl's errand.

Then there was Karl—and what Karl represented to Leonard. For years, Leonard hadn't paid much attention to his sexual preference. He'd successfully hidden his desire for male companionship—and his infrequent trysts to satisfy his desire—from the Marine Corps. He'd considered secrecy a minor inconvenience compared to the greater satisfaction he received from fulfilling his military missions. He should've been more intimate with Chris several years ago, but at the time, he was too focused on selection to general to consider the possibility of a relationship with a man. Now that he had both his promotion *and* Karl—he could compare them side by side and see that there was no contest. Karl was living proof—beautifully visual and deliciously tangible—that what Leonard had had with his ex-wife, he should be able to have with Karl. A system that punished people for their relationships was unjust and inequitable. Most importantly, such a system didn't deserve the ultimate sacrifice it often demanded. Lieutenant McAbe had given his life for a government that didn't want him. How often had that happened?

Everyone in the packed auditorium stood to sing *The Navy Hymn* and a bugler played taps. The memorial service was over and uniformed Marines walked quickly to the front to escort the families out of the chapel. General Neville, Eileen, Leonard and the other high-ranking officers stepped into the aisle. Leonard turned to follow the families and was astonished and pleased by the act of kindness he witnessed at the rear of the chapel. On this dark day, it was a glimmer of hope.

42

"Thank you, ma'am." *Leo's right as always. Lady's waiting here with a smile on her face, ready to do what he asked her. How does he do it? People will do anything for him. Shit. I know I will. God, I love him so much.* Karl took the small box, wrapped tightly in insulated packaging, and returned to the sedan to review his instructions. *Take the 55 south to the 405 south. Exit at Sand Canyon. Turn right into the hospital. Got it.* He started the ignition and put the car in reverse. *I should be there in twenty minutes, if fuckin' midmorning traffic's light.*

Karl looked in the rearview mirror, making sure no kids or anyone else had stepped behind the car. *What the fuck is that? What kind of perv is cruising me now?* He adjusted the mirror to focus on a car about a hundred feet away. *Let's see if the fucker follows me. Come on, baby, bring it on!* Backing out of the space, Karl stopped, put the car in drive and slowly rolled forward toward the street. *Holy shit! The bastard's following me! Hmmm, lemme see if he falls for this.* Karl slowed almost to a stop and pretended to look at something in the seat. *Asshole stopped too! Okay, motherfucker, I'm gonna see who the hell you are.* Karl raised his head quickly, getting a good look at the driver. "Motherfucking son of a bitch!" he said aloud. *I'm gonna go back there and fuck up your world, asshole!* Before he opened the door, though, he recalled Leonard's instructions. *No, Leo's mission is way more important. Revenge can wait.*

* * *

He'd been spotted and recognized. The chase was on and Zack needed fuel. With a move he'd practiced thousands of times, he reached swiftly into his pocket, retrieving the little plastic bag containing one-sixteenth of an ounce of the bitter crystalline powder. Squeezing open the ziplock top, he used a ballpoint pen cap to scoop a tiny portion of the chemical to his right nostril and snorted it. He'd graduated to smoking meth—occasionally injecting it—long ago, but sometimes the situation forced him to revert to more clandestine means of ingesting the awesome magical potion. As his brain began firing neurotransmitters across his synapses faster than the speed of light, he let out a rebel yell, speeding from the parking lot in pursuit of his prey.

Don, Jeanne and Lance stood in the back of the chapel, packed tightly with other mourners. Some recognized Don from the *Herald* and whispered to their neighbors. More people entered and someone fell against him. At first he'd feared an attack from an antigay zealot. Instead, a Marine corporal with frightened eyes said, "Excuse me," before disappearing into the crowd.

Robbi had explained that Marines were in two camps about the collision's cause, with a larger number blaming Patrick. Surveying the crowd, Don wondered who could be so insensitive as to accuse Patrick. His disadvantage was his junior status as a pilot-in-training—few people had known him. The lieutenant colonel's weakness was that he'd been a certifiable asshole, but some Marines admired tyrants. Maybe they hoped to become tyrants themselves.

Don no longer cared what anyone thought. His important life tools forty-eight hours ago—secrecy, protection and segregation into the personal and the professional—were now trivial. Control had been vital to his survival. After enduring tragedy years ago, his reaction had been to manage every part of his life, with the goal of preventing anything bad from happening again. Control had worked because he hadn't felt pain in a decade. But he also hadn't felt love—the vulnerable and surrendering form of love that separates humans from everything else on earth.

The January afternoon in Balboa Park with Eddie had been a turning point. Eddie's advice had prepared the way for him to meet Patrick that night. With Patrick, he'd charted a new course, creating a new man. Don knew, going into the relationship, that life ends quickly. When he was with Patrick, nothing existed beyond that moment. Being together, they had an intuitive understanding that the meaning of life was where they were—not in the past, not in the future and not in a far-off heavenly—or hellish—afterlife with a judgmental God or a vindictive Satan.

With Patrick, living in the moment had been the easiest, most natural thing in the world. The challenge for Don now was daunting. How could he live in the moment when the moments were so abysmal? How could he compare each new day ahead without Patrick to the hundred days with him? Don couldn't—and he shouldn't. The last hundred days had been a special treat, but the gifts going forward were the lessons he and Patrick had learned together, through each other.

I hoped that was you. Hearing Patrick's first words to him in his head, Don's tears rolled freely. How lucky he was to have embodied the hopes of a man as wonderful as Patrick.

Control was a joke—no, it was worse than a joke. Not only did it not exist, but its illusion had robbed Don of joy and growth. He'd imagined himself as a fighter, a guy who fearlessly combated the current by swimming against it. He'd couldn't have been more wrong. Before Patrick, Don's control fantasies had turned his life into a rancid puddle of stagnant water. He'd been so busy policing his life, constantly checking it to see that every part of it was in its proper place, that he'd lost sight of the world around him. True, he had wonderful friends, but now, with the gifts Patrick had given him, he'd be an even better friend, because he'd be a better person.

Never again would he pretend to be a heterosexual Marine. He'd always be himself and that's who the world would see. He'd stand tall and tough, but he wouldn't need to move—from now on he'd go against the current by remaining serenely still, watching the folly swirl past him.

The service ended and Marines walked in step to the front of the chapel to escort the families out of the building. The first group included a middle-aged woman and two adolescent children, probably the wife who'd walked out on the squadron commander. Don wondered if she blamed her husband, and if she did, whether she'd be honest if asked. Probably not. She had two sons to raise, and as long as she remained unmarried and her husband's reputation was intact, she'd receive the widow's pension. Chris Ashburn's family was somewhere in the group, but although he and Don had been close friends for a decade, Don knew nothing about his family.

Sorrow flooded Don's heart. The next couple was Patrick's mom and dad, and their son had characteristics of both of them. He had his mother's long, slender features and hair and skin color, but his eyes and gait were the same as his father's. Jeanne must've sensed Don's sudden reaction and its cause, and she put her arm around him for support—both emotional and literal. Seeing the McAbes leave the chapel, with Mrs. McAbe clutching the tricornered American flag, was tough. His tears poured more freely than at any time since the collision.

A woman ran over to Don and took his hand. At first he didn't recognize her because of his tears, but when she spoke, he knew it was Melanie. "You belong with us," she said, pulling him out of the crowd of mourners and into the group of families. Don dried his eyes, looking up in time to return Colonel Spencer's warm and knowing smile of solidarity.

Sharp curve ahead. Gotta slow down to get on the 405 south. Karl slowed down just enough to safely maneuver onto and over the flyover. *Fuckin' psycho MP's car is faster. Shoulda recognized Gared's sports car. Old cheap sports car, still faster than this goddamned Chrysler. Piece of shit. Leo deserves better.* Fortunately, morning traffic had decreased, and once he'd safely merged, he revved the engine to ninety miles per hour. *Bastard's on my ass. Time for a little evasive driving.* Jerking to the right across four lanes, Karl attempted to throw the MP off his trail by switching his right indicator on as if he were exiting onto Culver Drive.

Ha ha, motherfucker! Karl laughed as the other Marine reacted hastily, almost ramming a Mercedes. The Mercedes driver gave him the finger, which only seemed to anger the MP. Both the sedan and the sports car sped in the direction of the Culver off-ramp. *Now for the bait and switch.* Karl swerved the sedan to the left, missing the exit and continuing south on the 405. *Fuck! Dickhead made it back to the freeway.* Besides speed, the sports car had the advantage of greater maneuverability. *You're trying to stop me from gettin' this blood to the lab, aren't you, asshole? No way in hell are you gonna make me break my promise to Leo!* He hit the gas.

Sand Canyon exit, one more mile. At over a hundred miles per hour, he'd be there in less than thirty seconds. *Two—no three goddamned traffic lights. Fucker might ram me on the surface street.* Pondering a way out of his dilemma, Karl suddenly remembered what was just beyond the exit. *That'll throw him off my ass!*

The sports car pulled up to Karl's right side. *Son of a bitch MP might have a gun!* Karl swerved to the right throwing the full weight of the larger sedan against the smaller sports car. The car lurched across the freeway but the MP regained control, returning to Karl's side.

Jesus Christ, not now! Karl saw the California Highway Patrol but he couldn't avoid them or worry about them. *Arrest me, I don't give a fuck—wouldn't be the first time—just wait till I get this blood to the lab.* Karl had only one more exit. *Timing's gotta be perfect.*

The highway construction at the El Toro "Y" was just ahead. The project included a far left lane for high-occupancy vehicles. When finished, the lane would arc way above the congested freeways, giving carpoolers an overpass to the dreaded merge. Karl's plan was to trick the other Marine into taking that lane, trapping him on a route that'd take him far south of Sand Canyon Road with no easy way to return. Karl would be free to take the next exit and double back to the hospital, only a few minutes behind his original schedule.

Hello, Officer Poncharello. The CHP motorcycles had caught up and were part of the high-speed chase. *Calling for backup, are you?* The sedan had reached its maximum speed. *Shit, if this doesn't work, Ponch and Jon are gonna fuck everything up.* The officers maneuvered to the right side of the sedan and the construction site was mere yards ahead. A barrier blocked traffic from entering the ramp. *Low-riding sports car. MP can't see what's ahead of him.*

Karl couldn't see the end of the ramp and didn't know how far south it would put the MP on the freeway, but that wasn't his problem because he didn't plan to take the ramp. *Time for another bait and switch—last one was the dress rehearsal, now for the real thing.* The wooden orange-and-white-striped barriers loomed just ahead.

"Yippie ki yea, mothafucka!" Karl shouted as he closed his eyes and ducked below the steering wheel. *Sounds like a cyclone just ripped the house apart!* The large sedan broke through the barrier as if the construction team had made it from Popsicle sticks. *Twenty-five yards, point of no return—CHiPs are behind, not beside—out-fuck-ing-standing!*

In one swift motion, Karl jerked the sedan one lane to the right. He slammed on the brakes and the CHP motorcycles almost crashed as they swerved around to his right. After sliding to a halt, Karl put the sedan in reverse and made a hasty three-point turn.

Nice of the crew to leave this gap in the divider for me. Note to self— send Cal-Trans a thank-you card. Karl drove through the gap, entering the 405 north. "Get over it!" Karl said to the cars honking him as they swerved. Soon, he was part of the flow of traffic. *Okay, motherfuckers, where are you?* He looked over his shoulder, searching for the MP and the CHP. *Ha ha! Asshole fell for it this time!* He watched the MP in the sports car continue up the HOV flyover at more than one hundred miles per hour. *Where does that HOV lane end—ho-ly moth-er-fuckin' shit.* Suddenly Karl realized why he hadn't seen the other end of the flyover.

It doesn't exist!

"Oh, fuck!" Karl said, his eyes growing huge. More cars honked as he pulled onto the shoulder. He watched in shock as inertia carried the sports car several feet through the air before gravity pulled it onto the freeway below. The car hit the ground as if it'd fallen from the roof of an eight-story building, the equivalent height of the unfinished HOV flyover. Vehicles crashed in a chain reaction and traffic quickly backed up on the south side. *Don't forget your mission.* Karl hit the accelerator and sped north. In his rearview mirror, he saw the explosion, and a nanosecond later, he heard it. *Rot in hell, you filthy scumbag. Good fuckin' riddance.*

Approaching the Sand Canyon exit ramp from the south, Karl turned on his right signal. *Just what I thought.* The CHP had resumed their pursuit and weren't far behind. *Hospital one block ahead!* He pressed his foot against the accelerator and raced down the short stretch of road. Less than a minute later he arrived at the entrance to the hospital's ER. Leaving the sedan running, he grabbed the package and ran inside. The CHP pulled up right behind him. *Ha ha, just like my Leo said, somebody's waiting.*

"Are you the Marine that Colonel Spencer sent over? I was becoming concerned."

Karl handed the man the box. "Thank you, Doctor. Now it's my turn to be concerned."

The doctor looked confused but said, "You can wait here for the results if you'd like."

Over his shoulder, Karl saw the CHP officers. "Think I'll be waiting somewhere else."

"What makes you say—?"

The first CHP officer broke through the door. "Freeze!" he shouted.

A horrified look came over the doctor's face as another officer stormed into the hospital. Karl raised his hands in the air. "Hold your fire! I'm unarmed! I'm getting down on the floor!" With his hands high above his head, Karl got on his knees, fell facedown and placed his hands behind his back. "Doctor, Colonel Spencer needs the blood test results like yesterday."

"Oh—okay," the doctor said, scurrying away from the scene.

The first officer knelt down and placed a knee on Karl's back. For the second time in two days, Karl felt the cold steel of handcuffs against his wrists. This time, though, he was happy. "What're you smiling about, Marine?" asked the second officer. "You're in a lot of trouble."

"That's okay, ma'am. Mission accomplished."

"Gunnery Sergeant Hawkins showed up at the memorial service? That was foolish."

"I disagree, General," Leonard replied. "I thought it was a rare act of courage."

"Foolishness or courage? I suppose it's a fine line—a matter for the historians." Leonard didn't respond. He looked out the car's window as Corporal Reynolds drove by carrying Eileen and the Hammers to the officers' club. "The families decided to forgo the press conference?"

"More like boycott it, rather than just forgo," Leonard answered. "That's *not* a fine line. Hopefully we can join them soon." The two rode in silence to the headquarters building. A dozen news vans and three or four times as many reporters were outside, with some reporters randomly brandishing microphones like weapons at unsuspecting Marines. The general's driver sped past the media hoi polloi to the rear. He jumped out and punched the code to the general's private entrance. Leonard and the general hurried inside before the journalists spotted them.

"General Neville, the courtyard is overflowing with media for the press conference," said the chief of staff. "Congressman Coughlin is out front in the waiting area, along with the Naval Investigative Service agent, Jay Gared." The name "Jay Gared" sent chills down Leonard's spine. Despite Karl's statements minimizing the agent's involvement, he'd been an accomplice to Karl's kidnapping and beating. Although Leonard wasn't usually prone to violence—outside combat—he wanted to annihilate Jay Gared as painfully as he—or his sidekick—had hurt Karl.

"Shall we greet our congressman?" General Neville asked. The question was rhetorical and Leonard obligingly followed his superior down the suite's corridor to the waiting area. "Thank you for coming today, Congressman Coughlin."

"General. Colonel," Coughlin said curtly. "I was just speaking with the fine young investigator here about the case. Would you mind if he joined us for a little chat before the press conference?" The congressman's question was also rhetorical and the four men entered the general's office for a private meeting. After quick introductions around the small table, Coughlin said, "The reason I asked if Agent Gared could join us is that he has information that corroborates some—*disturbing* news I received last evening."

Leonard searched the agent's face for clues to his motivation. Karl had called him a "closet case." Although Leonard understood the psychological theories behind self-loathing and denial, in real people their ramifications were more complex than the books explained. Across the table sat a man who despised who he was so much that he'd destroy people's lives rather than face the truth about himself. Outwardly, though, Gared could've been a model in the investigative agency's recruiting brochure. He wasn't flashy, yet his understated appearance was sharp, and he paid attention to details such as the cut of his suit and the shine on his shoes. He'd placed a small stack of papers on the table and the corners were perfectly aligned.

"We should begin the press conference before the media freaks start a riot in your courtyard," Coughlin said. "I'll get to the point. Last evening my colleague, AJ Finkels, paid me a visit. Do either of you gentlemen know Congressman Finkels?"

"Doesn't he represent a large district in eastern California?" the general asked. Leonard didn't know Finkels, but eastern California meant one thing—an abandoned desert air base.

"Yes," said Coughlin. "He's the only Democrat from this state—or *any* state—I trust. If Republicans retake the House next year—which I think we will—my guess is that Finkels will switch parties and come out of the closet, so to speak, as a Republican. But that had nothing to do with his visit last night." Coughlin stood and paced, forcing the other three men to strain their necks to follow him. "This Friday I'm introducing a bill on the floor of the House. My bill will turn DoD Directive 1332.14 into a federal law banning homosexuals from the military. Clinton won't be able to tinker with military readiness, or use the military for his sick social experiments, simply by issuing an executive order. Finkels agreed to cosponsor my bill. On one condition."

Coughlin waited. The general asked, "What condition is that, Congressman?"

"Ridgecrest Airfield is an abandoned World War II Army air base near Death Valley. The runways remain intact and they're fifty percent *larger* than El Toro's runways. AJ asked that I not oppose any plan to close El Toro. In exchange for cosponsoring my bill, he's asked for my support in his proposal to move the Seventh Marine Aircraft Wing to Ridgecrest."

Leonard watched a trickle of sweat slide down General Neville's temple. The general spoke slowly. "Surely, Congressman, you informed Mr. Finkels that the costs to relocate this entire Aircraft Wing to Ridgecrest far outweigh the benefits. New aircraft hangars, an up-to-date control tower and modern barracks for the Marines would all have to be constructed. We don't have the personnel, the money or the time."

Coughlin walked to the table and folded his hands on the back of his chair. "General, we've discussed this dozens of times. The base closure commission will issue its recommendations Friday afternoon. If the commission decides closing El Toro and moving your Aircraft Wing to Death Valley are in the nation's best interest, I'll have to expend every ounce of political capital I have to block that move. Success still won't be guaranteed." He resumed pacing. "General Neville, Colonel Spencer, you both know how much I love the Marine Corps. Having this Air Station in the 57th district is my pride and joy. But let's face it—this is Orange County, California. The real estate under these runways is a gold mine. I'm one of the few congressmen in America whose district actually *loses* money by having a military base operating in its midst."

General Neville stood. Leonard had never seen him so angry. "You know as well as I do when this base is put on the chopping block, the pressure to turn it into El Toro International Airport will be insurmountable. Who will your constituents blame when jumbo 747s fly a few hundred feet above their multimillion-dollar homes? When airport traffic congests the freeways more then ever? No, you need El Toro to remain in the hands of the Marine Corps just as much as we do, so don't feed me this line of *bullshit* about how much we need you."

Coughlin smiled and returned to his chair. The general sat down. Leonard hadn't expected his outburst of profanity. Coughlin said to Gared, "Never thought you'd sit in on a conversation like this, did you, son?" Gared smiled but wisely remained silent. Coughlin softened. "Valid points—although my wealthy constituents will *never* allow a commercial airport in their backyards."

Coughlin opened a manila folder. "The only reason I've fought as hard as I have to keep this base open in the past is because I love the Marine Corps. And I *thought* the Marine Corps loved me. It *used* to." The congressman slid copies of an eight-by-ten photograph across the table to the other three men. As Leonard fished for his reading glasses, Coughlin explained, "AJ brought these photographs to me last night, along with other information."

As Leonard put on his glasses, the general summed up the revelation. "Holy shit."

Melanie and her mom waited with Don outside the chapel. Much of the crowd had dispersed before Jeanne and Lance exited the building. The other families were on their way to the officers' club for a less formal celebration of the pilots' lives. As Melanie made introductions, a staff car returned to the chapel parking lot. Don froze in place as he watched Patrick's mother step out. Melanie said, "Carol, this is Don Hawkins."

In the few seconds before she spoke, Don wondered what she might say—or do—to him. His decade-and-a-half of combat training had prepared him to deal instinctively with hundreds of scenarios but nothing like this. Finally, she said, "You were very important to Patrick, and over the last three months I could tell from his voice he was happier than he'd ever been in his life. Now I know why. My husband—Sean—isn't ready to meet you yet, but trust me when I say both of us want you to be present at Patrick's funeral in Chicago Thursday afternoon."

"I—I'll be there. And thank you, ma'am. I could never—say in words—how much this means to me." With tears in her eyes, she hugged Don and returned to the sedan.

Don was still processing what had just happened when Melanie's mom asked, "Will you join us at the officers' club?"

Jeanne and Lance looked at Don. "No, ma'am," Don said. "We're going to the general's building. We've got a feeling—someone needs to make sure Patrick's interests are represented."

43

"He's the same Marine," said Coughlin. Through his glasses, Leonard focused on the image. From a human perspective, it was harmless, even charming. A shirtless Hawkins unbuttoned McAbe's shirt as the men smiled and almost kissed. Their gaze showed genuine affection, the look of two people in love that only the best actors could imitate. From Coughlin's perspective, though, it was evidence of perversion by someone who'd publicly humiliated him.

"I didn't pursue the matter," Coughlin said, "because I thought the Marine Corps would handle it properly. But from what Congressman Finkels tells me, the Corps did nothing to punish this—this filthy *sodomite*. The regimental commander, Colonel Watkins, dismissed all charges of disrespect and insubordination. Apparently he didn't even bother to investigate whether Hawkins was queer. A shame, because with just a few hours of fieldwork, a private investigator uncovered *mountains* of evidence that he's a homosexual. Why didn't the Corps?"

"You'd have to ask the infantry," said General Neville. "At Camp Pendleton."

Coughlin ignored the general. "While waiting to see you today, coincidentally I happened to meet this bright young investigator. Know what he said? Go ahead, Agent Gared."

"I've had Hawkins under surveillance since January. But NIS's instructions were to halt investigations into homosexuality until Clinton's policy is resolved."

At the mention of Clinton, Coughlin shook his head in disgust. "Since *January*. It's the middle of May. I don't care whether it's Camp Pendleton or El Toro, if the Marine Corps had done its job, you wouldn't have needed a memorial service for five pilots. This press conference wouldn't be necessary. This homosexual lieutenant would've been discovered and kicked out of the Corps—or thrown in prison where he could've enjoyed all the sodomy he wanted."

"We don't know Lieutenant McAbe caused the collision." Leonard's voice was low, but inside, his temper flared to dangerous levels. The general shook his head, indicating that Leonard should be quiet about the investigation.

"Agent Gared is the investigator," Coughlin said. "He says the evidence indicates that McAbe was suicidal. Why else would he care about life insurance? Is that right, Agent Gared?"

"Yes sir. The other theory is that Lieutenant Colonel Hammer was drunk and distraught. But the laboratory tests showed he was sober at the time of the crash."

"There you have it, gentlemen. In a few minutes when we talk to the press, I expect—"

"Even sober, Lieutenant Colonel Hammer could've caused it. All the bad news he'd received would send the most stable person over the edge." Leonard seethed—not even his commanding general's glare could silence him. "We also haven't ruled out the possibility of equipment malfunction or human error. This—this newspaper article has misled everyone. People with no insight have publicly leapt to a conclusion for which the evidence is circumstantial—at best." Leonard was shouting. "This press conference is entirely too—!"

"Thank you, Agent Gared," the general said, rising to his feet. "That's all."

The agent stood to leave. "I have one question," Leonard said. "Am I correct in recalling from our conference call yesterday that you *were* at the hospital on Sunday?"

"Yes, Colonel. I was at the air show because I had Lieutenant—"

"Why was it that we didn't see you? At the hospital, I mean."

For the first time, the agent seemed surprised. "I was in back, talking to a doctor."

"Thank you," Leonard said. Neither the general nor the congressman had any further questions and the agent left the office. Agent Gared's demeanor had shifted near the end, unsettling Leonard. His response seemed inconsistent. A thorough agent—as Gared seemed to be—would've talked to the general regardless of the level of activity. Also, what investigative advantage had Gared hoped to gain by watching McAbe fly in an air show? Driving from San Diego and fighting crowds seemed like a tremendous amount of trouble with no obvious benefit. And if Gared had had Hawkins under surveillance for months, no doubt he'd also watched Karl for a long time. If so, perhaps Gared knew of his relationship with Karl.

"Let me clarify my interests." Coughlin's bitter tone brought Leonard back to the table. "A homosexual pilot intentionally killed himself and three other pilots. Dozens of people died as a result. This incident vividly illustrates—better than all the congressional testimony or newspaper articles—what happens when we let homosexuals in the military. McAbe committed this act of treachery. The sooner Americans know that, the better. When they do, I won't *need* Finkels to cosponsor my bill. I can tell him where he can shove his plans for moving your Aircraft Wing. Half the Democratic caucus will be knocking on my door, *begging* to sign on as cosponsors."

Coughlin folded his hands and smiled. "But Colonel, if I can't point to the news footage of the collision and say, 'Look what happens when we let gays in the military,' I'll need all the help I can get to pass my bill. And I won't have the political capital left over to keep this base open."

"Congressman, that's unconscionable," General Neville said. "You can't possibly—"

Coughlin held up his hand, silencing the general. He looked directly at Leonard. "Colonel Spencer, if you allowed a known alcoholic to command one of your squadrons and *he* caused this collision, I won't be able to guarantee your promotion to brigadier general."

"President Clinton guarantees my promotion. Not you, sir."

Suddenly Leonard put it all together. "How did you know Colonel Watkins's name?" As a member of the minority party, Coughlin wouldn't have the sway to block Joe's promotion, but—"Is the Honorable Mr. Finkels on the Armed Services Committee?"

"He is," said Coughlin. "That's what makes his cosponsorship so valuable—if I need it."

"He removed Colonel Watkins's name from the promotion list, didn't he?" Leonard asked. "He did it as a token gesture to show you how much he supports you. All because Joe—"

"I don't know what you're talking about," Coughlin said.

"You're playing games with a man's career. You lying, vengeful blackmailer!"

"Leonard!" the general shouted. "I need to speak to the congressman in private."

Jay couldn't believe his good fortune in meeting Edward Coughlin. Not only had he made a positive impression on his political hero, but the man was also on his side in the investigation. Jay exited the general's suite, descending the stairs to join the throng in the two-story Spanish-villa-style courtyard. He took a closer look at the photograph Coughlin had given him of Hawkins and McAbe. Comparing it to the *Herald* picture, Jay wasn't surprised at the similarities. McAbe's shirt was the same and the men were standing in identical positions in McAbe's apartment. Jay laughed and said, "See you're still up to your old tricks, Kate."

Colonel Spencer's antagonism surprised Jay but not enough to concern him. With Coughlin on his side, the colonel was outmatched. Didn't Colonel Spencer know the power of a man like Coughlin? The colonel's question about his whereabouts at the hospital was disturbing but no one could prove Jay's involvement in the blood swap. He'd safely locked Hammer's blood vial in the glove compartment of his car. Thinking about his car reminded him that Zack should be here. Scanning the crowd of hundreds, though, he didn't see his wayward protégé.

Leonard was angry with Coughlin and Gared, but was angrier with himself for losing his temper and for underestimating Coughlin's vindictiveness. He didn't have time to dwell on his anger, though. Slipping into the empty conference room, he called the doctor's direct number.

"Hope you're sitting down, Colonel. According to what we sent to the crime lab, Hammer's blood alcohol content was point two three—three times the limit to operate a moving vehicle."

"How do you explain the discrepancy with the report you sent to us yesterday?"

"I'm ashamed to admit it, but I can't explain it. Not only was the BAC way off, but I'm afraid we have two separate samples. They're not even the same blood type."

"Was another pilot's blood accidentally tested or reported under two separate names?"

"That was my first guess," the doctor said. "Going back, I discovered something really strange. Hammer's original sample wasn't from any of the pilots—including Hammer."

"Can I be sure the point-two-three blood alcohol reading is—?"

"—Melvin Hammer's? Yes sir. I've confirmed it three times and started an investigation into the cause of the discrepancy. Now, though, we don't know the source of the mystery sample."

Leonard heard General Neville and Coughlin's voices. "Thank you, Doctor. I greatly—"

"Colonel—quick question. How did you know—or even suspect—this discrepancy?"

"I didn't," Leonard answered truthfully, "but I always get a second opinion. When I called your technician yesterday, he said he'd shipped a second set to the county. I asked for an expedited analysis. Sometimes these 'Hail Mary' passes actually work. Now, Doctor, I can't tell you how grateful I am for your help but I really must—"

"Colonel, one more thing before you go. That Marine you sent over—he's in jail."

Lance scanned the crowd. "Where's Karl?" Jeanne and Don shrugged. "Holy shit!"

"Find him?" Jeanne asked.

"No. But I spotted somebody else." Lance pointed. "Jay Gared. Think he sees us too."

"At last," Don said. "The infamous Agent Gared out in the open. No car windshield or two-way mirror separates us." Seeing the man this clearly—the physical embodiment of his hatred—had a mixed effect on Don. Gared sent Don's emotional turbulence—already equivalent to a Category 4 hurricane—to a Category 5. On the other hand, Gared didn't have horns and a pitchfork. He looked almost innocent. He had an official bureaucratic appearance—maybe that's what made him so dangerous. He was an agent of the system, merely doing its vicious bidding. Looking up, Don saw Coughlin, another enemy, enter the courtyard. "Guess it'd be wrong to pound Gared into the concrete during the speeches. Keep an eye on him. It can wait."

"Leonard," the general said, "you must speak your conscience. But professionally, there are consequences beyond my—or anyone else's—control."

Leonard had waited until Coughlin exited the suite before opening the door to the conference room, giving him a few seconds alone with the general. "The hospital committed an error. Sledge's blood alcohol level was point two three. We *must* postpone this press conference."

"They what? No, I can't. Just say—just—whatever you say, don't point to any evidence. Vaguely state the theories. Say that we're continuing to investigate all possible causes." The general opened the door. "How could the hospital make such a stupid—?" He shook his head. "I'll introduce Coughlin. When he's through, you'll give a brief statement and answer questions. The staff judge advocate will be standing behind you and you may deflect questions to him. But *don't* talk about the conflicting lab reports. We'll sort that out later." General Neville caught up with Coughlin and escorted him along the second-floor walkway above the people.

Coughlin's face lit up when he saw the crowd and he frantically waved his arms. After the general's introduction, Coughlin started with his agenda, rehashing his old scripts. "We must do all we can to save our children and our families, our sons and daughters who we send off to fight our nation's battles from those with perverted values." He held a copy of the morning's *Herald* over his head.

"While our children protect us from enemies abroad, we must protect our children from enemies within. Enemies within our borders have an agenda to corrupt our children's minds and lives, disrupting their training with social engineering."

Don't point to any evidence. Vaguely state the theories. Say that we're continuing to investigate all possible causes. General Neville's instructions had been clear. *Don't talk about the conflicting lab reports. We'll sort that out later,* he'd said.

Leonard had succeeded by making calculated choices. His conscious instinct was to follow the general's order and hold off on a preliminary conclusion. Something else, though, something deep and primitive, told him that this was the moment, not later. In his heart, he knew the cause of Sunday's collision and today he had an opportunity to halt—or slow—NIS's investigation into Lieutenant McAbe's personal life. But if he chose that option, he could kiss his promotion good-bye and the Marine Corps would lose El Toro, an extraordinarily high price.

Two roads diverged in a wood, and I— Leonard heard lines from Robert Frost's fitting poem he'd learned in his youth. If he exercised patience and told the press to wait a few days, he could avoid disastrous consequences for himself and the Marine Corps.

I took the one less traveled by— Or he could seize this opportunity and end the tragic debate about the cause of the collision. If he couldn't end it, at least he could steer it in the right direction. As Coughlin neared his conclusion, Leonard thought about Karl and how much more good he could do for Karl and others like him working from within the system than on the outside. If Clinton allowed gays to serve in the military, they'd need a high-ranking advocate. He simply didn't have enough time to make this decision. Leonard would have to go with his gut feeling, the same feeling that had carried him to victory in so many battles in the past.

And that has made all the difference.

Don seethed as Coughlin spewed his hate-filled vitriol. Jeanne rolled her eyes and stomped her foot a few times. Lance made a few cracks about Coughlin's hair and suit, while questioning his choice of skin care regimen. The reporters paid little attention to the speech. Don suspected they were waiting to fire their questions at Colonel Spencer. Finally, Coughlin concluded. The crowd gave him polite applause and the general returned to the podium.

"As the commanding general, I'm ultimately in charge of everything that takes place within the Seventh Marine Aircraft Wing. Colonel Spencer is the commanding officer of the Marine Aircraft Group 79, headquartered at Camp Pendleton, and he is the officer responsible for the various investigative bodies that look into an unfortunate event like this. At this time, Colonel Spencer will make a brief statement. Afterwards, he will field your questions."

Colonel Spencer appeared from behind the general. Don held his breath, anticipating what he might say. "The past forty-eight hours have been the worst two days of my life. Many of you share that feeling. All Marines—especially the men and women of my Aircraft Group—are my family. With the loss of five pilots in one day, I can't express the grief I feel. The purpose of this press conference, though," Colonel Spencer said, pausing to glance at the congressman, "is to provide honest answers to some tough questions. After all, this is a democracy, right, Congressman? As such, the citizens deserve to know what happens in their military. Let's begin with the facts of which we're reasonably certain. First Lieutenant Patrick McAbe was gay."

Every reporter in the room copied the colonel's statement.

"Furthermore, he was in a relationship with an enlisted Marine, which goes against the Uniform Code of Military Justice for more than one reason." Don didn't like the direction of the colonel's statements. Maybe Karl had been starstruck by the colonel's rank and had uncharacteristically misplaced his trust. "Many of you are aware of the rumor that Lieutenant Colonel Melvin Hammer had alcoholic tendencies and that he may have been drunk at the time of his flight. Those of you with connections, though, are aware of a report from the El Toro Regional Medical Center showing that Lieutenant Colonel Hammer had no alcohol in his blood at the time of the crash. No doubt everyone here is aware of the Serviceman's Group Life Insurance form that McAbe assigned to his partner not long ago.

"But there are many facts we *don't* know. We don't know which pilots were in each helicopter nor do we know who flew lead in each helicopter as there was no communication with the control tower on the morning of the flight. The only eyewitness to the events immediately preceding the flight was Captain Pfeiffer. Sadly, he is no longer with us and we haven't located anyone he spoke to on Sunday—other than me. Most importantly, we will probably never know the motivations of each man in the cockpit at the time of the collision."

Jay grew concerned. Why didn't Colonel Spencer state the obvious? *Although the investigation is in progress, all preliminary evidence points to a despondent homosexual as the cause of the crash.* Jay wondered why Hawkins was here and if Karl was also present. Why hadn't Hawkins's battalion arrested him? Jay had spoken with the commanding officer yesterday. Lieutenant Colonel Ritter assured him that the Marines would coordinate with NIS and investigate the matter thoroughly. But Gunnery Sergeant Hawkins was here.

The colonel continued, "I want to thank Congressman Coughlin for focusing my attention on one particular aspect of this crash." The colonel turned to smile at the congressman, who returned a blank, unknowing expression. "Congressman Coughlin spoke of enemies." Jay hoped the colonel would follow Congressman Coughlin's statements. *Homosexuals are our enemies.* "In Vietnam, the enemy, though not always visible, was known. In *Desert Storm* our enemy was clearly identified. Throughout my career, I've dedicated my life to fighting the enemy, in keeping with the oath that I took. Whether it was the Russians, the Libyans, or the Iraqis, the enemy was apparent. Another part of our oath acknowledges that the constitution of the United States has domestic enemies as well as the foreign ones."

This would be an ideal segue. *Homosexuals are our domestic enemies.*

Instead, the colonel said, "Domestic enemies come in many forms. The congressman believes that homosexuals who are committed to defending America are our domestic enemies."

The speech had taken a wrong turn. The undisputable evidence was still on Jay's side, though. The press corps had grown

CODE OF CONDUCT   431

unnervingly silent. He hoped they weren't placing too much stock in Colonel Spencer's remarks.

"I counter that the gay servicemen and women valiantly serving in the military, even as I speak, are not our enemies, but our beleaguered teammates. No, Congressman Coughlin, domestic enemies are those who would have us compromise our integrity for political gain."

Jay watched the congressman's face turn bright red. Sweat formed on his forehead and he began to tremble. The colonel continued. "Domestic enemies also tamper with evidence to obstruct justice. To my shock, minutes ago I learned that the report from the hospital showing a lack of alcohol in Lieutenant Colonel Hammer's blood was based on a false blood sample. Someone deliberately steered this investigation away from its real cause. I'm convinced the final report of this investigation will show that Lieutenant Colonel Hammer had a blood alcohol level of point two three, almost three times the legal limit to drive in California."

Colonel Spencer's revelation felt like a blow across Jay's forehead. How had he known? What else did he know? If he knew the blood sample was bogus, tracing it to Jay wouldn't take long. He had to get away. The courtyard was packed but exits were open in three corners. He maneuvered to the nearest one.

Don was relieved. During better times, he might even say he felt ecstatic but today he was simply glad that finally something was going as it should. Perhaps the tide was turning. Not only was Colonel Spencer putting a voice to thoughts Don had kept inside for years, but the voice belonged to a highly respected officer and his audience was an interested media crowd.

He took his eyes off the agent for only a moment. When Don looked back to the spot where Gared had been standing, he was gone. "I'm gonna find him," Don said. Jeanne said she'd remain in place to find Karl and Robbi while Lance followed Don.

"Another fact is that on Saturday evening, I informed Lieutenant Colonel Hammer that he hadn't been selected for promotion to colonel. At the time I told him this, I know Lieutenant Colonel Hammer, if not intoxicated, was well on his way to becoming so. I suspect that he drank the rest of the night and, while under the influence of alcohol, bullied his way into the cockpit."

Don glimpsed someone making his way toward a side ext from the courtyard. "Over there."

"Today," the colonel continued, "I make one final stand against the enemies of my country. One hundred and seventy years ago, Commodore Perry sent a message to General Harrison after the Battle of Lake Erie. It was: 'We have met the enemy, and they are ours.' Forty years ago, at the peak of McCarthyism, a wise comic strip author paraphrased Commodore Perry's message. He wrote, 'We have met the enemy, *and he is us.*' The most sinister enemy this nation faces is us—what we all have in ourselves—the potential to let our fear-based hatreds dominate us, clouding our basic humanity. This nation will not be destroyed by a foreign adversary or an invader. What threatens us the most is a cynical lack of understanding about each other.

"This attitude breeds hatred, which compels men and women— our sons, our daughters, our brothers and sisters, and our friends— to hide their identity. In the military, we have pursued this attitude to the extreme, and we've done so under the false pretense of maintaining unit cohesion. When we have proper leadership, we will have unit cohesion. When we develop moral courage, we will do the right thing and end the senseless harassment and inquisition of our own people."

As Don and Lance neared Agent Gared, he increased his pace. Don sprinted. "Sorry, sir," he said when he ran into a man frantically taking notes.

The colonel's voice boomed through amplifiers to the overflow audience outside the courtyard. "There are several likely causes for Sunday's tragedy. As always, we look into the possibilities of an equipment malfunction or pilot error. Despite my belief that this is far too soon, I've been asked to postulate the most probable cause."

Don listened to the speech as he chased the agent. Why was Gared running? Had the colonel said something to make him want to flee? Don didn't care—he just wanted to catch the bastard. The colonel reached the finale. "Using my best judgment, my preliminary conclusion is that this accident was *not* caused by a suicidal gay pilot. In fact, I believe that First Lieutenant Patrick McAbe's actions, as well as those of Lieutenant Chris Ashburn and First Lieutenant Tim Roberts, may have saved the lives of thousands of spectators. I also believe that Lieutenant Colonel Hammer, while under the influence of alcohol, killed himself and three of his pilots."

"Stop!" Don shouted. The agent was a fast runner, but so were Don and Lance. When Gared looked over his shoulder, he bumped into two reporters walking briskly around the corner. The impact knocked Gared on the ground, and within a matter of seconds, Don was on top of him. "Why were you running, asshole? You the one turning everybody against Patrick?"

"Get off me, you fucking queer!" the agent shouted. A camera crew who hadn't made it into the courtyard caught the fight between the Marine and the NIS agent on film.

MPs approached with their guns pointed. "Break it up!" Don stood and brushed his pants.

Standing, Gared shouted at the MPs, "Arrest him! This is Hawkins—a known homosexual, I can prove it! Arrest him, I said!"

The MPs remained still, keeping their pistols pointed at the two men. They looked at Gared, then at Don. "What's going on here—Gunny Hawkins?"

"Someone get the colonel," Lance shouted. "Tell him Agent Gared was trying to escape."

"Thank you, Gunny Hawkins." Don turned to see Colonel Spencer, the general, Coughlin and others follow him out of the building. "Arrest the agent," Colonel Spencer said.

"Why arrest the agent?" Coughlin pointed at Don. "*He's* the one you should arrest!"

"There's probable cause to arrest Agent Gared for tampering with evidence, misleading investigators, falsifying official reports and obstruction of justice, just to name a few charges. Oh, and let's add evading arrest. Check with the judge to make sure it's done legally, but draw his blood and compare it to the samples at the hospital for Lieutenant Colonel Hammer."

"You have the right to remain silent." The military police officer slapped handcuffs on Agent Gared and shoved him into the squad car. "Anything you say—"

"Thank you, Colonel," Don said.

"Don't thank me, Gunny Hawkins. You're the brave one." Colonel Spencer turned to the general. "General Neville, I hope you'll excuse me—"

"Leonard, I'm afraid you've got questions to answer."

"I'll say," growled Coughlin. "I don't know where you came up with that nonsense about—"

"General Neville, Congressman Coughlin, I'll be the sacrificial lamb. Don't take your frustrations out on the Corps. This was my decision. Please keep the base open. But quite honestly, General, I don't feel like answering any questions. I've said enough today."

"What are you saying, Leonard?" the general asked. "What do you mean, 'sacrificial—'"

"General Neville, please convey to the commandant that I've tendered my resignation from the Marine Corps, effective—"

"Sounds great to me," said the congressman. "Your career's over anyway, Colonel."

"Under one condition." Leonard looked directly at Coughlin. "That you put Colonel Watkins back on the promotion list as soon as possible."

"Can't make any promises, Colonel Spencer," said Coughlin. "Except that I'll look into it."

"Leonard," said the general, "are you sure about this? Don't make a decision you'll regret."

"There won't be any regrets, General Neville. Please accept my resignation."

"Very well. On behalf of the commandant of the Marine Corps, and pending his final authorization, Colonel Leonard Spencer, your resignation is accepted."

"Thank you, General. Now, Gunnery Sergeant Hawkins, is your car nearby?"

"My friend Jeanne's car is, sir. Where are we going?"

"Whether it's my last act as a group commander, or my first act as a civilian, we've got to bail my driver out of jail."

44

"Well, Kathryn. How was your time at the resort?"

"Wonderful. I would've stayed until Friday—tomorrow I guess—but I had a message you wanted to see me? Sounded urgent." She remained apprehensive as the editor-in-chief of the *Washington Herald* showed her a seat and closed the door to his office.

"Yes, it is." He was a large man who spoke with a thick Southern drawl. Sitting behind his desk, he said, "Over the last couple of days—while you were at the spa—I've had some delightful conversations with a smart young man by the name of Ricky. He's the editor at a weekly in San Diego called the *Gay and Lesbian Times*. Are you familiar with that publication?"

"Vaguely. But I don't see what this has to do with me." She was annoyed. If she'd ended—

"This has everything to do with you." Kathryn became alarmed as his tone darkened and he picked up the pace. "In two days, Ricky has uncovered the start of what will be a huge scandal."

Kathryn smiled as this was familiar turf. "Sounds juicy. Should I pick up the trail?"

The editor-in-chief laughed, but it had a menacing sound. "Oh, heavens no. I've hired Ricky to come here and write the story for us. In fact, he's on a flight to DC as we speak. If he does a good job, I may be inclined to hire him to work here full-time."

"Oh." She became very concerned.

He pulled an eight-by-ten photograph out of a folder and slid it across the desk for her. "What can you tell me about this image?"

"It's—we took it the night I interviewed Patrick McAbe and Don Hawkins in Oceanside, shortly after we took the photograph we actually used—you know, in the Valentine's Day piece and then again Tuesday morning. We took this photograph more as—a playful shot. I thought it was sexy—it was only taken as a personal favor to Don and Patrick." She looked up at the powerful man in front of her. "Why did the photographer give this to you? It was never used."

"I didn't get this from the photographer. Oh no, ma'am. And I'm afraid that it *was* used, Kathryn. Only not by us here at the *Washington Herald*. You've heard of the *Washington Herald*, haven't you, Kathryn? The organization that pays your salary and funds your expense account!" His chubby face was red with rage and Kathryn's heart sank. She was busted. After more than a decade of uncovering scandals and reporting on everyone else's misdeeds, now she was the one who'd been scandalized. All she could do was sit stone-faced.

"You see, Kathryn, I received this photograph from Ricky, which naturally leads you, as an investigative journalist, to a whole series of questions, beginning with, *Who gave this photograph to Ricky?* Well, Kathryn, since you asked, a colonel in the Marines was responsible for getting this to him. So, you ask, *Where on earth did a colonel in the Marines get a photograph taken by a* Washington Herald *photographer if he didn't receive it from the photographer?* The mystery just gets deeper because it seems that Congressman Edward Coughlin—"

"But Coughlin wasn't—" She stopped, realizing she shouldn't have said anything.

"Coughlin wasn't what, Kathryn? Coughlin wasn't the one who paid you for this photograph? Is that what you were about to say?" Shaking his head, he stared out the window. "I've never been so disgusted! You're damn right Coughlin didn't pay you! I bet you don't know who paid for this, do you? I'll tell you, Ms. Angel. There's a group of *extremely* wealthy land developers and contractors out there in California. Seems they bought a bunch of land *real* cheap out in the desert, near an old abandoned Army airfield called Ridgecrest. This consortium—I prefer to call it a cabal— came up with a scheme to get a huge military unit out to Ridgecrest Air Field. If they succeeded, that land value would be worth fifty times what they paid for it overnight and the no-bid construction contracts would be lucrative. This cabal hired a consultant to find every way possible—legal, illegal, unethical, whatever—to make sure the Marine Air Station at El Toro closed and the Seventh Marine Aircraft Wing moved to Ridgecrest. Part of their scheme was to get Edward Coughlin on the side of the representative for Ridgecrest's congressional district, AJ Finkels." He pounded his pudgy fist on the desk. "Does this sound complicated to you because it sure as *hell* sounds complicated to me!"

Kathryn wanted to cry and it took every ounce of strength to stop her lip from quivering. Everything made sense now. These things were always about money and everyone was a mercenary. Including her. This time, though, it had blown up and she'd be the one to pay.

He continued more calmly. "Finkels knew the best way to get Coughlin on his side was to appeal to his ego. That's where your information came in. I'm sorry, *my* information came in. Finkels used it to convince Coughlin that the Marines didn't care about him, to get Coughlin so pissed off, he'd turn against them." He laughed, and said, "What a petty bunch of—but that's not our concern. What I can't figure out is why you'd sell something that doesn't belong to you, Kathryn." He clasped his hands together on top of his desk and leaned forward. "Maybe you weren't sure about how things work around here, but when we pay you to travel across the country and interview people and take their pictures, that information and those photographs belong to the *Herald*, not to you. And the *Herald* is not in the business of digging up dirt on people to sell to the highest bidder. If you wanna do that, there are lots of places in this town you can go. Why don't you do that because guess what? You don't have a job. *You're fired!*"

No one said "you're fired" anymore. Kathryn had written a piece recently on workplace discrimination with that as a premise.

But here was her boss, telling her in the most definite way possible she was fired. He pressed a button on his telephone. "Are the guards here yet?"

"Guards?" Kathryn was horrified. This was real.

"Yes, they're waiting," said the voice.

"Send them in." The door opened immediately. "Kathryn, these gentlemen here are going to be kind enough to walk you to your car. And it will be the last time you *ever* go through the doors of the *Washington Herald*."

"Thank you for driving up here on such short notice."

"Thank you for inviting me. I've admired you for over a decade, sir. I used to live in DC."

Coughlin smiled. "Good to hear. You won't mind living there again?"

"Not at all," said Jay.

"Good. I liked what you did on the El Toro investigation. I like your commitment to the job. Too bad it didn't turn out the way we wanted. Well, win some lose some. We've got to move on. Looks like the Senate's compromised with Clinton so 'gays in the military' is a dead issue as far as I'm concerned—at least for now." Coughlin walked around the desk in his Orange County district office. "I have my sights set on higher things and I need reliable and dedicated people to help me. Nineteen ninety-four will be the year of the Republican, Jay! We can take back the House of Representatives for the American people, but in order to win, we must play as dirty as—no, dirtier than—the Democrats. We need people with your investigative skills who aren't afraid to do anything— and I *do mean* anything—to dig up dirt on our enemies."

"Congressman Coughlin, this sounds like the job I was born to do."

"That's the spirit! Don't think I'll stop with Congress. After we're successful next year, I'm on my way to the White House in 1996 and I'll take you with me all the way." Coughlin returned to his notes behind the desk. "I'll pull some strings. These bogus charges against you will be dropped." He stood and extended his hand. "Welcome to my team, Jay. When can you start?"

"I've got a quick trip out of town tomorrow and Saturday. Back Sunday and Monday to close out my lease and move. I'll be in Washington by the end of next week." Jay shook his hero's hand, thrilled that, once again, he was the phoenix rising from the ashes.

"I need a round-trip ticket, nonstop, Dulles to San Diego, departing Monday. Return date is open-ended. First class."

"That will be $1,938, Ms. Angel. What credit card will you be using?"

Kathryn was stunned. "How much? You've got to be kidding!" For ten years her assistant had booked her trips using the *Herald's* travel agent. She hadn't paid attention to the costs. Now that she was freelancing, things were different. Although she'd saved a lot of money, she also had an extravagant lifestyle. Until she sorted things out, she'd have to—economize.

"What would you like me to do, ma'am?"

The tears rolled down her face. "Let's change that. To coach."

After booking her trip, Kathryn dried her eyes and reread the note her assistant—*former* assistant—had phoned to her this morning. How pathetic her life had suddenly become. On this desperate day, she was basing her hopes for the future on a cryptic message from an anonymous caller. *Compare DNA. Orange County— False blood sample in McAbe collision to San Diego evidence warehouse—stray hairs found in Edward L. Johnson death investigation.* Still, as she looked at the words, perhaps they provided the key to her comeback and her ticket to another Pulitzer. "Cheer up, Katie girl. You clawed your way up before. You'll do it again!"

45

Jay checked the address again: *8762 King Road, Northwest.* "Matches the number on the mailbox, but—" He stared in bewilderment. "This can't be right."

Just before Ollie fired him Wednesday morning, Jay had searched the military's information system for Zack's address in Atlanta. He wanted to pay his respects to Zack's mom, despite the problems Zack had caused him. Arriving in Atlanta, he'd rented a car and the agent had given him a map and detailed directions to Zack's mom's. Jay checked into a cheap hotel near the airport and drove north through the capital of the New South. Getting through the city took over an hour in Friday afternoon traffic. North of downtown, he'd exited into a posh neighborhood shaded by giant old oak trees with low-hanging limbs and covered in velvety-green flower-lined lawns.

After twenty minutes of twisting, hilly narrow roads, he reached his destination. Rather than being a run-down apartment building in a bad part of town, northwest Atlanta reminded Jay of the stylish suburbs of northwest Washington. The smallest house had to be four thousand square feet and the minimum lot size was over an acre. Pulling over to the side of the road, he sat in his car, debating what to do. He'd come all the way across America, so he should at least go to the door. They'd tell him he had the wrong address and he'd return to San Diego. He backed up, turned into the long driveway and parked in a roundabout in front of a majestic colonial house.

He climbed the steps to the front porch and rang the bell. A tall elegant African-American woman with suspicious eyes answered. "Is—I'm here to see—Mrs. Schein. I may have the—"

"Who may I say is here?" the woman asked politely, her eyes still on the alert.

"Um, I—I'm Jay Gared," he said. "I'm—I was—a friend of Zack's."

A short pretty woman with a sad and tired face appeared around the door. "Mr. Gared. I'm Geraldine Schein. Please come in." The first woman disappeared quietly into another room and Jay followed Mrs. Schein into the foyer. A crystal chandelier hung overhead, surrounded by a winding carpet-covered staircase made of dark wood, the kind Scarlett O'Hara could've waltzed down with grace. Mrs. Schein entered a small but elaborately furnished living room. "I'm Zack's mother. Please have a seat while I get my husband." Her accent was soft and pleasant. Besides antique furniture, the room had original artwork and Remington sculptures.

"I'm David Schein, Mr. Gared. Zack's father. Did you fly all the way from California?"

"Yes." Jay stood to shake the man's hand and all three sat down. Zack looked exactly like a much younger version of the man who'd introduced himself as his father. "I considered Zack a friend—but—but please forgive me if it sounds like I'm prying. Are you Zack's *step*father?"

The Scheins looked confused. "No. We've been married thirty years," he said. "I assure you we're both Zack's natural parents." The man pulled out a checkbook. "We're sorry about what Zack did to your car. I assume he borrowed it without permission or stole it. He was uninsurable, given his record, so I'll set things right with you now. Our lawyer gave me a form, if you don't mind signing it once we agree on an amount. Will $30,000 cover your loss?"

"David." Mrs. Schein looked at her husband disapprovingly.

"My apologies, Mr. Gared, I failed to factor in your trouble for coming all this way. I'll make it out for $40,000. How do you spell your name?"

Jay was stunned, almost speechless, but he spelled his name. "Has—have you *always* lived in this house?" he asked, reaching across the coffee table. "Never in an apartment building?"

"We bought this house when Zack was five," Mrs. Schein said. "when David was promoted to chief surgeon at the hospital. Before, we lived in Buckhead, not far from here."

"Mr. Gared, our son was a troubled soul. We tried as hard as we could. We gave him the most life could offer. The best treatment available from the most skilled doctors in Georgia—"

"Treatment?" Jay asked, putting the check in his wallet. "For what?"

Zack's parents looked at each other. "Zack had a severe case of borderline personality disorder," said Mr. Schein. "By itself, treatment might've worked, but Zack became messed up with drugs rather early on. BPD and addiction together are like fighting a multiheaded hydra."

"I'm not familiar with this condition."

"It's more common in women," said Mrs. Schein. "But it affects men as well."

"Zack had all the most common symptoms: Strong emotions that wax and wane frequently, intense—although brief—anxiety or depression. His biggest symptom was his inappropriate anger, which, I'm afraid, might've escalated to physical violence. I hope you never experienced that with him—if you're still his friend, even after what he did to you, my guess is you didn't."

"No," Jay said quietly, "I—he never physically confronted me."

"He also had difficulty controlling his emotions and he was very impulsive," said Mrs. Schein. "Another major symptom that may have led him to enlist was his fear of being alone."

"How did he join the Marines? Don't they screen for mental conditions and drug abuse?"

Mrs. Schein's face betrayed feelings of anger. "Those infernal recruiters persisted with their calls. When Zack turned eighteen, we couldn't stop him from joining. I went up to the colonel in charge of the recruiters, but he acted like I was a hysterical mother." Mrs. Schein wiped her eyes. "Do they screen? From your questions, Mr. Gared, I assume Zack wasn't truthful with you all the time. He lied to the military's so-called 'screeners' and told them he was fine."

"But the meth," Jay said, "I thought the military tested—did urinalyses on all—"

"Methamphetamines are in a person's system at most seventy-two hours," Mr. Schein said. "Even Zack could stay clean that long. As you can tell, Mr. Gared, my wife and I were compelled to learn much more than we ever wanted to know about behavioral disorders and drugs. I'm sorry Zack deceived you and destroyed your car."

A back door opened and slammed shut and a man who appeared to be Jay's age entered the room from a hallway. He wore a cut-off shirt and faded jeans. His muscular arms were tan and glistened with sweat from an afternoon working in the Georgia sun. Jay noticed a tattoo on his arm. As he stared, he thought it said USMC with a bulldog underneath.

"I'm finished with the hydrangeas, ma'am. They look beautiful."

"Thank you so much. I'd like you to meet someone. This gentleman is Jay Gared. He was a friend of Zack's in California." She turned her head from one man to the other. "My, my. You two resemble each other quite a bit. Don't you think so, David?"

Jay agreed. Meeting a twin for the first time was unnerving. The other man must've felt the same way because he was slow to shake Jay's extended hand. As he did, he smiled and said, "Nice to meet you, Mr. Gared. Were you in the Corps too? Or do you just like my tattoo?"

"I wasn't a Marine, but I see those a lot—just didn't expect to here. You knew Zack?"

"Oh, yes sir. I've worked in this neighborhood—and for Zack's family—for nine years. Ever since I got out of the Corps. I'm Sebastian."

Sebastian. Zack's upstairs former Marine friend who'd respected him.

"Sebastian was one of the few positive role models Zack allowed into his life," said Mr. Schein. "Became like an older brother to Zack. Took him camping and fishing."

Sebastian looked at the floor. "I sure am gonna miss him." Looking up, he said, "As much as I liked the Corps the four years I was in, I told Zack he shouldn't join, but he wouldn't listen."

"He never listened to any of us," said Mrs. Schein. "Not even to Sebastian. He wanted to be just like you, didn't he?" Sebastian laughed awkwardly. She said, "It was touching that Zack left his serviceman's life insurance benefits to Sebastian—"

"Rather than to a Vegas stripper, like he'd said he was going to do," said Zack's dad. "As horrible as this has been, it was the silver lining, I suppose. It was Zack's way of letting us know that in his heart, he was a good boy, we just couldn't cure his demons."

"Now I can start my own landscaping company," Sebastian said, "and name it after Zack."

"Congratulations! It's Sergeant Steiger and Sergeant Reynolds!" Leonard said. His interim replacement had promoted the couple meritoriously. Leonard, Don and Jeanne didn't attend the ceremony to protect them from any suspicion. Instead, Jeanne had arranged a dinner in honor of the two new sergeants on the deck of the restaurant on the Oceanside pier. "Who's this little guy?"

"This is Rocky," said Jeanne as Leonard scratched the dog's head. "He's part of the group."

Don faced Patrick's apartment. It was a sweet reminder of the man who'd made him feel so good about living. Sensing Don's emotions, Jeanne asked, "Mr. McAbe ever come around?"

"In his own way," Don said. "He spoke to me after the funeral. Not about Patrick, but about the Corps. His way of connecting. It meant a lot."

"We should be thankful for the baby steps," Lance said. "Better than no steps at all."

"Decide if *this* is baby steps or no steps." Jeanne read from the morning's paper: "'Senators reached a tentative proposal to halt the military's attempts to hunt down homosexuals but would continue to prevent gays and lesbians from serving if they are open about their sexuality.'"

"What a crock of shit," Karl said.

"It gets better," Jeanne said. "'Senator Sam Nunn, the Georgia Democrat who heads the Armed Services Committee, summarizes the policy as,' get this, '"*Don't ask, don't tell.*" It means that that the military won't ask new recruits about their sexual orientation or conduct investigations meant to ferret out homosexuals. But it would also impose a strict code of conduct that would address such questions as harassment, holding hands on base and same-sex dancing.' 'Don't ask, don't tell.' Have you ever heard of anything so fucking ridiculous?"

"Unfortunately 'Don't ask, don't tell' is how many people live their lives—gay *and* straight," said Leonard as he ordered another round of drinks. "There's an old saying that 'you're only as sick as your secrets.' But no one thinks the saying applies to them until it costs them."

Karl put his arm around Leonard. "But they say, 'What you don't know won't hurt you.'"

"Just the opposite is true," said Leonard. "What we don't know—or won't admit—is the most treacherous threat we face. Clinton's new law turns the closet into a dangerous vault."

"It says no more investigations?" asked Esther. "Hope that doesn't put me out of work."

"Listen to you!" said Robbi. "No more investigations—that's a *good* thing!"

"I'm kidding, honey, you know that."

"Who's going to stop them from investigating?" asked Jeanne. "There's no enforcement."

Don asked, "What's this 'don't ask, don't tell' shit do to Coughlin's bill?"

"Kills it," Leonard answered. "Turned out to be a bad week for our favorite congressman. His bill died in committee. No need for Congressman Finkels to sign on as a cosponsor."

"What's happening with the base?" Jeanne asked. "Is it closing?"

"Yes, El Toro is closing. Because I wouldn't go along with his plan, Coughlin refused to fight to save El Toro. But the way things turned out, Coughlin wouldn't have done any good."

"Will the Aircraft Wing move to the desert?" Robbi asked. "Marines will be so pissed off!"

"No," Leonard said. "Funny thing. The only reason the commission considered Ridgecrest in the first place was because some land developers bribed a few commissioners. General Neville was right. It would cost too much to move the Aircraft Wing to Death Valley."

"So, if El Toro is closing," Lance asked, "where are the 17,000 Marines in the wing moving?"

"San Diego. Miramar, once home of 'Top Gun,' will be Marine Corps Air Station Miramar."

Don hadn't expected this news. "The Corps's gotta be thrilled to move out of Coughlin's district. As long as they're going to Miramar and not Death Valley." Leonard nodded.

"Another Marine base in San Diego?" Lance asked. "Hot damn! The gay bars will be more crowded than ever. The Flame will be too, Jeanne. Maybe I'll stay in bartending."

Don looked at Jeanne. She'd already told him her secret but the others didn't know. "Got some news. I sold The Flame and I'm moving to DC. Can't be without my Robbi."

Esther hugged her friends. "I'm going to miss you all so much!" Returning to her seat, she asked, "What about you, Don? You stickin' around?"

"Don't know." He took a drink of his beer. "Thought about moving to Australia."

"Australia?" asked Leonard. "Can't say I'd blame you for that, mate."

"Been on three floats that stopped at Perth. Loved every second of it. But—don't know what I'll do. Weird as it sounds, I don't mind not knowing. Everything's an opportunity."

"Nice, ain't it," said Lance. "I just feel sorry for all those gay kids still in the Marines. The ones who're asking themselves, 'What the fuck did I get myself into?'"

"You mean like me?" asked Karl, with his arms around Leonard. "Yeah, life's tough."

"That reminds me what I wanted to share with you guys." Don

pulled a slip of paper from his pocket. "At the memorial service Tuesday, a young Marine bumped into me. Didn't know it at the time, but he stuck a note in my pocket. I was paranoid about getting assaulted by some violent homophobe. Well, listen to this. *'Dear Gunny Hawkins. If you read this then you did come to the service. I'm sorry for what happened but glad you are here – that took guts. I'm gay too. Before you I thought I was the only gay Marine. Now I know that's not true. Semper Fi.'*"

"Oh my God!" Jeanne exclaimed, "That is the sweetest thing I've ever heard."

"Was he good-looking?" Karl asked with a grin.

Robbi punched him in the arm. "You are *impossible*!"

Don noticed that Leonard had been sitting quietly for a few minutes. "Don, that note—it goes right to the heart of an idea I've had for a long time. Congress will pass this ridiculous 'Don't ask, don't tell' law this summer and years will go by before it's overturned to allow gays and lesbians to serve openly. In the meantime, Marines like this young man—or anyone—will need assistance. The government has a responsibility not to investigate under this proposal. Like Jeanne said, 'Who's the enforcer?' They should be held accountable to their own policy. The hell that we've all been through—with Agent Gared and Congressman Coughlin—situations like that should never arise again, even under a law as unappealing as 'Don't ask, don't tell.'"

"What're you getting at, Leonard?" Don asked.

"I've been looking for something worthwhile to do with the money my father left me. I think I've just discovered it. Karl's moving to Washington and so am I. I'll start an organization specifically to help gays and lesbians in the military."

Everyone cheered and applauded. Jeanne exclaimed, "That is so wonderful of you!"

"Jeanne, Don. I'd be honored if both of you would be a part of this organization."

Don was taken aback and Jeanne returned his open-mouthed stare. "We'll do it!" they said.

"I want to contribute the life insurance money from Patrick," Don said.

Leonard looked thoughtful. "Don't you think Patrick would want you to use that money to live? DC is an expensive town."

"Well, Chris and I had a deal too. He didn't want his evangelical family to get his SGLI—said they'd just give it to some antigay hate group. And I don't *have* a family so we signed our SGLI over to each other. Yep, Patrick wanted me to have his money, but to keep their memory alive, Chris's will be the first donation to the cause."

"That's a great idea," said Leonard. "Now we need to decide on a name."

"The first of many discussions." Jeanne looked at Don. "Australia's gotta wait awhile."

Jay returned to his motel room near the airport. Tomorrow he'd fly back to San Diego, pack his meager belongings into the back of a rental truck and start the long drive eastward. Although he'd be returning to the town he'd left not even six months ago, he was coming back to a better job and a better life. Despite his failures in San Diego, he'd been rewarded with a great future.

Another major symptom that may have led him to enlist was his fear of being alone. Jay couldn't shake Zack's mom's voice from his head. Zack was afraid of being alone too?

He stripped out of his clothes to take a shower. "You're looking good, Jay-man! I'd fuck you—*again*!" Jay looked in the mirror and saw his uninvited guest. They laughed together. "Bet you never expected to see me again, did ya'?"

"Actually, Zack," Jay replied, "I was wondering what took you so long."

Zack crossed the room, almost letting Jay touch his smooth, naked skin. "You takin' me to Washington, DC, ain't ya?"

"Do I have a choice?"

"I wish we had a better resolution for Eddie," Don said. "Something definite that I could tell his mom." Jeanne nodded in agreement as Robbi slipped Rocky a small piece of steak.

"Don't be so sure we don't," Esther said slyly. "Been meaning to tell you something."

449 CODE OF CONDUCT

"What have you done?" Jeanne reached out as the waiter handed her another glass of wine.

"After Ollie fired Jay Gared, guess who got the job of reorganizing his caseload?" Esther raised her hand. "That's right, yours truly. Finally I was able to review every page of Eddie's file, including Gared's handwritten notes."

"Eddie's your friend the Navy claimed committed suicide?" Leonard asked. Karl nodded.

"The forensics investigators discovered some hairs that appeared to belong to a Caucasian male trapped in the fabric on Eddie's sofa. Now that we know Jay Gared was at Eddie's that night *and* we know that Jay Gared substituted his blood for that pilot's—"

"This Jay Gared fellow caused a lot of trouble in a very short time," Leonard observed.

"Especially when Don was corn-holin' him on Channel 5—'*Get off me, you fuckin' queer!*' is what Gared was shouting," said Karl. "He looked fuckin' ridiculous!"

"What if the hairs belong to you?" Jeanne asked. "You were at his house just hours before."

"You shittin' me?" Karl said. "Eddie wouldn't let us sit on that sofa—said it was for guests."

"That's funny," Robbi said, "he always let *us* sit on it." Everyone at the table laughed.

"Besides, he always made me scrub the place after I used the bathroom," Karl said, pouting.

"So this is why Esther asked me all those questions," Lance said. The rest of the group looked perplexed. "Esther called yesterday morning asking if there was a way an analyst could tell if hair and blood came from the same person. That's exactly what I'm studying in molecular biology. The latest DNA testing kicks ass. If the hair and blood have the same DNA, there's a 99.999% chance it's the same person."

"Were you able to convince NIS to reopen Eddie's investigation?" Don asked.

"No. There's no way I could do that without blowing my cover."

"That's right," Jeanne said, "we're back to our dilemma of how do we use the information we obtain without revealing your identity. Let's think. What can we do—?"

"Already took the lead," Esther said. "I know she's not our favorite reporter, but—"

"Oh my God!" said Robbi. "You tipped off Kathryn Angel?"

Jeanne nodded. "Makes sense. She's smart. Even if she's corrupt, she's a good journalist."

"And she has a lot of time on her hands," Esther explained. "Ricky found out she sold information, just like Leonard suspected. The *Washington Herald* fired her."

"So there's justice in this world after all," Leonard said. "And now you've got a pro like her doing your dirty work for you. She'll obtain a confession out of Mr. Gared one way or another."

"I'm impressed," said Jeanne. "We'll be back East while you'll do great work on this coast."

"Hey, Don," Karl said. "Where're you going?"

Don pushed in his chair and said, "The sun's setting over the ocean and I—I'm going to—to make my own personal symbolic gesture. You're welcome to join me." He grabbed a bag from under his chair and headed for the railing at the western edge of the long pier. Rocky whimpered, fearful he was being abandoned, so Karl untied his leash and walked him over with the group. The restaurant's other customers stared curiously as the group of seven left their patio table.

"What's in the bag?" Lance asked. When Don removed his shiny medals made of anodized brass, Lance exclaimed, "Holy shit, Gunny Hawkins. That's quite a rack!"

"That's very impressive, Don. I was also part of *Operation Eagle Claw* and I was in Beirut." Leonard and Don locked eyes. "You've been through something like this before, haven't you?"

"Yes, Colonel, I have. And this time, I'm dealing with it much differently."

"So have I," Leonard said pensively. "And I'm dealing with things differently now too."

Don asked, "What was your—actually, I want to ask you more

about it, but not now. We've got many conversations ahead of us, Leonard. I look forward to getting to know you very well."

"Being the lone civilian in this group," Esther said, "I need to ask, what are all these medals for?"

"Lots of things," Jeanne said. "Granada, Panama, *Desert Storm*, to name a few. Mostly they mean Don did one hell of a job during his sixteen years in the Corps."

Don looked at the sky as a flock of birds flew noisily over the pier. The sun formed a semicircle atop the Western Pacific. Turning to Esther, he said, "What they mean is that I survived." He put the medals in his right hand and, with a broad sweeping motion, hurled them as far out into the ocean as possible. Just before they reached the water, the anodized brass caught a piece of the sun's brilliance and reflected it onto the group. "A glimmer of hope."

"Will you ever replace those?" Leonard asked as they turned back toward the restaurant. "Will you ever wear your uniform again?"

Don looked to the beach and saw Patrick's balcony, where they'd kissed so many times. "Someday I will. When the military—when America—does the right thing, ends this 'don't ask, don't tell' law and lets people like Patrick—and all of us—serve openly and without fear."

"That won't be anytime soon, I'm afraid. The battle lines have been drawn. We're in for a long, hard slog."

"In the end we'll be victorious," Don said as he smiled and put his arm on Leonard's shoulder. "Until then, Colonel, we've got a lot of work to do."

Epilogue

Clinton Proposes "Don't Ask, Don't Tell" Policy for Gays in the Military
By Ricky Shilts, Staff Reporter, *Washington Herald*

WASHINGTON, July 19, 1993—President Clinton announced his proposal today to ease the ban on homosexuals in the military. It allows gay men and lesbians to serve *if* they do not engage in homosexual behavior on or off base *and* are silent about their sexual identity. Although the Joint Chiefs openly revolted in January when Mr. Clinton promised to lift the ban outright, they praised the new policy. General Powell called this "an honorable compromise after difficult debates." He also said the military chiefs "fully, fully support" the plan. However, Representative Barney Frank, the openly gay Massachusetts Democrat who tried to end the ban, said the plan "falls short of where I thought we would be. This does not meet the minimum."

Mr. Clinton, though, said, "It certainly will not please everyone—perhaps not anyone—and clearly not those who hold the most adamant opinions on either side of this issue." The president's audience to announce his plan indicated how the balance of power has changed. It was an audience made up of military officers—no gay or lesbian representatives were present.

"Nothing's changed," said Jeanne Pruitt. "The devil's in the details." Ms. Pruitt was discharged from the Marines under "other than honorable circumstances" in 1987 after her command discovered she was a lesbian. "Who we love—whether it's God, country, Corps or a significant other—is an important part of who we are, even for members of the military. Maybe Mr. Clinton can live his life according to 'Don't ask, don't tell' but it's unconscionable for him to ask service members to make such an unreasonable sacrifice." Ms. Pruitt and Don Hawkins are coexecutive directors of MAG, the Military Advocates Group, a new organization dedicated to helping members of the uniformed services who face challenges under this new law.

Portions of the text of the "Don't Ask, Don't Tell" law, signed by President Clinton, November 30, 1993.
Fourteen years later, it remains in effect.

TITLE 10—§654. Policy concerning homosexuality in the armed forces

(a) Findings.—Congress makes the following findings:
... (13) The prohibition against homosexual conduct is a longstanding element of military law that continues to be necessary in the unique circumstances of military service.

(14) The armed forces must maintain personnel policies that exclude persons whose presence in the armed forces would create an unacceptable risk to the armed forces' high standards of morale, good order and discipline, and unit cohesion that are the essence of military capability.

(15) The presence in the armed forces of persons who demonstrate a propensity or intent to engage in homosexual acts would create an unacceptable risk to the high standards of morale, good order and discipline, and unit cohesion that are the essence of military capability.

(b) Policy.—A member of the armed forces shall be separated from the armed forces if:

(1) That the member has engaged in, attempted to engage in, or solicited another to engage in a homosexual act or acts . . .

(2) That the member has stated that he or she is a homosexual or bisexual, or words to that effect . . .

(3) That the member has married or attempted to marry a person known to be of the same biological sex . . .

(f) Definitions.—In this section:

(1) The term "homosexual" means a person, regardless of sex, who engages in, attempts to engage in, has a propensity to engage in, or intends to engage in homosexual acts, and includes the terms "gay" and "lesbian."

(2) The term "bisexual" means a person who engages in, attempts to engage in, has a propensity to engage in, or intends to engage in homosexual and heterosexual acts.

(3) The term "homosexual act" means—

(A) any bodily contact, actively undertaken or passively permitted, between members of the same sex for the purpose of satisfying sexual desires; and

(B) any bodily contact which a reasonable person would understand to demonstrate a propensity or intent to engage in an act described in subparagraph (A).